Velvet screamed . . .

. . . a long unearthly cry that made all the hair on my body stand at attention. Streams of black poured from her eyes in a rush and then, with her fingers hooked into ragged claws, she charged forward, throwing herself across the room at me with the kind of rage and despair that only the dead can muster.

I'd been wrong.

This was no harmless poltergeist but actually a full-blown spectre masquerading as a lesser ghost. And clearly, she intended to tear me limb from limb.

Instinct took over then, every fiber of my being shouting at me to run, and run I did. My body was already in motion before my brain had finished telling it which way to go, and as I pushed through the door, I gave it a hearty swing back in the other direction, slamming it shut at my back.

Something massive struck it, and I heard the wood crack quite clearly, even over Velvet's horrible cries.

I spun around to face it, only to have the room around me go strangely silent at that exact moment.

The sudden quiet was as alarming as the torturous shrieking cut off in my wake.

Just what the hell was *she . . .*

Turn the page for raves about *Eyes to See*.

Praise for *Eyes to See*

"Gritty, grim, yet surprisingly personal and poetic, *Eyes to See* is like nothing else in its field. Make time for this one."
—Seanan McGuire,
New York Times bestselling author of the October Daye series

"At last—something new under the urban fantasy moon. Nassise's visceral prose and dark, gritty settings propel the blind Hunt and his unique ghostly companions, Whisper and Scream, through an urban nightmare where nothing is what it seems."   —F. Paul Wilson,
New York Times bestselling author

"This is definitely an author to watch in the world of urban fantasy. Go out and grab or download a copy of *Eyes to See*; you won't be disappointed!"
—*Totally Horror*

"Joe Nassise's driven, sardonic hero, Jeremiah Hunt, sees a whole lot more than dead people in *Eyes to See*. Vividly set in Boston, the novel follows Hunt through a labyrinth of undead dangers and unexpected emotion as he seeks his missing daughter and finds an unearthly serial killer. The climax, both thrilling and moving, will stick with you."   —Alex Bledsoe, author of
The Girls with Games of Blood and
Burn Me Deadly

"This is a very well-written, dark, and gritty urban fantasy. Fans will love this and clamor for more. Excellent!"
—*drey's library*

"Very intense. I gulped this down and am looking forward to the promised sequel."
—Henry Leon Lazarus,
Weekly Press (Philadelphia, PA)

TOR BOOKS BY JOSEPH NASSISE

EYES TO SEE

JOSEPH NASSISE

A TOM DOHERTY ASSOCIATES BOOK
NEW YORK

This is a work of fiction. All of the characters, organizations, and events portrayed in this novel are either products of the author's imagination or are used fictitiously.

EYES TO SEE

Copyright © 2011 by Joseph Nassise

All rights reserved.

Edited by James Frenkel

A Tor Book
Published by Tom Doherty Associates, LLC
175 Fifth Avenue
New York, NY 10010

www.tor-forge.com

Tor® is a registered trademark of Tom Doherty Associates, LLC.

ISBN 978-0-7653-6575-0

First Edition: October 2011
First Mass Market Edition: July 2012

Printed in the United States of America

0 9 8 7 6 5 4 3 2 1

For my kids—
the four best things that ever happened to me

ACKNOWLEDGMENTS

I owe a debt of gratitude to a number of people for this one, not the least of whom are the instructors from the 2007 Borderlands Bootcamp: fellow writers Tom Monteleone, F. Paul Wilson, and Doug Winter, as well as editor Ginjer Buchanan, who assigned the writing exercise that resulted in this book's opening sentence and from which everything else followed; my German editor, Tim Sonderhuesken, who helped me find Jeremiah's unique voice; and my American editor, Jim Frenkel, who brought Jeremiah home to his native shore.

Special thanks, as always, to my wife, whose support and love make all of this possible.

I

now

I gave up my eyes in order to see more clearly.

I like to tell myself that if I had known then what I know now, I never would have made such a Faustian bargain, but the truth is that I probably would have done it anyway. I was pretty desperate in those days, the search for Elizabeth having consumed every facet of my life like a malignant cancer gorging itself on healthy cells, and I'd have tried anything to find even the smallest clue about what happened to her.

And yet despite my sacrifice, I'm not completely blind. I can actually see better in complete darkness than most people can in broad daylight. I can no longer see colors—everything comes out in a thousand different shades of gray—but at least I can see. Call it an odd side effect of the ritual I underwent, if you will. But the minute you put me in the light, everything goes dark. In direct sunlight I can't even see the outline of my hand if I hold it right in front of my face. All I see is white. Endless vistas of white.

Electrical lights are almost as bad, though with a pair

of strong UV sunglasses I can see the vague shapes and outlines of things around me. I lose details, of course; even up close, I wouldn't know the face of my own mother from that of a stranger, but I can tell the difference between a horse and a house.

Usually.

Enough to make my way about with the help of a cane, at least. If I have to have light, then candlelight is best. The weaker the better. At home, I prefer complete darkness. It tends to discourage visitors, too.

Tonight, for the first time in weeks, I had some work to do. The offer filtered down late last night through the handful of people who know how to get in touch with me for just these kinds of things. I don't have an office. I don't advertise my services. No "Jeremiah Hunt, Exorcist" business cards or any crap like that. Most of the time, I just want to be left alone. But occasionally, if the time and circumstances are right, I'll help out the odd individual here or there. I hadn't decided if I was going to take the job until reviewing the sorry state of my bank account earlier this morning. The monthly checks from the university still come in, the benefits of a well-negotiated severance package in the wake of Elizabeth's disappearance, but they are never enough for what I need. Searching for someone who may as well have fallen off the face of the earth isn't cheap. A quick infusion of capital goes a long way.

Even if it does mean facing off against a homicidal ghost.

You see, one of the consequences of my decision to relinquish my sight was a newfound ability to see the ghosts that surround us on a daily basis. Arthur C. Clarke once said that behind every man now alive stand thirty ghosts, for that is the ratio by which the dead outnumber the living. And while I haven't counted them all, I can say with confidence that Clarke was off by more than a few zeroes.

The truth is that the dead are everywhere.

They wander the city streets, drifting unnoticed through the crowds. They sit beside you on the bus, stand next to you in the supermarket checkout line; sometimes one or two of them might even follow you home from work like lost dogs looking for a place to stay.

That little chill you sometimes feel for no reason at all? That's their way of letting you know that they are there, watching and waiting.

They like to congregate in public places—subway stations, churches, nightclubs—anywhere that the living can be found in significant numbers. Some say they find sustenance in all that raw emotion, as if they were feeding off us like some kind of psychic vampires, but in the three years I've been watching them I've never found evidence to support that theory. I think it is more likely that they simply miss us. Miss being alive. When they watch us, their gaze is so full of longing and pain that it's the only explanation that makes sense to me.

The dead are everywhere and I can see them as plainly as you can see yourself in a mirror. The buildings around me might be as hazy as a summer fog, but the dead shine brightly even in the dark.

The feeling of the cab slowing down and pulling over snagged me out of my reverie and back to the present.

"Here you go, pal. Fourteen sixty-seven Eliot Ave. You sure you want to get out here?"

While I couldn't see what he was seeing, I could imagine the neighborhood with little difficulty, and understood his hesitation. I'd driven through the area in the old days and knew beyond a shadow of a doubt that it could've only gotten worse instead of better. West Roxbury is one of those places you avoid in midafternoon, never mind after dark; a warren of tenement buildings and three-family homes, all of them run-down and decrepit, long past their prime. Graffiti and gang signs are prominent and iron grilles cover the windows, even on the upper levels, scant protection against a stray bullet from the weekly drive-by but good enough to deter the casual crackhead looking for an easy score. The entire neighborhood probably should have been torn down years ago, but should have and will be are two very different things. The place will probably still be standing long after I'm gone; urban blight has a way of hanging around long after its expiration date.

"Yeah," I said. "This is the place."

I dug in the pocket of my jeans, locating the twenty by the triangle it had been folded into earlier, and handed it through the barrier, asking for a five back in change. I heard the driver shift in his seat, pull out his stack of cash, and shuffle through it. Another creak of old leather as he turned my way. Believing I was good and truly blind, which wasn't all that far from the truth, the cabbie put his hand through the narrow opening and pushed the bill into mine.

"A five it is, pal."

A discreet cough came from just outside my open window.

"That's no five. It's a single," said a low voice.

The driver was fast but I was faster. I grabbed his hand before he could pull it back through the barrier and bent it at the wrist. I heard him grunt in pain and I twisted his arm a bit harder, just to be sure he got the message.

Leaning forward, I took off my sunglasses with my free hand, treating the driver to a close-up of my face. Eyes that had once been as blue as the Caribbean Sea were now without pupils and whiter than snow, framed by the scars from when I had tried to claw them out of my head. It was an unsettling sight and one I had learned to use to my advantage.

"Thanks, pal," I said, drawing out the last word with a heavy dose of sarcasm, intentionally mocking him, my voice as dry as ice and just as cold. "Since you can't resist being an asshole, why don't we just skip the tip altogether, huh? Give me my nine fifty before I break this glass and knock you on your ass, blind or not."

As the cabbie scrambled to comply, I kept up the pressure on his wrist, more than willing to snap his arm in half if he tried to cheat me again.

Finally he found the right change and handed it back to me. I released his arm and then quickly climbed out of the cab, just in case he tried to get even by pulling away before I was clear and leaving me sprawled in the street.

The cabbie shouted a few curses at me but was apparently unsettled enough to leave it at that. He pulled away from the curb with a squeal of tires, leaving me standing on the sidewalk next to my Good Samaritan.

"Mr. Hunt?" he asked.

I nodded, not trusting myself to speak yet, my anger at the cabbie still bouncing around inside my head like an errant pinball.

"Joel Thompson, Mr. Hunt. We spoke on the phone?"

I recognized his voice, a thin, reedy warble that reminded me of a whip-poor-will. Not that we get many whip-poor-wills in Massachusetts, but you get the idea. I took a deep breath, forcing my anger back down into the shadows of my soul, put my hand out in the general direction of his voice, and waited for him to take it. He was clearly nervous; his palm was damp with sweat, and it didn't take a genius to recognize that I unnerved him almost as much as did the events that had forced him to seek me out in the first place.

Frankly, I didn't give a shit. Miss Congeniality, I was

not. All I wanted was the money they were offering, money that could help me continue my search for Elizabeth.

"Thanks for your help with the cab."

He brushed off my thanks, embarrassed for some reason I couldn't identify, and then told me that the others were waiting across the street in front of the building.

"Let's get to it then," I said.

He led me to the other side and introduced me to them one by one.

I could tell Olivia Jones was elderly by the thinness and frailty of her hand as I held it in my own. Frank Martin was her exact opposite, a veritable tank of a human being, his dark form looming over me in my limited vision, and his grip felt like it could have crushed solid steel. It was hard to guess anything about Judy Hertfort and Tania Harris, the two younger women in the group, other than the fact that both seemed to favor cheap perfumes I had a hard time identifying. Last but not least was Steven Marley. He was the only one to actually sound like he meant it when he said, "Pleased to meet you."

I could just imagine what I looked like to them, the ankle-length duster I habitually wore hanging loosely over jeans and a thick work shirt, like some kind of thin, ragged apparition out of the Old West, my face hidden behind a pair of dark sunglasses.

I could feel all of them staring at me, a combination of fear, anger, and uncertainty radiating off them like heat from the pavement in the heart of summer. Considering the circumstances, I couldn't be sure if it was directed at me or what I was there to do, so I let it go.

Like I said before, I didn't care either way.

I wasn't the one with the notoriety here, they were. You couldn't pass a newsstand or a television in the last few weeks without the Silent Six staring back at you, famous not for what they had done but for what they had failed to do.

Eight months ago a young woman, known on the street as Velvet, had been beaten, raped, and ultimately left for dead inside the tenement building behind us. Each of the individuals in the group in front of me had looked out of a window or door, seen the young woman arguing vehemently with her companion, and then had done absolutely nothing, not wanting to get involved. When she'd yelled for help, they'd ignored her. When she'd screamed in fear and pain, they'd pretended not to hear. And when she lay dying on the cold floor of her shitty little apartment, she did so all alone while her killer walked off, free as a bird.

If she'd been just another poor street hooker knocked off by her john maybe nobody would've cared. But Velvet, aka Melissa Sullivan, had been a third-year student at Northeastern University. She had gotten into more than a few things dear old Mom and Dad back home wouldn't have approved of, including a little tricking on the side to help pay for a growing coke habit. Unfortunately, one of her customers had decided that he wanted a little more than she was willing to give and had taken it from her by brute force.

Her white, middle-class parents blamed everything and everyone they could think of for the demise of their "precious little girl," conveniently forgetting that said little girl made a habit out of sucking off complete strangers in dark alleys for cash, a pretty glaring omission if you ask me. And of course they made sure that the evening news heard their version of the story loud and clear. You can laugh, but to hear them tell it, you'd think Velvet was a freakin' saint.

Before you knew it, the city had a media firestorm on its hands.

It was only later when the police caught the killer that

the Six found the courage to come forward and tell someone what they'd seen. To give them some credit, in the end it was their testimony that put the killer behind the bars of the maximum security wing at Walpole State Prison for the rest of his miserable life.

Apparently, though, Velvet felt their actions were a case of too little, too late.

And now she was making them pay for it.

I thought back to the call I had with Thompson earlier in the morning. He described being a captive in his own home; feeling watched, stalked even, whenever he was inside the building. Objects would fly off the walls or move around on their own, often without any warning whatsoever. His nights were spent in sheer terror as something seemed to hover at his bedside, waves of anger and hatred radiating off of it. Lately the presence in the building had become more aggressive, to where it was actually trying to do harm, opening elevator doors on empty shafts, shoving from behind when anyone dared to take the stairs.

I'd come here to put an end to all that.

Spirits come in a variety of types and sizes. At the bottom of the food chain are the haunts, little more than whispers in the dark. You can sense their presence, but they don't have any real physical form. Next you've got your standard apparitions, ghostly presences that repeat the same motions over and over again, like memories caught in an endlessly repeating loop. The city's largest public park, Boston Common, is full of apparitions, spirits of the criminals who were publicly hanged there during the late 1600s. Visitors often claim they can see the apparitions walking the path toward the place where the gallows once stood, only to vanish immediately upon reaching it. A step up from the apparitions, you have your actual ghosts, spiritual presences that are bound to our plane for one reason or another, unable or perhaps unwilling to move on. Ghosts are about as aware of us as we are of them and delight in showing themselves to us whenever they can. Poltergeists are a subclass of ghosts, able to move objects in the physical world through sheer force of will. The foghorn-blowing phantom that occupies the Baker Island Lighthouse is probably our city's best known example. Spectres are another subclass: ghosts that have gone insane and seek only to annoy, and sometimes harm, the living.

Rarer still, and at the very top of the hierarchy, are the shades. These are ghosts that, given the right opportunity and the right stimulus, have the ability to reclaim their living form even long after their original death.

I've gotten pretty good at identifying just what kind of ghost I'm facing off against from the descriptions of those who've encountered it. In this case, I was betting that Thompson's own guilt was amplifying the impact of the ghost's presence and that when I got upstairs I'd find an angry, but basically harmless, poltergeist waiting to be sent on her way.

With the introductions over, I got right down to business.

"You have my money?" I asked, addressing no one in particular.

There was a bit of a rustle, people shifting uncomfortably, and then the big guy, Martin, opened his mouth.

"Uh-uh. Do your job and then you'll get paid."

I turned my head in his direction, listening to his breathing, feeling his anger, trying to decide how far he was willing to push this, and then made up my mind.

"Fuck that," I said.

I turned away and stepped toward the street, my cane leading the way.

"Mr. Hunt?" a voice called.

That would be Thompson, wondering if I was really going to leave them.

Damn right I was.

I raised two fingers to my mouth and whistled shrilly for a cab, long practice having taught me just the right tone to use to cut through the sounds of passing traffic.

"Mr. Hunt! Wait!"

I stopped and let him catch up to me, though I moved my arm away from his touch when he reached out to hold it.

"Where are you going?" he asked, his nervousness now coming through loud and clear. "You agreed to help us!"

"I explained my terms on the phone," I said patiently. "I get paid, up front. And I keep the money whether I am successful or not. This isn't a fuckin' walk in the park, you know."

Jerking a thumb back in the direction of the group, I continued, "If Grape Ape back there doesn't want to play by the rules, then he can go right back to dealing with her on his own. No skin off my back."

I heard a car pull up next to me, figured it for the cab I was trying to flag down, and held out a hand in a signal for him to wait.

"You can't just leave us here with . . ." He waved his hands around, flustered and unable to make himself say it aloud.

I smiled, knowing it was not a pleasant sight. "Of course I can. I'm not the one who left her to die."

"It wasn't like that!" he said sharply.

Again, I really didn't care. His guilt or innocence made no difference to me.

He must have sensed that I wouldn't be moved on the topic, for his anger suddenly went as quickly as it had arrived. "Can you give me a moment to talk with them?" he asked.

"Sure," I said, filling my voice with disinterest. I needed the money, but I'd be damned if I let him know that. First rule of any negotiation: never let 'em know you're desperate.

The wait wasn't very long. Whatever he said to them must have worked, for Thompson returned after a moment and passed me an envelope. I could tell by the feel of it that it was thick with cash.

I told the cabbie I wasn't going to need him after all, made a quick check of the pockets of the duster I was wearing to be certain that my tools were still in place, and then asked the question that would separate the men from the boys.

"So who's going in with me?"

2

now

There was a long moment of uncomfortable silence. I could picture them standing about, looking everywhere but at each other, all of them hoping that one of the others would speak up so they wouldn't have to.

Eventually one of them did.

"I'll take you," Olivia Jones said into the silence.

You go girl! I thought, surprised at the old lady's bravery and sheer chutzpah, but then shook my head.

"I'm sorry Ms. Jones, but you won't be able to help me. I need someone strong enough to stand by my side and tell me what's happening during even the worst of the confrontation. If I need help, that person has to act as my eyes and be able to physically assist me in getting back outside."

I wasn't surprised when she didn't object. She seemed like a feisty old bird, but what I was asking was a lot for someone her age.

"Anyone else?"

More silence.

I decided to give them a five count. If no one volunteered by the time it was over . . .

Five . . .

Four . . .

Three . . .

"Fine. I'll do it."

It was Thompson again. Had to hand it to the man; he wasn't shy about stepping up and getting involved. Too bad he hadn't seen fit to do so on the night of Velvet's death. Might have saved himself and his fellow tenants a whole heap of trouble if he had.

Maybe he's learned his lesson, I thought, then snorted in derision at my own optimism.

Life just didn't work that way, I knew.

I quickly explained to him how it was going to work. I needed him to act as my eyes once we were inside, telling me everything that was happening around us, no matter how small or insignificant it seemed to him. "The Devil's in the details" went the old saying, and when it comes to ghosts, nothing is truer. They can't speak and often are limited in how much impact they can have on their physical surroundings, so you have to watch carefully in order to figure out what they might do next.

That's what made this situation so interesting. If what Thompson said was true, the sheer amount of power this ghost could call under its control was astounding. And the more powerful the ghost was, the more it knew. Death did that. Gave them some kind of connection to the world around them in a way they'd never had while alive, let them see and hear and know things that they had nothing to do with and no business knowing. It's true; the dead know our deepest, darkest secrets.

Understanding those secrets was a different story.

There was always a first time, though, and maybe tonight would be the night.

Maybe tonight, when I cornered this ghost and asked

her if she had seen my daughter, she'd put me on the road to finding Elizabeth.

Satisfied that Thompson understood his role, I let him lead me up the stairs and into the building. As I stepped over the threshold, the smell of the place hit me like a fist in the face. Mold and mildew mixed with the smell of too many people in too small a space, the stench of urine overlaying it all like a terrible garnish. It was enough to make me wish I'd lost my sense of smell along with my sight.

My face must have broadcast my reaction, for Thompson mumbled, "You get used to it," beneath his breath and then he took out his keys and unlocked something that creaked and rattled as he pushed it open.

"What's that?" I asked.

"Security gate."

I remembered it now from the news coverage. There had been some early speculation that someone had left it open behind them and that was how the killer had gained access to the building. That was before they'd understood that Velvet herself had let her killer in, that she'd not only invited Death inside but had taken him with her upstairs.

"Steel?" I asked.

"Iron. Heavy son of a bitch, too," he said, as he swung it back into place with a loud clang that echoed in the small space.

Iron.

One part of the puzzle solved.

"Let me guess: this place has bars on all the windows, too, right?"

He grunted. " 'Course it does. Every place on the block does. Upper floors, too. Damned thieves would climb the fire escapes and rob us blind if we didn't."

"And those are iron, too?"

"Yep. Harder to cut through."

Like running water, iron is anathema to a ghost. They can't cross it. Was it possible that Velvet wanted to leave and simply couldn't?

I thought about it for a moment and then dismissed the notion. The security gate wasn't permanently closed. If she wanted to get out, all she had to do was wait by the gate for someone coming in or out to open it and then slip on past.

No, she was here for some reason.

Not daring to take the elevator, Thompson led me down the hallway until we reached the emergency stairwell at the other end.

Like most tenement buildings, this one was poorly lit. The dimness allowed me to see the vague outlines of the steps ahead of me as Thompson started up.

I followed.

I felt her the minute I put my foot on that first step. You know that feeling you get when you know someone is watching you, that sense of pressure in your mind, that creeping sensation at the base of your neck? That's what it's like for me. Except in my case, rather than sensing the living, I'm attuned to the presence of the dead.

Just as they are attuned to me.

She was somewhere on one of the floors above me and I knew beyond a shadow of a doubt that she was now as aware of me as I was of her.

I could tell that she wasn't happy that I'd come to pay her a visit, either.

Thompson was climbing the stairs ahead of me, oblivious to both my split-second hesitation and her presence high above us, and so I dutifully followed behind. He was rambling on, probably to help calm his nerves, telling me that Velvet's apartment was on the fourth floor and that she had been murdered inside. No sooner had he said the word *murdered* than the temperature in the stairwell dropped from a cool seventy-five to somewhere below freezing.

"Jesus!" Thompson said, startled. "I can see my breath."

It wasn't just the cold that had the man's teeth chattering in his head.

He was scared.

To tell you the truth, so was I.

Cold spots are nothing new to paranormal investigators. The accepted theory is that ghosts use the ambient energy in a given space, including heat, to manifest themselves or to fuel other types of supernatural activity. Usually the temperature differential is no more than a handful of degrees, the kind of thing that you need an infrared thermometer to confirm for sure.

What was happening now was something else entirely.

I could actually feel the frost as it formed beneath my fingers where they gripped the metal railing. The air took on that harsh, biting quality it gets in the depths of winter, when every breath seems to burn a little going in and out. Goose bumps rose all over my flesh and I was suddenly glad for the coat I wore.

What the hell had I gotten myself into?

But it didn't stop there.

A sudden, overwhelming sense of despair washed over us. One moment we were perfectly fine and the next, drowning in a sea of emotion. It was the helplessness of a young child lost at the county fair without a familiar face in sight, the horror of a prisoner facing a life sentence in a six-by-eight box of a cell, the utter hopelessness of watching your family slaughtered horribly before your eyes while you lay bound on the floor, unable to do anything to stop it, all rolled up into one neat little package. It thundered into our heads as if put there by God Himself.

I staggered beneath the weight. If it hadn't been for the lodestone hanging around my neck, I would have been utterly defenseless. As it was, I was nearly driven to my knees. I'm not a geologist or a trained parapsychologist. I don't understand what it is about lodestone that makes it an effective defense against ghostly activity any more than I understand how my microwave works. That doesn't stop me from using either one, however, and I've made a point of carrying some lodestone with me whenever I think I'm going to face off against something otherworldly. I learned early on that there are plenty of things out there that don't hold our best interests at heart, so when it comes to the supernatural, I'm a firm believer in the old Boy Scout motto: *Be Prepared.* So today I had a good-size piece on a thin silver chain strung around my neck.

Unfortunately for Thompson, I hadn't brought enough to share and he was left to face the full force of the psychic attack on his own.

It proved to be too much for him.

He collapsed with a grunt, crashing into me with barely any warning, his dead weight nearly sending us both tumbling back down the steps to the landing below. Only my grip on the ice-cold railing kept us upright and prevented a sudden and decidedly uncomfortable end to the business at hand. As it was, I ended up with a fat lip from the elbow I took in the face as he toppled backward, unconscious.

Velvet didn't want any guests, it seemed.

Tough. She'd made the mistake of pissing me off, and when I get angry I have a tendency to not think too straight. Rational decisions, like getting out of there before she could do further harm to either me or Thompson, just didn't enter into the equation. I tended to get all "full speed ahead and damn the torpedoes" and shit.

Like now.

Rather than making my slow and careful way back down the stairs with Thompson's unconscious form in my arms, I laid him down gently on the steps, felt for the railing, used it to maneuver my way around his body, and continued upward.

The pressure was still there, the weight of the emotions that she was sending down onto my shoulders like an extra fifty pounds I had to carry to the top, but I gritted my teeth, shouldered the burden, and put one foot in front of the other, again and again, until I reached the second floor.

I stopped on the landing and listened for a moment. I could hear the thump of a radio turned too loud somewhere down the hall and beyond that a baby crying, but these were normal sounds, the kind of things you'd expect.

Just another night in the Rox.

Satisfied that nothing was amiss, at least not here, I continued upward.

About midway to the third floor, the pressure in my mind backed off, and by the time I hit the fourth-floor landing, it had vanished altogether. Either the sweet, saintly Velvet was feeling regret about knocking my companion unconscious or she was conserving energy for her next attack.

It didn't take a genius to figure out which was more likely.

A lone lightbulb illuminated the hallway before me. To anyone else it would have been a weak and unsteady light, but this close it rendered me effectively blind, and that wasn't something I wanted at this point. I already had enough to be worried about. Wrapping my hand inside the sleeve of my duster, I reached up and smacked the bulb sharply with my fist. There was a tinkle of falling glass and the light vanished, leaving me standing on the edge of the stairwell in the sudden darkness.

A very welcome darkness, given the fact that I had no trouble seeing in it.

The hallway stretched out before me, half a dozen doors on either side, all of which were tightly closed. The apartment I wanted was at the very end of the hall, facing me.

Number 43.

The place where Melissa Sullivan, aka Velvet, had met her end.

I started toward it, moving confidently through the darkness.

The first of the apartment doors swung open as I passed, slamming into the wall with a booming crash. Just as quickly it slammed closed again.

Ignoring it, I continued forward.

The second door did the same, as did the third, and then the rest of the doors all along the hallway quickly followed suit, slamming open and then shut, open and shut, over and over again, until the narrow space was filled with the booming sound of their cacophony.

Unable to force me to back down, Velvet was now trying to scare me off.

Sorry sister, but that's not going to work.

I marched determinedly down the hall, ignoring the ruckus around me, until I stood before her apartment. The door was slightly ajar, as if beckoning me to enter.

Was it an invitation or a trap?

I didn't know.

There was only one way to find out.

3

now

I nudged the door the rest of the way open with my foot, allowing me to see beyond it, into the apartment itself.

Thompson had explained the layout to me on the way up the stairs earlier so that I would know what to expect when he led me inside, but with night having fallen and the shades drawn, it was dark enough that I could actually see fairly well. The place was a one bedroom, set up railroad style, a long stretch of rooms from front to back; a short entryway led into the kitchen, which in turn led into first a living room and then a bedroom. The front entrance was directly opposite the door to the bedroom at the far end and, with both doors open, I could see all the way to the rear wall where Velvet's ghost stood with a forlorn expression on her face, in front of the grime-covered window, staring out through the iron bars at the side of the tenement building next door.

Like most ghosts, she shone for me brighter than the living, surrounded by a faintly luminous silver-white glow that made her seem to pop out of her surroundings. As I stepped across her threshold, she turned slowly in my direction, giving me a better look at her.

She was a gaunt, hollow-eyed shell of her former self, dressed in the tattered clothes her killer had left on her body. She was hanging in the air about a foot off the floor. Her long hair was tangled and clumped together in certain places with a dark, sticky substance that I took to be blood. She stared at me for a moment, her eyes burning with intensity, and then she seemed to lose interest, her gaze falling to the floor before she turned back to face the window again.

I waited to make certain she wasn't about to do anything crazy and then made my way through the apartment with slow, measured steps. I kept my gaze on her the whole time, ready to take action if she decided to object to my presence. My caution was unnecessary, however, for she never even looked at me after that first penetrating glance, allowing me to reach the bedroom without incident.

So far, so good.

Now that I was inside, it was time to see what I could do to send her on her way.

There are quite a few methods for making an unruly ghost abandon its current haunt. Thanks to some trial and error over the last few years, I've settled on several techniques that I prefer and I always start with the ones that are the least intrusive.

I start by simply asking the ghost to leave.

I spoke to her firmly, using her full name to reduce the chance of her acting as if she didn't know that I was speaking to her.

"Melissa Anne Sullivan. Your life here is finished. It is time to leave this place and move on."

I always feel a bit pompous spouting off like that and it makes me want to wave my hands around in the air in front of me like I'm some kind of amateur magician, but this time I managed to squelch the impulse. Still, I couldn't argue with the results. Seventy-five percent of the time the tactic actually works and the ghost moves on to wherever ghosts go.

Unfortunately, this was not one of those times.

Velvet ignored me.

A little more pressure was apparently required.

Reaching into the inside pocket of my duster, I withdrew a few items: a reporter's notebook and pen, a cigarette lighter, and a small white candle. I scribbled a hasty note on a clean page of the notebook, and then tore it free. I put it on the floor and stood the candle on top of it.

Velvet stirred slightly, proving she *was* paying attention after all, but she didn't move from her position by the window. After a moment's hesitation, I continued with what I was doing.

I picked up the lighter and lit the candle.

The flame flared brightly and then bent at a forty-five degree angle until it was pointing directly at Velvet, almost as if in accusation.

Her head came up slowly in response.

The note and candle ritual has been around for centuries. You can find reference to it in texts as ancient as Artemidorus's *Oneirocritica* and Cicero's *On Divination*. I'd personally used it on more than a handful of occasions, and each time it had done the trick. The writing on the paper acted as a physical representation of my desire, in this case my command for Velvet to depart, and the flame represented the earthly element needed to "charge" the command and force the ghost to obey.

From a ghost's perspective, it's a bit like being manhandled out the back door by a couple of heavyweight bruisers with no necks, whether you wanted to go or not.

Apparently Velvet didn't care for the treatment.

This close, I could see her aura change in response to

my actions, could see the anger sparking off her now in thick black streaks, and beneath that the red splatter that was her pain and the faint, luminescent sheen of blue I'd come to learn was fear. Three emotions that didn't play well together in the living, never mind the dead.

The fingers of my left hand absently rubbed the lodestone hanging around my neck as I felt myself shiver at all that raw emotion.

Velvet stood her ground, ignoring the banishing and refusing to leave.

She wasn't happy with recent events though, and she let me know it. The temperature in the room dropped like a stone; even as I watched, frost blossomed on the window and spread out across the glass. Along with the cold came the first true poltergeist activity I'd seen so far tonight, the bed beginning to rock up and down on its four legs, banging out a staccato rhythm against the floor.

It was time to bring out the heavy guns.

From the depths of my outer pocket I withdrew a can of red spray paint. Velvet's eyes were following my every move by this point, but she still hadn't given any sign that she intended to try to physically stop me, so I continued with my preparations. Turning to the door, I uncapped the paint and sprayed a big red X right across it from one corner to the other.

An old wives' tale says that ghosts don't like the color red and, oddly enough, it happens to be true. In fact, ghosts will go out of their way to avoid it, the same way you and I might cross the street to avoid a nasty-looking dog. Some say it's because of the vibrations the color gives off, others that red reminds them too much of blood, and therefore of life. I didn't really care one way or the other. All that mattered to me was the knowledge that with the door marked in red, Velvet wouldn't cross that barrier if she had any other option open to her. The window was already sealed off thanks to the iron grille, and with the door now secured, her options were dwindling fast.

I was hoping that at this point she'd decide to go peacefully.

I was done with being polite, though. She'd resisted the simpler methods at my disposal. Now I had no choice but to get a little rough.

Velvet's watchful demeanor changed the second I pulled the clump of sage out of my other pocket. Gone was the casual disregard; now she stared directly at me and the black taint of her aura intensified until it drowned out the other colors.

I'd come too far to stop now though. I was being paid to get rid of her. She didn't belong here, not anymore, and I'd gotten pretty good at enforcing my will in situations like this.

I repeated my request for her to leave, this time with a bit more force, and then touched the sage to the candle flame. As the dried herb began to smolder, it gave off a thick, unpleasant-smelling smoke, which I began to wave around the room and at Velvet herself. Smudging, it was called, and, like the note and the candle routine, it was supposed to drive off the ghost.

The bed was bouncing up and down harder now and the drawers of the dresser in the corner began slamming open and shut as Velvet fought back against my efforts. She was stubborn, holding her ground against the noxious fumes, refusing to move on. I kept my head down but my gaze fixed firmly on her as I hunted in my pocket for the last item I needed to finish the banishing.

Something flew through the air and just missed smashing into my head. It took me a moment to realize that it was a dresser drawer. I glanced up, only to jerk my head to the side as another swept past not an inch in front of my eyes. A third slammed into my stomach, momentarily driving the breath from my lungs.

Better hurry up, Hunt . . .

My hand finally found the cloth pouch I'd been rooting around for and I pulled it free, slipping the drawstrings open as I did. Velvet's figure was swelling as she drew power from the air around her, and I wasted no time in pouring what was inside the pouch into the palm of my hand and flinging it in her direction.

The finely ground iron dust struck her full in the face.

I had a brief, fleeting moment to think I'd bested her at last and then everything spun out of control.

Velvet screamed, a long unearthly cry that made all the hair on my body stand at attention. Streams of black poured from her eyes in a rush and then, with her fingers hooked into ragged claws, she charged forward, throwing herself across the room at me with the kind of rage and despair that only the dead can muster.

I'd been wrong.

This was no harmless poltergeist but actually a full-blown spectre masquerading as a lesser ghost. And clearly, she intended to tear me limb from limb.

Instinct took over then, every fiber of my being shouting at me to run, and run I did. My body was already in motion before my brain had finished telling it which way to go, and as I pushed through the door, I gave it a hearty swing back in the other direction, slamming it shut at my back.

Something massive struck it a resounding blow on the other side, and I heard the wood crack quite clearly, even over Velvet's horrible cries.

I spun around to face it, only to have the room around me go strangely silent at that exact moment.

The sudden quiet was as alarming as the torturous shrieking cut off in my wake.

Just what the hell was she . . .

I began backing my way across the living room, unable and unwilling to take my eyes off the door. As I went, I dug in my pocket for my last line of defense, a small hand mirror.

I'd barely made it halfway across the room when something struck the door with incredible force, blasting it right off its hinges and directly at me.

I threw myself to the ground, feeling the weight and heat of the door's passage as it whistled by me.

The impact with the ground jarred the mirror loose from my hand. It bounced across the floor, out of sight.

"Noooo . . . !" I cried involuntarily, fear filling my throat. Without that mirror, I was done for. I had to find it!

I scrambled forward on elbows and knees, searching, as Velvet came after me.

Come on! Where the hell is it?

A wave of freezing cold washed over me and I knew she was almost upon me. If I didn't find it fast . . .

There!

As those claw-tipped fingers reached for my tender flesh, my fingers finally found the mirror's edge. I grabbed it and I swung my hand up and around, thrusting the mirror out in front of me, directly into her path.

Velvet's gaze went to the mirror's surface, and in the split second before the reflection snagged her I thought I saw her eyes widen in surprise.

For the living, a mirror is simply a convenience, a way for us to see that we don't look like complete idiots when we leave the house in the morning, but to the dead, it is oh, so much more.

Ghosts can use mirrors as portals, passageways from one place to another, in much the same way that hobgoblins can travel from shadow to shadow. Most people recognize this, even if only on a subconscious level. That's how the custom of covering the mirrors in the home of the deceased during a wake originated; no one wanted the dead man's ghost showing up and scaring off those who'd come to pay their respects. The same reasoning explains why the best funeral homes in any city expressly forbid hanging mirrors inside their halls.

But mirrors also have other uses, and I'd specially prepared this one for just such an emergency as this. Held to the place by the violent circumstances of her death and all the iron covering the entrances to the building, Velvet would have probably gone on haunting the place indefinitely. Unable to reach the individual who had stolen her life away from her, she was using those who'd failed to help her as his surrogate, taking out all her hatred and rage on them instead. She likely could have left at any time had she wanted to. After all, what woman's apartment didn't have a mirror in it somewhere? But she'd become focused on vengeance and was ignoring the means at her disposal to let go and move on to whatever was next.

I was simply forcing her to do so.

This close she couldn't resist the pull of the way between worlds, something that seems to be true of every ghost I'd encountered so far, and as a result her headlong rush changed just enough to bring her into contact with the mirror's reflective surface.

A flash of searing cold passed through the mirror, frosting its face, and then the glass cracked with a loud snap that echoed in the sudden silence that fell over the apartment in the wake of Velvet's disappearance.

Working quickly, I pulled a piece of black silk out of my pocket and wrapped the mirror in it. With its surface broken, the ghost was now trapped inside the glass, at least temporarily. In time it would either move on to whatever stage of the afterlife was next or discover a passage back to the real world through a connecting portal. Either would take some effort, which left me some time to dispose of the mirror as I saw fit without worrying about Velvet coming after me.

I slumped back against the ground, exhausted.

It was over.

Nearby, something clattered to the floor.

I sat up hurriedly, afraid that there had been more than one entity holed up inside the apartment, but the room behind me was empty. Nothing looked out of place, either.

I knew I hadn't imagined it, though. The sound had been quite distinct. Something had skittered across the bedroom floor, as if pushed by errant hands, and I had the sudden overwhelming urge to find what it was. My gut told me that I couldn't just turn my back on this. I had no idea why, but I knew it was important.

I've learned to trust hunches like that.

Back in the bedroom I got down on my hands and knees and went over the floor with the proverbial fine-tooth comb. It took a while, but eventually I found it, tucked away under the baseboard against the wall by the window where Velvet had been standing. It was a small locket, maybe silver, maybe gold; it was hard to tell in the gray haze that was my vision. The kind of locket a girl might wear on a chain around her neck, and from the amount of dried blood on it I could tell that Velvet had probably been holding it when she'd died. If the cops had searched hard enough they would certainly have found it, as it wasn't that far out of sight, but obviously they hadn't cared as much about some dead hooker as the captain led the press to believe.

I couldn't see the image in the photograph that lined the inside of the locket: another side effect of my Faustian bargain from years before. And not just photographs, but paintings, too. They all looked to my strange new vision like deep gray Rorschach blotches, and I knew them for what they were simply because they were the only things that appeared that way. This one was no different.

The picture didn't really matter though. It was the locket itself that was important.

To those in the trade they were known as fetters, physical objects that tied a ghost to a certain location. Fetters could be anything, from a childhood toy to a prized personal possession to a loved one the ghost refused to leave behind. In the short time I'd been doing this kind of thing, I'd seen my fair share of them and could recognize them by the way they pressed against my senses in much the same way as the ghost to which they were tied.

The locket had been Velvet's fetter, her link to this place and time.

I scooped it up and put it in my pocket. If you were going to haunt somewhere, there were a thousand better places in this city to do so than a run-down tenement building in the heart of the Rox.

Taking one last look around the apartment, I turned and headed for the door.

My job here was done.

4

then

I can't remember my first kiss or the first time I said "I love you" to the woman I would one day marry, two events most people would consider to be quintessential moments in a man's life, but I remember each and every detail, no matter how trivial, of the horrible afternoon when Elizabeth disappeared. They are etched indelibly on the surface of my mind, a grotesque and terrifying mosaic that I can recall at will, anytime, anywhere. It is as if the universe wants to be certain that I don't forget even the slightest detail, wants me to be able to relive it all in a heartbeat, complete with high-def and Dolby surround sound.

Anne was gone for the weekend to the spa in Westport with her girlfriends—their annual pilgrimage, I liked to call it—and I was alone in the house with our daughter. It had been raining all day, one of those cold October rains that seeps into the very marrow of your bones and chills you from the inside out. I'd spent much of the morning locked away in my study, working on the translation of a *manuscript that had just come in from Iraq. I could hear the television playing in the room down the hall and knew Elizabeth had settled in for her afternoon ritual of watching Scooby and the gang chase down the latest villain. She'd be there for at least an hour and that gave me the time I needed to get the translation under way.*

I was working from computer scans of an ancient scroll found in the desert by an American army patrol, and it required all my attention to correctly decipher and translate the Chaldean script that covered the pages. What I had intended to be an hour session quickly turned into two, then three. At last I was done. I leaned back in my chair, closed my eyes, and smiled in achievement.

That's when I noticed the quiet of the house around me.

That's weird, I remember thinking.

Elizabeth was a boisterous child, with five times the energy any one person deserved. If she was quiet, that usually meant she was up to something.

My thoughts still on the work I'd completed, I left the study and went in search of my daughter.

The living room where she had been watching cartoons earlier was empty, as was the bathroom adjacent to it. The television had been turned off, so I assumed she'd had enough of Scooby and had gone off to her room to play. A glance at my watch let me know how long things had gone on; it was almost time for dinner.

"Elizabeth?" I called.

No answer.

"Elizabeth? Where are you, honey?"

Only silence.

The quiet was getting to me and I felt the first faint stirring of unease in the pit of my stomach.

I tried to ignore it, telling myself that nothing was wrong.

Assuming she must be up in her room listening to her radio with her headphones on, I climbed the stairs and moved down the hall. Her bedroom was halfway down the hall on the left, just before my own.

I knocked once, waited a minute, and then opened the door when I didn't receive a reply.

The room was empty.

I didn't react at that point. Who knows, maybe I should have. Maybe if I had run outside right then and there I might have been able to save her. Or, at the very least, gotten a good look at whoever had taken her. But hindsight is always twenty-twenty and nothing in that moment suggested that five years would pass without a clue to her whereabouts or fate. Elizabeth was an active child; I was sure I'd find her somewhere else in the house.

I wandered from room to room, calling her name as I went. I checked the living room, in case she had gone back to watching television. She wasn't there. I checked the kitchen, thinking she might have gotten hungry and gone looking for a snack, but that room was empty as well. I even went back upstairs and stuck my head in the spare bedroom, for she sometimes liked to curl up in there and watch the cars drive by on the street outside. No dice.

It was only when I wandered back past her room that I noticed the draft. The curtains had been drawn, covering the window, but even from the hallway I could see them billowing away from the wall as they caught the breeze from outside.

A sense of dread swept over me in that second and somehow I knew.

Elizabeth was gone.

Parents experience a unique kind of fear. It is at once more visceral and more paralyzing than any other fear, a cold, clammy hand that squeezes your heart until your very blood starts to drip from between its fingers. It invades your mind like an alien presence, disrupts your *thought processes and ratchets your emotions right off the scale, until you can't possibly think straight and every second is an eternity, an eternity where all you can do is think about all of the terrible things that could have happened to your precious child.*

Fear overwhelmed me, freezing me where I stood, my pulse pounding in my ears. All I could do was stare at those billowing curtains and imagine my daughter's body lying on the frozen ground two stories below.

Getting my legs to move took a Herculean effort.

I yanked the curtain back, exposing the open window. The lower half had been pushed upward as far as it would go. With these old windows that was a good foot and a half, at least half again as much as Elizabeth would have needed to slip out.

Bracing myself, I stuck my head out into the rain and looked down.

The ground below me was clear.

I gasped in relief, not realizing until that moment that I had been holding my breath, but that relief was short-lived, for she was still missing.

"Elizabeth?" I shouted, from the top of the stairs, hearing my voice echo through the rest of the house. "This isn't funny now Elizabeth, come out here right now!"

The house mocked me with its silence.

Panic took over then, a panic fueled by years of news reports about missing and abducted children, of small bodies found broken and twisted in the dark and lonely places of the world. I raced frantically through the house, shouting her name, demanding that she come out right this instant or there was going to be hell to pay.

Of course she didn't answer me.

Now, years later, I'm convinced she was long gone by then. I have this memory, real or imagined, I'm not sure, of a thump I heard from the room above me while in the midst of my translation efforts. Nothing drastic, nothing that caused me any sort of alarm at the time, just a brief thump, like when a heavy book falls to the floor.

A heavy book.

Or maybe a young child.

When she still didn't respond to my calls, I dashed outside, running around the yard, hoping against hope that she had simply decided to put on her raincoat and go play in the puddles. But there was no sign of her anywhere.

Dripping wet and shivering with cold, I came back inside and dialed the police, the fear thick in my throat.

They were quick in arriving. They always are when the welfare of a child is at stake. But by then it was too late. Elizabeth had vanished, and I would spend the next five years searching in vain for even a hint of what had happened to her.

I was still in the midst of that search when I found Whisper.

Or rather, Whisper found me.

5

now

With the threat to my life now over, I sagged against a nearby wall and caught my breath. That had been a bit too close for my liking and I needed a minute to compose myself. When I was ready, I went in search of my employer.

Outside the darkness of the closed apartment, the lights in the hallway interfered with my vision and I was forced to negotiate the stairwell by keeping one hand on the banister all the way down. I kept waiting to trip over Thompson's unconscious form, but I never did, and suspected he'd beaten a hasty retreat the moment he'd come to; I know I would have had our positions been reversed.

I made it back outside to find the group, including Thompson, waiting for me. I'm convinced more than half of them didn't expect me to return, but then again I was used to people underestimating me due to my condition. Annoyed, I felt like telling them I was blind not helpless, but it wasn't worth the trouble.

I gave them a quick rundown of the events as they had occurred and did what I could to assure them that Velvet would not be returning to pay them a visit anytime soon. Their troubles were over. Then, before they could ask too many questions about where the ghost had gone, questions I honestly didn't have answers to, I walked down the street to the corner and hailed a cab.

As I climbed inside the vehicle, the cracked mirror in my pocket feeling curiously heavy, my cell phone began to ring. I pulled it out and answered it with a simple, "Hunt."

"I need you on the Hill," Detective Stanton said in his usual annoyed tone, and then rattled off an address.

Apparently I was Mr. Popular tonight; first a job and now some paid consulting with the Boston PD. I was pretty well worn out from all I'd just been through, but I knew better than to argue with Stanton. He had me cold and I knew he'd squeeze me for every ounce he could get. Being called out abruptly like this was a minor inconvenience compared to what he could do to make even the shattered remnants of my life considerably less comfortable, so I told him where I was, explained it would be at least fifteen minutes before I could get to his location, and sat back to wait out the ride.

Beacon Hill lies just north of Boston Common and is the city's most upscale neighborhood. Founded in the late 1790s, it still retains much of its original character, with brick-lined sidewalks, perpetually burning gas lamps, and narrow streets that often change direction without notice. It was built with old money and old money still maintains it. Even the slightest changes to its mix of Victorian, Federal, and Colonial Revival architecture are strictly regulated, and there is enough social and political power floating about in the neighborhood that uniformed police officers can often be found guarding public parking spaces for their wealthy patrons. The Hill was only a short physical distance from where I lived in Dorchester, but in every other sense, the two neighborhoods were worlds apart.

The sudden onslaught of cobblestones beneath the tires let me know when we turned onto Seventh. Three more blocks and we'd be there. A few minutes later the car pulled over to the right and came to a stop, engine idling. I paid the driver, turned down his offer of help, and got out.

I stood on the sidewalk for a moment, getting my bearings. The wind had picked up during the drive over and it diffused the sound around me, making it seem to be coming through gossamer curtains, but I could still hear the casual conversation of the officers standing watch at the door of a brownstone nearby. I withdrew my cane, extended it, and made my way toward them.

The officers couldn't miss my approach, a tall thin figure dressed in black tapping the tip of his cane against the pavement in front of him, and so I wasn't surprised when one of them challenged my presence.

"I'm sorry, sir, but you can't come in here."

I kept moving forward, knowing they'd be hesitant to touch me because of the cane, as if blindness was an infectious disease or something, and spoke without stopping.

"I'm Hunt. Jeremiah Hunt. Stanton called for me."

I passed them, reached the front steps, and started upward as the patrolman continued to object, telling me this was a crime scene and I wasn't allowed inside.

Like I didn't know that already.

Idiot.

I hadn't gone more than another step or two, however, before I heard the door above me open and a gruff voice said, "It's okay, Williams. I've got it."

Homicide Detective Miles Stanton gave me a moment to fold up my cane and put it in the pocket of my duster.

Then, taking my arm, he guided me up the stairs and in through the front door.

"Took you long enough, Hunt."

He had a deep baritone voice and a gruff attitude to match, exactly what you would expect coming from a short, stocky fireplug of a man. This time, though, there was also a little tremor in his tone, a slight quivering that wasn't usually there.

That was a bad sign.

I'd known Stanton for several years, ever since the initial investigation into Elizabeth's disappearance. While we certainly weren't friends, I couldn't say we were enemies, either. That would require us to see each other as equals, something neither of us was willing to do. Stanton clearly thought of me as an inferior, to be ordered around at will, and I, well, I tried not to think of Stanton at all.

Most days, it worked out pretty well for both of us.

"Here. Put these on."

He handed me some bunched-up fabric and I knew from prior experience that I'd been given a pair of booties made from stretchable cloth. They went over the outside of my shoes, like old-fashioned galoshes, and were intended to keep me from contaminating the crime scene, preventing me from tracking in anything from outside on the bottom of my shoes. The fact that I had to wear them told me that the scene hadn't been fully processed; the body was still in place. Without worrying about which end was the front and which was the back, I used Stanton's arm for balance and pulled the booties over my shoes.

"All right," I said, once I had both feet on the ground again. "What have we got?"

Stanton didn't answer.

Another bad sign.

He just took my arm and led me through the house and up a flight of stairs to the second floor.

As we headed down the main hallway I started to get nervous and decided I wasn't going any farther until I got some answers out of him. I pulled my arm free and stopped. "Come on, Detective, cut the bullshit. You've got to tell me something."

I could sense his gaze on me for a long moment before he answered. "All right, fine," he said, and I was surprised to hear the strain in his voice. "We've got a homicide, obviously. A woman named Brenda Connolly. No sign of forced entry. No sign of a struggle. In fact, there isn't much of anything except the body itself."

His voice got a little catch in it when he said the word "body." A sighted person never would have noticed, that's how well he hid it, but I had trained my ears to take the place of my eyes and to me his discomfort was as plain as day.

He didn't say anything for a long time, and I was finally forced to prompt him. "And?"

Stanton blew out his breath in frustration. "And it's bad," he said. "So bad that it's probably better that you can't see it."

Stanton had been on the force a long time. I imagined he'd seen just about the worst things that human beings could do to one another. If what he'd seen had made him this uncomfortable . . .

But he wasn't finished. "Look, Hunt. You know how it is. People don't get murdered on the Hill. Especially not like this. The pressure to wrap this up quickly is going to be intense. If I don't come up with something soon, the captain is going to have me punching parking tickets in Southie before the week's out."

While I would be perfectly happy to see Detective Stanton demoted to little better than an errand boy, I knew he'd be less than thrilled. And when Stanton wasn't happy, he had a habit of making my life equally miserable. So if I wanted the freedom to continue the search for my daughter, I'd have to help him out as best I could.

He started walking again and I shuffled along beside him, our booted feet whispering against the hardwood floor. His voice hardened and regained its usual steel. "I'm sure I don't have to remind you about the rules. You're here to do that thing you do and identify the killer. Period. There isn't any room for fucking up, got it?"

Gotta love him. Even when he desperately needed my help, he still had to put the screws in.

Nice.

But the truth was that it didn't even bother me all that much anymore. Maybe once upon a time I might have cared, but no longer. Stanton could say and do whatever he wanted; in the end, finding Elizabeth was all that mattered. He was nothing more than a means to an end.

Helping him out kept my access open to the latest information about my daughter's case. I'd been declared persona non grata years ago, thanks to Anne's machinations, and Stanton was my only link to the occasional lead that came in. I'd do backflips if that was what he wanted, provided the flow of information continued.

I was here to use my skills to give Stanton a jump start on his investigation. You see, Stanton thinks I'm psychic. Has ever since the day we first met. I can't say that I blame him; if I saw someone do what I'd done that night, I'd probably believe they were psychic, too. Working with a psychic was even becoming respectable, in some areas. As long as the other homicide dicks at the station didn't find out what he was doing, Stanton was perfectly happy to use my particular set of skills as he saw fit.

Psychic he could deal with. It was something he could get his head around.

Believing I can see dead people and communicate with them?

Not so much.

Which was fine with me. Trying to explain the nuances of my relationship with the dead would have been too much for *both* of us.

Sure, there were days that I wished the dead could speak directly to me, but there were just as many others when I am equally thankful that they cannot. Like the times when they just pop in uninvited. That *always* creeps me out.

Besides, I don't need them to speak; there is a lot I can learn just by observing what they do at the scene of the crime.

So I come whenever Stanton calls, I keep my eyes open, and give him whatever I can pick up at the scene. In return, he keeps me up to date on my daughter's by now very cold case. Tit for tat. Everybody is happy.

When we reached the end of the hallway he pulled back slightly on my arm, bringing me to a halt.

"The body's in the bedroom in front of you. I know you need peace and quiet to . . ." he hesitated, searching for words, ". . . do what you do, so I'm just gonna wait out here in the hallway. Holler if you need me."

He guided me inside the room and the click I heard over my shoulder told me he'd closed the door behind him on his way out.

I immediately felt the heat of the crime scene lights set up around the room. Even if I hadn't, the whiteout before my eyes would have been enough to clue me in to their presence. No way was I going to take a chance of fumbling around trying to turn them off, though. Since I had no idea where the body was and didn't want to accidentally stumble on it the hard way, I stayed right where I was. My inability to see anything meant that I was going to need Whisper's help.

I raised my face to the ceiling and extended my arms out to either side, palms up. Closing my eyes, I called out softly.

"Come to me, Whisper. Come to me."

As I called her name, I pictured her doing what I wanted, having learned over time that a bit of positive reinforcement went a long way to helping the summons to be successful.

I repeated my request, over and over again, until at last I felt a presence join me and her cold, slim hand slip inside my own.

One thing was for certain: my growing headache was going to get considerably worse before the day was done.

6

now

"Lend me your eyes," I said to Whisper. I kept my voice low, respecting the quiet emptiness of the room around us and the still, unseen presence of the dead.

There was a moment of dizziness, startling in its intensity, and then the taste of bitter ashes flooded my mouth and I could see again.

Sort of.

Looking through the eyes of the dead is a sensory experience unlike any other. It had taken me weeks to get used to it in the early days. Now, several years later, it barely made me flinch.

If you'd asked me ahead of time what I thought the dead might see from their place on the other side of life, I would have probably described a visual representation of hell on earth, all dark shadows and wet, oozing rot, the miasma of a thousand different dark emotions swirling amidst the entropy that was the lot of all of us in the end.

The reality, however, is startlingly different.

The first thing you see is this incredible explosion of color, ten times brighter and more vivid than anything I remember from before my "sacrifice." Right about then you realize that you aren't alone, that the supernatural denizens of the world around you are now clearly visible. From that first glance you understand that we regularly interact with creatures far stranger and deadlier than you ever previously imagined. It's not that they weren't there before, it's just that humans rarely recognize them for what they are. Ghosts don't have that problem. They see everything, from the fallen angels that swoop over the narrow city streets on ash gray wings to the changelings that walk among us unseen, safe in their human guises. The glamour-like charms that supernatural entities use to conceal themselves from human sight are no match for the eyes of a ghost.

But perhaps the cruelest irony is the fact that the dead can see all of the emotions that they can no longer experience as fully as they had in life. And not just the emotions of the living, either. Objects can gather and hold emotional residues as well. A child's teddy bear might glow with the pure white light of unconditional love, while the hairbrush used to brush a woman's long, glossy hair might reflect the scarlet eroticism felt by her husband as he wielded it night after night over twenty years of marriage. Each and every object gives off an aura of some kind and the more important the object is to its owner, the brighter the glow. In my own home, the photograph of Elizabeth that stands on the mantelpiece practically burns with the harsh, silver light of my regret and lack of forgiveness.

When I take over Whisper's sight, I have to deal with all that emotion, too. How the dead manage it is beyond me.

I glanced down at her, noting for what seemed the thousandth time the vacant way that her eyes wandered thanks to my commandeering her vision. As always, I was struck by her resemblance to Elizabeth. Same dark hair, same bright eyes. Even that impish little grin Elizabeth used to wear can be seen on Whisper's face from time to time, when something causes her to forget, even if just for a moment, the ghostly existence to which she was condemned.

She and Scream had just shown up one day, not too long after my sacrifice. I don't know what drew them to me or what makes them stay. I do know that I can count on them whenever I need their help, something I can't say about many of my so-called friends among the living.

Along the way these two ghosts and I have discovered that we are bound together in some kind of mystical fashion. When I need to, I can borrow Whisper's sight or Scream's strength. Sometimes both at once, if the need is great enough. But I don't do it often. Linking with one of them for too long leaves me exhausted. Linking with both often ends with me lying unconscious on the floor.

Sometimes looking through Whisper's eyes can be difficult; tonight the view was pretty good. It was more or less upright and squared off and through it I was able to take a good look around.

The writing immediately caught my eye. Black marker on white walls will do that. I spun in a slow circle, drinking it all in, stunned by what I was seeing. Sumerian pictographs. Chaldean script. Egyptian hieroglyphics. Norse runes. A few languages that I didn't recognize, but if I had to hazard a guess I would have said they were as old as the others, if not older.

Thanks to Whisper's unusual ocular powers, the letters seemed to lurch in different directions, like insects trying to escape the touch of the light. They gave off a patina of emotion, from hunger to pain, from desire to obsession, but the one underlying feeling that shone through without question was one of menace. Whoever put them there knew what they were doing. The feeling seeped under the skin in much the same way that water seeps beneath the earth, slow and sure, going where it wills, unfettered and untamed.

Despite my familiarity with most of the languages, I didn't immediately recognize any of the phrases displayed around me and I knew it was going to take a bit of effort to decipher just what it all said.

I noticed the body as soon as I could tear my gaze away from the writing on the walls. It was hard to miss. It was only the fact that once upon a time, in what seemed like another life, I'd made my living translating ancient languages at Harvard that had kept me from focusing on it right away.

She'd been beautiful once. Long blond hair that fell just past her shoulders. A narrow waist. Strong, sculpted legs. Her nakedness made it easy to see that this was a woman who had liked to take care of herself. But the position and stillness of the body stole the illusion of life away like fog in the sunlight, turning beauty into horror.

Her flesh had an odd blue-green tint to it. I stared at it for a few minutes, nonplussed. It was way too early for the discoloration to have been caused by decomposition, and the fact that it covered every square inch of her flesh that I could see ruled out postmortem lividity as well. Her aura still lingered, which was also unusual. You didn't see that with a Normal, which meant she was something either more, or less, than human.

She was kneeling, her hands clasped together in front and her head angled upward toward the heavens.

I walked across the room and maneuvered around the body until I could see her face.

Her mouth gaped wide in a silent scream and empty sockets stared back at me where her eyes should have been. She had not died easily, that was for sure.

You had to look closely to see the fishing line that had

been used to keep her forearms and hands tied together, but once you had, it was easy to see everywhere else it had been used to secure her in place. Her legs had been tied together at the thighs, knees, and ankles, and long stretches of fishing line had been run back to the bed and nearby armoire to hold the body upright.

I reached out and touched one of the lines, noting the tautness of the fishing wire and the artfulness with which it had been used. From the other side of the room, you weren't even able to see it.

Which was exactly the point.

I knew instinctively that the killer had wanted it to appear that the woman had simply been kneeling in the corner of her room, praying.

I wasn't a crime scene investigator by any stretch of the imagination, but I'd seen enough episodes of *Law & Order* and *CSI* to know that the positioning of the body was a strong clue to the motivation of the killer. I took a few minutes to study it carefully.

Stanton was right; it *was* creepy. Very creepy. Staging the body like this had required patience and ingenuity. The killer had taken his time, binding the body and then securing it in place, using the natural process of rigor mortis to stiffen the corpse into the desired position. He hadn't worried about being interrupted before he was finished, which suggested that he'd known ahead of time that he wouldn't be.

Turning my attention from the corpse, I glanced around the room, making certain the woman's ghost wasn't still lurking about, but Whisper and I were the only ones there.

Relax, Hunt. Don't get all spooked before you really need to.

I wandered around the room for a bit, trying to get a feel for who the woman was, what she'd been like. A person's bedroom can tell you volumes, if you know how to look. That she was wealthy was immediately obvious. The address alone told me that, but the exquisitely handcrafted furniture, the thick silk bedsheets, and the closet full of clothing with designer labels also spoke of a life of leisure without concern for expense. None of it, however, showed any real emotion attached to it. They were symbols of status and that was all.

The stack of books on the nightstand, on the other hand, glowed with the brilliant sheen of hope.

I walked over and picked a few off the top of the stack. They were all contemporary romance novels, bestselling hardcover stuff by Nicholas Sparks, Nora Roberts, and the like, though there were a few trade paperbacks in the bunch by authors I didn't recognize. Up-and-comers, I assumed. Apparently the princess in the castle was still waiting, and pining for, her Prince Charming.

The armoire was covered with photos of her standing with various celebrities. Most of them were local folks, the kind you'd meet at a major charity fundraiser here on the Hill, but here and there were pictures of the victim with the occasional movie star or Broadway actor. The latter were always in slightly larger frames, so that they stood out a bit from the rest. I thought it would have made more sense to have the entire set out in the front room somewhere where they would have been seen. Just who she thought was going to see them here in her bedroom was beyond me, but then again, I didn't know much about the victim's dating habits. Maybe they were right where they needed to be after all.

A master bath, complete with the largest Jacuzzi tub I'd ever seen, jutted off one side of the bedroom, but a quick look told me that there wasn't anything significant inside.

Having exhausted my meager investigatory skills, it was time for Whisper and me to get down to business and give Stanton something he could work with.

I steered the two of us back over to the corpse and then knelt beside it, pulling Whisper down next to me. Leaning over, I told her what I needed.

She shrugged, as if my request was no big deal, and who knows, maybe to her it wasn't. She reached out with her free hand and laid the tips of two of her fingers inside the victim's empty eye sockets.

I felt Whisper's fingers squeeze my own, warning me, and then a freight train roared through my skull, wheels churning and horn blowing, tracks rattling thunderously beneath its wheels, filling my head with a cacophony of sound that brought its own shipment of raw pain. I expected it, but that didn't make it any easier to bear.

I waited until the train passed and the pain stopped before slowly opening my eyes.

The last few minutes of Brenda Connolly's life played out before me as witnessed through her own eyes, just as she had lived through them, with a little extra thrown in thanks to Whisper's unique nature.

She'd been getting ready to go out, that much was obvious. I caught a long flash of smooth thigh as she sat down on the stool in front of her cosmetics mirror. She'd been a good-looking woman; there was no doubt about that. As Whisper and I watched, she carefully applied makeup to her already flawless face. When she was satisfied, she wandered into the walk-in closet, chose a sleek black dress, and then slipped into it before returning to the mirror to admire the way it showed off her figure. She spent a few minutes fussing over the right shoes to wear, finally settling on a pair of high-heeled black pumps that accented her shapely calves and gave her a few extra inches of height.

She was giving herself a final once-over in the full-length mirror when motion behind her caught her eye. A man appeared in the mirror, standing behind her in the doorway. He was dressed in a dark, ankle-length coat that dripped rainwater onto her expensive flooring. The wide-brimmed hat he wore was pulled low enough that it covered his face in shadow.

She must have known him, for a smile spread across her face and she moved to join him by the door with a clear sense of eagerness that made her seem younger than her years.

I waited for him to lift his head as she drew closer, to give me a look at his face, but he never did. He kept his head down and his hat on. At the last minute he opened his arms and she practically flung herself into them. Her eyes were closed as she lifted her face for a kiss . . .

That's when the vision faded.

Apparently she hadn't been conscious for whatever had happened next.

I cursed beneath my breath as Whisper brought us back to the here and now. I hadn't gotten much in the way of information. Her visitor had been male, a bit over average height and had apparently been someone she'd known. For all I knew he was her boyfriend and not her killer.

At least it was a place to start.

As I got back to my feet, I inadvertently kicked something with the side of my shoe and sent it skittering across the floor. Retrieving it, I saw that it was a small charm in the shape of a winged fairy, the kind of thing a young girl might wear on a charm bracelet. It was fashioned of silver, and a good deal of care and detail had been used in its construction. It had tiny eyes, a pixie nose, and the faintest traces of swirling designs in the center of its wings.

It seemed so out of place that for a long moment I just stared at it. Where had it come from? More importantly, what was it doing here? It didn't fit the scenario; it didn't feel like something that belonged to the victim, nor could

I imagine it as the type of item the killer would have left behind.

It was oddly familiar, like I'd seen it before, but when I tried to focus on it the feeling slipped away and I knew better than to chase after it. It would come when it was good and ready to do so and not a moment earlier. On impulse, I slipped the charm inside the pocket of my coat.

With Stanton waiting in the hall for whatever I could tell him, I took a few minutes to gather my thoughts, trying to figure out what it was that I was going to say and what I was going to keep to myself. When I was ready, I positioned myself so that I was facing the doorway, said thank you to Whisper, and braced myself as she left me on my own.

As she faded away into nothingness beside me, the light stole my vision from me, and with it came a wave of fatigue so strong that all I wanted to do was lie down right then and there and go to sleep. I fought it off and made my way to the door instead.

Stanton caught me as I stumbled out into the hallway. "Well?" he asked, a bit impatiently.

I shook him off and stood on trembling legs. "You're looking for a man," I told him wearily. "Over six feet and roughly two hundred pounds. Big hands."

"What about his face?"

I shook my head. "I didn't get a look at it. But he was wearing a long dark coat and a wide-brimmed hat. Someone must have seen him. Folks like that aren't exactly inconspicuous in this neighborhood."

"Anything else?"

I thought about it for a long moment, then, "Gloves. He was wearing thin latex gloves, like a surgeon."

So much for fingerprints. I knew Stanton was thinking the same. Still, the description was more than they'd had to go on before I'd been called in. That was something at least.

"Anything else?"

I shook my head.

"All right, Hunt, good enough."

I knew that was as close to thanks as I was going to get, so I took it for what it was worth and followed Stanton back down the stairs to the first floor. The medical examiner's men had arrived while we were upstairs and Stanton's hands were suddenly full directing them to the body and passing along the necessary information to the uniforms so they could start canvassing the neighborhood, looking for anyone who might have seen the mysterious perp.

In the resulting confusion, I slipped out the front door and made my way down the street.

7

now

Behind Hunt, the creature wearing the face of Officer Marcus Williams stood on the steps and watched him go, a smile spreading across its features.

Everything had gone accordingly to plan.

Now only time would tell.

Meanwhile it would continue carrying out its orders, for it was imperative that the Master's suspicions not be aroused. For the plan to work, Hunt had to have time to put it all together.

But what if the clue left behind hadn't been interesting enough to capture his attention? What if Hunt decided not to get involved after all?

That wouldn't do.

Wouldn't do at all.

It would have to think of something else, a surefire way to keep Hunt in the midst of things until he figured out for himself what he was supposed to do.

It turned back toward the chaos that was the crime scene, ready to play its part to the hilt, but its thoughts were still on the strange human who had just left and what it could do to ensure that he remained a part of the investigation.

It thought it knew just the thing.

8

then

In the aftermath of Elizabeth's disappearance, my house filled up with strangers. Old man Weinstein, my normally recalcitrant neighbor, was the first to arrive; he'd heard me screaming Elizabeth's name while I was frantically racing around the backyard and had come over to be certain everything was all right.

It was Weinstein who'd let the police in when they arrived. The group moved like a cyclone, all frantic activity and thundering noise. Three uniformed officers searched the house and yard, as if I hadn't just spent the last half hour doing so, while a pair of detectives, one male and one female, sat me down on the couch in the living room and asked me a lot of questions. Questions to which I didn't have many answers. What was Elizabeth doing before she disappeared? What was she wearing? Had she been upset about anything? Had she spoken to anyone on the phone?

To my shame, I had no idea about any of it.

We spent an hour, maybe more, going through it over

and over again. In the back of my mind I knew they were looking for inconsistencies, but I had nothing to hide and couldn't have hidden anything even if I had wanted, my mental state having been torn to ribbons as the horror of it all descended like a black cloud over my mind.

Somewhere in the midst of it all Anne returned home. I have no recollection of her arrival, just a hazy memory of looking up as I fought to come up with an answer to what should have been a simple question, only to find her standing on the other side of the room, tears streaming down her face as she stared at me in disbelief. I think that it was at that point that our marriage became irrevocably broken. Sure, it lingered for a while, nearly two years, but the damage had been done right then and there. It simply took us a while to recognize the cracks that ran beneath the surface, cracks that just became too deep and too wide for us to do anything about.

But that was for later. At this point we thought Elizabeth might still be found and Anne wasn't going to waste a precious second if there was a chance of bringing her back to us. Recognizing my utter uselessness, she stepped in and took over, giving the police a precise description of what Elizabeth had been wearing that morning, the places around the neighborhood she liked to go, who she liked to play with, the whole nine yards. The information galvanized the investigation, as the police finally had a place in which to start. As everyone jumped into action, I was left alone on the couch, staring off into space, appalled at my inability to help search for the one person I loved more than life itself, my own failings staring me starkly in the face for perhaps the first time in my life.

Yet despite all the confusion and noise going on around me, it was the silence that was deafening. A silence that stood four feet tall. A silence with long flowing hair and a shy, tender smile that could melt your heart in an instant, that shouted from all the things she'd left behind: the dollhouse in the corner of the playroom, the stack of Disney videos leaning haphazardly against the television, the half-finished picture resting on the coffee table, its bright colors mocking me with their cheerfulness.

The silence of the dead is a terrible thing, but it is a silence with a sense of finality to it, an air of completion. The silence of the missing is anything but. It communicates without words, its message clear and unhindered. Find me, it screams, find me, and your heart breaks to hear it so loud in the empty places that should be filled with laughter and the joyful sounds of life. It follows you wherever you go, tugging on your sleeve, reminding you every second that something is wrong, something is missing. You can't ignore it, you can't escape it, and eventually, no matter what you do, it drives you insane with its insistent cries. Parents of missing children live their days in a special corner of hell reserved just for them and I'd just joined the club with fanfare and fireworks.

I might have been drowning in self-pity and shame, but the well-oiled machine that was the Boston Police Department never hesitated.

Uniformed officers were brought out in droves, given the photograph Anne had produced, and sent out to speak to the neighbors, looking for anyone who might have seen Elizabeth, alone or in the company of a stranger. The license and registration of every car in the vicinity were run through the registry's computer systems, looking for one that might be out of place, that didn't belong. The crime scene people came in and began to systematically go over every square inch of Elizabeth's bedroom, hoping to find a piece of physical evidence that would *give them a starting point in identifying who might have taken her. I remember my wife being fingerprinted, and then, when it was my turn, feeling a strange sense of shame and guilt as they rolled my fingers in the black ink and pressed them down on that small white card. For exclusionary purposes, they said, and I simply nodded, not caring if it was true or not. I found out later that they even brought in a team of tracking dogs and set them to work in the fifteen acres of woodland that butted up against the back of my property.*

After searching for hours, they came up empty.

Technicians were brought in to wire my phones, in anticipation of the ransom call we were all expecting. My wife and I were instructed to keep the caller on the phone as long as we could. The longer the trace the better able the police would be to narrow their search area and focus in on the exact location. If the kidnappers were stupid enough to call in on an identifiable line, the police might even be able to get a physical address. The tape also could be analyzed for background noise, voice patterns, and a hundred other identifying criteria that could be used to build a psychological profile and help narrow the list of suspects.

By this time the press had gotten wind of what was going on and our quiet suburban street filled up with news vans from the local network affiliates, WCVB, WBZ, W this and W that. Their reporters and cameramen stomped around in my front yard, blocking traffic and generally making an annoyance of themselves until the police erected a cordon around the property to hold them back. Word went out on the wires that a young girl had gone missing, presumed abducted, and we all waited with bated breath for a call that never came.

In the end, it made no difference.

None of it.

Elizabeth had vanished as surely as if she'd never existed in the first place.

It wasn't until later, when a witness surfaced claiming to have seen Elizabeth in my company an hour after I'd reported her missing, that suspicion came to rest on me.

9

now

Despite my fatigue, I didn't feel much like going straight home. I wanted to wash the sight of that dead woman out of my mind, and I knew just the place to do it. I wandered a short distance down the street from the murder scene and then I raised my hand and waited for a cab to show up.

You'd think that in this day and age a cabdriver would think twice about picking up a guy who refused to take his sunglasses off after dark, but thankfully that wasn't the case. The first driver who saw me pulled over without hesitation and I opened the door and climbed inside, nodding at the ghost of the middle-aged woman who already occupied the rear seat. She moved over to make room for me, as if she actually filled the space in which she sat, and I didn't have the heart to tell her differently.

I directed the driver to take me to Murphy's in Dorchester. He grumbled a bit, not wanting to go to that part of town at this time of night, but when I flashed a few bills at him he shut up and drove.

If Beacon Hill is Boston's playground for old money and the nouveau riche, then Dorchester is home to the common joe. Annexed by Boston in the mid-1800s, Dorchester, like its neighbors South Boston and Roxbury, is one of the so-called streetcar suburbs, named for the areas connected to the city by the railroad and streetcar lines laid at that time.

Because of its size, Dorchester is often divided for statistical purposes. North Dorchester consists of the area north of Quincy and Freeport Streets, including the major business district known as Uphams Corner and the Harbor Point area, home to the Boston campus of the University of Massachusetts. South Dorchester, on the other hand, is bordered on the east by Dorchester Bay and on the south by the Neponset River, and contains dozens of smaller ethnic neighborhoods in which families have lived for generations, places like Meeting House Hill, Neponset, Four Corners, and, of course, Savin Hill, the predominantly Irish neighborhood that I currently call home.

It's a rougher section of town than most people will admit, and the cabbie's reluctance to go there at this hour wasn't surprising. Ethnic lines still ran very strong in the old neighborhoods and people protected their own. God help you if you were caught in the wrong neighborhood with the wrong family background after dark. I'd been living there long enough that I'd gradually been accepted as a local, but I think my right of passage had more to do with an unvoiced sense of pity over my blindness than anything else. Whatever it was, I wasn't going to object.

Murphy's was the only Irish pub in Boston run by a Russian. Perhaps the only one in all of Massachusetts for that matter. And not just any Russian, mind you, but one with the sheer stones and thickheadedness needed to fend off the Irish mob's attention every time they decided that bringing Murphy's back under their wing was a priority. The owner's name was Dmitri Alexandrov, and rumor had it that he'd won the place from its previous owner, Sean Murphy, in an all-night poker game on New Year's Eve in 1998. Rumor also claimed that Dmitri tore Murphy limb from limb with his bare hands when Murphy tried to welsh on the bet, but you know how rumors are—you can never quite separate the truth from the bullshit.

A few blocks before we reached our destination, my fellow passenger opened her mouth and vomited up a thick mass of ectoplasmic residue that slopped all over the back of the seat in front of her. The driver might not have been able to see the spiritual mass dripping off the leather next to him, but the thick cloying stench of week-old garbage that came with it couldn't be missed. I immediately felt his attention on me in the rearview mirror.

I pretended not to notice, for, after all, how could a blind man see such a thing? He sniffed indignantly a few times, but apparently didn't have the backbone for anything more because he kept his mouth shut and stopped staring.

As soon as the cabbie looked away, I dug into the pocket of my coat and pulled out one of the envelopes I habitually carried. This one held a mixture of ground rosemary, hazel, and mint, just the thing for an unwanted ectoplasmic spill. I waited until the driver's attention was captured by something on the street and then poured a handful of the mix in the shape of a simple glyph onto the seat beside me.

The reaction was immediate.

The scent of fresh herbs replaced the stink of garbage and the ectoplasm faded to a mere shadow of its former self.

The old lady got out of the cab in front of Murphy's at the same time I did, and I watched her for a moment as she slowly made her way up the street, until at last she faded from view. As I dug in my pockets for the fare, the cabbie finally found his nerve.

"Hey!" he said sharply, pointing at the crushed herbs on the rear seat beside me. "Take your trash with you."

I pretended not to hear him as I sorted through the bills in my hand.

He wasn't content to leave it at that. "I said pick up your trash. You no mess up my cab!"

That did it. I was trying to do the man a favor and all he could do was bluster and yell. He wanted the herbs out of his cab? Fine. I'd take the herbs out of his cab.

I dropped the bill on the seat beside me, swept the sweet-smelling mix into my hand, and climbed out of the car without another word.

With the herbs gone, the ectoplasm would rapidly regain its full strength. And it wouldn't fade until sunrise.

Good luck getting another fare tonight, you ingrate.

I left the curb behind and crossed the short distance to the bar's front door. Pushing it open, I stepped inside, then cautiously made my way across the crowded floor to the bar and took a seat at the first empty stool I could find.

"Evening, Hunt. The usual?"

Dmitri. I couldn't see him, the light in here being far too bright, but I turned my face in his direction and nodded. I'd been coming here a few times a month for the last several years and that was the extent of our conversation each and every time. I'd order my drink, Dmitri would deliver it with quiet efficiency, and then he'd leave me alone. Just the way I liked it. Regardless of how Murphy's had actually come under his control, one thing could be said about Dmitri: he was a damned good bartender.

He put my glass of Johnny Walker Black down exactly six inches in front of me, right where he put it every time, allowing me to find it without difficulty. It was little things like that that made me really appreciate him. He didn't ask me where I wanted it, didn't try to put it in my hand or anything like that, just treated me like every other customer he served, and in doing so made me feel normal again, even if it was only for a few minutes. It was what kept me coming back, rather than frequenting any of the twenty or so other pubs in the area.

Word on the street said that Dmitri was a fixer, the go-to guy for those in need. If you were looking for something, no matter what it might be, he could get it for you, no questions asked. There was a price to be paid, obviously, and his services didn't come cheap, but then again, you get what you pay for and Dmitri was rumored to be well worth the cost.

I didn't know if there was any truth to it all, didn't care either way, really, but I did know that Dmitri was one of the Gifted, just like me.

There are all sorts of creatures living on the streets of this fine city, and after getting over my shock of discovering that they existed in the first place, I'd split them into broad groups just to try to keep them straight in my head.

First you have the Normals. They're your average, everyday people, without any particular abilities beyond those that the good Lord has graced them with, be they good looks or the ability to figure out the square root of 6,849,531 without the help of a calculator. If I had to guess, I'd say that the Normals make up at least 95 percent of the city's population and live in blissful ignorance of the creatures that walk, and sometimes hunt, among them.

Then you have the Preternaturals, creatures out of myth and legend that live among the rest of us like wolves among sheep. Frankly, there are far more of them than I ever expected or am comfortable knowing about. Vampires, revenants, and shapeshifters. Goblins, ghosts, and ghouls. Nagas. Chimeras. Kengu. Lamia. Spider folk. The list goes on and on. Demons of every shape and color are particularly prominent among the upper reaches of Boston society life, and in the years since I've gained the ghostsight I've even caught a glimpse here and there of their opposite numbers, the angels.

Finally you have the Gifted. That's what I have taken to calling those of us who, either by nature or design, have abilities above and beyond the average. The woman born with the sixth sense. The guy who suffers a terrible head injury, and awakens with the ability to hear the thoughts of those in the room with him; the dowser who can find anything with his dowsing rod; or the necromancer who can raise the dead, provided they haven't been gone too long: humans who have gained the ability to tap into the supernatural essence of the world and use it for their own means.

Sometimes their abilities are the results of deliberate effort and practice, like those who focus on ritual magick and sorcery. Other times they're simply nature's way of stirring the pot. If you could do something the average individual could or should not be able to do, you got lumped in with the Gifted.

An odd side effect of the ritual that had taken my sight was the ability to "see" people for who they really are. Normals, Preternaturals, or the Gifted; it doesn't matter. I can see them all. They might hide by shielding themselves with a powerful glamour, but then the presence of the glamour itself will tell me that they are not what they appear to be. It is similar to what I'd experienced when viewing Brenda Connolly's corpse, a faint shimmering aura, though the aura is much stronger in those still among the living. I know the physician in charge of the emergency room at the Deaconess on Monday nights is really a ghoul, for instance, surreptitiously feeding on the life essence of those who can't be saved. And at least one, maybe two, of the nuns at the Convent of the Blessed Mother are succubi, gorging themselves on the suppressed lust and erotic dreams of the newly initiated. Things like that.

Dmitri is no different. When he's near me I can feel him pushing against that same spot in the back of my brain that responds to the presence of the dead, but in a different way. When I use what's left of my sight to look at him, I can see the slight shimmering that surrounds him, a hazy aura that clearly marks him as one of the Gifted.

I've never tried to find out more. I figure he's entitled to his privacy, just as I am. He serves good whiskey and that's enough for me.

A quick glance around the room showed me a couple of other pockets of luminescence, which meant the crowd tonight wasn't entirely Normal. I wasn't surprised; given who and what he was, Dmitri's bar tended to act as a sort of meeting place for all kinds of creatures.

Facing front again, I sat and nursed my drink, thinking about what I'd seen back on the Hill.

I'm not a trained investigator like Stanton, but it doesn't take a genius to know that the police had a real problem on their hands. Given the wealthy victim and the neighborhood where the crime occurred, the pressure to solve the case quickly was going to be incredible. When you throw in the fact that the killer probably wasn't human—a reasonable assumption considering how easily he'd slipped in and out of the Connolly residence—things really looked bad.

There was no way Stanton was going to solve this one easily.

And he probably wasn't going to solve it at all without my help.

I pulled out my phone and hit the 3 key. I had a homicide cop on speed dial. I didn't even want to think about what that said about my social life.

He answered with his usual laconic, "What?"

From the noise in the background I could tell he was still at the crime scene. "M.E. get there yet?" I asked.

"Just finished up. They're getting ready to take out the body."

"When's the autopsy?"

He snorted. "You kidding me? With all the pressure on this one, they'll probably start in the ambulance."

Cop humor. There's nothing darker. "I want to see what I can do with the writing on the walls. Can you get me photos?"

There was a moment of silence and then he said, "Okay." Stanton didn't ask what the hell a blind guy would want with crime scene photos, and he gained some points in my book for not asking. Probably thought I was going to have someone describe them to me or something. If only it were that simple . . .

Stanton did have a question though. "Think you can translate them?"

"Gonna give it a shot. Once upon a time, I was good at that kind of thing."

"Yeah. Once upon a time."

"Fuck you, too, Detective."

I spent a few minutes explaining how I needed the photos to be taken and he dutifully grunted in all the right places, letting me know that he was taking notes. Stanton was a decent detective, perhaps even better than most. If he was going to do something, he'd do it right the first time and save himself a lot of grief. When I was finished with my explanation, I paused for a second, debating, and then decided to say it anyway. "Don't worry. We'll get him."

Stanton laughed. "I don't remember thinking otherwise, asshole," he said, and hung up.

Serves me right for trying to be friendly.

I turned back to my drink and reminded myself not to do that again.

I0

now

From a booth in the back corner, Denise Clearwater watched as Hunt hung up the phone and went back to nursing his drink. For about the tenth time that night, she asked herself the question that had been haunting her for days.

What in Gaia's name did this man have to do with her?

She'd come tonight hoping to find an answer.

Hunt had first intruded on her life three weeks before. She was in the midst of erecting a set of wards inside a client's home when she'd seen his face reflected in a nearby mirror. His appearance had startled her so badly she'd botched the warding, sending her magick snarling wildly away from her, something that hadn't happened to her since the early days of her training. It had taken her several long minutes to regain control. By the time she'd turned to look, it was as if he'd never been there at all.

She saw him again a few days later, watching her

from the other side of a crowded subway platform. Curious, she cut through the crowd and approached him, intending to ask just what the hell he thought he was doing following her, only to discover that he'd vanished. The spot where he'd been standing was occupied by a middle-aged businessman reading a newspaper. Denise had glanced sharply around, looking for Hunt. The stairs off the platform were behind her and she knew there was no way he could have gotten past without being seen.

It was at that point that she'd realized that he hadn't ever been there at all, that the visions were just that, visions, and were for her alone. Similar events had happened a few other times in her life, when the universe at large, or maybe even Gaia herself, decided she needed a little push in the right direction. As a hedge witch, Denise was able to use the power inherent in nature to bend reality to her will. Usually it wasn't anything drastic, just a nudge here or there, when she thought the situation demanded it, though she had the power to do so much more if the need arose.

The trouble with visions was that they were always so damned cryptic, full of hidden meanings and messages that took time and effort to sort out, and this one was no different. She'd always done her best to interpret what she was being shown and to use that information as well as she could. She hadn't always been successful, but she'd given it the old college try. So far, she was having no luck.

As the days passed, Hunt's unexpected appearances became more frequent, until it had gotten to the point where she would see him whenever she used her scrying mirror, the most common tool of her trade. She'd be looking for someone else and there he would be, on the edge of the image, staring off into the distance as if searching for something.

After seeing him a few times, she did her homework.

His face was familiar, and it didn't take her long to remember why. The case had made national headlines for a while and local ones longer still. She knew about the daughter who had gone missing from his home years before and now she understood just who it was he was searching for in her visions.

She asked Dmitri if he remembered the case and was surprised to learn that Hunt came into Murphy's a couple of times a week for a late-night drink. She decided it was time for the two of them to meet and tonight she'd come down early so she wouldn't miss him.

He wasn't what she'd expected. In her visions he appeared as he had shortly after his daughter had disappeared: a good-looking, well-dressed guy who was obviously on his way up. Apparently the mighty had fallen, and fallen hard, for the Hunt who walked into Murphy's that night would never be mistaken for that other man. His blindness was surprising, yes, but perhaps more interesting was the change in the way he presented himself to the world. Gone were the finely tailored clothes and the carefully groomed hair. In their place were a loose-fitting Henley jersey, a well-worn pair of jeans, and disheveled hair. His face was thinner and he clearly needed a shave, but where he had appeared stiff and stuffy before, now he simply looked comfortable.

Tattoos peeked out beneath the pushed-up sleeves of his jersey and where it hung loose about his neck. Denise couldn't see them clearly from where she sat, but she knew the old Hunt never would have let anything so hip be permanently etched onto his skin.

Denise knew just from looking at him that there were deeper changes than those that met the eye, too. Despite his outward appearance, or perhaps because of it, he gave off an air of strength, of inner confidence, that you saw only rarely and then usually in the faces of those who'd survived a major disaster. A flood, a hurricane, something like that. He looked like someone who'd been through the heart of the fire and come out changed, but intact, on the other side. He also looked older than the thirty-seven that she knew him to be.

Losing a child will do that to you, she thought.

She wondered what happened to cause him to lose his sight and made a mental note to ask Dmitri about it later when she had the chance. For now, though, it was time to do what she had come to do.

She slid out of the booth, grabbed her backpack with one hand, and, slinging it over her shoulder, started threading her way through the crowd toward where Hunt was seated at the bar. Her athletic figure and long, dark hair caught the attention of several of the male patrons she passed on the way, but after one of the more overzealous of them received a swift knee to the crotch for grabbing her arm, the others left her alone.

She sat down on the empty stool next to Hunt, waving at Dmitri for a drink as she did so. She leaned toward the man she had come to see.

"Can I buy you a drink?" she asked, over the noise.

He turned those dark sunglasses in her direction. "I'm sorry?"

"I asked if I could buy you a drink."

"Why would you want to do that?"

The question caught her off guard. She didn't have a ready answer so she simply shrugged, thinking even as she did it how stupid it was to shrug at a blind man. "Why not?"

His lips tightened into a thin line. "No, thank you. Maybe another time."

Before she could say anything further Hunt abruptly stood up, laid a folded bill down on the bar next to his empty glass, and left without another word.

Denise looked at Dmitri. "Well, that's a first," she said,

with a puzzled laugh. "Getting shot down by a blind guy. I must be slipping."

The bartender scowled. "You don't want to get mixed up with the likes of him, Denise. He's trouble."

She nodded. "You're absolutely right, Dmitri. I *don't* want to get mixed up with him." She looked back at the door through which Hunt had disappeared. "But trouble or not, I don't think I have any choice in the matter."

II

then

It was almost a week after my daughter disappeared when the witness came forward. She claimed to have seen a girl matching Elizabeth's description in the company of a man at a rest stop on I-93 shortly after she had been reported missing.

Martingale, the detective in charge of our case, called to let us know about the witness and to caution us not to get too excited. We get hundreds of these a week, he said, and only a slim few ever pan out. Despite being told to stay home, Anne and I hurried down to the station house in the hope that we might just have our first lead.

The witness patiently answered all of the detectives' questions and then spent two hours going through the albums of mug shots, looking at felon after felon, trying to find one who looked familiar, who might have been the man she'd seen in the rest area with Elizabeth.

When that process came up empty, they sent a sketch artist into the interview room to work with her. If they could get a reasonable facsimile of the man's face, we could release it to the media, which always brought in more information. Someone, somewhere would see the guy and call it in.

What seemed like hours later, Detective Martingale came out of the interview room, saw us waiting in the hall, and gestured for us to join him in the room next door. We were happy to oblige.

"Did we get anything useful?" I asked, coming in the door.

The detective was just sitting down at the conference table and waved us into a pair of chairs opposite. Anne and I sat down side by side. I gave her an encouraging smile and, taking her hand in my own, repeated my question.

Martingale's expression was noncommittal as he said, "Well, that depends, Mr. Hunt. Before I get into what the witness had to say, I need to go over a few details of your testimony with you, if that would be all right."

It wasn't. I'd been over it a million times, could practically recite it verbatim by now, but when a cop asks you if it was all right you can't say no without looking like a suspect.

I smiled tightly. "That would be fine."

Martingale asked me all the usual questions: What time did I notice her missing? What time did I report the problem to the police? What had I done from the time I called 911 until the time the police first showed up at my house? Could anyone else vouch for where I was during those specific time frames? It was the same bullshit we went over every single time I spoke with them and I could feel myself rapidly getting annoyed at what I saw as a useless waste of time.

The detective must have noticed my irritation, for he smiled his lazy smile at me and asked if everything was all right.

"No problems here," I answered, the same stupid smile plastered on my own face.

We went over it all again, this time with him checking my responses against the answers in the file in front of him. Right when I thought I couldn't take it anymore, Anne stood up.

"This is ridiculous, Detective. We've answered your questions again and again, and frankly I'm getting sick of it. I'm sure my husband is as well. You're treating us more like suspects than grieving parents and I'm not going to tolerate it any longer!"

Anne was angry, angrier than I had seen her in some time.

Rather than answer her verbally, Detective Martingale withdrew a piece of paper from his file and slid it across the table.

"That's the sketch our witness came up with, the face of the man who was allegedly seen with Elizabeth just two hours after her disappearance."

"Oh, my God!" Anne exclaimed, her hand going to cover her mouth.

I was too shocked to say anything.

It was all I could do to stare at the face on the paper in front of me.

My face.

"Now maybe you can understand why we had to go over all those details again," the detective said.

"This can't possibly be right," Anne said.

Martingale just looked at us.

I suddenly felt guilty and I hadn't even done anything wrong. I couldn't imagine what it would be like to be in this room and know that you had committed a crime.

Anne wasn't having the same reaction, however.

"This is bloody well ridiculous, detective, and I guarantee you that you'll be hearing from our lawyer first thing in the morning. How dare you? How DARE you?"

Martingale finally held up his arms in a calming gesture. "Now take it easy, Mrs. Hunt. When you've calmed down, you'll know that looking into this was necessary and . . ."

Anne cut him off, the indignation in her voice turning it to liquid steel. "Don't tell me it was necessary, you son of a bitch. My daughter is out there somewhere, still missing, and you're following up on half-assed theories that have her out on a Sunday afternoon joyride with her father while we were all answering questions in our dining room? Is that the kind of incompetence we can expect on this case? Did you even bother to check the time logs and match those up with the internal reports?"

Martingale was speechless; Anne's vehemence was startling in a woman of her small stature, and I suddenly understood just what it was that made my wife such a good lawyer. No matter what the situation, she was convinced she and she alone was correct.

I was glad she was on my side this time around.

Perhaps recognizing that he was way out of his intellectual league, Martingale did the smart thing and backed off. He apologized for the inconvenience, thanked us for coming down, and got us out of the police station as quickly as he was able.

12

now

I caught a cab outside of Murphy's and rode home in silence. Having learned from previous experience that the sight of my all-but-boarded-up home made taxi drivers uncomfortable, I had the cabbie drop me off at the top of the block and walked the rest of the way.

I live on a quiet, dead-end street and my house sits at the very end of the block, set back from the road and off by itself. It had cost Anne and me a pretty penny when we bought it fifteen years ago—a three-quarter-acre lot that backed up onto public land and had a fair degree of privacy was practically unheard of in an inner-city neighborhood like ours, so we'd jumped at the chance to make it our own. Anne had just made partner, I was working to get tenure at the university, and with dreams of having a family it seemed like the perfect place for us to spend the next several decades of our lives.

I doubted that she would even recognize the place now.

The ground-floor windows had all been covered with plywood, which kept out the light and let me function relatively normally inside my own home, no matter what time of day or night. The yard was overgrown and the mailbox sagged on its pole.

I'd added a six-foot-high wrought iron fence around the entire property. In order to get as much as I needed I'd had to buy it from a number of local suppliers, but the peace of mind it provided was more than worth the effort.

And the cost.

The gates barring the entrance at the front of the property had once stood before the largest cemetery in central Ohio, but the chains and padlocks had come directly from Sears by mail order. Still, they did the trick, which was to keep out the unwanted, both the living and the dead.

Speaking of which, as I drew closer I could feel the usual collection of ghosts gathered outside my gates. I had no idea what they wanted or why they felt the need to congregate there, but more often than not that's what they did, staring in, as if they were expecting me to do something for them. Maybe they came simply because I knew they were there. Maybe the presence of Whisper and Scream drew them; I don't know.

The border of my property was as close as I was willing to let them get, however.

As I approached, the crowd backed off a bit, the lodestone around my neck doing just what it was intended to do. That gave me enough room to unlock the chains securing the gates, slip inside, and relock them behind me. Turning my back on the dead, I headed for my house.

A paved walkway led from the gates, across the overgrown lawn, and to the front door. Even if I hadn't been counting my steps, the gurgle of gently flowing water let me know when I was nearing the house itself. I'd dug the moat by hand last spring over the course of two weeks. Talk about backbreaking labor. The trench had to be three feet deep and as level as possible to support the semicircular pipe that lay within it, and that kind of precision isn't easy when you're blind and essentially digging in the dark. Still, I'd gotten it done without any major disaster and had then borrowed Whisper's sight to conquer the hardest part of the project, installing the pumps that keep the water endlessly recirculating around and around my home.

The iron was my first line of defense; the running water my second. As both were anathema to a wide variety of supernatural creatures, it would take something pretty powerful to get past them, but if something did, there was still one last barrier that they would have to deal with.

Scream.

He was usually there to greet me when I came home, but tonight I didn't feel the weight of his presence and I was frankly too worn-out to care.

The day's events had gotten to me. Death was never easy to be around, and being reminded of my obligation to Stanton at the same time certainly didn't help. My head was pounding from all the time I'd spent linked to Whisper, and the blatant come-on at Murphy's—by one of the Gifted no less—had set my teeth on edge for some reason.

All in all, it had been a particularly shitty day.

I crossed the moat and made my way up to the front door. Once inside, I went straight to my desk and took out a large padded envelope. I slipped the mirror out of my pocket and, keeping it wrapped up tightly, slid it inside. I scrawled a quick note to a guard I knew at Walpole Prison, added that to the envelope's contents, then addressed the outside of the envelope to his attention.

A day or two from now, that mirror would end up in the cell of a certain inmate. And maybe, just maybe, Velvet would have the chance to teach her killer a little something about fear in return.

But my good deed didn't do anything to improve my mood. The house seemed particularly cold and empty to me, even more so than usual. Maybe it was the nature and brutality of the crime I'd been called to witness. Maybe it was the interaction with Whisper and the tendency she had to remind me of Elizabeth. Maybe I was just too damned tired to think straight. It didn't really matter what caused it, just that I felt it like an icy hand had reached inside my chest and squeezed for all it was worth. I missed my wife. I missed my daughter. I missed the life we had, a life full of laughter and happiness and hope for the future.

A life wiped away in the space of a few minutes of inattention.

And I had only myself to blame.

Wearily, I climbed the stairs to the second floor and walked into Elizabeth's bedroom, needing to feel close to her, even if it was only to quiet the silent screaming of my heart.

I'd left the room just the way it had been on the day she disappeared; her unmade bed still dominated the small space, her Nancy Drew books still lay scattered across the surface of her desk, right next to the drawing of the cat she'd been making for Halloween. Her clothes still filled the drawers of her dresser and the space inside her closet, her toothbrush still occupied its spot in the cup holder in the bathroom.

I cleaned her room regularly, so that when she came home again, it would all be ready for her.

I lay down on her bed, bunching the Scooby-Doo sheets against my face, searching for the faint scent that had once filled them, the last bit of evidence that my daughter had actually ever existed.

Eventually, I slept.

I3

now

True to his word, the next morning there was a package from Stanton containing a thick sheaf of photographs waiting just inside my gates. The courier even had the decency to read the sign and call the house, leaving a message on the answering machine to let me know it was there.

I threw on a t-shirt and jeans, then made my way down the walk to retrieve it. Back inside, I grabbed the first of what would prove to be many cups of coffee, my usual vice, and got down to work.

I closed my eyes and summoned Whisper.

Or rather, I *tried* to summon Whisper. She didn't respond. I spent ten minutes pushing the sending with all my mental strength, trying to feel that presence, that connection that told me she was nearby.

Nothing.

I didn't want the entire day to go to waste, so reluctantly I decided I was going to have to get some other help. The fact that I knew how to banish a ghost from a particular area also meant that I understood how to keep one hanging around beyond its natural desire to leave. I didn't do it often, but it appeared I didn't have any choice at this point. I needed to see the photographs, and there was only one way I could do so.

I needed someone else's eyes.

I opened my desk drawer, took out the battered old harmonica I kept there, and went back down to the front gate. It's commonly recognized that music can tame even the most wild of beasts, but it is less widely known that it also has the same power over ghosts. Find the right tune and, like the Pied Piper with the children of Hamlin, you could lead a ghost anywhere.

I stood inside the gate for a little while, watching the crowd that gathered there. I needed a ghost strong enough to withstand the strain for several hours, but not one that was going to be difficult to control or send on its way once my work was finished. It took me about twenty minutes, but at last I found him.

He was young, probably in his midtwenties when he died, and he had that lost and disoriented look that the newly dead usually have. That would mean he wasn't 100 percent comfortable in his new state and would respond better to the things he used to know, like music and the sense of being home.

I started slowly at first, pushing out a few lines of song here and there, looking for the right genre and the right tune to capture his attention.

It was "Turn the Page" by Bob Seger that finally did it.

The minute I broke into that opening sequence, his head came up, his eyes lost their focus, and he was lost in a sea of memories. The music called to him, caught his soul and spun him about, and I knew I had him. Still playing, I unlocked the gate, waited until he was just outside, and then opened it wide enough to let him slip inside.

He followed me up the walk and inside the house without incident. While he stood enrapt in the tune, I called up my music library on my computer, put the song on infinite loop, and, when his attention was distracted by the competing strains, I reached out and borrowed his sight.

While not as powerful as the live music I'd been playing, the recorded tune kept the ghost distracted and docile enough that I was able to turn my attention to the photographs Stanton had sent over and try, at last, to get some work done.

I started with the Chaldean script. It was a descendant of ancient Aramaic and having risen somewhere in the neighborhood of the second century BC, was perhaps the oldest language of those found at the Connolly crime scene. Because it was cursive and written from right to left, it would, given my lack of sight, be the hardest for me to deal with, so I wanted to be as fresh as possible when I tackled it.

Having asked Stanton to have his crime scene techs arrange the shots in a particular sequence—first a wide-angle shot showing all the writing on each individual wall, then photos of each group of words or phrases on that wall, and finally individual shots of each letter or glyph itself—I went through them in the same order.

I spent some time familiarizing myself with each image, noting those that were immediately recognizable and briefly puzzling over those that were not. Because I was "seeing" them through a different medium, the strangely malevolent feeling that had nearly overwhelmed me the night before wasn't present, but I hadn't forgotten it. Just the memory of it made the hair on the back of my neck stand on end. The feeling reminded me to proceed with caution as I set to trying to translate in earnest.

Doing so, however, was much more difficult than I expected. I was able to recognize many of the individual letters and a good number of the words they formed, but that was as far as I could go because none of the word groups fit together into coherent phrases.

After a long, frustrating hour, I put the Chaldean aside and turned my attention to the Norse runes.

They were the version of Old Norse known as Elder Futhark, which consisted of twenty-four runic symbols typically arranged into three groups of eight. They dated from around 400 AD, and very few scholars outside of Scandinavia specialized in them. Fortunately, I was one of those few.

I immediately recognized the P-like symbol that meant "joy," as well as the R-shaped one that stood for "ride" or "journey." A few of the others also looked familiar, though with minor differences, such as the crossbar on the rune meaning "need" being drawn straight instead of being slanted to the right.

But it didn't take me long to realize that the same problem I'd run into dealing with the Chaldean was present with the runes as well. The letters and pictographs themselves were correct, in the sense that they were actual parts of the language in question, but none of them were fitting together with any coherent meaning. As word after word and phrase after phrase turned out to be gibberish, I began to wonder if the whole thing might be some kind of code.

Like most boys, I'd played around with secret codes a bit in my youth. The two most common and easily utilized ciphers are those that either transpose the letters in the message or substitute some other letter for those desired. In the former, a simple word like "help" might become "phle" while a substitution code might use the next letter in the alphabet after the one desired, causing it to read "ifmq." Once you knew the particular cipher used to make the message, it was usually an easy matter to decode it back into its original form.

My stand-in was starting to flicker and I knew I wouldn't be able to keep him around much longer. Rather than try to break the code, I spent the next half hour copying all of the symbols on the various photographs into my journal, so I could view them again without assistance. It was a good thing I did, too, for no sooner had I finished than my ghostly companion faded away, the energy needed to sustain his corporeal form drained at last.

I was tired, but determined to find an answer. I kept working, and I was still struggling with it when later that afternoon Stanton arrived to take me to Brenda Connolly's autopsy.

14

now

Boston's City Hall has to be one of the ugliest buildings ever designed by man. It is a multistory concrete bunker that looms over an equally depressing plaza, the former created by three academics with minimal building experience who won the competition held to design the place and the latter by the equally overrated I. M. Pei, who thought a featureless plane with stick figure statues would be just the kind of place to attract "the masses." The inside is no better, for it is filled with dank, concrete corridors that always seem clammy to the touch. The center houses an open-air atrium, which, given New England's penchant for being cold and wet more often than being sunny and warm, is simply a waste of useful space. The building is dark and depressing, a monument to technocracy that seems to suck the life out of you the minute you walk through the doors. It is somehow poetic justice that it was here that the city planners placed both the registry of motor vehicles and the city morgue, as if spending too long in one might lead you to end up in the other.

After parking the car, Stanton led me inside the building and off to the left of the lobby where a set of stairs took us down a level to the subbasement that housed the morgue. He stopped outside the entrance before we went in.

"The M.E. doesn't know who you are, and I want to keep it that way. If you leave your sunglasses on and don't say anything, we should be fine. He'll think you're some punk agent the feds sent over to annoy me."

He paused, searching for the right words. "I know this isn't your usual thing, but give it a shot anyway. Like you said last night, it doesn't hurt to cover all the bases."

Fair enough, I thought, nodding to show I understood. I didn't tell him that unless the ghost of the dead woman was sitting in there with us, I probably wasn't going to learn a damn thing. I intended to milk Stanton's misconception of me as psychic for as long as I could. After all, the truth was so much harder to swallow. Why ruin a good thing if I didn't have to?

The room was far too bright for me to see anything but a mass of solid white, so I was forced to rely on my other senses. The smell of antiseptic hit me like a wave as I passed through the doors. Beneath it I could pick up several other odors: the dusty tang of old blood, the burning stench of cut bone, the cloying spice of the medical examiner's aftershave.

The room was quiet except for the voice of the M.E. as he dictated the findings of his external exam into the microphone I knew to be hanging over the autopsy table. I followed Stanton's footsteps over to the table, where he and the M.E. exchanged the usual banter. I pretended disinterest and in the process I thought I heard Stanton whisper something about "the fuckin' feds." I knew he was just establishing my cover and so I pretended not to hear it.

I didn't need to see the room around me to know what the place looked like. Institutional gray walls, probably with the paint discolored here and there with moisture stains. A bank of stainless-steel drawers that housed the recently deceased lining one wall. Stark luminescent lighting that left little to the imagination.

In short, it was depressing as hell and I couldn't even see it.

There was a certain heaviness to the room's atmosphere, a palpable sense of anxiety and anger, and from the pressure in my head I knew that the living weren't the only ones present. The ghosts hung back and didn't bother us though, so I left them alone as well. No need to get them stirred up over something that didn't concern them, and I was too worn out to utilize their senses anyway.

When the M.E. got down to the real business of the autopsy, meticulously taking apart Brenda Connolly's body, piece by piece, I settled on distracting myself with trying to categorize the activity going on in front of me based on the sounds that were made. The hum and whine of the bone saw were obvious, as was the crack of the splitter used to separate the ribs from the sternum. I didn't know what the gurgling sound underlying it all was, but something told me I really didn't want to know anyway, so I left it alone.

After a while my thoughts drifted back to the mysterious writing and the code I'd been trying to break at home. I knew that unless I stumbled on a key sequence and was able to decode that, I could very well be working on cracking it for months, if not years. I simply didn't have that kind of time.

Still, there was something naggingly familiar about it, as if I had seen it before and all I needed to do was remember where in order to break it. But even that little fact eluded me.

Something Stanton said caught my attention, and I tuned back in to the conversation going on before me.

"Do you know what might have caused it?" Stanton was asking.

"No. I've never seen discoloration like this before. It resembles postmortem lividity in some ways," he said, referring to the phenomenon in which the blood will settle in the lowest part of a corpse and darken the flesh in that area as a result, "but it's clearly not that. It's almost as if the entire surface of her body was bruised at the exact same moment and with exactly the same amount of force, but the only condition I know of that can produce a result like that is being exposed to a vacuum. Somehow I doubt you found outer space in her living room."

Don't be so sure, Doc, I wanted to say, but I resisted the urge and kept my mouth shut.

"There's no damage to the tissue itself however, so we can also rule out radiation or other high-frequency wavelengths."

I could feel Stanton's impatience rolling off him in waves and wondered how long it would take for him to blow.

Not long, as it turned out.

"All right, let's cut to the chase. How'd she die?"

Harrington didn't hesitate. "I don't have the foggiest idea," he said.

Not the response Stanton was looking for, apparently.

"C'mon, Doc, don't give me that. You've got to know something."

I could almost hear the M.E. shake his head.

"I'm not yanking your chain, Detective. I don't have any idea what killed this woman."

I heard a clank and then the rustle of pages and figured Harrington had picked up the woman's chart.

He went on. "Aside from the strange state of her dermal tissues, and of course her missing eyes, I can't find any other sign of external injury. No gunshot or knife wounds, no evidence of strangulation or blunt trauma."

Stanton grunted. "So her heart gave out. Wouldn't be the first time, right?"

"I thought so, too, Detective, but the exam showed her heart to be in excellent shape, with no evidence of myocardial infarction. Nor have I found any evidence of a stroke."

"Poison? Toxic exposure to some chemical?"

"Nothing that showed up on the primary toxicology screens."

Stanton grunted in annoyance. "So what you're telling me is that whatever did this to her skin somehow also killed her, but in a way that you can't detect?" Stanton's tone told me he was well beyond mildly annoyed at the lack of answers and was moving rapidly into his "tell me what I want to know or I'm going to beat the living shit out of you" mode.

It was time for me to cut in.

"Tell me about the eyes, Doc."

I could feel Stanton shooting daggers at me with his gaze, but I ignored him and kept my attention on Harrington instead. He, at least, seemed thankful for the change in topic.

"Hmm. The eyes. Nasty bit of work. Based on the nicks that can be seen around the edges of the sockets, I'd say the killer inserted a knife between the flesh of the socket and the edge of the eyeball itself, then simply applied pressure to pop the eyeball free. A quick cut through the ocular nerve is all it would take from there."

"But what's the point? Why would anyone do that?" I pressed.

"How the hell should I know? I'm not a psychiatrist. Maybe he wanted a souvenir. Or maybe the lack of sight meant something to him personally."

"Meant something?" asked Stanton. His tone said he'd

gotten his anger under control, but I could practically hear the tightness of his clenched jaw and knew it wouldn't take much to make him lose it.

Harrington's voice took on a professorial quality, one I recognized rather easily, for I had a tendency to slip into the same pedantic mode myself, and I wondered briefly where he did his teaching. Harvard? Maybe Boston University?

"Meant something, yes, that's right, Detective. Surely you remember your tenth-grade Shakespeare? The eyes are the window to the soul?"

I recognized the famous line from *The Taming of the Shrew* right away, but when Stanton made no comment I decided now was not the time to share my love of literature.

It didn't matter. Harrington's question had been rhetorical anyway. "Perhaps the killer took the eyes as a symbol of his complete mastery over his victim. From his view not only did he take her body, but he also took her soul, if you will. But like I said, I'm not an expert, so you'd best check with someone who . . ."

Stanton cut him off. "Yeah, yeah, fine, Doc. We get it." He paused, as if something new had just occurred to him, and then asked the question aloud. "Was she alive or dead?"

The M.E. gave him a confused look in return. "I'm sorry?"

"The vic. Brenda Connolly. Was she alive or dead when the killer took her eyes?"

"Oh. Alive. Definitely alive."

I remembered the malevolent feeling I'd gotten staring at the symbols on the walls the night before and found myself wondering just what the hell was loose in our city.

And how the hell we were going to stop it.

15

now

By the time I left the M.E.'s office, afternoon had faded into evening. With my thoughts still churning, I hailed a cab, intending to go home, but we'd only covered half the distance before I asked the driver to pull over and let me out. I needed to think, and walking usually helped me do that, so after ascertaining from the cab driver just where I was, I headed off down the street on foot in the direction of home.

For some reason that I can't quite pin down, no one ever bothered me when I was out on my walks. The hustlers and the homeless, the gangbangers and the drug dealers, they all left me alone. It was almost as if they sensed something wrong with me, as if what I had been through had left some kind of taint on me that those operating on the level of their baser instincts could recognize, making them steer clear of me. The same seemed to hold true for the unnatural denizens of the city streets, though in their case it always felt more like they were granting passage to one of their own.

At any rate, I was able to walk the streets at just about any time of day or night without being afraid of getting mugged or run over by some punks joyriding in a car that wasn't their own.

Tonight, like most nights, come rain or shine, there was a group of streetwalkers congregated on the corner of Sullivan and Tremont. I could hear them calling out to the passing cars as I approached, asking the drivers if they wanted a "date" for the night. Even though all I could see at this point was their vague outlines, I knew that despite the cooler fall temperatures they were still clad in the usual assortment of hip-hugging shorts, high heels, and low-cut blouses. Conflicting perfumes warred with each other for dominance; I was convinced that standing amidst them for any length of time was sure to permanently damage your sense of smell.

They fell quiet as I reached their little group, stepping back and out of the way to let me pass. I could hear a whisper here and there at the periphery, the experienced ones telling the newcomers to stay clear of the "freak with the creepy eyes." I was used to it and didn't let it bother me.

After I'd passed, one woman shouted after me from out of the crowd.

"Hey, Ray!" she called, apparently in the belief that all blind men were named after the famous piano player or something equally stupid. "Tell me somethin'. Do ya like what you see?"

Her wisecrack was greeted with gales of laughter from the other ladies of the night, as if it was the funniest thing they'd heard in the last week. But the joke, which wasn't that funny to begin with, was now so old and stale that it had about the same effect on me as the breasts I knew from prior experience were being bared behind my back. I raised a hand and waved without looking, which only sent more laughter in my direction.

Any other night, their antics would have been forgotten long before I'd even reached the end of the block. But tonight they lingered, mixing with the unease that had accompanied me ever since leaving the medical examiner's office. Before long I was in a completely foul mood, cursing the memories the women's teasing had conjured up—memories of time spent with Anne, of her laugh, her smile, the simple pleasure of holding her hand in mine or the feeling of her warm back pressed against my chest as she slept soundly beside me.

I realized with a start that the bitter taste in my mouth was envy. It had been so long since I'd felt the soft touch of a woman's flesh on my own, inhaled the scent of clean skin mixed with perfume, wrapped my arms around my partner. Hell, it wasn't even the absence of sex that had me so riled up. It was the idea that they took the human companionship that came with it for granted.

For one long piercing moment I missed Anne almost as much as I missed Elizabeth. My stomach cramped and I found myself on my knees, my mouth open as if I were about to vomit all over the place. I gagged, once, twice, but nothing came up and after a few seconds my stomach muscles eased off and I could breathe again.

I fought my way back to my feet, pointed myself in the direction of home, and tried not to think of all I had missed during the search for my missing daughter.

16

now

On the other side of town, the creature discarded the face of Officer Williams. In its place the creature put on the face, form, and clothing of the twenty-eight-year-old woman who ran the art gallery across the street from where the creature now sat, watching the front door from the safety of its car. It had parked on the opposite side and several yards up the street from the gallery itself, giving it a decent look at the entrance without making its presence obvious to the casual passerby.

An open magazine sat on the passenger seat, and from behind the wheel the creature glanced at the photograph displayed there, double-checking the individual in the picture with the one who was currently approaching the gallery from the south.

"James Marshall," the caption said, "Back Bay's Own Master Carver." A tall, thin, unassuming man, Marshall was the type the average person could pass on the street and never even notice, but the creature wearing the face of Marshall's part-time manager and occasional bedmate knew the reality was far different. No matter how hard Marshall tried to mask it, the glow of power leaked through his shields, the shimmer of arcane energy looking like a cloud of fireflies surrounding his form.

It checked the list it held in one hand; Marshall's name was the fourth from the top. After it took care of him, there would only be another eight more to go, four of them right here in Boston.

Time was running out.

If it was going to finally free itself from the Master's clutches, it needed to accelerate the process. Tonight, it would take the next step.

It watched as Marshall unlocked the door to the gallery and disappeared inside. After a few moments, lights went on in the loft above; Marshall was settling in for the night.

Time to go.

It stepped out of the car, casually glancing up and down the street as it did so, checking to be certain it was unobserved. Satisfied, it crossed the street and walked over to the gallery entrance.

It held the car keys up to the lock, pretending, and then reached out and calmly turned the doorknob, snapping the entire locking mechanism in the process.

Opening the door, it slipped inside.

Marshall had left the lights off, and the creature that had been sent to confront him did the same. It didn't need the lights anyway; it could see perfectly well in all but complete darkness, and there was enough light filtering in from the street outside that it might as well have been moving in broad daylight.

It had entered the wide warehouselike space that Marshall used to display his artwork and took a few moments to peruse the collection, moving from room to room, curious about the individual it had been sent to kill.

The sculptures were strange, twisted things, the wood from which they were made warped and pulled into shapes it was never meant to take, and for a moment the creature wondered if its prey had somehow sensed he was being pursued. Was he right now waiting for it in the darkness above?

For a moment its pulse quickened, the thought of a worthy adversary after all these years filling it with excitement, but then it realized how unlikely such a scenario was and it brought itself back under control. No, its quarry didn't know it was coming; they never did. The Master might remember the events of that night in the distant past, but those he enacted his vengeance against never did.

This time would be no different.

It had wondered about that before, why the knowledge had been lost, why the threat was no longer guarded against, but the answers to those particular questions were beyond its grasp. Not that it minded; as it was, the situation allowed it to carry out its own plans without fear of discovery or reprisal. The Master was too wrapped up in his own efforts at escape, and his victims were too stupid to see what was happening right before their very eyes.

Which was just fine as it provided the opportunity it needed for its own schemes.

On the other side of the room was a spiral staircase that led to the living space on the floor above. The sound of a television drifted down from above; the creature used the noise to mask its approach.

When it was in position near the staircase, it reached out and gently pushed one of the nearby sculptures off its pedestal.

The resulting crash couldn't be ignored, and when the television was snapped off and footsteps sounded on the floor above, it congratulated itself on its planning. A light went on at the top of the steps, illuminating the staircase and a thin stretch of the first floor in front of it, though it didn't reveal the unwanted visitor hiding just beyond. Marshall's voice floated down into the darkness to where the creature hid, waiting.

"Who's there?" he asked.

The pitch of his voice was higher than usual, evidence of the fear that coursed through his system at the thought of an intrusion in the middle of the night, and the creature lying in wait smiled in recognition of the sound. It flicked its tongue out into the darkness, like a snake testing the air, and its grin grew wider at the peculiar flavor that met its unnatural senses.

Fear has such a delightful taste, it thought to itself, sharp and pungent, with a unique aroma all its own. It should know; it had spent the last two hundred years inspiring it in more victims than it cared to count, and it knew all its varieties and variations.

"I said, who's there?" Marshall called again.

When he received no reply after several moments, he tried a different tact.

"I'm warning you," he said into the darkness, this time with a bit more force but even less conviction. "I've got a gun and I'm going to call the cops if you don't get out of here right now!"

It nearly laughed at the man's bravado, but it knew that doing so would ruin all its fun, so instead it stepped into the thin slash of light that splayed across the floor in front of the staircase, revealing itself, a seductive smile already set on its beautiful, stolen face.

"Gina!" Marshall exclaimed. "You startled me."

It could hear the relief in his voice, could see him visibly relax now that he recognized that his mysterious visitor wasn't a threat.

Fool, it thought.

It was almost too easy.

"Did you forget something?" Marshall asked.

It didn't say anything, just looked up at the man standing on the steps above it with hunger in its eyes, hunger it didn't need to fake, and let the body it had assumed do the rest of the work. It wasn't difficult; a certain quirk to the mouth, a certain pose, and the man above knew exactly why his girlfriend had unexpectedly shown up in the middle of the night.

Marshall laughed and just like that his fear fled, replaced just as quickly by excitement and lust.

"You could have called, you know."

"Then it wouldn't have been a surprise," it said, and its voice was a perfect copy of the rich contralto of the woman whose body it wore.

The smile still on its face, it climbed the stairs toward its unsuspecting prey.

☩

Later, when it was finished, when what it had come to collect was safely stored and ready for delivery, when the body had been posed appropriately and the markings left scrawled haphazardly across the walls as they had been at the last scene, it withdrew another small figurine from its pocket and flicked it across the room. The charm bounced a few times before coming to rest on the far side of the bedroom, near one wall.

As before, the charm was not in the Master's plan; he would, in fact, be furious if he ever found out about them.

The risk was worth it, however.

This time Hunt wouldn't be able to ignore the obvious. And when he made the proper connections between the current events and those that happened five years ago, he wouldn't quit until he had chased the clues back to their source.

And, at long last, it would be free.

Satisfied, it resumed the form it had used when entering the gallery two hours before and left the scene as swiftly and as quietly as it had come.

17

then

I thought the first month was bad, but it wasn't even worth comparing to the endless weeks of fear and anxiety that followed. Every time I heard the doorbell I was convinced the police would be waiting on the doorstep with terrible news. Every time the phone rang I imagined a flat, lifeless voice telling me that they had found my daughter's body and were going to ask me to come down to the station to make an identification. Each time I was wrong my anxiety level went up a notch because the possibility still remained. What I'd imagined could still come true.

It wasn't any way to live a life.

Eventually, I stopped trusting the police to do their job and began to look into things on my own. I went through the police reports, examined the interview files, double-checking every detail. I chased down every lead no matter how inconsequential, looking at everything they had already been through and then some.

When I couldn't stare at the computer screen any longer, I took to the streets, driving the neighborhoods, searching the back roads and alleys looking for my daughter. The chances of finding her this way were so remote as to be astronomical, but that didn't stop me from trying.

Whenever I grew tired I reminded myself that my little girl was out there somewhere, lost and afraid, and that it was up to me to find her and bring her home. Whenever I wanted to throw up my hands and give up, I thought of her smiling face and pushed myself that much harder because of it. I wouldn't rest until she came home, I told myself over and over again, and slowly but surely the search began to take over my life.

I didn't realize just how much until that day in late March, seventeen months after Elizabeth had vanished.

"I'm leaving."

I was so engrossed in looking through a stack of notes I'd made over the last several months, odd scraps of paper with nearly indecipherable scribbling about potential sightings and the occasional police alert over some other missing child, that I didn't even look up when Anne spoke.

"Okay," I said absently. "When will you be back?"

"I won't."

I'm embarrassed now to say that it took several minutes for her reply to filter through to me. When it did, I looked up in confusion to find her standing at the door to my office. Behind her, in the hallway before the front entrance, I could see several suitcases.

"What are you doing?" I sputtered, half-rising out of my seat. "Where are you going?"

She looked at me calmly. "I'm leaving, Jeremiah. For good."

I didn't understand. "But you can't leave," I said, gesturing vaguely back at the computer screen and the stacks of file folders on my desk. "We've got to find Elizabeth."

"Elizabeth is dead."

Her tone was flat, cold.

"What?!"

I couldn't believe what I was hearing. It had only been a little more than a year since we'd lost our daughter. I knew there were plenty of cases on record where kids had been found years after their disappearance. Shawn Hornbeck. Natascha Kampusch. Elizabeth Smart. There was still hope.

There was always hope.

Apparently Anne didn't think so. *"Elizabeth is dead, Jeremiah. Probably has been for a long time."*

I stiffened and felt my anger flare. *"Don't say that!"*

"It's the truth."

"No, it's not. She's out there. I know she is!" I was practically spitting with sudden, unrelenting rage.

Anne sighed and looked away for a moment. When she turned back, I expected to see tears in her eyes, but there weren't any. She'd burned through her sorrow long ago. Somehow, I hadn't noticed.

Her voice was calm, level.

"Look at yourself. You haven't changed your clothes in more than a week."

Confused, I glanced down. I had a vague memory of getting dressed, but I couldn't be sure if that was earlier that morning or earlier that week. The proliferation of coffee stains on my shirt suggested the latter, though even that wasn't a reliable indicator. I drank a lot of coffee.

"You stink. Literally. I can't even remember the last time you had a shower."

For that matter, neither could I, but I wasn't about to give her the satisfaction.

"I'm getting close, Anne, I know it," I said, my eyes straying back toward the pile of paper, torn between dealing with her sudden announcement and losing my train of thought. *"She's out there and I'm going to find her."*

She shook her head. "No, you won't. You're a mess, Jeremiah, and every day it gets worse. You're obsessed and it's killing you. Killing us."

"So you're just going to walk away, is that it? Forget Elizabeth? Forget us?"

I'd meant it to hurt, but she didn't even flinch.

"I'm not forgetting anything, Jeremiah. It's you who's forgotten. Forgotten that there is more to life than staring at photos of missing children and scouring police reports. Forgotten that there is a time to grieve and a time to move on with your life. Forgotten us."

That last part was said with more than a hint of longing, but I was too far gone in my self-inflicted madness to even notice. Maybe if I had, things would have turned out differently. Maybe she would have stayed and the collision course I was headed toward could have been averted. I'll never know, because I did the one thing I shouldn't have.

I got defensive.

"Oh, so suddenly I'm to blame for all this, huh? Why don't you just say what you really mean, Anne? You've been dying to say it for over a year now, so have the balls to just put it out there on the table instead of hiding behind all this bullshit. Go on, say it. It's my fault Elizabeth disappeared, right? Right?"

It was stupid. I know that now. But at the time all I could hear was my conscience screaming the same thing it had been screaming every single minute of every single day since Elizabeth had disappeared: it's your fault.

Anne stared at me for a while without saying anything. Then, in a soft voice, she said, "Get help, Jeremiah. Get help before it's too late."

Without another word, she turned, picked up her suitcases, and walked out of my life.

18

now

I'd shed my anxiety and self-pity by the time I reached home. After undressing, I flopped onto my bed and quickly fell asleep. To my amazement, it was the first night in a long while that I slept restfully. Apparently I'd needed it, too, for I didn't wake until midmorning the next day. After a cup of coffee and a bagel, I went back to work trying to translate the writing on the crime scene walls.

Stanton called just before noon.

"Well? What have you got for me?" he asked.

I ignored the impatience in his tone and tried to give him a decent summary of what I'd achieved. Which, when you got right down to it, wasn't all that much.

He wasn't fooled.

"Come on, Hunt? That's the best you've got? I thought you were supposed to be an expert on this stuff?"

"I'm working on it, Stanton. I just need a bit more time."

He grunted. "Time's not something we've got a whole helluva lot of, Hunt. Step it up. I need some answers!"

Asshole, I thought, as he hung up without saying anything more. I was working as hard as I could, for heaven's sake!

But his call did what it was more than likely intended to do—guilt me into working harder than I had been doing. Now that I had copied all the symbols onto paper, I could work at my own pace and without any ghostly assistance by simply doing so in the dark. I couldn't see photographs or paintings, but my own drawings were no problem for me. I spent the next four hours trying every type of code I knew of and then some. Substitution codes. Transposition codes. Numeric ciphers. Multiletter ciphers. You name it, I tried it, until my journal was full of my scribbling and false starts.

And I still came up empty.

Eventually my head hurt so much that I wandered into the living room and collapsed onto the sofa, intent on taking a short nap before getting back at it.

A loud buzzing woke me from a dream of being chased though endless corridors by six-foot-tall hieroglyphs with arms that threatened to squeeze me to death. I didn't need a psychiatrist to tell me that my failure to translate the markings on the walls of Brenda Connolly's bedroom had gotten under my skin and made me more than a bit exasperated.

The sound was the audible alarm I'd installed at my gate to let me know when someone was waiting outside. I stumbled tiredly over to the wall control and hit the talk button.

"This had better be good," I said, without the slightest sense of humor.

"Shut up and unlock the gate, Hunt."

Stanton. Great. To what did I owe this dubious honor? I thought.

Throwing on a t-shirt and a pair of jeans, I walked to the end of the drive, unlocked the gate, and let him follow me back up to the house. I returned to the kitchen for a much-needed cup of coffee.

I heard him come into the room just as I opened the cupboard.

"What happened?" I said over my shoulder as I got a mug out and reached for the coffeepot. I'd set it to brew a new pot shortly after lunch, which meant it was several hours old, but coffee was coffee, and with the afternoon I'd had so far I needed a cup to jump-start the system. "Wife throw you out?"

Stanton was too busy fumbling around in the dark and cursing beneath his breath to respond to my jibe. I chuckled at seeing him out of his element.

He wasn't amused.

"Christ, Hunt! I know you're blind, but can't you at least turn on some lights for your guests?" he asked.

I was opening my mouth to toss a witty reply in his direction about not having invited any guests when he apparently found the light switch on his own.

Blazing white light flooded the room, drowning out my sight. I flinched at the sudden assault on my unprotected eyes, squeezing them shut to avoid the blinding brightness, and managed to pour the coffee that was intended for the inside of my coffee mug all over my hand.

Now it was my turn to curse.

He ignored my outburst, and the spilled coffee. "Get dressed," he said.

"Why? We going somewhere?" I asked, as I fumbled my way to the sink and shoved my hand under cold water.

"Back Bay. We've got another body."

Shit.

Any thought I'd had of eating went right out the window. Blind or not, a murder scene on a full stomach was not something I wanted to experience. "Let me change my shirt and throw on some shoes," I said wearily.

Stanton drove. I sat in the passenger seat of his department-issue Crown Vic, letting the sun shine on my face through the window and trying to dispel the lingering sense of discomfort a visit to a crime scene always brought with it. I wondered what we were going to find this time.

Apparently, Stanton was learning how to read my thoughts.

"Guy's name is Marshall. James Marshall. Makes custom wood furniture, sculptures, shit like that. Has a gallery and loft apartment on Newbury Street."

Known to some as America's Most Desirable Neighborhood, Back Bay stretches from the Charles River to the Mass Turnpike and contains cultural landmarks like Copley Square and the John Hancock Tower. It was best known for its expensive shopping and housing areas. Having a house there was seen as a certain measure of social status. If you lived in Back Bay, you had made it.

'Shit like that' must pay pretty damn well, I thought, as Stanton went on.

"Marshall's gallery manager got worried when she couldn't reach him this morning. Finally asked the building super to go in and take a look." Stanton chuckled. "Gotta give those guys credit. Sometimes I think they find more bodies than we do," he said, as he swerved around a corner.

There are certain situations where I am perfectly happy being blind. Driving with Stanton is one of them. I had my feet braced against the floor and a death grip on the doorjamb, and I still bounced in different directions as we swept down the street. Stanton used the siren multiple times to clear the way ahead, never once slowing down but simply trusting that the other drivers would get the hell out of his way, and I suspect we had more than our fair share of close calls. Having to look out the windshield and watch it all happening probably would have made me nauseous.

Eventually we arrived at our destination, and as I thankfully got out of his car and put my feet back on solid ground, I realized that there was a crowd gathered in front of Marshall's brownstone.

A crowd made up entirely of ghosts.

I could feel them standing in a loose semicircle before us, and I knew without having to see them that they were all staring at the building toward which we were headed.

What did they know that we didn't?

A chill ran up my back, and I suddenly didn't want to have anything to do with this case. But then Stanton was taking me by the arm, leading me toward the front door, and whatever thought I'd had about objecting to being here faded as quickly as the ghosts we passed through.

I felt a single shadowy figure separate itself from the watching pack and come toward us. *Whisper. What was she doing here?* I wondered.

She caught up with us before we reached the building, slipping her little hand in mine. Apparently she wanted me to see whatever it was that was waiting for us inside, for she loaned me her sight without my having to ask for it.

That was a first.

Fool that I was, I didn't have the common sense to be worried about it, either.

A uniformed officer met us at the building entrance. Stanton flashed his badge and we went inside without a word.

The brownstone's lower floor had been converted into a private gallery, the wide space carved into minishowrooms with temporary dividers. The smell of heated iron and shaved wood filled the space. Each room held three or four different pieces of artwork, everything from small, tabletop carvings to giant, surreal pieces of sculpture made from wood and iron. As we passed the first of the minishowrooms, I caught sight of a particularly large piece that rose twisting and turning toward the cathedral ceiling. Through Whisper's ghostsight the wood and iron were transformed into a thousand human hands all reaching for the sky high above, and the sculpture pulsed with an eerie sense of yearning.

After that I kept my gaze on the floor and away from the artwork around me.

Stanton led me to the rear of the brownstone and up a cast-iron spiral staircase to a large, well-lit apartment. Like most lofts, it was a mostly open floor plan, with the kitchen blending into the living room space just beyond. The far wall of the apartment was made of glass, allowing a breathtaking view of the city. Sunlight streamed in through the window, a sharp contrast to the tragedy we knew we'd find elsewhere in the space.

At an impatient gesture from Stanton, the uniformed officer guarding the bedroom door found something else to do. Once the guard was out of the way we entered the room and stepped around to the other side of the enormous bed that took up a good portion of the room. There, on the floor facing the far corner, was the body of the victim.

Where the last body had been posed kneeling in prayer, this one had been left prone in complete supplication, though it had the same strange coloration as the first. The man was lying with his face down and his arms stretched out over his head, his palms flat against the floor.

Stanton, not knowing I could see the corpse, took a moment to explain its positioning and condition to me. I figured he wanted to be certain I understood the connection between the two killings. "We're guessing that he died sometime last night, maybe even yesterday afternoon, based on the state of the body. We'll know for sure once the M.E. has a chance to get him on the table."

I thought that rigor mortis would move the body out of position, so I asked Stanton why it hadn't.

"His hands and feet have been nailed to the floor," he said, with no more emotion than if you'd asked him the time of day, and as I watched his gaze take in the body and the rest of the room around him, I understood why. It was like a switch had been thrown somewhere in his mind and now the scene had transformed for him; rather than being a horrible tragedy it had become a peculiar puzzle to be solved. He now had two bodies killed in similar fashion and—you could see it in his eyes—he wasn't going to stop until he had caught whoever had done these horrible deeds. He didn't have time for emotions; they would just get in his way.

I wondered if I could ever be that analytical.

And in the same heartbeat realized that I already was. After all, hadn't I driven off my wife and all my friends, given up my life, all in the name of finding my daughter?

Perhaps Stanton and I were more alike than I thought.

Now that was truly frightening.

"Okay, Hunt. Give me something I can use." With that he clapped me on the back and walked out of the room.

Right. No pressure.

Whisper was already with me, so we got right down to business. She reached out and placed her hand against Marshall's remains.

I withstood the roaring freight train and the sudden avalanche of pain. When it passed, I opened my eyes, expecting to see the events as they had transpired several nights before.

Instead, all I saw was the room in front of me, dead man and all.

I turned and looked down at Whisper. With her head bent forward and her eyes squeezed tightly shut, she was the picture of concentration. It was obvious that she was doing what she could to conjure up the events of the past, but this time it wasn't working. I let her work at it for a few more minutes and then gently told her to stop.

She did so reluctantly, and the expression on her face said she wasn't happy with her failure. I didn't know what the problem was. Maybe the killer had done something to mask his actions, though why he didn't do it the first time around if he did it this time was beyond me. Maybe it was simply a function of how much time had passed. Either way, we'd come up bone dry.

Until I turned away from the corpse and discovered that we were no longer alone.

The ghost of James Marshall was watching us from just a few feet away. He appeared as he had in life: a tall, thin man with dark, curly hair, dressed in a neat pair of chinos and a button-down dress shirt. Only the emptiness in his eyes and the flickering image of his form gave away the fact that he was no longer among the living.

Before I could say or do anything, Marshall strode forward and passed right through me!

A wave of intense cold rushed throughout my body as my skin made contact with his ghostly form. With it came a cascade of mental images: Marshall in gloves and safety glass, working on one of his sculptures; Marshall watching the sun set from the big glass window in his apartment; Marshall kneeling amidst a grove of white birch trees, with his head bowed as if in prayer.

But it was the very last image that held me spellbound, for it showed him rearing up in agony from his kneeling position in the grove, his hands trying to force back the dark, shadowy shape that appeared to be trying to envelop him from the head down.

As Marshall's ghost stepped away I fell to my knees,

momentarily drained of energy. It was all I could do to hold on to Whisper's hand, desperate to keep my link to her open, in case there was something more for us to see. My mind was working furiously, trying to decide if Marshall's actions had been meant to cause some harm to me. I didn't think my system could take another encounter like that. If he did it again, I was going to be in serious trouble.

Thankfully, that didn't seem to be on his agenda. When I had caught my breath and was able to raise my head again, I found him standing near one of the walls, watching me closely. He held my gaze for a moment and then pointed with one spectral finger at the wall beside him.

Just then the door to the bedroom opened and Marshall's ghost vanished as swiftly and as silently as it had come. I heard someone enter the room behind me and knew without looking that it was Stanton.

"You all right, Hunt?"

I nodded in reply to Stanton's question, too stunned by what had happened to speak. I've been seeing ghosts for several years now. I knew they could communicate with me if they chose; Whisper, and even Scream, were proof of that. But I'd never had any other ghost do so until now.

What exactly had Marshall been trying to say? And why had he vanished when Stanton had come into the room?

"Did you see anything?" Stanton asked from the doorway.

Suddenly deciding to keep Marshall's appearance to myself, I said, "No. It's as if the whole room has been wiped clean."

I glanced toward the door as I climbed to my feet, only to find that Stanton had already left the room.

In the wake of my failure to help him, I had apparently been dismissed.

19

n.o.w

Denise dreamed.

In her dream she was walking, in the depths of a wide tunnel somewhere underground. A drainage system. A mining shaft. Something like that. The walls were smooth and uniform, clearly man-made, and every fifty feet or so a light hung from the ceiling above, dimly lighting the way ahead.

She wasn't alone.

Hunt was hurrying down the hallway with her, pulling her along with one hand; the incongruity of being led by a blind man was not lost on her.

That was what dreams were like though, full of inconsistencies that nature would never allow in the real world.

But this was no ordinary dream. It had that peculiar sense of inevitability that she had come to recognize as a hallmark of her precognitive visions, short glimpses of a future that might be, could be, but would not necessarily be true.

She ignored them at her own risk.

Her bare feet splashed through a puddle of dank water and Hunt glanced back at her sharply, raising a finger to his lips in the signal for silence.

But he was too late. The damage had been done.

An inhuman wail echoed from somewhere back down the passage behind them. The sound of it set her heart to hammering in her chest and filled her with dread.

Something was following them!

"Run!" Hunt shouted, hauling her forward as he followed his own advice and took off at a pace she never would have imagined possible for a man in his physical condition. They ran for all they were worth as the sounds of pursuit drifted down the hallway behind them.

Hunt never faltered, never hesitated, even when the hallway branched in different directions. She stumbled along in his wake as best she could, but she was already exhausted from the first confrontation with . . . She couldn't remember the details, but a vague memory loomed dark and painful in the depths of her mind, and she knew she couldn't keep up this pace much longer. They had to find help soon or it was all over for both of them.

They ran on.

The corridors seemed to go on forever; more than once Denise stumbled and nearly fell. Each time Hunt caught her and supported her for several steps until she could move again on her own. She liked to think of herself as tough, but it was obvious that it was only Hunt's strength and determination that kept them moving forward.

It wasn't enough, though.

The sounds of pursuit were growing closer and one look at Hunt's anxious face let her know that they weren't going to make it.

At the intersection he skidded to a stop. Pointing up

the right-hand corridor he said, "Dmitri is waiting for us at the end of that passage. Just stay in the main hallway and you can't miss him."

"What about you?"

Hunt shook his head, ignoring the question. "Remember, straight ahead until you find Dmitri. Now go!"

"Hunt?"

Another eerie howl echoed through the halls then, much closer than before; at the sound of it Hunt shoved her forward. "Go!" he shouted, pointing again at the right-hand tunnel. "Run!"

Denise ran. She couldn't help herself. Whatever it was that was following them filled her with such atavistic fear that she had no choice but to run, and run for all she was worth.

She told herself she would find Dmitri and return with him to help, but deep in her heart she knew it wouldn't matter. Hunt would be dead long before they could return.

She glanced back, wanting one last look at the man who was sacrificing himself so she would have a chance to survive.

Hunt stood in the center of the hallway, his back to her. For just a moment she thought she saw two other figures standing there with him, a little girl on his left and a large hulk of a man on his right, but then the corridor curved ahead of her and she lost sight of him.

She ran on, praying to Gaia to keep him safe.

She hadn't gone more than a half-dozen steps farther when a terrible, pain-filled cry filled the tunnel around her and she stumbled and fell . . .

. . . only to wake up on her couch, her heart hammering in her chest and a cry for help on her lips.

Doing what she could to calm down, she glanced at her watch.

10:15.

It had been just after six when she'd put her head down to rest for a minute. She hadn't intended to fall asleep, but obviously Mother Gaia had other plans for her. She knew that was where the dream had originated, for rather than fade with the passage into wakefulness, the details of her dream lingered, further proof of its precognitive nature.

Her Goddess was trying to tell her something.

Had been trying ever since Hunt had first appeared to her in that mirror in her client's apartment.

Determined to try to speak to him once more, Denise pulled on her shoes, grabbed her coat, and headed out the door. If Hunt kept to his usual routine, she'd find him at Murphy's.

This time, he wouldn't blow her off so easily.

20

now

Marshall had been trying to tell me something, and I was determined to figure out just what it was, but there was no way I was going to be able to do so with Stanton and the rest of the crime scene crew milling about. I needed a place to hole up for however long it was going to take for them to clear out and then go back on my own.

Thankfully, I knew just the place.

I was getting out of the cab in front of Murphy's when I heard a woman call my name. The events of the last few days had left me short-tempered and easily annoyed, so I did my best to pretend I hadn't heard.

I paid the cabdriver and stepped away from the curb, using my cane to guide me. I'd only gone a few feet when I felt a hand grab my arm.

"Let me help you, Mr. Hunt."

My nose told me what my eyes could not. It was the woman from the other night. The woman who smelled of cinnamon, coffee, and just a touch of jasmine. I'd noticed her scent when she'd asked to buy me a drink and it was peculiar enough that I remembered it. Had a hard time forgetting it, in fact, and the way it made me feel only increased my irritability.

I disliked being touched, even by a woman who smelled like that, and I yanked my arm out of her grip. "Don't touch me," I said, a bit more forcefully than was really necessary, but I just couldn't seem to help myself. "I don't need your help."

"Sorry."

I could tell by the change in her tone that I had hurt her feelings. *Good*, I thought, *maybe she'll leave me alone*.

No such luck.

"Would you like me to get the door?" she asked.

I planted my feet and refused to move. For all I knew she was a terrific human being, but for some reason she made me so damned uncomfortable whenever she got close that it practically made my skin crawl.

Rather than answering her question, I asked one of my own.

"What do you want?"

"Just to talk, that's all."

"Not interested."

I moved forward, hoping she wouldn't follow.

"Well, then, how about that rain check? You know, for that drink?" Her tone was back to being cheerful, hopeful, but this time I could hear the effort behind it.

I stopped and turned to face her. Now I could see the faint shimmer of an aura around her, marking her as one of the Gifted, and the sight only increased my impatience. The last thing I needed was to be involved with another freak like me.

"What the hell is it with you?" I asked, my tone conveying my rising anger. "Can't you see I want to be alone? Are you so hard up that you have to hit on a blind guy?"

"No. Nothing like that . . . Goddess, is . . . is that what

you think?" she stammered. She sounded like the remark threw her off.

I didn't care. The events at Marshall's were on my mind and I didn't want to be bothered any longer.

"Look. I don't know who you are or what you want, but I really just want to be left alone. Go bother someone else."

Apparently she finally got the point, because she didn't try to stop me as I pushed my way inside Murphy's.

☩

I gave them four hours and then caught a cab back to Marshall's neighborhood. I had the cabbie drop me off two blocks from the scene. From there I made my way down the street with my cane and a little help from Whisper. She led me right past the front door and its thick ribbon of yellow crime scene tape, giving me a chance to glance inside and see if there were any lights on. When I saw that there weren't, we ducked down the alley just beyond the entrance and climbed the low fence at the back that surrounded the postage-stamp-sized backyard. After that, it was a simple matter to jimmy the door lock with the tire iron that I'd borrowed from Dmitri and was carrying under my coat.

I hadn't made it halfway through the gallery before I ran into trouble, though.

"Don't move, asshole."

The voice came from my left. The sound of a pistol being cocked accompanied it. That was enough to make me freeze where I stood.

So much for getting in and out with no one the wiser.

"That's it. Just stay right where you are."

A flashlight clicked on and shone directly in my face.

I threw up one hand to shield my face from the light

and beside me I felt Whisper mimic the action with her own hand.

A guard moved out of the shadows beside me and I wanted to hit myself for not realizing that the gallery would have wanted to protect its investment in all that artwork. Given the way the world worked, I wouldn't have been surprised to learn that the prices probably soared through the roof when word of the artist's murder got out. As the guard moved closer I got a good look at him and was relieved to see that he was wearing the uniform of a private security company rather than that of the Boston PD.

A rent-a-cop I could handle.

"Thought you could just help yourself, did you? The poor schmuck's only been dead since this morning and the grave robbers are already on the prowl, huh?"

He kept the gun trained on me with one hand while using the other to pull a walkie-talkie off his belt. Bringing it to his mouth, he prepared to call in some backup. With the gun pointing at my chest, there wasn't much I could do to stop him.

Thankfully, Whisper and I hadn't come alone.

"You might want to look behind you," I said calmly.

The security guard scoffed. "Keep your mouth shut, asshole, or I'll shut it for you." He thumbed the switch on his radio and brought it up to his mouth.

Whatever he was going to say never made it past his lips as Scream chose that moment to make his presence known.

If Whisper was my angel, then Scream was my devil incarnate, all rage and mayhem bound up in human form. At just a hair above seven feet, even in death he was a towering giant of a man. His fists were like sledge-hammers, his legs as thick as oaks, and he had the disposition of a junkyard bulldog that had been kicked one too many times and now intended to take the leg off the next person who came too close.

Of course, the guard couldn't see him, not the way I could. But Scream has his own unique way of letting you know he is there, filling the space around him with a sense of fear, doubt, and apprehension that follows him like a cloud. Being in his general vicinity makes most people uncomfortable; being right beside him could make you literally sick with fear. I've never experienced it myself, for whatever reason I seem to be immune, but I've been told that it is like living through all your very worst fears at the same moment: the things that haunt your psyche in the deepest dark of the dead of night; the things that no matter how hard you try you can never seem to get away from.

Scream swam into view behind the security guard like a hazy mirage, insubstantial at first and then with increasing solidity until we were staring at each over the guard's shoulder.

Imagine a face that is all harsh planes and sharp angles. Now hollow out the cheeks and sink the eyes deep into their sockets. Add the gaping hole of a gunshot wound above the left eye and a shock of white hair, and you'll have a close approximation of what Scream looks like to me when he graces us with his presence.

I nodded in his direction.

Of course, the guard couldn't see him, but that didn't mean he didn't feel Scream's sudden presence. As I watched, the guard glanced down at his arm—the one holding the gun—and his eyes widened noticeably. Suddenly he began shrieking at the top of his lungs.

"Get it off! Get it off me!" he screamed, flailing about, the gun in his hand completely forgotten as he sought to dislodge with his free hand whatever phantom creature he was seeing in his mind's eye.

I moved to one side, out of what I hoped was the line of fire, and waited for it to end.

Apparently the guard was seeing more of them now, for he cast his gun aside and with both hands began frantically to brush at his arms, face, and chest. He was breathing heavily, practically hyperventilating, and an eerie keening sound was coming from his mouth. As I watched, he turned and ran for the doorway, desperate to escape.

He was so distraught that he missed the opening by a good two inches, running directly into the doorjamb at full speed, his forehead slamming into the unyielding wood surface with a loud thud, knocking him senseless.

I moved in quickly, snatched his weapon from the floor, and then secured him with his own handcuffs. From the size of the knot already forming on his forehead it looked like he'd be out for a good long while.

With that taken care of, the two ghosts and I quickly made our way back through the apartment and up to the second-floor bedroom where Marshall's ghost had made its appearance earlier that afternoon.

It was dark enough now that I could see fairly well on my own. The body was gone, moved to its temporary home in a steel drawer at the morgue. The holes in the floor where the spikes had been driven into the polished hardwood were visible, dark shadows on the glossy surface. I wondered if Marshall was still alive when those spikes had been used and then decided that I didn't really want to know. Some details were better left unknown.

I went directly to the wall Marshall's ghost had pointed at and began to search. I wasn't sure what I was looking for, but I figured I'd recognize it when I found it.

Fifteen minutes later, I was still looking.

I moved back a few steps and sat on the floor, staring at the wall. My head was starting to hurt from all the time I'd spent looking through Whisper's eyes today, and my frustration was building by the minute. What the hell was I missing? What had Marshall been trying to tell me?

My attention kept coming back to that wall and the nagging suspicion that something about it just wasn't right. I sat and stared at it for a while. I got up, paced around, and stared some more.

It was the pacing that did it.

A suspicion blossomed in the back of my mind and grew with each step I took. To test it, I went back down to the lower floor and paced off the room directly below. Forty-eight steps from one side to the other. Returning to the upper floor, I did the same thing.

Thirty-six steps.

It was a false wall.

My subconscious recognized the differences in the room sizes even if my conscious mind had not. That was what had been bothering me. It was also what Marshall had been trying to make me see.

Once I knew what to look for, I found it quickly enough. The switch was along the floor seam, right where it could be nudged with one foot while standing in front of the wall. When tripped, it made a soft click and a door gently slid open in front of me.

Seeing what lay on the other side, I could only stand there, gaping in astonishment.

Before me was a grove of white birch trees. The full moon in the sky above gently splashed the grove in its silvery light and I could hear the leaves whispering together in a gentle wind. Somewhere in the back of my mind it registered that it was too cloudy to see the moon tonight, but since that was the least of the inconsistencies that I was looking at, I just let it go with nothing more than a mental shrug.

Clearly, this shouldn't be possible and yet there it was.

The surface of the gravel path that led from the door deeper into the grove was splashed with something dark just a few feet in, and the sight of it drew me like a magnet. When I knelt next to it, the pungent smell of blood met my nostrils. It didn't take a blood splatter expert to understand I was looking at that place where Marshall had met his end; there was too much blood for it to have been anything else. It was splashed across the trail in a wide pool and had dried into a thick stain.

At the very edge, something glowed with a faint luminescence.

If I had been looking at it with ordinary eyesight, I never would have seen it, but in the strange wavelength that was Whisper's ghostsight it stood out like a beggar at a yacht club. I moved closer and got down on my hands and knees to take a look.

It was roughly five inches across and just this side of translucent, like the skin of a snake after it has been shed. Even as I watched, the aura about it slowly faded, until if I hadn't known where it was already I never would have been able to pick it out against the stony background. Afraid I might lose it, I gently lifted it off the ground and slid it into an envelope from my pocket.

Instinctively, I knew that this must be what Marshall had wanted me to find.

I stood up, staring down the gravel path to where it disappeared into the trees and the darkness up ahead. I wondered where it led. *Maybe that was how Marshall's killer had gotten out of the apartment,* I thought.

As I headed in that direction, though, Scream materialized directly in front of me. His massive arms were held across his chest and with a shake of his head he made it plain that I was to go no farther.

"Screw that," I said, and tried to go around him.

Without a change of expression, Scream picked me

up and tossed me back through the open doorway into the apartment proper.

I bounced once when I hit the floor and then slid for a few feet before coming to rest against the opposite wall. My arms burned where Scream had touched me, the type of burn you get from touching something intensely cold, and I lay there, astounded that he'd been able to affect the corporeal world in such a fashion.

Apparently there was more to Scream than I had ever imagined.

My connection to Whisper had been cut off when he'd separated us, but I didn't need my sight to recognize the click of the latch as Scream closed the door to the hidden room and disappeared along with it.

Okay, I can take a hint. No grove exploring for me.

I gave myself a moment to catch my breath and then moved to get back up on my feet. As I put my hand on the floor to steady myself, I encountered something small and metallic. I scooped it up and brought it close to my face to take a look.

It was a tiny figure, maybe a dog or even a pony. Something with four legs at least.

I didn't need to see it to know it was another charm like the one that had been left at the Connolly crime scene.

Except this time, with a jolt every bit as shocking as having a needle jammed unexpectedly into my eye, I recognized it!

21

now

I have to get home.

The thought kept repeating itself over and over again in my mind as I left the crime scene behind and frantically tried to flag down a cab on the street outside.

I have to get home.

The proof I needed was there, in the long-unused jewelry box on the bureau in my missing daughter's bedroom.

I have to get home and I have to get there NOW.

The cab ride seemed to take forever, and I know I didn't make a new friend by constantly haranguing the cabbie to drive faster. I didn't care. All that mattered was what I would find when I got home.

For the first time in almost five years, I thought I had a solid lead on those who had taken my daughter from me and nothing was going to stand in my way of proving it, one way or another.

After what seemed like forever, we reached the top of

my street. I broke my usual rule and directed the cabbie right to my front gate. I didn't even wait for him to tell me the fare, just dropped a handful of bills in his lap as I got out of the car and dashed for my front door.

In the house.

Through the living room.

Up the stairs and down the hallway to the last room on the left.

The pair of bracelets had been a birthday gift from Anne and me when Elizabeth had turned seven. They'd been designed to our specifications by a local artist named Jean Luc Lafayette, making them a one-of-a-kind gift. He'd cast the figurines in silver and carved the same trademark mandala design into the base of each.

Elizabeth had been wearing only one of the bracelets on the day she'd vanished.

The other still rested inside the cedar jewelry box she'd purchased to store them in.

I burst through her bedroom door and hurriedly crossed the room to where her dresser stood against the far wall. I snatched the container off the top, my hands shaking as they upended the contents of the box onto the top of her bureau.

It took only a matter of seconds for me to find the matching bracelet and to examine the design carved into the base of the figurines.

I slid to the floor, my legs no longer able to support my weight as the full impact of what I'd just discovered washed over me.

The designs were the same!

There was no doubt about it. The charms I'd discovered at the crime scenes had come from the bracelet Elizabeth was wearing the day she'd disappeared. Either the killer had crossed paths with Elizabeth or he was the abductor himself.

Vertigo gripped me, and it took me a moment to regain control. For the first time in five years, I was looking at a solid lead.

I needed to get the police on this right away. They had the manpower and resources to deal with it swiftly and effectively. I snatched up the phone, punched in Stanton's cell number, and . . .

. . . hung up before it could ring.

Excitement warred with trepidation in my heart. This was the first piece of evidence that had surfaced in literally years of searching, the first tangible clue to what had happened to my daughter.

A clue tied directly to a cold-blooded killer.

That didn't bode well, and it meant that I had to approach this with more than a bit of caution. *Think before you act, Hunt. Think.*

What, exactly, had the police done for Elizabeth over the last five years?

Sure, they'd come out to the house at first, done the usual canvass of the neighborhood and such. But even then they hadn't been convinced that she'd been abducted. Even then their questions had been closer to insinuations: *Had she ever run away before? Was there a reason she might have run away? How was I getting along with her in the days before she disappeared?*

And then there had been that business about her being seen with me hours after I'd reported her missing, the need for them to "take every lead into consideration." The trip to the police station and the polite questions in the interview room, as if I had something to do with it.

It hadn't taken them long to give up on her, either, just a few short months before her file was moved to the cold case unit, just another example of a runaway who hadn't come home.

Except my daughter hadn't run away.

She'd been taken.

The charm in my hand was proof of that.

I realized that I'd long ago lost any confidence in the idea that the police were going to be able to help find my daughter. Wasn't that why I'd taken the search into my own hands? Why should I think that things would be any different now?

The cops were after a killer; they wouldn't be looking out for my little girl.

I thought back to Stanton's demeanor at the first crime scene. He'd been agitated, clearly upset with the direction the investigation was going. He'd called me in to give him that little extra edge he needed to solve the case quickly, and I had a hunch that it hadn't been my expertise in ancient languages that he'd wanted, either.

The investigation had been only a few hours old when he'd called me in. Stanton couldn't have even talked to all the neighbors yet, never mind thoroughly examined the crime scene. He'd taken one look at that body and immediately asked for my help.

Suddenly, I wanted to know why.

What did he know that I didn't?

It was like a puzzle with too many missing pieces. I knew it all went together somehow, but I didn't have any idea what it was supposed to look like, let alone where to begin.

One thing was certain.

I wasn't ready to trust Stanton or the police with what I had discovered just yet.

Come morning, it would be time to do a little investigating of my own.

22

then

In hindsight, Anne's leaving saved me from myself. Without her as a crutch to lean on, I was forced to pay attention to life around me again. She'd been buying the groceries, paying the bills, washing the clothes. With her gone, I had no choice but to do these things for myself and it was that return to routine that kept me from falling over the edge of the cliff into despair.

The crazy-eyed lunatic raving about saving his daughter disappeared. His replacement was a man driven by ice-cold focus and a determination that nothing would get in his way.

Or so I thought.

My next run-in with the police told me I didn't have everything as together as I thought I did.

I had gone into the city to follow up on a tip about some street kids living inside the Callahan Tunnel, thinking Elizabeth might be among them, and was tired from dodging traffic all day while searching for their hiding place. The fumes from the rush-hour traffic were getting

to me, and I'd decided to call it a day when the car carrying Elizabeth drove right past me.

I saw her, plain as day, from my position on the access
ramp at the mouth of the tunnel. She was sitting in the
back seat of a white Mercedes in the far lane, on the opposite side of the highway from where I stood. She was
staring out the window, lost in thought, and I saw her
face clearly as she drove past.

"Elizabeth!" I shouted, dashing out into traffic without thought for my personal safety.

Horns blared, brakes squealed, and it was only the
heaviness of the traffic that kept me from getting killed.

That or the fact that God keeps a special eye out for
crazy people.

"Elizabeth!"

Traffic had slowed and I caught up with the car pretty
quickly. I bent over and peered into the window.

"Elizabeth! It's Daddy, Elizabeth! It's Daddy!"

The girl inside recoiled.

"No, honey, it's me. It's Daddy." I knew I didn't look
like I had when she'd been taken, so I frantically tried to
comb down my long hair and turned sideways to let her
see my profile so she could recognize me.

The car pulled ahead suddenly.

"No! You're not taking her away from me again!"

I ran to catch up. "Give me my daughter, you son of a
bitch!" I screamed, as I yanked on the door handle while
banging on the window with my other hand.

The driver, a wimpy-looking guy in a three-piece suit,
tried to speed up, tried to get away, but I'd be damned if
I was going to let that happen. I'd found her and no one
was taking her away from me again. Never again!

I pumped my legs and hung on for dear life. Thankfully the traffic ahead had become backed up again and
the driver had no choice but to slow down. When he
did, I threw myself across his windshield, trying to block

his view of the road ahead and prevent him from moving forward.

"Give me my daughter! Elizabeth!"

Unknown to me, one of the cars I'd raced out in front of had been a Metro police cruiser. The cop inside had watched everything unfold and had quickly turned his vehicle sideways, blocking off traffic from closing in behind us, and had then exited his vehicle, racing to catch up with us.

By throwing myself across the hood of the other man's car, I'd inadvertently given him the time to close the distance.

The first time I knew he was there was when he shouted at me to freeze.

My daughter Elizabeth was in that car. There was no way in hell I was listening to anyone until she was safe in my arms.

"Give me my daughter!" I screamed again.

The cop, not getting the response he wanted, radioed for backup and moved in to bodily remove me from the vehicle.

That earned him a kick in the mouth as I grabbed hold of the windshield wipers to keep from being pulled off, struggling against his efforts to dislodge me, screaming all the while.

The next thing I knew, there were 50,000 volts of electricity surging through my body and I jerked around on the hood of that car like a fish out of water.

Apparently the cop had decided that I was an imminent threat to those in the Mercedes and shot me with his Taser.

When I came to, I was lying handcuffed on the pavement a few feet away from the vehicle. The officer was standing beside the driver and a teenage girl with long, dark hair. He was asking them questions and taking notes on the pad he held in one hand. When the driver noticed *that I was awake, he pointed at me and the cop came over.*

"Are you okay, sir?" the cop asked politely.

While he still held his notebook, his other hand had moved to the butt of his pistol.

"Tell that son of a bitch to give me my daughter," I gasped out, still recovering from the effects of having that much electricity shot through me.

"Is that your daughter over there, sir?" he asked, watching me closely.

My voice was coming back. "Not the teenager, you idiot. The little girl. The little girl in the back."

I craned my head around, looking for Elizabeth. Where had they put her?

"Those are the only people who were in the vehicle, sir. Just that gentleman and his teenage daughter."

"No." I shook my head. "NO," I said, more forcefully this time. "I saw my daughter in the backseat. She was there." I turned and caught the driver watching. "Give me Elizabeth!" I shouted at him.

Several other squad cars appeared at that point, along with an ambulance. I was checked out by the paramedics and then transported to the police station to "cool off."

In the end, I got lucky. The driver decided against pressing charges, and the cop took pity on me and declined to charge me with assaulting an officer, so after spending the night in jail, I was released.

To this day I'm still not convinced I didn't see her sitting there, in the back of that car, staring out the window.

23

now

Once I'd made up my mind that I was going to handle this without the police, it was clear that I was going to need help. Dmitri was the obvious choice. He had the connections and resources I needed to answer the questions I was suddenly asking myself, so as soon as it was reasonable to do so I headed for Murphy's.

Looming at the forefront of that list of questions was why Stanton was so anxious to wrap up the investigation quickly. It didn't fit with his normally meticulous approach to a crime scene. The same was true of his recent emotional behavior. His anxiety seemed misplaced, almost as if there was something he wasn't telling me. Which wouldn't be a surprise, actually, as this was Stanton we were talking about.

Still, I didn't like being in the dark, no pun intended. And if what they said about Dmitri was true, he was the perfect person to get me the information I needed. I had two items that I was certain had been in the presence of the killer. Now I needed the right kind of person to help me track them back to their owner.

I'd learned a lot about the world since my daughter had disappeared. One thing I knew beyond a shadow of a doubt was that much of what people thought of as bullshit was anything but, when it came to the supernatural. Sure, for every legitimate precognitive there were a hundred, no a thousand, charlatans, but that didn't take anything away from those who really could do the things they claimed to do.

Right now, I needed to find a certain type of individual, and I hoped Dmitri could help me.

The place was locked up tight when I arrived, but I pounded on the door anyway until Dmitri came to see who was stupid enough to be that annoying at this hour of the morning.

"Hunt," he said, noncommittally, when he opened the door.

"Mind if I come in?" I asked.

"Be my guest," he said, and ushered me through the door.

It was quiet inside, peaceful actually, a far cry from the way it was at night. It smelled better, too, the smell of fresh Pine-Sol and other disinfectants overlaying the usual nightly scents of beer and sawdust. Dmitri moved to turn on more lights, but I intercepted him before he could do so.

"Mind leaving those off?" I asked.

He hesitated, then shrugged. "Suit yourself."

With the curtains drawn and most of the lights off, I could see fairly decently in the dim interior. I followed him across the room to the bar itself.

"Drink?" Dmitri asked, as I climbed atop a stool and he took his usual place behind the counter.

"Coffee, if you've got it," I said, buying some time

while I tried to think of how to approach the issue that I'd come here for.

In typical fashion, Dmitri fetched me my drink and then stepped back and silently waited for me to tell him why I was pounding on his front door at what had to be, for him, an ungodly hour.

He knew that I occasionally acted as a consultant for the police on certain unusual cases, so that seemed the safest tack to take with him now. "I need some help with a couple of things," I said, and then explained about the two recent murders and how I'd gotten involved in them. "Detective Stanton has asked me to look into using some, well, let's call them less conventional methods of investigation."

"Like you?"

I knew from past experience that Dmitri didn't understand just what it was a blind guy could do for the police department. He'd never come right out and ask, wasn't his style, but occasionally he tossed out a line like that one, looking to see what I would say.

I smiled, letting him know I knew what he was doing, and shook my head. "Much less conventional than what I do."

"Less conventional than bringing a blind guy to a crime scene? That's pretty out there, I'd say."

I shouldn't have been surprised that Dmitri knew I'd been physically present at both murder scenes. Like I said, he had contacts everywhere, and if it was worth knowing, Dmitri eventually heard about it. I tried to laugh it off.

"Cops. Who can understand them?" I said.

"Apparently you do, since you're working for them."

If I'd been using Whisper's sight, I knew I would have seen him staring hard at me in that way he does when he thinks there's something funny going on. Sitting and listening to people all day had sharpened Dmitri's bullshit detector and it seemed he wasn't going to let me get by without some kind of explanation. He wanted to know what it was I did for the police. If I didn't tell him, I risked losing his help.

This was new. He'd never forced the issue before. Then again, I'd never come to him for help before.

I weighed my options and decided that it might be time to come clean, given the seriousness of the issue.

Whether he believed me or not was another story.

"You want to know what it is I do for the cops, is that it?"

I could almost hear his shrug. "You said it, not me. I'm just a bartender, remember?"

That was the biggest load of bullshit I'd heard in a while, but I wasn't going to challenge him on it. Instead, I asked, "What do you know about transference?"

"It's a psychoanalytical term that refers to what happens when a therapy patient places certain feelings or emotions onto the therapist. By doing so, they give the therapist the opportunity to respond in a way that is different from the response of the person on whom the feelings are based, thereby giving the patient a chance to heal," he answered matter-of-factly.

Color me shocked. The big bartender sounded like a college professor, for heaven's sake.

"Right. What I do is something similar to that. I'm a sensitive. I can pick up stray thoughts from other people, particularly when they happen during periods of high emotion."

"So you've got ESP? Cool. Tell me what I'm thinking."

So much for the college professor. "No, I don't have ESP. At least not in the way you're suggesting. I can't read minds or anything like that. I just feel things, emotional echoes I guess you could call them, that occasionally give the police a clue that can help them find who they are looking for."

"And now you need something better than that?" He actually sounded disappointed that I couldn't read his mind.

"I have something that we think belongs to the killer. I need someone who can find the link between the object and the killer, who can follow that link back to the source and tell us where to find him."

Given that he was one of the Gifted, I wasn't surprised when he didn't even blink at my request.

"You need to talk to Denise Clearwater," he told me.

"Who?"

"The good-looking brunette from the other night."

I had no idea who he was talking about.

Dmitri chuckled. "Sorry, sometimes I forget you really are blind. Just about any other warm-blooded guy who comes in here would know exactly who I was talking about with that description. She's pretty hard to miss."

He still hadn't answered the question.

"Great, so she's hard to miss. Who the hell is she?"

Sometimes he can be so exasperating.

"Oh, right. Remember the woman who asked to buy you a drink the other night?"

Uh oh. "The one who smells like coffee and jasmine?"

"You noticed that, did you? I'm impressed."

Shit! Of all people, it had to be her.

"How can she help?" I asked, with far less enthusiasm in my voice than before.

He grunted at the change. "Best she tell you that herself. Not my place to tell other people's secrets."

"There's no one else?" I asked.

"You want the best, she's the best."

Great. Just fucking great.

"How do I find her?"

"She comes in about once a week. Usually Fridays."

I shook my head. "I can't wait that long, Dmitri.

People's lives are at stake. I need to talk to her as soon as possible. Preferably today."

He drummed his fingers on the bar for a moment, thinking. I let him take his time. Rushing him wouldn't get me anywhere.

"What else?" he asked, after a moment.

"What do you mean?"

"You said you needed help with a couple of things. So far you've only talked about one. What's the second?"

I hesitated, uncertain how to proceed. *Exactly how do you ask someone you don't know very well to commit an illegal act on your behalf?*

"Something about the investigation doesn't feel right. Stanton's too anxious, too focused on wrapping this up quickly for it to be an average, everyday homicide. There's something he's not telling me."

"And you want me to find out what that something is?"

"Yes."

There, I'd said it.

I needn't have worried. He took it all in stride without even a second thought.

"I can hack the police department's database, if that's what you want, but it will cost you."

If I'd been a sighted man, I probably would have blinked at him in dumb surprise. I'd expected him to tell me he'd put some feelers out on the street, reach out to his contacts, that sort of thing. Hack the police department's database? That was something else entirely.

"How much?" I found myself asking.

He named a figure I thought was reasonable, and so, before I could change my mind, I agreed. We shook on it, sealing the deal, and that was that. Dmitri explained that it might take him anywhere from several hours to several days, but that he would call when he had something.

Business concluded, he offered to show me out.

"Clearwater?" I prompted gently instead.

He grumbled a bit, still not entirely convinced of the necessity of what I was after, but that didn't stop him from taking the phone out from beneath the bar.

"I'm gonna regret this, I just know," he said under his breath, but the telltale sound of the rotary dial ticking back to the left let me know he was making the call.

While I waited I mused on the fact that Dmitri must be one of the few people left on the planet who preferred a rotary-dial telephone.

Some people are even weirder than I am.

I heard him say something into the phone by way of greeting and then he stepped away from me, talking in a low voice. I could have listened in if I'd wanted to, my hearing vastly improved from the years of relying on it so much, but I gave him the privacy he wanted and didn't. After a few minutes of discussion he hung up and walked back over to me.

"She has a place in Brookline. A basement-level apartment over by Boston College. She's there now. I'll call you a cab." He wrote down the address for me on a scrap of paper to give to the driver.

I thanked him, paid for my coffee, and got up to leave.

As I reached the door he called out to me. "Be nice, Hunt. She's a friend of mine." I could feel him glowering at me and it spoke volumes without saying a word.

"Sure, Dmitri. No problem," I told him.

Having Stanton pissed off at me was one thing. Getting Dmitri mad was a different story entirely.

24

now

The cab dropped me off outside her Brookline address, and I managed to negotiate the narrow stairs down to the front door of her apartment without tripping and killing myself. It helped that her outside light was off and the illumination from the streetlamps didn't penetrate down this far thanks to the angles involved. I knocked sharply several times.

It took a few minutes but eventually the exterior light went on, blinding me. I heard the door in front of me open.

"I thought you wanted me to leave you alone?" she said, when she saw that it was me.

"Yeah, well . . ." I let the statement trail off, uncomfortable with saying more.

She wasn't going to be satisfied with that, however.

"Yeah, well, what?" she said, her tone sharper this time.

"I . . . uh . . . um . . . I need your, uh, help."

"You what? Sorry, can't hear you, Hunt."

I sighed. *Why'd she have to make this so difficult?* I stood up straighter and said clearly, "I need your help."

"You need my help?"

"Yes."

"No."

"No? No, I don't need your help?" *What the hell?*

"Yes, you need my help. No, I won't give it to you. G'night, Hunt."

The door closed in front of me with a sharp click. It wasn't quite a slam, but it was close. The light went off.

"Shit."

I stood there for a moment, at a complete loss. It had been years since I'd asked anyone for help and the fact that she just up and turned me down suddenly pissed me off. I wanted to pound on her door, tell her exactly what I thought of her, rant and rave and generally make a scene. Trouble was, I couldn't afford to antagonize her any further. I didn't know anyone else who could do what I needed to have done. I couldn't go to the police, and Dmitri had been clear that she was my best bet. Clearwater was it, my only hope.

Restraining my baser impulses, I knocked a second time.

When there was no answer, I did it again, a little harder this time, in case she hadn't heard me from the other side of the apartment.

My anger flared further when she still refused to answer. After all, I knew she was in there. She was doing this just to stick it to me.

Fine. Two could play at that game.

I turned around, made my way back up a couple of steps that led to the street above, and sat down, determined to wait her out.

Ten minutes went by.

Fifteen.

I was just about to say "fuck it" and give up when I heard the door unlatch and open.

"You still here?"

I swallowed my annoyance. "Yes, I'm still here."

She didn't respond.

"I need your help. And I'm sorry about what happened earlier." Then, after another moment of silence. "Please."

At last she relented. "Maybe you'd better come in." She turned away and disappeared inside, leaving the door open behind her.

Breathing a sigh of relief, I got to my feet, negotiated the steps in front of me, and entered her apartment.

The moment I crossed her threshold, I went blind.

Totally, truly blind. Not the blindness I get when I'm around too much light, that sense of being caught in a whiteout. No, this was more like having an iron box dropped over my head and sealed up tight, cutting off not just my sight but also my senses of hearing and smell. It was so unexpected that I literally staggered, crashing sideways into what I think was a coatrack and sending it and me tumbling to the floor in a jumbled mass of limbs and loose coats.

"I knew it!" Clearwater crowed in triumph, her voice coming to me from far away, as if I was hearing it through deep water.

Extracting myself from the tangle, I got slowly to my feet, groping for the support of the wall beside me. I reached out with my mind, trying to get my bearings, searching for anything that could help me orient myself, a hint of light, a snatch of sound, the slight trace of Clearwater's unique scent.

Nothing.

I suddenly felt very vulnerable.

"What the hell just happened?" I asked, not surprised

to hear the little shakiness in my voice. I wasn't used to being at someone else's mercy and didn't like the feeling in the least.

"You stepped across my threshold."

"So?"

"My entire house is warded, Hunt. A Mundane wouldn't have felt anything at all yet you act as if the whole place suddenly caved in on your head. Ergo, you're not a Mundane."

A Mundane?

"I have no idea what you are talking about."

I had my back to the wall now, my hands flat against the surface behind me, ready to use it for leverage if I needed to push off it suddenly. Trouble was, I'd gotten disoriented in the fall and didn't know which direction was out. I could make a run for it and wind up deeper inside her apartment instead of out the door where I wanted to be.

"Stop playing games, Hunt. Dmitri and I have known there was something different about you for a while now. He might let you get away with that act you put on, but I won't. Especially if you want my help. Now start talking."

As I struggled to figure out how to answer her, I heard a loud click.

I knew that sound from a hundred different cop shows.

It was the sound of a pistol being chambered in front of me.

"Is that a gun?"

"Yes," she replied.

My heart rate went up a few notches.

"Are you planning on using it?"

"Only if I have to."

She sounded almost bored.

I was quite certain she knew how to do so, too. Apparently my time was running out.

"What do you want to know?"

"Are you here to harm me?"

What a curious question. Like I would tell her if I was? "No, I just need your help."

She was quiet for a moment, long enough for me to wonder if she had left the room. All I could hear was the pounding of my own heart.

Abruptly, the veil over my senses lifted. Clearwater must have been very close—I could smell that particular scent of coffee and jasmine that she gave off like perfume—and my hearing went back to normal. I still couldn't see, she had too many electrical lights blazing away for that, but at least the sense of being lost in nothingness went away.

"Take my hand. We're going to go into the living room to talk, and I'd rather you didn't trip and break your neck on the way. After that, if I believe you, we'll see about that help."

I didn't want to. What I wanted to do was get the hell out of there; I didn't like feeling so helpless. But then I thought of Elizabeth, and I visibly swallowed my pride and took Clearwater's hand, letting her lead me into the living room where she put me in a seat across from her.

"Talk," she said.

So I did. I told her everything. Well, almost everything. I told her about my missing daughter and just how far I'd gone, and still would go, in order to learn what had happened to her. I told her about my subsequent discovery that the world was full of things that the average person couldn't see, some dark and terrible, some truly majestic, and how I'd been blessed or perhaps cursed with the ability to actually see them for what they are. I even explained my affinity for the dead and how I'd somehow managed to befriend two particular ghosts who I'd taken to calling Whisper and Scream. Last but not least, I told her about the work I'd been doing for the police and the two crime scenes to which I'd recently been called.

She sat calmly through it all, as if discussing gruesome murders and meandering spirits was something she did every day. I kept waiting for her to freak out and order me out of her home, but it never happened.

Taking her silence for permission to continue, I went on.

"At the second scene, I found this."

I withdrew the envelope from my pocket and passed it to her.

There was a moment of silence as she opened it and looked inside.

"And?"

"And I need someone to help me determine what it is and, if possible, track it back to the person it came from."

"And you think I can do that?" she asked.

I nodded, knowing how crazy it sounded but not caring much about that at this point. "Can you?"

She laughed.

"I should hope so, Hunt," she replied. "I am, after all, a pretty decent witch."

25

now

A hedge witch, actually, as I found out moments later. Historically, they were the village wise women, the local healers and seers, the ones you went to when you needed that little extra something. The term originated from the fact that the witch usually lived out beyond the hedge, or the boundary of the village. That area was considered part of the unknown, the wilds. The hedge witch lived on the boundary between the known and the unknown, between this world and the next, and was seen as one who walked in both. Gradually the name also began to be applied to those who were wise in the ways of the natural world, who explored the great mysteries of nature.

Clearwater explained all this to me as I sat there on her couch, the piece of stolen evidence sitting in an envelope on the table before us. I wasn't worried about getting shot anymore, which was a relief, but I wasn't sure what her reaction was going to be with regard to my end run around the police.

She, however, had other concerns.

"What's your take in this?" she asked.

"What do you mean?"

"Why are you doing this? What's in it for you?"

I shrugged, trying for lighthearted. "Just doing my civic duty. Ma'am."

"Bullshit." Her tone brooked no argument. "You don't even like people, so I don't see you as the altruistic type. Out with it."

I could feel her scrutiny and something deep inside told me that if I wanted her help, I couldn't lie. Not here, not now.

I reached into my pocket and withdrew the charms from Elizabeth's bracelet. I'd been carrying them around with me ever since realizing they'd belonged to her; they made me feel somehow closer to her, gave me hope that at last things might be turning around. I showed them to her.

"These belonged to my daughter. I found one at each of the crime scenes. Whoever he is, he knows what happened to my little girl. I intend to find him before the police do."

I didn't say anything more. I didn't need to. My tone was enough to let her know what my intentions were if I succeeded.

She was silent for a few moments.

"What can you tell me about the tissue sample?" she asked finally.

I told her how I'd gone back to Marshall's loft and discovered it near the spot where his body was found. I didn't mention the hidden room or the mysterious birch grove, as I didn't see how they were relevant.

"You realize that whatever it is, it probably isn't human." She stated it as fact.

I wasn't surprised; I'd suspected as much. "Is that a problem?" I asked.

"No, not really. Just something to be conscious of,

that's all. If we're going to try and trace it back to its source, it pays to be aware of such things. There are plenty of creatures out there that value their privacy and don't like being spied upon."

"So you'll do it?"

"Of course," she said, sounding as if there had never been any doubt.

She led me into the kitchen and sat me down at the table. She left me alone for a moment as she went to gather what she needed for the working. I could hear her banging around in another room, muttering to herself, and something about it made me laugh. I made sure to have the smile off my face by the time she returned. When she came back, she put several items on the table in front of us.

"We're going to use a scrying mirror for this working. Think of it as a crystal ball, but one that is flat instead of round, okay?"

"Sure."

"In the same way that we all have a unique genetic signature, we also have a unique magickal signature. Call it a spiritual fingerprint, if you want. And as any competent worker of the Arts will tell you, that spiritual fingerprint can be used for all kinds of mischief. In this case, we're going to use it to zero in on our suspect."

"Will he know that we're looking for him?"

I couldn't see the smile on her face, but I could hear it in her tone.

"Not when I'm the one doing the looking."

She talked me through what she intended to do. "A successful scrying depends upon many things: the strength of the one doing the working, the nearness of the subject, how strongly the subject does *not* wish to be seen, and a hundred other factors that are too esoteric to go into right now.

"The mirror will act as our focus. At first we won't

see anything, the mirror will simply appear like any old mirror, just as it does now. But as our seeking gets closer to its target on the ethereal plane, it will begin to shine brightly and ripples will run out from the center, as if someone had dropped a stone into a pool of water. The faster those ripples occur, the closer our seeking is to its target.

"If the working is successful, we'll see the ripples stop, the center of the mirror will clear, and we'll be able to see our target as if we're watching a show on television."

As I was way out of my league, I took her word for it. Who was I to argue with a witch?

"Because we are attempting to spy on a possibly other-worldly creature, I'm going to cast a ward around us just to be safe." She explained that wards were one of the mainstays of modern magick and were used to form a shell of protection around a specific location, person, or object. They came in two types: minor and major. Minor wards were just what the name implied, minor magicks that could be used to protect an object or a location for the short term. These could be performed by a single individual with limited preparation, often on the fly, which is just what she intended to do now. Major wards were another story entirely, intended to last indefinitely and requiring several days of preparation by a sorcerer with considerable power, using the assistance of several acolytes. Major wards were not undertaken lightly, and the slightest mistake could have disastrous consequences.

"Isn't the house already warded?" I asked. I remembered all too vividly my arrival.

"Yes, but it's only a generic warding and keyed to me alone. This one, while much smaller, will be more specific to our particular task and therefore offer more protection for both of us. Shall we get started?"

She picked up something from the table and a moment later I heard her strike a match. She blew on something, probably to get the flame to catch, and then the sweet smell of incense wafted into the air around us. I was reminded of the way the priest would use an incense burner to bless the congregation on high holy days. She must have been doing something similar, because I could hear the soft clanking of a chain as she moved in a circle around the table.

"O Guardian of the East, Ancient One of the Air, I call you to attend us this night. I do summon, stir, and charge you to witness our rites and guard this Circle. Send your messenger among us, so that we might know that we have your blessing, and protect us with your holy might."

A light breeze caressed my cheek, ruffling my hair. Within seconds the breeze strengthened to become a wind. I could imagine it stirring the incense smoke around us into a thick cloud.

The smoke stung my eyes and tickled my nose. I heard the flutter of wings, as if a great bird had suddenly flown into the room, and somewhere in the back of my mind I could hear its shrieking cry of hunger and warning, but it lasted for only a few seconds and then was gone.

I heard her strike another match, and the scent of a vanilla candle banished that of the incense. She moved around us again, this time in the opposite direction.

"O Guardian of the South, Ancient One of the Flames, I call you to attend us this night. I do summon, stir, and charge you to witness our rites and guard this Circle. Send your messenger among us, so that we might know that we have your blessing, and protect us with your holy might."

There was no mistaking the sound of a roaring fire, nor the heat that streamed off of it. Suddenly frightened, I almost rose from the table but Clearwater's hand on my shoulder gently held me in place.

She poured something into a cup or a bowl and then

put it in the center of the table before calling out a third time, using the same ritual words but this time calling for the Guardian of the West, Ancient One of the Waves.

Her final words were almost drowned as a thunderclap boomed throughout the room. No sooner had its echoes died away than rain poured from the ceiling, hammering us in a torrential downpour. Something large and wet loomed overhead, like a wave about to break over us. But in the next instant it disappeared and I was dry again.

She was quiet for a moment, doing something, but I couldn't tell what. We'd had air, fire, and water already, however, so I could guess what was coming, the element of Earth, the Guardian of, I figured, the North.

When she was finished, Clearwater sat down next to me again at last, and as she did a new kind of tension filled the air, as if every molecule had gained an additional charge.

"Well now, that should do it," she said. "Let's see what the mirror has to show us."

We sat in silence at first, but after a couple of minutes, she said, "We're getting something."

I leaned forward eagerly, desperately wishing for Whisper's presence so I could see. I wanted to look upon the face of the person who had done this. I thought of asking Clearwater to turn off the lights, but realized that even that wouldn't help; the mirror was now glowing with a light of its own.

"Yes, yes, we're getting closer, closer . . ."

I felt my blood pounding in my ears. *Let's have a look at you, you son of a bitch!*

"Got you!" she crowed.

Clearwater's next comment took me by surprise, however.

"It's a woman," she said, and I could hear the confusion in her voice. "A woman with long blond hair."

A woman?

"No, wait, it's a man. Late sixties, I'd say, long white hair and beard. He's wearing a striped suit and it looks like he's walking down a city street, I don't know where, it doesn't look familiar. The buildings look old, worn out. Wait a minute! Now it's a younger man. He's standing in Central Park, I recognize the Beresford building in the background."

Central Park? What the hell . . . ?

It didn't stop there. For the next several minutes the image of our target morphed again and again, showing her more than twenty different individuals from all walks of life. Male, female, young, old, thin, fat, tall, short—you name it, we saw it. Or Clearwater did, rather. I just sat there in my personal darkness, growing more and more frustrated. Finally I couldn't take it anymore.

"Enough! Shut it down."

We sat in silence for a couple of minutes, lost in our own thoughts.

"Does that happen often?" I asked, thinking that maybe it signaled a failed sending or something.

"I've never seen anything like it."

So much for that theory.

"Theoretically, it shouldn't happen," she said. "It's almost impossible to interfere with a sending of that nature. You can block it, but if that was happening we wouldn't get anything at all. I just don't get it."

Neither did I.

But we weren't finished.

We still had the charms from Elizabeth's bracelet.

26

now

I laid the pewter figurines on the table in front of me.

"Can we try the sending with one of these?"

I could hear her push them around a bit with her finger. She was quiet a moment, and then asked, "Are you sure you're ready for this, Hunt?"

"What do you mean?"

She sighed. "Come on, don't be obtuse. What if I zero in on your daughter's location and, well . . ."

It took me a moment, but then I understood what she was trying hard not to say. I took a deep breath and let it out slowly as I considered the implications.

It had been five years since Elizabeth had mysteriously vanished from our house. In that time I hadn't found a single trace of her. Not one. Until now. This was my chance to change that.

While I didn't like to admit it, to myself or anyone else, I knew that Elizabeth might be dead. The police certainly thought so. They'd told me time and time again that most successful recoveries happen in the first seventy-two hours after a kidnapping and that after that, the chances of the victim living through the experience go down exponentially with each passing day. They had taken the active detectives off the case and sent her file over to the cold case division, where it got looked at once every three months as a matter of routine only. No one on the force was looking for my daughter; it was up to me and me alone.

I'd gone down some pretty strange roads since she'd disappeared. I saw no reason to stop now. If Clearwater had even a hair's breadth chance of locating her, I was in.

I felt myself nodding, slowly and then with more emphasis. "Yes. I'm ready to do this," I said to her. "I *want* to do this."

"Okay. If you're sure?"

"I am." A pause. "Except . . ."

"What?"

"I can't just sit here and listen to you tell me what's happening. I need to *see* this."

I could practically hear her frown as she said, "I don't see how that's going—"

I cut her off. "There is the possibility that I'm going to see my daughter for the first time in five years. You can't keep that from me, you just can't." I hurriedly explained how I could sometimes borrow Whisper's sight as my own. "All I have to do is call her; she'll come, I know she will."

There was a long moment of silence.

"I'm sorry, Hunt, but that's—"

I interrupted her again. "Don't give me that. Lower the shields, or whatever the hell you call them, and let her in. I *have* to see for myself."

I was rapidly getting exasperated, and when that happens I need to move, to let the energy out before it consumes me from within. I would have gotten up to pace, but I was afraid not only of breaking the circle but of walking into a piece of furniture and looking like a fool. I settled for bouncing my right knee up and down, like a junkie waiting for a fix.

Clearwater gave me a moment to get control of myself, and then said, "If you'd let me finish. I was going to say that I cannot alter the wards to let the ghost in; it would break the sanctity of the circle and then we would not be able to continue again until the morning."

She sounded like a schoolteacher talking to an errant child. It worked, too; I was suddenly ashamed of my outburst.

"Besides, you don't need your pet gho . . . um . . . Whisper, to see what I'm seeing."

"I don't?"

Another sigh. "You really are new at this, aren't you, Hunt?"

I decided *that* didn't need an answer.

"If you can borrow the eyes of the dead," she went on, "you certainly shouldn't have any trouble doing the same with the living."

Her comment stopped me in my tracks and left me speechless.

Borrow the eyes of the living?

I didn't know I could do that; had never even considered doing it, actually. I suddenly wondered what else I didn't know. What Clearwater might be able to teach me.

This was turning into quite an interesting night.

She explained the process, telling me that the ability was already there, as evidenced by the times I'd linked with Whisper; I just needed to learn to use it in a different way.

Apparently it was all about belief. She lost me a bit explaining how the consensual belief in the present reality paradigm generated the world that we all exist in, how that reality could be bent and shaped by those whose willpower was stronger than the willpower of those around them, but I got the general gist of it and was ready to give it a try.

"Concentrate on visualizing the end result," she said. "See yourself 'borrowing' my sight, seeing through my eyes."

I did as she asked.

I imagined looking around the kitchen, seeing it as if for the first time, but nothing happened.

"You have to give it more. You have to believe. Forget what you know, that your eyes no longer work the way they used to. Imagine them working in a new and different way, just as they do when you borrow the eyes of the ghosts around you."

I tried again.

I put everything I had into it, straining my mental faculties to do just as she asked. I wanted more than anything to see what that mirror had to show me. I don't think I'd wished that hard since the days I'd believed in Santa Claus and maybe not even then.

Perhaps that was my problem. My desire was so strong that it apparently messed up whatever connection Clearwater expected me to generate, for I remained firmly ensconced in darkness.

"Nothing?"

I shook my head.

"That doesn't make sense," she said softly, more to herself than to me. If my hearing hadn't been so acute I probably would have missed it altogether. "You should be able to do this."

She wasn't ready to give up, not just yet.

"Here, take my hand," and, without waiting for me to do so, she reached out and grabbed one of mine where it rested on the tabletop.

It was like striking a match; the minute our hands came in contact, whatever spark was needed to jump-start the connection arced between us and light flooded my senses. I found myself sitting at the table, staring back at my own face from the seat opposite, and my stomach did a half gainer before I got it back under control.

"Are you all right, Hunt?"

I nodded.

Then, realizing that by borrowing her sight I'd left her blind in my stead, I said it aloud. "Yes, I'm okay. You?"

"I'll deal with it for now," she replied, her voice shaking slightly, but she squeezed my hand as she said it, which I took as a good sign.

I could see again.

Son of a bitch! I could see again!

I sat there, numb with amazement. Clearwater's sight must have been better than mine ever had been, for everything came through with a clarity that I'd never experienced before. And unlike the times I'd borrowed Whisper's sight, with its odd perspectives and accompanying flashes of emotions pouring off of every object, the view from Clearwater's eyes was perfectly normal.

I glanced around the kitchen, taking it all in. It was a comfortable room, cluttered in a lived-in way, with pots hanging above the stove in haphazard order and a few unwashed dishes sitting on the counter by the sink.

I didn't care; it was gorgeous, the best kitchen I'd ever seen.

"Thank you," I managed to get out, through a throat clenched tight.

"My pleasure," she replied, and the warmth in her voice told me she meant it.

Now came the hard part. I was going to have to be *her* eyes. She was going to conduct the scrying ritual just as she had before, but this time I was going to be the one letting her know what it was showing us. She gave me a moment to collect myself, and then we both turned our attention to the mirror on the table in front of us.

The wards were already up, the scrying mirror already prepped and available, so when she bent her head over it she was able to get a response much quicker than the first time. As I watched, the surface of the mirror darkened and then began to churn, sending little waves outward from the center just as she'd explained earlier.

I could feel her excitement growing, not just physically but mentally as well, as some of her emotions leaked across the link that mystically bound us together. Her thoughts were there as well, faint itches at the edges of my consciousness, like ants crawling across the surface of my skin. I couldn't understand them; I was simply aware of their presence.

I could see the mirror's surface start to smooth out. "We're getting something," I told her, and then a scene fell into place before us.

Elizabeth sat on the floor of a room somewhere, playing with a doll I didn't recognize. The room itself was unfamiliar as well, with cinder-block walls painted a drab cream color. It was a bedroom, as evidenced by the institutional-looking bed with its thin mattress and iron frame, so different from the canopied cherrywood bed that Anne and I had bought her for her sixth birthday.

My pulse was pounding, and I thought my heart might climb right up and out of my chest. My grip on Clearwater's hand grew tighter; I didn't want to take a chance that we might accidentally sever the connection between us.

I was looking at my little girl.

Alive and unharmed!

Then reality asserted itself as I realized that the Elizabeth I was looking at was no different physically from the Elizabeth who had disappeared from my home five years before.

Five years and she hasn't changed? That can't be right.

I said as much to Clearwater.

"Unfortunately, that's one of the problems with this kind of clairvoyance. The images we see can be from the present or the past and we don't always have as much control over that as we'd like."

She explained that she would try to focus in on Elizabeth's current location now that I'd confirmed we'd latched onto the right arcane signature.

I could feel her release more energy into her link with the mirror and for a moment it seemed to respond. A new image began to form, hazy at first and then with more clarity. I watched as part of a building began to come into view; I could see a tall iron spire, maybe a weathervane or something similar, and the textured surface of what appeared to be a tiled roof.

The image was growing, spreading across the surface of the mirror, and I found myself silently urging it on as I realized that the mirror might just be showing us where Elizabeth was currently being held.

More of the setting appeared. It was definitely a building, a large one at that, with what appeared to be multiple wings. A mansion, a hospital, something like that, I thought, but I still couldn't see it clearly.

"Can we get it to focus any better?" I asked in a whisper, not wanting to break her concentration too much but unable to resist asking.

She grunted, a noncommittal acknowledgment that she'd heard me, and seconds later the image began to shift into focus, slowly becoming clearer and more visible.

Abruptly, there was a third presence in the link with us.

It was completely unexpected, an unwanted and alien presence, something that just didn't belong. The connection between Clearwater and me had felt smooth and natural; this one brought with it a sense of pain and anguish. And as each second passed the pain grew worse.

I could feel Clearwater's astonishment alongside my

own, could feel her growing concern as she sought to isolate us from whatever it was that was now staring back at us from the location we had linked to in the mirror before us. Whoever or whatever it was, it was strong; there was no doubt about that. I could feel its anger, could sense its rage at our trying to focus in on its hiding place, and, with the strength of a hammer blow, that rage poured back at us from the other side, slamming into us, disrupting our thoughts, blurring our senses of self as we were lost together in the feedback of that attack.

In the midst of it all I felt my hand slip from hers, but the link between us did not break. The newcomer was apparently holding the link open as it sought to locate us just as we had done the same in reverse.

Clearwater fought to protect us, to pull us free from the assault, and in the process something about the link between us changed.

I'd been dimly aware of her thoughts and emotions at the edge of our link, but it had been like skimming the surface of some vast ocean. Everything had seemed so far away, so distant. Nothing had been clear. Nothing had been in focus. But now I was suddenly immersed, the surface giving way and plunging me deep into the depths, battering me from all sides like a ship lost in a storm. I grew dizzy from all the emotions: pity and pain, fear and curiosity, wonder and shock. I could sense her horror at the loss I had endured with Elizabeth's disappearance, her amazement at my unwillingness to let her go even after all this time, and, perhaps most surprising, her attraction toward me despite it all.

It was heady stuff, coming on the heels of the glimpse we'd caught of Elizabeth and of my being able to see normally again after so much time in my own personal darkness. Emotion flooded through me, like the raging waters that pour forth from a shattered dam. Her attraction coursed through my veins, the incredible intimacy of the moment transposing itself into sudden desire stronger than any I had ever known. She tried to pull back from the table, but I caught her arm and drew her bodily toward me, bending my head for a kiss, all thought of the invading presence now forgotten in the flood of endorphins and emotional bliss.

The slap caught me totally off guard, never expecting that kind of response given what I'd just caught churning through the depths of her mind. My head rocked back from the blow . . . and my thoughts cleared.

In that instant I understood that whatever was in the link with us was feeding the feeling, trying to overwhelm us with emotion as it stole deeper and deeper into our heads.

The kitchen was spinning before me as I stumbled away from the table, fighting to retain my sense of self. The pressure and pain in my head was overwhelming. Out of the corner of my eye I could see Clearwater holding on to the edge of the table as if for dear life while her other hand danced across the tabletop, searching for something she couldn't see.

Just as I thought we were finished, that whatever it was in the link with us was going to overwhelm us completely, her hands found what they were after—the mirror. She picked it up and smashed it down on the tabletop.

The link shattered instantly, followed a heartbeat later by the crack of the glass itself as the surface of the mirror returned to normal and reacted to the blow it had just been dealt.

My ability to see vanished, as did the horrible pressure in my head.

I could hear myself gasping, something I hadn't known I was doing, and over by the table I could hear Clearwater saying, "No, no, no," over and over again to herself.

I let myself slump to the floor and fought to catch my breath.

After what seemed like forever, I heard her approach and felt her hand on my arm.

"Hunt?" She tried to go on, but her voice seemed to fail her.

I answered the unspoken question anyway. "I'm okay. How are you doing?"

Her laugh was shaky, but at least it was a laugh. "Remind me never to offer to help you again, okay?"

I chuckled along with her, but what I really wanted to do was scream. We had been so close!

Suddenly I had to get out of there.

I didn't say a word about what had passed between us, though whether out of concern for her feelings or just simple cowardice, I don't know. Instead I thanked her for her help, found my way down the hall through a combination of touch and memory, and let myself out the front door.

27

then

The world turned and time continued to pass, without a single clue as to what had happened to Elizabeth. That didn't stop me from continuing my efforts to find her. I tried it all, too. I printed up fliers by the tens of thousands and handed them out wherever I went. I hired private investigators to follow up on any lead that surfaced, no matter how small. I worked the telephone like crazy, consulting experts in law enforcement, child abduction, and kidnapping, searching for some new method or procedure that hadn't yet been tried. I went on local cable shows and pleaded my case, asking for the safe return of my daughter. Radio show after radio show followed, as I tried to reach as many people as possible. I even paid for my own television commercials carrying the same message. Someone, somewhere, had to have seen her or those who had taken her.

When conventional approaches failed to produce results, I turned to more esoteric methods. Anything that had the slightest chance of success was fair game. I called *every church in the phone book, asking to be put on their prayer list, and did the same thing with every synagogue and mosque as well. I consulted fortune tellers and card readers, hoping to turn up a clue to what had happened to Elizabeth. I had myself hypnotized on several occasions, thinking that my subconscious might hold the key, might contain that little piece of information that would send us down the right path. Dowsers. Psychics. Remote viewers. Voodoo hougans. Santeria priestesses. UFO-abductee groups. I even had tattoos of mystical symbols inked across my body.*

You name it, I tried it.

None of it worked.

By the time I met the Preacher, I was primed for what happened next.

It was a chilly November afternoon. The sun was hidden by a thick blanket of slate gray clouds that pressed down from above, like the weight of the entire world hanging above my head, and the screen door smacked loudly in its frame as it slammed shut behind me.

I'd just come from a meeting of local psychics who, it turned out, were about as authentically precognitive as a slab of granite, and disappointment burned like a bonfire in my heart. I had been so sure, so convinced that these were the people who were finally going to give me that lead I was looking for, the one solid piece of evidence that could help me discover what had happened to Elizabeth.

Instead, they'd tried to cheat me out of what little money I had left.

I might have been obsessed, but I wasn't an idiot. I left one of them lying on the floor with a bloody nose as payment for my trouble and got out of there as quickly as I could.

Heading down the street toward my car, I glanced at my watch. It was just after 4:00 p.m. The Atlantic Paranormal Society was hosting a guy at the local union hall in Quincy who was supposed to be a world-renowned dowser. If I hurried, I could catch the last part of his talk and see if I could hire him to find Elizabeth.

There was a small park at the end of the street. I'd parked on the opposite side, unable to find anything closer, and with time at a premium I cut across the grass rather than walking all the way around.

That decision changed my life.

The Preacher stood atop an old wooden crate in the middle of the park, shouting out his message. His arms were outstretched, his palms extended up toward heaven, his head thrown back as if to catch whatever faint vestiges of sunlight might sneak through the clouds. His raspy voice echoed in the still air.

"Repent, for the end is near! The horsemen shall ride and blood shall flow in their wake. Confess your sins and receive salvation before it is too late!" His clothing was an assortment of obvious castoffs, some too small, some several sizes too large, and his long, matted hair was partially obscured by a grimy baseball cap. A shopping cart full of plastic garbage bags bursting with discarded junk stood a few feet away.

I didn't need some religious rabble-rouser getting on my nerves, so I gave him a wide berth as I continued on my way. I was annoyed enough as it was already.

I'd walked only a few feet farther when . . .

"I can help you find her, you know."

The phrase was spoken so matter-of-factly that at first I wasn't certain I'd heard him correctly. My steps slowed, then they stopped altogether as I tried to puzzle it out.

Into the silence the voice came again, and this time there was no mistaking what was said. "I can help you find her."

I turned, looked back.

The man now stood upright, his arms at his sides. His face was angled away from me, still looking upward at the setting sun, and the falling waves of his hair kept his features obscured, but somehow I knew he was talking to me.

"Excuse me?" I asked.

"Your daughter. I can help you find her." As he spoke, the Preacher slowly turned to look at me, revealing two empty sockets where his eyes should have been. The edges of the pits were raw and inflamed, as if their former occupants had been ripped free from their moorings and tossed aside, forgotten. Those empty sockets stared at me with furious accusation.

The sensation of being seen, being watched, by that ruined face sent chills racing through my body. Trapped by his eyeless gaze, I suddenly had a hard time finding my voice. When I did, it came out weak and uneven. "What do you know about my daughter?" I stammered.

The Preacher jumped down from his perch and moved forward without hesitation. He crossed the distance between us unerringly, without a single misstep, until just a few feet stood between us. A wave of bitter cold traveled before him, an arctic wind stolen from the depths of the north, and I was suddenly enveloped in its hoary clutches. I felt dizzy, overwhelmed, as if the cold was affecting my thoughts, numbing my capacity to think. As if from a distance, the other's voice reached my ears faintly, hollowly. "I know she's missing. And I know you can find her, if you have the courage. If you care enough about her to do what must be done."

I took a step back, my nerves jangling. "Who are you? What do you want with me?"

"Who I am is unimportant. I want you to find your daughter, and I'm the only one who can give you the knowledge you need to do so."

"You know how to find my daughter?"

Rather than responding verbally, the man reached inside his shirt and withdrew a parcel wrapped in a stained *cloth and tied with what appeared to be twine. He offered it to me.*

Whatever it was, the sight of it made me instantly nauseous, as if my body instinctively knew something I did not. I stepped back a step without realizing I was doing so.

"What's this?" the stranger asked, surprised. "Don't you want to save your little girl?"

Despite my growing fear, I croaked out another response. "I don't need your help."

The other laughed. "Of course you do, you just don't know it yet." He slipped the package back out of sight. "No matter. Everyone comes to me in their own time."

A grinning leer crept over his features, and the sight of it was enough to finally jar me out of my daze. I turned away without a word and continued across the park to my car. Once inside, chilled to the bone and wondering if I would ever be warm again, I turned the heater on high.

My encounter in the park had used up valuable time, and I knew that now I could never make it across town before the APS meeting ended, so I turned the car toward home instead.

It was completely dark by the time I arrived, so, once inside, I walked through the house turning on all the lights. Knowing what was out there, I'd grown uncomfortable with the darkness.

My stomach was grumbling, reminding me that I hadn't eaten since breakfast, and so, once the lower floor was blazing like a shopping mall at Christmas time, I wandered into the kitchen to get something to eat.

The parcel was sitting on my kitchen table.

Same stained wrapping. Same dirty twine.

The Preacher's words came back to me like a whisper on the wind.

"Everyone comes in their own time."

I edged past the table to the sink, stared out the win-

dow into the night, looking for God knows what. There was no way the old man could have beaten me home. I knew that. It was simply impossible. And yet . . .

I turned back to the table.

The package sat there, unmoving, daring me to unwrap it and see what was inside.

Just how the hell had he . . . ?

An accomplice.

He was working in conjunction with someone else! He must have called someone as I was leaving the park. Someone who knew where I lived, who could get inside the house to leave the parcel on the table.

With that thought came the realization that I might not be alone in the house. I snatched the carving knife from the rack at my side and brandished it at the empty room in front of me.

After a few moments of standing there and feeling stupid, my fear gave way to anger. This was my house and I'd be damned if I was going to be afraid in my own home!

I set off to search the place and drive out anyone I found hiding there, never realizing the real threat was right there in front of me on the kitchen table.

It took me a half hour to cover the entire house, but by the time I was finished I was certain that if there had been anyone there earlier, they were gone now. Satisfied that I was alone, I went back into the kitchen and sat down in front of the parcel, the knife close at hand, determined to get to the bottom of things. No sooner had I done so than the strange wave of nausea I'd experienced in the park returned, stronger this time. I gripped the edges of the table and swallowed hard, forcing a sudden surge of bile back down. I sat with my eyes closed, unmoving, until it passed.

When it had, I opened my eyes and examined the package in front of me.

The twine that held it together had been tied multiple times into a complex knot, and I could see right away it would take some doing to untie it. Rather than waste the time needed to do so, I picked up the knife and cut through it. The layers of cloth fell open, revealing another parcel inside the first. This one was smaller, about the size of a thick hardcover book, and was wrapped in newspaper pages held together with a thick dollop of red wax. Some kind of seal had been pressed into the wax. There may have been writing on it, but I wasn't able to decipher it.

The newspaper tore easily, revealing the treasure inside.

A book.

An old book, actually. Yellowed pages. The dry, musty smell of old parchment. A weathered cover of leatherlike material with more than its fair share of cracks. When I reached out to trace it with the tip of my finger, something strange happened.

The book shifted beneath my touch, as if trying to escape.

I yanked my hand back in surprise.

I stared at the book in a kind of sick fascination, the way one stared at a bad traffic accident, disgust and horror mingling with a deep-seated need to see, to understand, to know just how bad it was.

Tentatively, I reach out again.

This time the cover yielded slightly to my touch but didn't pull away. Maybe I'd just imagined it. Something still didn't feel right, though. The book was warm, pliable, like a living thing rather than an inanimate object.

I half expected to hear it breathing.

Horrified, yet still strangely enthralled, I gently pushed the cover open.

28

now

The events at Clearwater's had left me full of conflicting feelings. My thoughts were a jumbled mess, and as a result the rest of the afternoon passed slowly with little to show for it. The idea that Elizabeth had been, and might still be, in the presence of something powerful enough not only to sense the link Clearwater had crafted with her magick but to use that portal for its own dark ends was terrifying because there was absolutely nothing I could do about it. I didn't have the power or ability to create a link like that on my own, which meant I was going to have to rely on others for help. I was perceptive enough to know that doing that wasn't one of my strong suits; it never had been, and, in the years since Anne had left, what little social skill I'd possessed had gone south mighty quick.

All in all, I was starting to think I'd been better off not knowing anything.

The phone rang, startling in the stillness of the house.

I grabbed it before the harsh ringing could make the pounding in my head worse than it already was.

"Hunt," I said gruffly, leaning against the nearby wall.

"It's me," Dmitri said.

At the sound of his voice I stood up straighter. He wouldn't be calling unless he'd found something. I felt my adrenaline start to flow.

"What have you got?"

His refusal to answer the question directly spoke volumes. "Can you come down here?"

I didn't need to ask where "here" was. There was only one place I'd ever seen Dmitri and that was at Murphy's.

"When?"

"Now."

"On my way."

I took a quick shower and changed my clothes, then grabbed some spare money out of my dresser. As an afterthought, I stuffed the photographs from the crime scene into an old satchel and took them with me; maybe Dmitri would be able to make heads or tails out of them when I couldn't.

When Dmitri let me in twenty minutes later, Denise Clearwater was already there, waiting.

The memory of the attraction I'd felt for her earlier was hovering in the forefront of my mind, so it was all I could do to mumble a hello. My face felt like it was burning with embarrassment and with it came the realization that somewhere along the way I had stopped referring to her in my mind as Clearwater and had moved on to Denise. That was enough to make me be sure to sit with a few bar stools between us so there wasn't any chance of us accidentally touching and forging another link.

I knew that she and Dmitri must have shared stories already, otherwise she wouldn't be here, and I wondered just how much she had told him.

With my luck, probably everything.

Yet Dmitri didn't seem upset. At least not with me. Given how he'd specifically told me to behave before sending me to see her, that made me think that maybe she hadn't told him everything. Which then made me question why, which only made my already pounding head hurt even more as I tried to work the angles.

I think I was happier being a recluse.

Dmitri might not have been upset, but he did appear more subdued than usual, as if something heavy was weighing on his mind.

There were a few minutes of small talk as Dmitri passed out cups of coffee, and then he got right down to business.

"Your detective friend is lying to you."

I shrugged. "I know. Question is, how much?"

"It's bad, Hunt. He's playing you, angling for a promotion or something equally stupid."

I waited for him to continue.

There was a long moment of silence, long enough that I wondered if he and Denise were mouthing words to each other over my head. Dmitri spoke up once more.

"Let's go down to my office. I've got a few things to show you."

A door behind the bar opened onto a staircase leading down into the basement where all the bar's essential supplies, including its liquor, were stored.

"Watch your step; the stairs are getting a bit old," Dmitri said as he started down. "There's a railing on the right, Hunt. It should support your weight if you don't lean on it too much."

Great.

I hesitated at the top, not liking the creaking sounds rising up from the staircase as it worked to support Dmitri's weight.

"Let me help you, Hunt," Denise said from behind

me, and I felt her grasp my arm just above the elbow, as if she intended to help me negotiate the first step.

This time the link was almost instantaneous. Sight flooded in like the tide, revealing the staircase ahead of me, a sagging old structure that was everything I had expected it to be: weary with age and worn smooth by the passage of many feet. Just as Dmitri had said, a makeshift railing was tacked onto the right-hand side, though it looked less able to support my weight than the steps themselves. About halfway down the staircase a bare lightbulb hung down from a wire. As my eyes adjusted to the sight, I could see Dmitri's broad back disappear into the depths of the room below.

Memories of what had happened earlier that afternoon slammed to the forefront of my mind. I turned my head and hissed in Denise's direction. "Let go!"

"No," she replied, and the steel I'd heard in her voice earlier was back. "Dmitri said you need to see this and that's exactly what he meant. You need to *see* it. Now shut up and get moving. I've been here before; I won't fall."

Dmitri's voice wafted back up the stairs to us, apparently having heard the exchange. "She's right, Hunt. Stop being so damned independent and let her help."

She'd shared everything all right.

"What if . . ."

Denise was already shaking her head. "It won't happen again, Hunt. Frankly, if I'd given it an ounce of thought before forging the link, it wouldn't have happened in the first place. Don't worry; this time there won't be any bleed through."

I took her at her word; what else could I do?

The storage room spread out before us at the bottom of the staircase. Large steel shelves had been erected throughout the space, containing everything from paper products to what seemed like endless rows of liquor and cases of beer. Dmitri led us through the man-made maze until we reached the other side, where we were greeted by the sight of a dead-bolted and padlocked door. Our host removed a thick set of keys from his belt and unlocked it.

"Welcome to my inner sanctum," he said with a grin and pushed the door open.

The room was small, but well lit, the bright, overhead fluorescents a vast change from the gloom of the storage room through which we'd just passed. It was climate controlled as well; I could hear the hum of the air conditioning over the soft whir of the computer equipment that lined the walls. Much of it I didn't recognize, though all of it looked to be top-of-the-line stuff. It was clear that Dmitri hadn't skimped when it came to outfitting his operation, a view that was only reinforced when you caught sight of the modular workstation on the far side of the room that contained not one, not two, but half a dozen linked flat-screen monitors that were currently running some kind of search. Photographs and background information on a wide variety of individuals were flashing past at an amazing rate, and when the computer found something that apparently matched the search criteria, it shunted that record to a separate, stand-alone screen which already contained quite a few individual dossiers.

Dmitri crossed the room and took a seat in the leather chair in front of this high-tech command center. Sliding a keyboard in front of him, he went to work, his fingers flying across the keys as he spoke.

"You asked me to see what the police were hiding. Aside from the photographs of the aliens at Area 51 and the truth about who actually killed Jimmy Hoffa," a flash of teeth as he grinned at us over his own joke, "it seems that the good boys in blue have been, how shall I say it, lying through their teeth?"

I grabbed the two extra chairs that were waiting nearby, and both Denise and I settled in beside him as he punched at the keys some more.

"You told me Stanton had summoned you to witness *two* murder scenes, right?"

"Right," I said. "One on Beacon Hill and one in Back Bay." The way he'd emphasized the *two* made me ask, "Are there others?"

He nodded. "Oh, I'd say so."

Another few seconds of additional keyboard work and then the right-most monitor responded by beginning to display a series of photographs in evenly spaced rows.

"Forty-seven others, in fact, going back almost two decades. Funny how your faithful police detective failed to mention them."

I could only stare along in dumbfounded shock as image after image appeared on the monitors in front of us. Most of the victims were male, but there were more than a handful of females as well. The victims ranged in age from teenagers to the elderly, with the youngest being seventeen and the oldest eighty-seven. The locations were scattered all across the US, with two in Mexico and one in Canada.

"Tell him what you told me," Denise said.

Dmitri shrugged, as if to say why not. "An interagency task force was set up six months ago, apparently after some rising star at Quantico managed to draw a link between some of the victims. The man in question, Special Agent Robertson, also got himself placed in charge of the newly formed task force. First thing he did was have the techies create a database to keep track of the growing number of cases that fit the profile of their killer. All I did was tap into that database."

He said it matter-of-factly, as if breaking into a highly secure federal law enforcement database without being detected was something any child over the age of five could do.

Dmitri had already printed out the individual dossiers and now handed them over to me. By the way he did it I knew that he and Denise had already been through the same files, so I didn't waste time digging through them myself.

Instead, I said, "Tell me."

Dmitri turned back to his computer and pulled up a new image. This one was a map of the US with the locations and dates of the killings plotted on top of it.

"By plotting the killings chronologically, we can start to get a sense of just what this guy has been up to," Dmitri said. "Near as I can tell, the killings stretch back fifteen years. They started sporadically, separated by thousands of miles and several months. Then, about five years ago, they began to occur at a faster pace and appeared to be grouped in a more efficient manner, without the crisscrossing of the country that had been a hallmark of the murders prior to that point."

Denise spoke up from beside me. "Then, in the last several months, the killer focused all of his efforts in New England."

Dmitri punched a few keys and the marked killings appeared on the map as a giant spiral, circling in toward the Greater Boston area where the latest two murders had occurred, those of Brenda Connolly and James Marshall.

"Holy shit," I said, almost to myself, as I realized the depth and scope of what had been happening for the last fifteen years. *How the hell had Stanton kept this from me? And more importantly, what did this have to do with Elizabeth?*

My thoughts whirled at a frantic pace. At first glance one might think that Elizabeth was just another of the killer's victims, albeit an unrecognized one, but I refused to believe that. For one, all but two of the other victims were adults, and in both of those cases the victims were young boys in their early teens. Serial killers are typically creatures of habit, using the same techniques, attacking similar individuals, often remaining in the same geographical area. There wasn't a single other case where a child as young as Elizabeth was the target, which was a good sign. For another, all of the bodies of the killer's victims had been left where they eventually would be found. None of them had been hidden away. None had been left for more than a week before being found. Discovery, and the impact it had, seemed to be part of the killer's modus operandi. He wouldn't have changed that for a single victim and then gone right back to what he'd been doing before.

No, whatever the killer's tie was to Elizabeth, it wasn't because she was simply another one of his victims.

I gave it some thought and realized that something about their explanation was bothering me.

"You said it took them a while to connect the killings. Why is that?"

Another shrug. "The data is stored on different computer networks depending on the agency involved. The FBI doesn't share its data with the state police, the staties don't share with the locals, and so on. With so many of the killings happening in different parts of the country and with considerable time between them, no one put it all together.

"It wasn't until somebody phoned in an anonymous tip that they started to look outside their own little boundaries. I would have loved to have been a fly on the wall when they started figuring out how long it had all been going on, right under their noses!"

"I thought all the changes after 9/11 were supposed to prevent stuff like that from happening?" I asked.

"You're right; they are. The thing is that they haven't

implemented more than five percent of the changes they were supposed to implement, so . . ."

I frowned. It had to be more than that. *How could they have missed the obvious?*

"You mean the writing didn't clue them in?" I asked.

Dmitri turned in his chair to face me. "What writing?"

29

now

"On the walls. The Hebrew and Chaldean and . . ."

My voice trailed off as I realized neither of them had any idea what I was talking about.

I pulled the photos out of my satchel and handed them over. Because I wanted Denise to see them as well, I convinced her to break the link between us, returning me to my usual state of blindness.

"You actually understand this stuff?" Dmitri asked, flipping through them.

"Yeah. Once upon a time I read that stuff for a living." For the first time in five years, I suddenly missed my days as a professor at Harvard. Strange the lives we lead . . .

Dmitri pulled a picture out of the stack. "This is Old Norse, right?"

I had him describe it to me and then said, "Yes," surprised that he'd recognized it. "How did you know?"

"I had a great aunt who taught some of it to me and my brother when we were kids."

"Your great aunt taught you Old Norse?" Denise asked, as if she hadn't heard him correctly.

"Believe it or not, yes. My father's family was Russian, but my mother's side was Scandinavian. They met in Finland, during the war, and later, after they were married, we used to visit her sister in Kajaani." His voice grew a little distant as he remembered. "We'd wanted a code we could use just between the two of us. My brother and I, that is. Aunt Natalia was a bit of a history buff, taught us some of the symbols so we could leave messages for each other that our parents couldn't read."

He laughed at the memories. "Drove 'em nuts for months, we did."

I didn't care about his happy childhood. All I wanted to know was what the writing in the picture he was holding actually said.

"Oh," he replied, when promoted. "It's nothing. Gibberish."

"What?"

"Well, I'm not an expert or anything, but from what I'm seeing, you've got someone who knows the individual runes but not how to put them together into coherent phrases. The letters, or rather the words, are correct, but not the combinations they make."

He pointed at a particular line in one photo. "Like this one. 'Sky water stone blue' would be the literal translation. Which, in English, pretty much means nothing. Like I said. Crap."

He did the same thing for several of the other photos. All of which echoed my original thoughts when I'd looked at them the first few times.

"Could it be some kind of code?" I asked, testing my current theory out on him.

"Sure. It could be. I mean, anything's possible, right? We're talking about a psychopath after all, but I don't see what the point would be."

Denise jumped in. "What do you mean?"

"Look," he said, flipping through the various photos. "You've got what, four, maybe five different languages here?"

Despite the fact that I couldn't see what he was referring to, I nodded. There were actually six, but I understood his point.

"The killer is already using languages that are ancient, ones that are practically forgotten by all but a handful of people like Hunt here. The message is therefore obscured, mysterious, unreadable to the average joe and certainly nothing the cops are going to understand right off the bat. Isn't that why they called you in, Hunt?"

"Yes."

"So why go through the trouble of putting it into some kind of code, especially one that's so obscure that the cops run the risk of never decoding it? The killer would want to make it hard, but not impossible."

"If what Hunt says is true, and I have no doubt that it is, what we've got right now is impossible. And that doesn't make any sense."

Unless you simply wanted to get someone's attention, I thought.

Like mine.

"So you're saying there isn't any evidence of writing like this at any of the other crime scenes?"

From the rapid clicking I heard, I knew that Dmitri had gone back to poking through the computer files. After a few minutes of searching, he said, "Nope. Nothing."

"You're sure?"

"Yeah, I'm sure."

The messages had been for me.

The realization hit me like a freight train. The killer was specifically trying to get my attention. First with the writing and then with the charms. And I was getting close, too; I could feel it, like the electrical tension in the air before a storm. My subconscious knew I was on the right track and was urging me on, but I hadn't had the time to work it all out yet.

I stopped my musing when I realized the room had gotten strangely quiet.

"Ah, guys? What's up?"

"Just a sec, Hunt," Dmitri said. In a softer voice, one not meant for me, he asked, "What is it?"

I felt Denise shift uncomfortably in the seat beside me. "I've seen this man before. Is there a better picture?"

Dmitri's fingers tapped at the keyboard. He explained what was happening as one of the monitors filled with the victim's personal information while another held a full-size image of the man's face.

"Joshua Barnes," Dmitri read. "Of Lancaster, Pennsylvania."

The name meant nothing to me. Nor did it mean anything to the other two.

"Can you go through them one at a time?" Denise asked.

Dmitri complied, putting the larger images up one at a time.

A few more passed before Denise pointed to another, this time of a blond woman in her late forties. "I've seen her, too."

Pages from a different police report must have replaced those on the monitor as Dmitri matched the photo to the file and said, "Angela Travis. Clarkston, Georgia."

The names meant nothing to me.

"Keep going. Let me see the rest," she said.

One by one the photos flipped passed. When Denise had gone through them all, we reactivated the link and I took a turn. I was keeping a silent count in my head and we were almost to the end when Dmitri flipped to another photograph and I felt my heart stop.

My hand whipped out as if of its own accord and pointed to the screen.

"Son of a bitch!" I said. "That's Scream."

30

then

It didn't take me long to read the entire book.

If I had read it that first year following Elizabeth's disappearance, I know that I never would have given it another thought. I would have scoffed at the information it contained and brushed it off as fanciful imaginings, alien to my rational point of view.

But my confidence in modern rational thought had eroded over the passing years as science failed me time and time again. It wasn't a big step to go from psychics and tarot-card readers to a belief in magick.

For that's what the book contained.

Magick.

Rituals, actually. Dozens of them, designed to help you impose your will on reality. Everything from finding the love of your life to cursing your worst enemy and the seven generations that came after him. Rituals to bring you wealth and power. Rituals to make your sex life better. Rituals that let you speak to the dead. You name it, it was in there.

There was only one that I was interested in, however.

It must have been a popular page, for the book naturally fell open to it when I leafed through the text.

"To See that which is Unseen" it said at the top of the page.

I seized on it the way a drowning man seizes a lifeline. Lost was the same thing as unseen, wasn't it? And if Elizabeth was unseen, the ritual should help me locate her. At the very least it should let me know if she was still alive, something I believed fervently in the depths of my heart.

The Preacher was right. This book would help me find my daughter. I was certain of it!

The ritual required a number of unusual ingredients, and it took me several days to gather them all together. Some I could find fairly easily around the house, others required a bit more effort. Eventually I had everything I needed. The weather had gone sour by then, however, and I was forced to wait three more days until the rains stopped. I used the time to memorize all the incantations and to walk through the process in my head over and over again, so that I would be prepared when the time came.

By midweek the rains stopped and the skies cleared.

At last, I was ready.

I chose a dark, moonless night. Not only did the ritual require it, but it would also give me another benefit. While I was long past caring what my neighbors thought of me personally, I knew that certain elements of the ritual would give them an excuse to call the police, and I couldn't have that. The darkness would help protect me from prying eyes.

I washed thoroughly, as the instructions specified, scrubbing every inch of my body in the shower until my skin glowed pink with the effort. Once I was finished, I lathered up again and began the slow process of shaving my entire body, starting with my arms and working my way down across my chest to my groin and ending with my legs. It was slow work, my hands shaking from the concentrated effort and the knowledge that if I cut myself I would be forced to go back and start the whole process of purification all over again, but I managed to get it done without mishap. When I stepped out of the shower, the cool air teasing my flesh like the touch of phantom fingers, I felt oddly naked in ways that I'd never considered. I dried off and then padded across the room on bare feet to the sink. The pair of barber's clippers were already waiting and it took only a few more minutes to give myself a buzz cut, which itself was then removed with some shaving cream and a fresh razor. By the time I was finished I was barer than the day I'd slid out of the womb.

I gave myself a once over in the mirror, dried the dampness from my scalp, and then dressed myself in the ceremonial robe I'd made from a pair of black silk sheets I'd dug out of the back of the linen closet earlier. For just a moment the memory of the last time Anne and I had used those sheets surfaced, but I stuffed it back down into the cellar of my memory and slammed the door on it as quickly as possible.

The backyard seemed to be the best place for the ceremony. It was shielded from the neighbors' view by a ten-foot fence and a row of mature oak trees. It was also large enough to lay out the twelve-by-twelve sacred space that the ritual called for. I had spent the afternoon getting it ready and was confident that all was prepared.

Taking a deep breath and trying to control my excitement, I stepped outside and began.

I drew the proper symbols in the grass of the backyard with the coarse salt that I had purchased from the grocery store, a representation of the element of earth. To represent the element of Fire, I lit backyard tiki torches and then jammed them into the ground in the proper locations within the symbols I'd just drawn. Earlier that day I had uprooted the bird bath from the side yard, cleaned it out, and filled it with bottled spring water. It now stood off to one side of my ritual space, representing the element of Water. The element Air was provided by a battery-operated fan I'd found in the attic.

With all four elements represented, each arranged in its proper place according to the cardinal point of the compass that it corresponded to, the grid was finished.

It was time for the second half of the ritual.

Of all the items the ritual called for, the goat had been the hardest to obtain. I'd been forced to roam the suburban farms south of the city until I'd found one that even had goats and then go back several nights in a row until one of the damned beasts came close enough to the fence for me to grab it without raising too much attention. It had kicked a bit at first, leaving what would turn out to be a decent sized welt on my left thigh, but I got it into the car and back to the house without too much difficulty.

I unclipped the goat from the dog run I'd been using to keep it from wandering out of the yard and led it over to the center of the circle, next to the largest Tupperware bowl I'd been able to find inside the house. It already held a mixture of various herbs that I'd picked up at the local apothecary, as well as a handful of Crisco cooking grease to give it a paste-like consistency.

Positioning the goat so that its throat was over the bowl, I straddled it, using the pressure of my thighs to keep it from moving. I grabbed the goat around the muzzle with my left hand and hauled its head back to expose its neck.

I was all ready to begin the ceremony when the damn thing bleated at me.

That one little sound nearly undid it all.

Hearing it, I couldn't help myself.

I looked down.

A pair of round, dark eyes stared back up at me.

In the space of a heartbeat the goat went from just another piece of equipment I needed to complete the ritual to a living, breathing creature, one that I was about to slaughter with my own hands.

My hands began to shake.

My throat went dry.

I couldn't do this.

Then the voice of the Preacher came back to me.

"I know you can find her, if you've got the courage. If you care enough about her to do what must be done."

That was enough to steel my resolve. My grip tightened and I closed my ears to the goat's increasingly nervous cries. I'd tucked a straight razor into the bathrobe tie I was using as a belt, and I withdrew it now, holding it open in my right hand. I raised my arms to either side and shouted the words of the incantation to the dark sky above. When I was finished, I pulled the goat's head up even higher and slashed its throat with the straight razor.

Or, at least I tried to.

Expecting my straight razor to slice without resistance through the goat's hairy hide, I was surprised to feel my hand jerk to a stop when the blade caught on a particularly tough piece of flesh only halfway through the job. Blood splashed, hot, thick, and pungent, while the animal twisted and jerked from side to side, trying to get away.

I almost let go, too.

Blood pumped from its neck in thick spurts with every beat of its heart. It got everywhere: on my shoes, on my legs, on my arms; somehow I even managed to smear it across my freshly shaven scalp. I was disgusted, horrified, but I knew I couldn't leave the poor beast like that. I had to finish the job.

I jerked the blade free, causing a fresh spout of blood to erupt in the process, and then made another attempt, slashing the beast's throat in the other direction.

With its throat now completely open to the night air, the goat died swiftly.

The blood was everywhere, but thankfully enough of it landed in the bowl for me to do what I needed to do, and that was all that mattered.

I shoved the carcass to one side, out of the way, and then knelt in the bloody grass next to the catch bowl, extending my left hand over it.

I used the razor to slice my palm and then let the blood dribble down into the bowl to mix with that of the goat and the rest of the ingredients.

As the blood flowed, I sang the final incantation in a shaky, pain-filled voice, and then, with the chant completed, I dipped both hands into the bowl and smeared the resulting mixture over both my eyes.

After all that had happened, my stomach nearly erupted in protest. The blood was thick and hot, like warmed honey, and it dripped down my face in thick rivulets. Some of it pooled at the corners of my mouth and pried its way inside, so I could taste it, rank and unappealing.

Gorge rose in my throat, but I forced it back down, refusing to let anything spoil the ritual.

Nothing happened.

I knelt there—blood dripping down my face, my hand pulsing with pain, the corpse of a murdered goat only a few feet away—waiting.

Still nothing.

I don't know what I expected, but nothing certainly wasn't it.

A hundred questions swam through my mind: Had I said the incantations right? What about the mixture, had I combined the ingredients properly? What if I dabbed some more of the bloody mess on my eyes, would that make it work better or screw it up?

As I frantically pondered those questions and more, the sane, rational side of my brain tried to reassert itself.

Of course it didn't work, you idiot! *it told me.* Magick isn't real. Everyone knows that!

Much to my surprise, I listened to that voice. I got up from the tableau in the backyard with disgust pouring out of me. I scrambled inside the house without a backward glance and made it to the bathroom before I finally lost control and ended up vomiting repeatedly into the toilet.

When the storm had passed, I stepped into the shower and tried to scrub the image of that goat's neck beneath my knife from the forefront of my mind. I was in there a long time, and when I came out, I still didn't feel much better, though my skin was nearly raw from all the effort.

I needed a drink and I needed it now.

I dressed quickly and left the house behind. There was a package store three blocks down that was open late; I could pick up a bottle of tequila there and drink until I couldn't see straight. It sounded like the perfect idea.

The strangeness hit somewhere in the midst of that second block. My eyes were fixed firmly on my destination, that neon Budweiser sign in the store window like a beacon in the night, when a kind of pressure wave rolled over me. It was as if the fabric of reality was a giant sheet and someone had just lifted up a corner and snapped the whole thing in my direction. I stumbled and went down on one knee.

What the hell was that? *I wondered.*

I had no sooner completed the thought when a longer, more powerful jolt rose up from the ground beneath me and enveloped me in its grasp. It was as if I'd grabbed hold of a high-tension electrical cable, the power coursing through me like a living thing. The current had its way with me, spreading my arms out to either side and throwing my head and body backward until I was almost folded in two.

It went on for who knows how long and then snapped off as quickly as if someone had thrown a light switch.

I collapsed to the ground, my heart beating wildly and my blood coursing through my veins.

When I got up again, everything had changed.

The world around me was sharper, clearer, as if I'd been walking around with gauze in front of my eyes for my entire life and now it had been stripped away.

In those first few seconds before my eyes burned themselves out, I saw it all.

I saw it all and was afraid.

3 I

now

"Who?" Dmitri asked.

"Scream," I repeated, still in shock at what I was seeing. I took a moment to fill him in on my history with the ghost of the man on the screen in front of us.

Turned out that Scream's real name was Thomas Matthews. He'd been an auto mechanic in Chicago before he was found dead on the floor of his shop. As in the rest of the killings, the autopsy had not turned up a discernible cause of death, but it did make note of the strange discoloration of the man's skin.

"This guy has been following you around for how long?" Dmitri asked me.

I did some mental math. "Almost a year now, I'd guess."

A quick check told us that Matthews had died fifteen months ago, according to the police reports. Which meant it hadn't taken him long to track me down.

But why? What did he want from me?

A new line of thought occurred to me.

"Dmitri, can you check the Matthews file and tell me if he had any children?"

"Just a sec . . . Yeah, looks like he had one. A daughter named Abigail." He hesitated a moment as he continued reading. "Huh," he said finally, "says here she went missing several weeks before her father's death. Apparently there was some question at the time as to whether or not he was involved."

I opened my mouth to ask another question, but Denise beat me to it.

"Is there a photograph?"

Dmitri hunted around for a few minutes but came up empty. "I can send a remote spider into the Chicago PD's network, hunt for the original file, but that's going to take a while."

"Do it," I said absently, my thoughts churning. I was willing to bet my left hand that Whisper was the ghost of Matthews's daughter, Abigail. Now all I needed to do was find out what they had to do with the killer and what the killer, in turn, had to do with my daughter, Elizabeth.

I turned to Denise. "You said you recognized some of the others? From where?"

It was strange watching her eyes moving absently in their sockets and knowing that it was because I was currently using her sight. It didn't seem to bother her, at least not at the moment as she said, "Our scrying session. There might be more, too. It's hard to be certain of the faces when I only saw them for a few moments."

I assured her that was fine and that it was enough that they looked familiar. It proved that the first part of our session hadn't been as big a failure as I'd thought. We'd made a connection, just as we'd hoped, but we'd somehow connected with the victims rather than the killer.

I wondered why. What did they have to do with the tissue sample we'd been using as our focus?

My head was pounding, a combination of the link I'd

been maintaining with Denise and all the new facts I was trying to assimilate. I wasn't going to be able to keep this up for much longer.

I knew the answers were here, somewhere, but I just couldn't get past my own fatigue to put them together. I said as much to the others as I let the connection between Denise and me go dead once more. It had been a long day, one full of surprising revelations. I was mentally and physically worn-out and needed to get some sleep before tackling things any further. We agreed to call it a night and to regroup again the next day. Denise even volunteered to drive me home, and I gladly took her up on it. As for Dmitri, he promised to keep digging through the files, looking for more information that might link all of the victims together.

We said our good-byes to him and left Murphy's behind. Denise took my arm and led me up the road to where she had parked her car.

I pictured her driving something small and sporty, maybe a Saturn or a Mazda. The throaty roar that sounded from beneath the hood when she fired it up told me I had been way off.

Despite my exhaustion, I couldn't help but smile. "You drive a muscle car?" I asked, incredulously. I never would have imagined it.

"Traded in my old clunker for this beauty," she said. Knowing I couldn't see it, she didn't stop there. "It's a 2008 Charger, with a 6.1 liter Hemi V8. 425 horsepower and 420 pounds per foot of torque."

Her infatuation with muscle cars was an entirely unexpected side to her, and I almost laughed aloud at hearing it.

I say almost, because she chose that moment to stomp on the gas and we shot away from the curb like a rocket on full thrust. It was all I could do to keep my heart in my throat and to hang on for dear life.

Still shy about having people, including my new friends, know where I lived, I had her drop me off at a house a few doors up from mine and then waited for her to drive off before making my way down the rest of the block.

As I walked, I considered what I'd learned.

At first, none of it made any sense. *Why the hell had Stanton kept all this from me?* But after I thought about it for a time, I gradually came to understand. Stanton had been in the doghouse professionally since the case that had first brought us together a few years ago. He was an exceptional cop, but one not prone to political moves, so in the eyes of the power-hungry personalities that ran the department, his rising star had gradually begun to dim and eventually burn out. If he wanted to advance beyond detective, he needed to make a name for himself, and the only way to do that was with a big case.

A multistate killing spree was just the thing.

Stanton hoped to break the Reaper case on his own, and he was using me to do it!

Now all of his nagging little phone calls and nightly check-ins made sense. He was keeping tabs on me, just in case I stumbled on something that could help him break the case wide open and let him catch the killer before the cops assigned to the task force could.

It was a pretty decent plan, actually. Without any way of knowing it, Stanton had actually chosen the person most likely to solve the case for him. With Dmitri's and Denise's help, and the information we'd put together to date, we were probably several steps closer to the killer than the task force.

I reached my front gate and pushed it open. Maybe it was my preoccupation with trying to figure out Stanton's angle in all this. Maybe it was simply my exhaustion finally catching up with me. Whatever it was, it kept me from noticing the things I should have, and so I entered my house with absolutely no warning of what I was walking into.

I closed the door behind me and stepped forward before my vision had fully returned. I hadn't gone two steps before something struck me across the shins and I fell forward, only to strike something else. As I lay there in pain, my vision finally cleared enough for me to see that I had tripped over the coatrack that usually stood to the right of the door but had fallen on an end table. Both of them had been strewn across the floor like inanimate land mines.

I fought my way free and regained my feet, keeping one hand against the wall to help avoid losing my balance a second time, and took a good look around my living room.

My place had been trashed.

The antique end tables that had stood on either side of the couch were in pieces in the middle of the floor. The cast-iron lamps that had sat atop them were twisted into odd, pretzel-like shapes that would have horrified my ex-wife had she been there to see them, especially considering the insane price she'd paid for them at a craft fair in Kennebunkport years ago. There was something black and bulky that seemed to be growing out of my kitchen sink, and it drew me like a magnet. As I got closer, I realized it was half of my flat-screen television; the other half was scattered into a thousand pieces all over the kitchen floor.

But it was the condition of the den at the back of the house that really knocked me for a loop. My books and papers, years of research and notes on Elizabeth's abduction, lay scattered about, and it would take me hours to sort through them, even with Whisper's help.

A sudden prickling along the base of my spine caused

me to turn and look back along the hallway to the front door. It was open, despite the fact that I was certain I had closed it behind me.

Even worse, a crowd of ghosts had gathered there, staring down the hall at me.

I had a split second to think *Oh shit*, and then my attention was torn away from them as something rushed at me out of the darkness of the bedroom to my right.

I tried to backpedal, to get away from whatever it was, but the destruction around me tripped me up. Expecting several feet of open space, I was surprised when my heels jammed up against something solid and I went over backward unexpectedly.

The fall saved my life. The strike aimed at my throat grazed the surface of my neck instead, drawing a thin line of blood rather than the hot gush of life-sustaining fluid that my attacker had apparently been going for.

Even as I hit the floor, I was scrambling to get out of the way while trying to get a sense of what it was I was up against. I had a momentary flash of a man-sized target tossing my stereo cabinet at me as I rolled frantically to the side.

My attacker followed in a heartbeat, throwing himself on top of me, using his weight to try to pin me to the floor. He was broad-shouldered, I could tell that from the ease with which he held me down, and he weighed a ton, as if his entire body was one mass of solid muscle. I fought back frantically, knowing that if I didn't dislodge him quickly I was dead meat.

I twisted and turned, bucking up and down as I did so, trying to slip out from underneath him. I kept waiting for the knife he'd used to cut me earlier to plunge into my flesh, but it never came. Maybe he'd lost it in the struggle. I didn't have much time to relish the idea, however, for, rather than stab me, he chose that moment to bring his forehead down in a swift blow to my own that had me seeing stars.

The impact stunned me for a moment and that was all he needed to open a big gash down one cheek.

So much for him losing that knife.

I needed help and I needed it quickly.

"Scream!" I shouted at the top of my lungs.

My shout surprised my attacker, made him ease up slightly, allowing me to slip partially free. With one arm loose I began to hammer at him with my fist while simultaneously trying to work my way up into a sitting position where I might have some better leverage.

The intruder reared back and slammed a punch of his own into my face, jerking it to the side, and so I happened to be looking at the wall right at the moment that Scream ran through it.

The ghost moved with all the grace of an avalanche, but it was good enough for me as those powerful legs propelled him across the room in our direction.

The guy on top of me never saw him coming. As the intruder reared up to deliver another strike, Scream barreled straight into him.

But rather than pass through my attacker as I expected him to do, as Marshall's ghost had done to me the night before, the two of them collided with a vicious smack that sent them both tumbling across the debris-strewn floor.

The killer was apparently more, or less, than human.

Scream's touch bore out the truth of that thought. A half second later, it stripped the illusion from the creature in front of me, revealing its true nature. Gone was the shadowy image of a human attacker. In its place was something straight out of one of my nightmares. A wide, circular mouth filled with razor-sharp teeth sat in the center of a featureless expanse of flesh. Slight indentations marked where its eyes should be, and, instead of a nose, it had two small slits in the center of its face. The hands I thought had been holding knives were in fact four-fingered appendages that ended in viciously curved claws.

That mouth opened and a howl like a buzz saw gone berserk erupted from it.

Scream disappeared as swiftly as he had come, but I knew he was still around, for I felt his strength flow into me before I even asked for it. I jumped to my feet, searching for something to use as a weapon. The leg of what had once been my kitchen table lay nearby, and I snatched it up, brandishing it like a club. If I had been facing the creature with just my own abilities, the table leg probably wouldn't have done much good, but with Scream's supernatural strength added to my own, I was ready to bash the creature into next week.

Unfortunately, the creature was a far better fighter than I was. I took a swing with my improvised weapon, extended myself too far, and spun back around just in time to get smacked in the side of the head with a blow that knocked me clean off my feet and left me unconscious on the floor.

32

now

Denise had driven only a few blocks when she noticed that Hunt had forgotten his satchel. It was sitting on the rear seat, right where he'd put it when he'd gotten into the car. For a moment she wondered if he'd left it there on purpose, an excuse to see her again, and then realized how ridiculous she sounded. Hunt was a grown man, not some lovesick teenager.

And isn't that too bad, a voice said in the back of her mind.

Denise snorted. Okay, so yes, she did find Hunt sort of attractive, she could admit that to herself, but now certainly wasn't the time to make anything of it. Not when there was a bloodthirsty killer running around loose and the two of them were up to their necks in trying to stop it.

Since she'd only gone a couple of blocks, she decided to turn around and go back. He'd want to know the information and photographs in the satchel hadn't been lost.

And it gives you a chance to see him again.

Shut up! she told herself, but there was a hint of a smile on her face as she said it. Sometimes you just couldn't argue with yourself.

It wasn't hard for her to locate the right house; if the boarded-up windows hadn't given it away, the general atmosphere of doom and gloom that hung about the place certainly would have. Pulling up out front, she realized something was wrong when she saw the shattered remains of the gate hanging in front of the property.

That's not good.

She threw the car into park and got out, eying the gate while trying to watch the house at the same time. The boarded-up windows didn't surprise her; Hunt had mentioned them the night they'd talked in her home. The feeling of impending dread that seemed to envelop the house was new, however.

Denise had the sudden sense that she wasn't alone.

She spun around, her hands coming up ready to protect herself, but there was no one there.

A little jumpy tonight, aren't we? she asked herself and then brushed it off as a bad case of nerves, more than likely caused by what they had learned earlier.

She considered calling out, announcing her presence, but then decided against it. No sense calling attention to herself if those who'd come calling were still hanging around inside, now was there?

Denise continued forward.

Halfway to the front door she found the remains of what looked like a moat. An honest to God moat! It was in ruins now, but there was enough broken PVC pipe and pooled water to allow her to figure out that that's what it had been.

What the hell was it for? she wondered.

She knew there were plenty of supernatural creatures

rumored to be unable to cross running water, including witches, and wondered if that was what this was all about. Had Hunt erected the fence and then installed the moat in an attempt to keep something out?

A glance at the ruins of the gate and the wet remains of the moat reminded her of how successful he'd apparently been and that increased her anxiety over Hunt's well-being another notch.

For the second time in less than ten minutes she wondered if he was okay.

You certainly aren't going to find out sitting around out here, she told herself. *Get your ass in gear.*

When she reached the front door, she hesitated. Every window in the house had been covered with sheets of plywood and nailed shut. She wondered if that was due to paranoia on Hunt's part or if it was designed to allow him to make the most of his unusual ability to see in the dark. The door itself stood partially open and through it she could see evidence of a struggle: a coatrack and end table that had apparently stood in the foyer now lay on their sides in the middle of the floor, the delicate wooden table in pieces.

But it was her concern over the power of Hunt's threshold that caused her to delay, even if only for a few brief moments. As the old saying goes, a home is a man's castle, and that was especially true when it came to supernatural entities, she knew. If a house has been lived in for any length of time, it begins to exert a protective energy around those who live inside, a type of mystical shield, if you will, that is designed for one specific purpose: to keep out the bad guys. That shield was centered in the main entrance of the dwelling. For a practitioner of the Arts like herself, the power of a threshold could be strengthened, enhanced so much that it could be used as an offensive weapon should some mystical creepy-crawly try to breach its protections.

Denise wasn't certain just how much Hunt knew about the supernatural world around him. From what she'd seen so far, not much, but it still paid to be careful.

Putting her hands out in front of her, palms up, she reached out with all her senses and felt for the power inherent in the threshold.

To her surprise, all she found were a few tattered wisps of energy still clinging to the doorframe.

Something had gone through the door's threshold uninvited. Doing so had triggered one heck of a backlash, but it had also destroyed the threshold defense itself.

Denise felt her heart jump into overdrive, and she took a couple of deep breaths to calm herself. *Focus, witch*, she told herself, *focus*. There were only a few creatures powerful enough to destroy a threshold like this, and she was certain she didn't want to meet any of them in the dark unprepared.

Cautiously, she pushed aside the door and stepped into the pitch-dark interior.

She reached for the light switch and then hesitated. Hunt's sight depended on the darkness; if she turned the lights on she might blind him at a crucial moment. If she didn't, she herself wouldn't be able to see. In the end she settled on a compromise. With a sharply worded command she conjured up a ball of flame small enough to carry in her hand but bright enough to light her way. It was also something she could douse quickly if she needed to. "Lamp" in hand, she moved forward.

She entered the small foyer that opened onto a living room, where there was further evidence of a struggle. A long leather sofa had been knocked over backward and several of its cushions lay scattered about the room. More than one of them held deep gashes that looked like knife cuts, but which could just as easily have been made by claws.

Neither one suggested particularly good news for Hunt.

Denise had the definite sensation that time was running out. She didn't have time to search the whole house; she had to act quickly. She had no idea where the notion itself came from, but she trusted it anyway. Such was the life of a hedge witch.

No sooner had she stepped inside that house than someone reached out and ran fingers up her cheek.

Her free hand flew to her face, batting away the sensation, and she spun around, ready to blast whoever had had the audacity to touch her into oblivion with a major spell . . .

. . . only to find the room around her empty.

Now facing the other way, she felt another set of hands brush across her shoulders, and then a finger slowly slide down the center of her back.

Each time she whirled to face the threat, and each time she found herself still alone.

Voices started speaking to her then, voices so soft that she could barely hear them, but there was no mistaking that they were there. Just as there was no mistaking the glimpses of movement she was getting out of the corners of her eyes at the same time.

Clearly, she was not alone.

It was time to show them that she wasn't without skills of her own. If they wanted to hide in the dark around her, then it was time to shed some light on her surroundings.

She spoke a second command and the light in her hand flared brightly, lighting up the room around her like the sun and causing whatever had been in the room with her to flee the brilliance.

At the same moment she saw Hunt. He was lying face-down on the living room floor, unmoving, amidst another pile of debris.

Rushing to his side, she dimmed the light again and ordered the ball of flame to hold position a few feet in the air in front of her, allowing her to examine Hunt in its glare.

A quick check showed that while Hunt was unconscious, he didn't appear to be seriously injured. He had a cut on the side of his face, and a few others on his hands, but that was about the worst of it.

She couldn't leave him here, but no matter what she did she couldn't wake him. Looked like she was going to have to carry him.

But even that turned out to be problematic, as she didn't have the strength to heft him up over her shoulder and move more than a few feet before she was forced to let him slide back down to the floor.

He was too heavy.

"My scrying mirror for a levitation spell," she muttered under her breath, scowling because she had never bothered to learn one.

She was going to have to do this the hard way.

Grabbing his arm in both her own, she hefted his head up off the ground and began dragging him through the house, hoping he'd wake up before she was forced to do this all the way back to her car.

33

now

I awoke the next morning on an unfamiliar couch in an unfamiliar living room. Or, at least it was unfamiliar until I caught a scent on the pillow I was using. Jasmine and cinnamon.

Denise.

What the hell was I doing at her place?

I sat up and attempted to rub the sleep from my eyes, only to yank my hands back into my lap when one of them brushed against the deep cut along my cheek.

"Don't, or you'll start it bleeding again," Denise said, as she came into the room. I could smell the coffee she carried from nearly six feet away.

"Is that for me?" I asked, and moments later accepted it gratefully when she slid the mug into my hands.

She made me turn my head and spent a few minutes dabbing at my face before slapping a few bandages over it and pronouncing me as good as new.

"That's great," I said, "but I'd feel much better if I could remember how I ended with my face slashed up in the first place. And what I'm doing here instead of at my place?"

I could almost hear her frown. "You don't remember what happened?"

"Ah . . . no."

At that moment I honestly didn't. I tried to remember what had happened after we'd left Murphy's. The last thing I was clear on was entering my house and finding it trashed, only to have something rush out of the bedroom . . .

"Holy shit!" I said, jerking to my feet as my instinct for self-preservation kicked in at the memory of what I'd faced off against the night before. I was lucky I didn't dump the coffee all over myself in the process.

Denise caught me by the shoulders and eased me back down onto the couch.

"Easy, Hunt. It's gone now and everything's okay. Just try to relax, all right?"

Relax. Sure, easy for her to do. She hadn't been almost ripped to shreds by a faceless thing from the back side of the beyond. If it hadn't been for . . . um . . .

I hit a blank spot in my memory.

"How'd I get out of there?" I asked, and was glad when Denise pretended not to hear the slight quaver in my voice.

"I dragged you out," she said, and explained how she'd found me in the house in the aftermath of what looked like a struggle.

Her comments brought it all back to me: the fight in the darkness, the way Scream had answered my call for help, the sight of the creature with its human disguise torn away. I was shocked to be alive, given the fact that I'd fought a hand-to-claw battle against the supernatural predator that had murdered forty-seven other individuals in its killing spree so far. It made me want to pull the blanket back over my head and simply go back to sleep. Maybe if I did, I'd wake up from this crazy dream.

Additional sleep wasn't in my immediate future, though.

"Now that you're back on your feet, it's time we got going," Denise said, getting up from the couch next to me.

"Going where?" I asked.

"To see the Magister," she replied. That, apparently, was all the explanation I was going to get, for she refused to answer any more of my questions, claiming we didn't have time for long-winded answers.

So be it, I thought.

It wasn't as if I had any better ideas.

We cut through the city, crossed the Charles River into Charlestown, and then headed north on Route 1 toward the coast.

"Mind telling me where we're headed?" I asked, doing my best not to give away the fact that her driving made me nervous as hell. Imagine only being able to see dark, featureless shapes as you rocketed by them at what felt like one hundred miles an hour, and you'll have an idea what I was experiencing.

"I told you, to see the Magister," she answered, as she swerved around some other driver unfortunate enough to be driving on the road with her. Horns blared behind us as we passed, and I found myself actually rather happy to be blind; I really didn't want to know how close we'd just come to scraping the paint off that other car.

I kept my thoughts on the conversation. "You've said that already. I just don't understand why we're going to see a judge."

"Not just a judge. *The* Judge. With a capital *J*." She was silent for a moment and then, "The Magister is our local historian, the practitioner of the Arts who has been chosen to keep a record of all that has happened in this region, mystically speaking, since the time he took office. I spent a summer training under him a few years ago and I learned a lot."

Here I was expecting some heavy-duty magickal enforcer or something and instead I get a . . . librarian?

"And we're going to see him because?"

"I think I know what it is that we're facing. I want to run the idea by the Magister, see what he says."

Which was all she would say on the subject until we arrived at the Magister's home half an hour later.

Marblehead is an old town with a lot of old money. I'd been expecting one of the posh mansions that lined many of the town's major roads and so was surprised when we pulled up in front of a rinky-dink little cottage right on the water itself. I say cottage only because of its size; while it was only a vague shape in front of me, I think I've seen storage sheds that were a bit bigger than the building we parked in front of. Still, Denise said we'd arrived and got out of the car, so I followed suit.

A cold breeze was blowing in off the water, and the air had the sharp tang of sea salt in it. The water itself must have been very close, for I could hear the breakers crashing against the shore, and I realized that it had been a long time since I'd seen the sea.

I made a mental note to pay it a visit when all this was over.

I came around the car and together we headed for the front porch. We hadn't taken ten steps before I heard the door ahead of us open and a welcoming voice call out.

"Denise, my dear. It's been too long. How nice to see you again!"

She stepped forward and climbed the few short steps to the porch. The two blurring shapes ahead of me merged for a moment as she gave him a hug. Curious, I triggered the other half of my sight, wanting to see if this "Magister" was human, as she and I were. The shimmer of Denise's aura, the special glow that marked her as one of the Gifted, was clearly visible to me, but when I looked at her companion I was surprised to see that he appeared completely normal.

That doesn't make sense . . .

As I reached the steps, Denise reached down to give me a hand up.

"Magister, this is . . ."

"Jeremiah Hunt. Yes, yes, I'm well aware of Mr. Hunt. In fact, I've been looking forward to this day for some time. Good to meet you at last."

His hand was old but his grip still strong. As I shook it, I felt whatever glamour he was using falter just the slightest bit and suddenly the strength of the man's aura shone forth like a miniature sun, a rainbow of colors so intense that it was like nothing I had ever seen before. While I didn't know exactly *what* he was, I did know that the Magister was in no way human. Not with power like that.

My librarian crack had been way off, it seemed.

As he turned to lead us inside, I tried not to think about why the local version of Gandalf might be "well aware" of me and what someone with that kind of power could do if he decided all this was my fault.

The Magister led us inside to the living room, got us settled on the couch, and headed into the kitchen to get us some coffee, an action I heartily agreed with. While he was gone I leaned close to Denise and asked, "Are you sure this guy can help us?"

"No, but it's our best option at the moment. Besides, he's been around for just over two hundred years. He's forgotten more than everything you and I've ever known combined, so if something like this has happened before he's likely to have heard about it."

She patted my hand reassuringly. "Don't worry; he's not going to bite. Just let me do the talking."

Getting bitten wasn't something I was worried about. Getting turned into a stone statue for knowing about him in the first place, well, that was another matter entirely. Not being able to see it coming made it worse. But I trusted her, so I sat back, kept my mouth shut, and let her do the talking just as she'd asked.

Once the Magister had rejoined us and coffee had been distributed all around, Denise let him know why we'd come to visit. She laid it all out for him. The multiple killings stretching back fifteen years. The unusual way in which the victims died. Her two attempts at scrying out the location of the killer. My daughter and her apparent connection to the killer. Even the assault on my house the night before and her subsequent rescue of yours truly from a horde of rampaging ghosts.

It made quite a story.

If I didn't know her, didn't know the things she could do or hadn't experienced half the events in the story right along with her, I'd be questioning her sanity right about now.

The Magister had no trouble believing what he was hearing though. "So what do you think it is?" he asked us.

Denise took a deep breath, let it out again, and then said in a rush, "It's a fetch."

The fear in her voice was crystal clear.

The Magister, however, wasn't convinced. "That's a pretty big leap of faith, isn't it?" he asked.

"What the hell else could it be?" she answered hotly. "You heard Hunt. It can change shape and form at will, can enter protected dwellings as if the wards and threshold do not exist, and it has been seen masquerading as a human to fool its victims. It has to be a fetch!"

They started to argue the merits of their opposing

points of view, but I cut them off. "Would somebody mind telling me what the fuck a fetch is?" I asked, glancing back and forth from one to the other.

Denise sighed. "Sorry, I forget that you are new to all this. Fetch is the old term. The more common name is doppelganger. Double walker, if you want the literal translation of the German."

That was one I had heard before. "A body double?"

"Yes and no. That's the modern definition of the word, the one most people know. Like you said, it is usually used in referring to the idea that everyone has an alter ego, an evil twin if you will, who does the things they wouldn't normally want to do. The yin to their yang."

"But that's not what we're referring to here," said the Magister.

"No, it's not," Denise agreed, almost reluctantly. "Some say that when a sorcerer gets powerful enough, it can create a kind of double, a physical representation of the darkness in his soul that he can use to carry out certain tasks that he can't do himself. Because the creature is created out of magick, its flesh is malleable, unfixed, and it uses that ability to take the form of any creature it has come into contact with in the past. The longer a fetch exists, the more forms it can take.

"Legend has them being used for everything from messengers to body doubles to assassins. They are completely inhuman and are crafted with a certain animal cunning that makes them extremely dangerous, especially given their resistance to pain and injury.

"The creature that attacked you matches the physical description of a fetch."

I frowned. "But how do we know for sure? And more importantly, how do we get rid of it?"

The Magister sighed. "That's the problem. We really don't know. No one has seen a fetch in at least a century or two. It takes incredible power to create one; I don't know of anyone powerful enough to do so right now."

"That doesn't mean it hasn't happened," I said, and Denise agreed.

Unlikely was a far cry from impossible.

"So what you are really saying is that we're not only fighting this doppelganger-fetch thing, but also the sorcerer that created it?"

"Unfortunately, yes. Fetches don't act of their own accord; they carry out the wishes of their masters."

"Well isn't that just great." It was bad enough we were dealing with some shape-shifting supernatural beastie. Now we had to deal with its sorcery-wielding creator, too.

We all sat there for a few minutes, thinking.

"All right then, riddle me this," I said. "What's the point of crisscrossing the country? Wouldn't this thing be safer staying in one place, where it knows the territory, knows where to go to ground if things get too hot?"

There was a moment of silence as they considered my question, then the Magister spoke up. "I would think it had something to do with the victims. Have you uncovered any ties between them, any reason why the doppelganger or its master might be after them?"

Denise answered. "Not a strong one, no. I did see several of the victims when I attempted to scry out the location of the killer, but that's all we've found to date."

"Was there anything common to the victims you did see?"

"I don't think so," she replied. "At least nothing obvious. It was a mix of men and women, of varying ages."

Listening, I decided maybe a fresh pair of eyes might be useful. I picked my satchel up off the floor and pulled out the photographs of the victims that Dmitri had printed out for us. I passed them to the Magister.

I could hear him flipping through them, occasionally stopping to take a longer look.

"These are the most recent victims?" he asked.

He must have been holding up their pictures, for Denise said, "Yes, the one on the right is Brenda Connolly and the one . . ."

". . . on the left is James Marshall," the Magister finished.

"How did you know?" I asked. I was certain we hadn't mentioned any of the victims' names during our conversation so far.

"Because I know them," he said. "They are both practitioners of the Arts."

34

then

Isaiah 44 says that we know nothing and understand nothing. That our eyes are plastered over so we cannot see. That our minds are closed so we cannot understand. In those few seconds, I finally understood just what the writer of Isaiah was trying to say. The scales had been ripped from my eyes and suddenly I could see.

Really, truly see.

I've never been so frightened in my entire life.

The world was not the safe place I had always believed it to be. I know that's a strange statement coming from a man whose daughter was stolen right out from under his very nose. But I would venture to say that you are no different than I was at that time. Despite all the horrible things in the world—rapes and murders and child abductions, wars and bombs and terrorist acts, car accidents and crack babies, torture and teen pregnancies—despite all that, the vast majority of us go through life like sheep, thinking that it can't happen to us.

Go on, tell me I'm wrong.

The funny thing is, nine times out of ten, we're usually right.

We live in these little plastic bubbles, content with our lives and our jobs and our families, and the evils of the world rarely touch us. We nod sagely at the television when some pretty-boy politician tells us we need to do something about it, but then we go right back to scarfing down our fast food dinners and our five-dollar cups of coffee, and nothing changes.

I was that way, too. Even after Elizabeth was taken from me, even after Anne walked out, I still thought that the world was basically benign and that it was only man's impact that was turning isolated parts of it sour.

I can't tell you how wrong I was.

The world is a cesspit.

A cesspit full of creatures you can't possibly imagine, all waiting to literally devour your heart, your mind, and your soul.

That night I had my first glimpse of them. What I saw scared me to the core.

In the darkness beneath the hedge lining the edge of the street, shadows danced and moved, their yellow eyes gleaming as they realized that I could see them at last.

The ghost of a young boy stared down at me from the limb of a nearby tree, the rope he'd used to hang himself still coiled about his neck. Just by looking at him I could tell that it wasn't the suicide that he regretted, but the fact that he'd done it improperly and had hung there for an hour, slowly strangling to death, instead of dying swiftly from a broken neck.

But the creatures that circled overhead, drawn by the power unleashed in the ritual I'd conducted, were the worst. They had wide leathery wings like those of a gargoyle, with claw-tipped hands and narrow heads complete with horns. Smooth, featureless faces that stared down at me, faces without eyes that could somehow see, *faces without mouths that still let me sense the cruelty and hunger that radiated from them in waves.*

And just as I looked up to see them circling high above, they looked down and took notice of me as well.

I had discovered the monsters in the world.

But, in turn, they had discovered me.

35

now

The Magister's revelation had startled Denise and Hunt both, but it had also made a lot of sense in her view. The doppelganger had been crisscrossing the country because it had been hunting the Gifted as victims. It had taken time to track them down and identify them, which was what caused the erratic nature of its movements. The converse of that, of course, was the realization that five years ago something had happened to make the doppelganger's job easier. Its selection process and travel movements had become much more refined, with far less repetition and waste.

Hunt's daughter had been taken five years ago.

She said as much to the others, but none of them were able to come up with any reason for the two events to be linked, except for the fact that none of them believed all that much in coincidence.

Eventually they ran out of ideas, and Denise decided they had learned all they could.

Ever the gracious host, the Magister led them to the door.

"It was good to see you again, my dear," he said, giving her another hug, and Denise agreed. She'd had forgotten how pleasant it was to just be in his presence.

"We'll have to get together more often," she replied, and meant it.

The Magister smiled and then turned to Hunt.

"You have an interesting destiny before you, Mr. Hunt. If I may, I'd like to offer you a small piece of advice."

Hunt shrugged, as much a sign of approval as he was likely to give.

But rather than say it aloud, which was what Denise expected, the Magister bent over and said something in Hunt's ear.

Drawing back, the Magister extended his hand. "Another day, Mr. Hunt."

Hunt regarded the man's hand as if it was a snake about to bite him, but after a moment he took it in his own and shook. Then, without another word, he descended the steps, walked over to her car, and climbed inside.

"You've got your hands full with that one, my dear," the Magister said and then stepped back inside his home and closed the door behind him before she could say a word in reply.

Frowning, she stared at the door and then turned to gaze at the car where Hunt sat staring out the front windshield, an annoyed expression on his face.

What the hell?

She'd missed something important, that was clear. She just didn't have any idea what.

"What was that all about?" she asked.

"Damned if I know," he said and wouldn't say anything else, no matter how often she asked about it.

Eventually she stopped, and they were both silent for

the rest of the way home, lost in their individual thoughts. Once back at Denise's apartment, they separated to give themselves some time to think about what they had learned. Hunt headed straight for the sofa while Denise ended up in the kitchen.

A half hour later she was still pacing back and forth across the kitchen floor, disturbed by what they had learned. If the killer was indeed a doppelganger, then their efforts to apprehend it would be even more difficult than she'd first expected. Their only hope would be to track the creature to its source and try to eliminate both it and its master.

Problem was, they didn't even have a place to start. All her efforts to track the creature had ended in naught. She depended on her magick, and to have it fail her like this was particularly troubling.

As she pondered the problem, it occurred to her that Hunt had been present in the room when she'd tried to zero in on the killer. Perhaps his presence there had caused some kind of interruption in the process, had thrown it off track somehow. After all, he'd admitted that he really didn't know exactly what that strange street preacher had done to him. Maybe lingering traces of whatever it was that had transformed him had interfered with her scrying?

It was certainly worth another shot.

This time, she would use something a bit more powerful than her mirror.

She checked on Hunt and found him tossing a bit restlessly on her couch. Knowing he needed the rest, and not wanting him to get up and disturb her in the midst of the scrying, she cast a small spell over him that sent him off to sleep and was sure to keep him there for several hours. When she was finished, Denise headed straight for the bathroom.

When she'd first moved in, the cast-iron tub that took

up most of the already small room had seemed an extravagance, but over the years she'd managed to adapt it to her work and now she was grateful she'd decided to keep it.

She filled the bathtub with water, then sprinkled rose petals, rosemary, and several other herbs onto the surface of the water. The plants' natural properties would help focus the energy she was going to be directing at the water, potentially allowing her greater range and clarity for her scrying.

When the tub was properly prepared, Denise took some time to steady her breathing and clear her mind of extraneous thoughts. It took her longer than expected, a testament to the stress of recent events, but at last she was ready.

Taking a deep breath, she passed her hands over the surface of the water, reaching deep within herself for the power needed to activate the working.

As if moved by unseen hands, the flower petals and herbs were pushed to the sides of the tub and formed a circle around its edge, leaving the center clear. A breeze sprang up out of nowhere and blew across the water, making the water ripple outward from the center in a series of circles until an image began to form. It did so slowly at first, just a hint of color here and there, a snatch of the whole, and then with a bit more energy. A street scene flashed into focus, there and gone again, before resurfacing several moments later. The image wavered, failed, and then solidified.

Denise found herself looking down the length of a city street at night, toward the front entrance of a nightclub a short distance away. It was an incredibly clear image, allowing her even to read the billboard above the club's front door. "One night only—Raging Lovers, featuring Sean Williams," it read. The club looked familiar, but she couldn't place it off the top of her head.

The image shimmered, began to drift apart, and so she poured more power into the working, doing what she could to maintain the connection, somehow knowing that what she was seeing was important.

The image winked out.

"No!" she cried, shoving as much power into the working as she dared. "Come back!"

Much to her surprise, it did, though now her perspective had changed. She was crouched at the mouth of a concrete tube, the kind used to run culverts beneath city streets, and could see through it into some kind of cavern or room at the other end. A street artist stood there, his back to her. He was young, probably not long out of his teens, and was dressed in the baggy pants and formless sweatshirt favored by so many of that generation. He was using colored chalk to draw a picture on the cement wall in front of him, but she was too far away to see what he was working on.

She knew without seeing it, however, that the image was important. It was what she had been brought here to see.

She began to make her way toward the artist, intent on seeing what was drawn there on the wall in front of him, but she hadn't gone half the distance before the scene before her began to grow hazy and indistinct. Recognizing that the scrying was in danger of failing, Denise drew upon the last of her reserves, pushing as much energy into the link as she was able to, but it was no use.

Before she reached the other end of the tunnel, before she could see what the artist had been working on, the sending winked out like the flame on a candle.

"Come on, come on," she said, as she struggled for several minutes to bring the image back again, but it was no use.

Exhausted from the effort, she let it go.

"Shit!"

She wanted to slam her fist into the side of the tub in frustration, but the truth was she was too tired to do even that. She settled for slapping the water, which only served to get her a bit wet and did nothing to calm her down.

She'd been so close.

She got up, furious with herself for losing the connection. There had been more that she'd been meant to see, she was certain of it. The sense of having missed something important, something vital, churned in her gut. Given the fickle nature of this branch of the Art, she might not ever have another chance.

Unless . . .

Denise rushed into the living room and over to the stack of newspapers in the corner. The club was real, the marquee outside the door familiar because she had seen it recently. She was certain of it. If she could find the club, she might be able to find the artist. If she could find the artist, she would find the paintings.

And that would give her a chance to understand their importance.

She dug through the stack of discarded newspapers until she found the most recent weekend edition. Sitting down on the floor and spreading it out before her, she flipped through the pages until she found the arts section. From there it was just a matter of looking through all the ads to find the right one.

There!

It was small and unobtrusive, a simple black-and-white announcement. "One night only—Raging Lovers, featuring Sean Williams." The same wording she'd seen on the marquee during the working. She knew that the Raging Lovers was a local band that had made it big; she remembered seeing them several years ago before they had really hit their stride. They'd come back to Boston for a single night's show at the club where they had started out, Dante's Heaven, which wasn't all that far from Lansdowne Street and Kenmore Square.

All she had to do was go to the club and then begin scouring the streets in the club's vicinity, looking for the culvert she had seen.

Shouldn't be all that tough, she thought. Still, it might do to have some company.

Returning to the living room, she crossed to where Hunt was sprawled across her couch, and tried to counteract her own spell, but it was no use. He was out for the duration it seemed.

She picked up the phone and called Dmitri, but got his answering machine instead. Nor did he answer his cell phone. And the sleeping spell she'd put on Hunt wouldn't wear off for a few more hours yet.

She couldn't wait. She needed to check things out now, before it was too late. She didn't know where the conviction came from, but trusted it just the same. That was how her life worked sometimes.

She'd have to go alone. But that didn't mean she wasn't going to take precautions.

She walked into the bedroom. On a shelf in the closet sat a large steel case. She took a minute to punch in the four-digit combination to unlock it. Opening the lid, she removed the handgun inside. It was the same one she'd held on Hunt the other night, a Sig Sauer P226. It had been a gift from her friend and occasional ally, Cade Williams, after a particularly grueling encounter with an infernal creature on Long Island a few years before. More than anything, that incident had shown her that sometimes her magick wasn't enough to protect her. Sometimes the task at hand required a more conventional defense.

It was a hard lesson to learn, but one she'd taken to heart.

She stared down at the weapon, then ran the fingertips

of one hand over the Templar Cross etched into the grips. Once, long ago, that particular symbol had been a symbol of honor, fidelity, and martial prowess. Now most of the world considered it and the organization it represented nothing but relics of the past.

She knew differently, and that knowledge made her smile.

It had taken a while, but just recently she'd returned the favor Cade had done her. Her karmic debt was paid in full, the wheel back in balance. That, too, was a good feeling.

She put the gun down on the shelf in front of her and withdrew the shoulder holster from the lower portion of the safe. She strapped it on and adjusted it to be comfortable. After loading her weapon, she made sure the safety was engaged and then slid it into the holster. From there it was simply a matter of throwing a few supplies into a shoulder bag, selecting a coat that would hide the telltale bulge of the firearm, and she was ready to go.

Since she couldn't leave a note for Hunt, she decided to call Dmitri again and leave a message on his answering machine. She felt better having someone know where she had gone.

Thanks to the hour, traffic was light, and it didn't take her long to get to Kenmore Square. She used the valet parking in front of Dante's and then, when no one was looking, wandered away down the street. Only a few short minutes later she was standing across from a large construction site, staring at the dark opening of the culvert she had seen in the vision.

The light from the streetlamps didn't penetrate down here, so she stopped for a moment and took out the high-powered flashlight she'd brought along. She also drew her firearm. Armed and able to see, she moved ahead confidently.

She paused at the opening of the culvert and listened. Nothing.

She thought about calling out, then quickly abandoned the notion, not wanting to give anyone who might be inside advance warning that she was coming.

All right, Denise, she said to herself, *let's do this*.

She walked, ducking, through the narrow tunnel and stood up in the wide stone chamber on the other side. Her flashlight picked out images drawn on the walls, some large, some small, but the narrow beam of light didn't let her get a good look at them.

Thankfully, she could do something about that.

Putting the flashlight inside her shoulder bag, she removed a large crystal from it instead. She held the crystal in her left hand and passed her right hand over it several times in a complicated pattern while saying a few words in ancient Etruscan, the language of the Greek forebearers who had begun the worship of Gaia, her patron deity. A spark flared in the depths of the crystal and then grew until it shone with the brilliance of a spotlight. Holding the crystal up above her head, Denise took a look around.

The entire space was covered with drawings, just as she'd seen in her vision, and the artwork wasn't just amazing, it was spectacular. It had all been drawn with colored chalk on the flat surface of the walls and floor, but drawn in such a way as to make it look like three dimensions, to give a feeling of life to that which was essentially lifeless. The pictures were incredibly varied in subject matter and detail.

This guy could make a fortune, she thought as she looked at the images. Three men in suits falling into a bottomless well. A Tyrannosaurus rex coming right out of the brickwork, its mouth open wide to consume her. A waterfall cascading into a swimming hole that looked so real she was almost ready to dive in. A winter wonderland complete with falling snow and a jolly snowman. There were movie stars coming down the red carpet, rock stars performing on stage, even an image of a Mickey Mouse face that seemed to wink at you as you went past.

There was a break in the images, a long blank space before they started again, as if the artist wanted to keep the second set of images away from the first.

There were six pictures in all in the second set, and from the moment she laid eyes on the first one she knew that this was what she had been meant to see.

Denise was staring at an image of her own face.

The artist had caught her in midmotion as she turned in his direction so that her face was in profile. Her gaze was hard, her mouth set in a determined line, her hair damp with sweat. The likeness was incredible, as if she'd been standing in the room posing for the artist when he'd drawn the image.

She moved closer, raising the light for a better look, and that's when the picture moved, the face turning fully in her direction, the mouth opening as if to shout.

Denise jerked back in surprise, almost dropping the light as she brought the pistol up in front of her, ready to defend herself if the need arose.

Nothing happened, however.

She held her position until her heart stopped hammering and the urge to blast the creepy thing off the wall passed.

A glance at the image showed her only what she'd originally seen: her face in profile, caught turning toward the center.

"Easy, girl. You're scaring yourself."

But when she brought the light closer to the painting a second time the image moved again, repeating the same sequence, and this time, in the depths of her mind, she thought she heard a voice cry out Hunt's name.

Her voice.

Sweet Gaia!

When she lowered the light, the painting went back to normal, just as it had when she'd stepped away the first time.

It's activated by the magick in the crystal.

Even as the thought came to her, she knew she was right. To test her theory, she raised the light again and watched the face go through its metamorphosis once more.

The artist had been one of the Gifted, and he'd imbued his art with a touch of his power!

"Yep, that's you all right," Dmitri said, staring at the painting in front of him. I'd already seen it through Denise's sight and agreed with him.

It *was* me.

After finding the paintings, Denise had called Dmitri and asked him to join her as fast as possible, though only after he'd made a stop at her place to pick me up. He apparently had a key, something I didn't want to give too much thought to, to be honest, and shook me out of my sleep with a simple, "Denise needs us."

Now we stood together in the tangle of the construction site, and I listened as the other two discussed just what the pictures meant. The first three didn't require much interpretation, as they were just simple portraits of the three of us from the shoulders up. We were surrounded by darkness in each image, though that might have simply been the artist's idea of background.

The other three, well, those were a bit different.

The first showed a group of figures rushing toward a small, indistinct structure in the background. Dmitri thought it looked like a small cabin or fishing shack, while Denise and I saw it as a house of some kind, but there was no way to tell who was right as it was shrouded in shadow and therefore hard to identify. The figures were dressed in hooded cloaks and had their backs to the viewer, so there wasn't much to go on there, either. About all that could be seen clearly was the sword one of the figures carried in its raised right hand. Thanks to the artist's Gift, the figures would rush forward in silence when you turned your head to look away.

The second painting had a thick forest filling the foreground and behind it, looming in the distance, a fortress-like structure that could have been a castle or a prison of some kind. Once again, there wasn't anything in the image to indicate a place or time period that could help us discover something new. Nor was the building in the image detailed enough for us to identify it.

The third and final painting in the sequence was the one that interested me the most, however. It was an image of a young girl's face. She'd been caught looking down at the floor, her long hair partially obscuring her face, but what remained was enough for me to recognize Whisper, or, to use her given name, Abigail Matthews. But what really made me sit up and take notice was the discovery that if you looked at the picture long enough, the young girl would lift her head and smile back at you. When she did so, her features changed from being those of Abigail Matthews to those of my long-lost daughter, Elizabeth. The minute you looked away, the painting would return to normal.

It was clear from the way these six paintings were set off from the rest that they were meant to be viewed as a group and the central theme among them only reinforced that idea. The problem was, we didn't know what they were supposed to be telling us. Nor had we seen any evidence that the artist was still around, so asking him or her seemed to be out of the question as well.

While the other two argued over the benefits of waiting until the artist returned, I found a comfortable spot on the ground and tried to think things through.

We'd managed to put a lot of the puzzle pieces together in the last forty-eight hours, but we were still a few bases short of a home run. We knew the killer was targeting the Gifted and that there seemed to be some kind of specific selection process in place for determining who would be the next victim. We knew that my daughter Elizabeth was somehow involved, as the killings had become more focused, more directed, after she'd been taken. We also knew the killer wanted me to be aware of her involvement, otherwise, why leave the charms from her bracelet for me to find at the last two crime scenes?

But it was at that point that we began to hit gaps in our knowledge big enough to drive a truck through. Who was next on the killer's list? One of us, maybe? And what was the purpose behind the killings?

Even worse, the Magister has said the fetch might be operating on behalf of the master that created it. That meant there might be another player we hadn't even encountered yet, one that the Magister had warned would have access to an incredible amount of power. We hadn't even been able to track its pet killer, never mind the mastermind itself.

Things were not looking up.

As Denise and Dmitri continued to argue, I turned my head and found Whisper standing a few feet away, watching me intently.

"Hello, Abigail," I said gently.

A horrified look came over her face, and I instantly regretted using her given name, never expecting that it might have painful associations for her. I quickly amended my welcome, calling her by the name I'd bestowed upon her, Whisper, and inviting her to my side.

She walked toward me, the solemn expression never leaving her face, but instead of stopping she continued past until she stood directly in front of the paintings in question. At that point she turned and extended her hands in my direction.

Even I could figure out what that meant.

Heaving myself to my feet, I walked over and knelt down in front of her, putting myself at her level.

I heard Dmitri call my name, obviously having noticed my strange behavior, but I ignored him, keeping my attention on the ghostly form in front of me.

"Is there something here you want me to see, Whisper?"

She nodded, and lifted her hands toward me again.

I took one in each of my own and I imagined that this time I could feel the strength of her father in those delicate little fingers. Who knows, maybe I did. I closed my eyes and braced myself against the dizziness I knew was coming. I stayed that way until the taste of ashes filled my mouth, the signal I'd come to associate with the transfer of sight from her to me.

Opening my eyes, I could see my companions standing nearby, watching. Through the veil of the ghostsight they were something to behold, bastions of strength and power wrapped in human form, and I was suddenly glad that they were standing with me in this crazy endeavor. I knew, without even having to think about it, that I never could have done this on my own.

Whisper hadn't given me her sight to have me admire my companions, however, so I turned my attention to the images painted on the wall before me.

The artist had been far more talented than we had

given him credit for. Seen through the unique perspective that was Whisper's ghostsight, the paintings took on entirely different dimensions, coming to life in a way that they simply could not when viewed through the lens of the mortal world.

The first three showed each of us, Denise, Dmitri, and me, moving through an old, abandoned structure of some kind. The walls were composed of crumbling cement and rebar, with a few flashes of brick seen here and there. There was nothing in the images to help me identify the location, however, so I moved on to the next.

The clustered group of figures rushing for the fishing shack, as Dmitri called it, clarified themselves into a group of five men and one woman, moving with a definite sense of purpose toward a cabin constructed of split timber and rough-hewn logs. The door of the cabin was open and a man stood waiting for them just inside, his face hidden in the shadows of the door. A powerful sense of rage rolled off him, clashing with the determined sense of justice and responsibility that poured off the approaching group.

But it was the fifth painting that really captured my attention, for the vague shape behind the trees had now coalesced into a building that I recognized.

The Castle on the Hill.

I suddenly knew, beyond any shadow of a doubt, that that was where we would find our quarry.

37

now

The fetch moved through the crumbling hallways with ease despite the darkness that lay over them. It could see nearly as well in complete darkness as it could in the light, something in which it had taken immense pleasure over the years as it had moved through the world on its own. Being able to hunt in the dark had become its own personal challenge, and it had spent the last two centuries honing its skills in a thousand different places around the world.

That is, until its master had awoken from his long sleep and called it back into service.

The fetch was still angry about that, and it was for that very reason that it had set its current plan in motion. Centuries of existence on its own had turned the fetch into something more than a dark twin of its creator; it had begun to think and act on its own.

And it valued its freedom.

Should the Master's plans be carried to fruition, the fetch would go back to being a servant and a slave, if it lived at all. That could not be allowed to happen. Of course, defending against it was going to be difficult.

The fetch was an extension of the Master, and carried a piece of the Master's very soul within it. Because of this, the Master could control the fetch's actions, could demand its loyalty and even take control of its physical form from time to time as needed.

The fetch had spent many years figuring out how to hide its actions from its seemingly all-knowing master, but in the end it had done it. It had found a way.

And on that day it'd begun its bid for freedom.

Soon, very soon, it knew, the final victim would be taken and the Master would have the power he needed to bring his long-dead body back to life. When he did that, the fetch's fate would be sealed, for it would no longer have any physical advantage over the one who had created it. If it was going to act, it would have to be soon.

But first, he needed to allay any suspicions the Master might be having, and that meant continuing the harvest as had been planned.

Reaching the immense chamber that had once served as the hospital's gymnasium, the fetch moved to the center of the room and waited patiently.

For several long moments nothing happened. Then, in the far corner, deep in the heart of the darkness that lay there, a shape began to coalesce. It took some time, gathering substance from the murk around it, but eventually it resolved itself into an oversized human face, one with eyes of molten glass.

The face thrust itself in the fetch's direction and said in a voice like grinding stone, "Why have you disturbed me?"

The fetch bowed its head in a gesture of humility. "I have brought you another of your enemies, Master."

The Master's face churned and roiled, reshaping itself

with every passing moment, but the fetch had long grown used to seeing it and ignored the subtle changes.

"Come," the Master said, eagerness dripping from his voice like honey.

The fetch walked forward and stood directly before the Master. This close the difference in size between the two became obvious; the Master's face was at least six times the size of the fetch's own. It hovered there, looming above the fetch. Had he chosen to do so, he could have opened his mouth and swallowed the fetch whole.

But that was not what the Master wanted.

Leaning back its head, the fetch opened its mouth wide and convulsed the muscles of its stomach. Like a bird regurgitating food for its young, the fetch coughed up what it had been storing for its Master.

A thick gray cloud poured forth from the fetch's mouth, roiling and churning with a life of its own. In its depths images flashed and voices could be heard, the accumulated memories of a lifetime, the sum of the experiences that had made the victim the person he had been in life right up until the horrible moment when the fetch stole his soul away.

And just as quickly as it appeared, the cloud was sucked into the maw of the hideous creature that had once been human and desired to be so once more.

With every soul it consumed the Master moved one step closer to its goal.

The fetch hated him for it.

But it took comfort in the fact that soon its deliverance would be at hand.

38

now

After returning to Murphy's, the three of us sat around debating our next course of action. Denise was in favor of trying to convince some of the other mystical talent in the city to join us before taking on the fetch, which would take time, time we didn't have. Dmitri and I favored more direct action—taking the fight to the enemy then and there. The fetch didn't know we were coming, and our best chance was to do something about it before things changed.

In the end, Dmitri and I won out, but not before agreeing with Denise that we all needed some food and a bit of rest before trying to beard the fetch in its own lair. As it was already almost noon, Denise suggested we all go home and regroup again later that afternoon. That would give us several hours to get organized and prepare ourselves for what was to come when the sun went down.

I didn't argue. I still wasn't up to full strength after my tussle with the fetch the night before. A hot meal and some relaxation would do me some good.

I was halfway up the walk to my house before I remembered that the doppelganger had trashed the place. It didn't look any better now than it did last night. I was too damned tired to deal with it at the moment, though. Instead, I flipped the couch back upright and settled onto it for a short nap.

The police came for me shortly after three.

I was in the kitchen, getting something to eat, when the front door of my house shattered under the impact of a breaching ram. Cops in tactical gear swarmed inside.

"Police! Get on the floor! On the floor now!"

For the briefest of moments I considered reaching out for Scream and resisting. I was tired and having a squad of armed men charge into my home uninvited put me in a bad mood. The thought of the bloodbath that would result if one of those cops got nervous and pulled the trigger kept me from doing so, though. Especially since the one most likely to wind up dead would be me.

Lights went on around me, stealing my ability to see and making the odds even worse for my side. Blind and surrounded by armed men, I did as I was told.

I kept my hands above my head and got down on my knees. Someone shoved me from behind, forcing me to the floor face first and smashing my nose against the linoleum hard enough to make me see stars and draw blood. A knee landed in the center of my back, assuring I wouldn't try to get back up, while hands grabbed my arms and wrenched them around behind me. My hands were secured together with a zip tie and that was it, I was done.

There were several shouts of "Clear" from the other parts of my house and some of the tension seemed to drain from the room as they realized I was alone. The knee withdrew from my back and hands grabbed me and pulled me to my feet.

"What's your name?" a voice asked.

I kept my mouth shut and didn't say anything.

The voice tried again, this time louder. "What's your name?"

"I'm blind, asshole, not deaf."

The blood dripping from my nose was making me more irritable than usual. Which was pretty damned hard to do.

The voice ignored my wisecrack. "Note that the suspect refused to give his name but that a visual check confirms him to be Jeremiah Hunt. Mr. Hunt, I have a warrant for your arrest. You have the right to remain silent. Anything you say can and will be used against you in a court of law. You have the right to have an attorney present during questioning. If you cannot afford an attorney, one will be appointed for you. Do you understand these rights as I have read them to you?"

I went back to keeping my mouth shut.

"Note that the suspect refused to answer. All right, wrap it up and let's go."

Hands grabbed me on both sides and led me out of my house and down the walk to the street. We reached the squad car and one of the two men escorting me let go to open the rear door. I felt the other man tense, as if he thought I might take that opportunity to make a break for it. I could just hear the newscaster now: "Blind suspect dodges officers, makes amazing escape, film at eleven."

Riiiight.

A hand was placed on my head and I was lowered into the backseat. The door was shut behind me, locking me in.

"Hell of a mess," I said to the ghost of the man sitting in the backseat with me. He had needle tracks up and down his bare arms and dried vomit on the front of his T-shirt. He didn't reply, just sat and stared, like they always do.

Tired of being treated like a second-class citizen, I put my hand on the ghost next to me and borrowed his sight.

I was shocked by what I saw.

It seemed the entire Boston tactical squad had been deployed to take me in! Armed officers surrounded the house and two different assault trucks were pulled up at the curb. Snipers were set up along the roofs of the houses down the street, and I could see several standard Metro police cruisers at either end of the block, keeping back the traffic.

News vans were already arriving, their telescope-mounted cameras trying to get a look at the action taking place.

I heard a car door slam to my left and turned in that direction.

Stanton's Crown Vic was parked a couple driveways over, and he stood next to it now, watching. His face was carefully blank, and I wondered what was going on behind those eyes.

Wondered, too, what this was all about.

"What are the charges, officer?" I asked, as the two patrolmen got into the front seat.

Now it was their turn to play dumb. One of them looked back at me, the move revealing his badge and the name tag above it. Bartlett, it read.

I filed the name away for future reference.

Evidence teams from the forensic unit showed up as we were leaving. *Good luck*, I thought to myself, considering the state the doppelganger had left my house in. I had no clue what they were looking for, but whatever it was, it certainly wasn't going to be easy to find in that mess.

39

then

To this day I don't remember how I managed to get back to my house, never mind inside. If I had to guess, I'd say that the instinct for self-preservation took over. I'd never before made that walk without being able to see, but my body must have known where it was going and taken me there when I needed it to.

However I got there, I woke up to find myself stretched out on my kitchen floor, though at the time I had no idea where I was. It was dark and it took several moments of frantic thrashing about, touching everything nearby, until my hands found the kitchen sink and I figured out where I was.

My eyes burned for days.

Nothing I did would stop it. I tried flushing them with water. I tried putting a cold compress on them. I tried to sleep with an ice pack tied around my face. Nothing helped. It felt like a blowtorch had been turned on at the heart of my eyeballs and was burning them up, millimeter by millimeter, from deep inside.

More than once, I wanted to claw them out of my skull.

I cursed the Preacher for deceiving me, swearing over and over again that if I ever got my hands on him I'd tear him limb from limb. I cursed myself for being stupid enough to listen to him in the first place.

But the anger was just a cover for what I was really feeling.

Fear.

Cold, stark terror, to be exact.

With every passing second I was excruciatingly aware that they were out there.

Watching.

Waiting.

My fear of them nearly consumed me.

I spent every waking moment in utter terror, sleeping only when I absolutely had to, and then in fits and starts that did little to ease my frayed nerves. I was certain that at any moment they were going to burst into my home, determined to seek out and devour the stupid human who had been audacious enough to pierce the veil that hid them from view. I cringed at the slightest sounds, from the creak of a floorboard above me to the tap of a branch against the window in a light breeze. Every sound was a threat, every silence the mask behind which a fiend from hell was creeping up on me.

Imagine suddenly realizing that everything you'd ever feared as a child was real. Every demon, every ghost, every hideous thing you'd ever seen at the movies or watched on television, everything you'd ever read in a book or conjured up in your fevered mind was, in truth, a reality. The bogeyman not only existed, but was coming to get you. That was how I felt every second of the day, and I knew I'd either go crazy or die of a heart attack before long if I didn't find a way to control it.

In the end, I couldn't save myself.

I needed Whisper to do that for me.

She just showed up a few days after I'd lost the ability to see in the sunlight. I don't know what called her to me or how she found me, but I'll be forever grateful that she did. I didn't see her arrive, couldn't in fact, but I felt her sudden appearance the same way you feel it when someone is watching you. That tingling sensation along your spine, that crawling feeling that you are no longer alone.

To be honest, I thought I was done for. I thought one of the things I'd seen outside that first night had finally come to claim its reward.

I'd been hiding away in a crawl space inside my bedroom closet, as far from the outside windows and doors as I could possibly get. I hadn't dared venture out and was weak from hunger and thirst. One minute I was alone and the next I felt her there with me. I tried to push myself deeper into the narrow space, frantic to get away, and I'm not ashamed to say I let out a shrill scream when I felt her hand on my shoulder.

Pain exploded in my head—fierce, pounding pain—and the world around me spun down into darkness as I passed out in fear.

When I awoke, I could see.

Not the way I had before, for my own vision was forever lost to me, but in that strange new way I've taken to calling ghostsight.

My salvation sat in front of me, rocking back and forth, her eyes wandering vacantly.

I don't think I can express the sense of wonder I felt in that moment, the sheer gratitude that poured out of me when this little dead girl reached out and ran her fingers across my face, memorizing my features by touch because she had loaned me her eyesight. If it hadn't been for her, I'm sure I wouldn't have made it out of that first month.

With time, I learned to call her when I needed her. We couldn't really communicate, not in any useful sense of the word, as she either wouldn't or couldn't reply to anything I said, but she was more than willing to listen, and I enjoyed her company. She was always so quiet, so gentle, that I began to call her Whisper and after a while the name stuck. It was as good as any, I guess. It was Whisper who taught me, through simple trial and error, that I could use the senses of the other ghosts around me as well, but I have never been as comfortable with them as I am with her. Maybe it is simply because she was my first.

Or maybe it is because she reminds me so much of my missing daughter.

I don't know.

I'm just glad she's here.

40

now

"Where the hell is he?" Dmitri asked.

Denise shook her head; she didn't know. The agreed upon meeting time had passed more than an hour ago, and Hunt still hadn't showed up. Nor had he called. She was starting to get worried.

He'd been adamant that the fetch was holed up in the crumbling remains of the old Danvers State Hospital, known to many of the locals as the Castle on the Hill. Denise had to agree; if you were looking for a spooky old place to hide out in, you couldn't do much better than that place. When she'd objected to the three of them facing off against the thing alone, Dmitri had taken Hunt's side. They needed to get a look at the thing, see what they were actually up against, and the best time to do that was now, before it discovered that they were on to it. Reluctantly, she'd agreed.

And now Hunt was missing.

They passed another ten minutes in silence.

Finally, Dmitri had had enough.

"Fuck him," he said. "We can do this alone."

"I don't know, Dmitri," Denise said. "Maybe we should check the hospitals or something."

"Nyet!" the big man replied, and his slip into Russian let her know just how upset the entire situation was making him.

"If he is in the hospital, then there isn't anything more we can do for him. But every minute we waste is another moment in which that thing could kill another of us, maybe someone you or I know personally. We have to find out what we are up against, and we have to act on that information as soon as possible."

He snagged the duffel bag of equipment he'd assembled earlier and turned for the door. "We don't have any more time to waste."

His reached the door and turned back to face her. "Besides, what good is a blind man on a combat mission anyway?"

As much as she hated to admit it, Denise realized Dmitri just might be right.

41

now

They left me sitting in the interrogation room for close to two hours. I'd watched more than my fair share of *Law & Order* episodes and I knew the drill, knew that they were trying to soften me up for what was to come. They must have thought that being left alone, blind and unable to see, would just heighten my anxiety and make me more willing to talk.

Thing was, that kind of approach just wasn't going to work with me. Number one, I wasn't guilty of anything. We could sit here for weeks on end and nothing would change that. Number two, the blind spent an awful lot of time alone in the dark or, in my case, the light, and it didn't make us uncomfortable the way it did the sighted. And, number three, the room wasn't anywhere near as empty as they thought it was.

I had the dead for company.

There were three of them. I could see them sitting there, watching me, waiting for heaven knew what. The room felt heavy with their anger and sorrow, and the weight of it made me wonder how many confessions had been influenced by their unseen presence. I understood how people could get very uncomfortable with them hanging around.

I resisted the urge to steal a look through their eyes, as I was tired enough already and knew this was likely to be a long session. Instead, I leaned back and thought things through. I went over everything I'd done since Stanton had called me out to that first murder scene. I considered every detail, no matter how trivial, looking for a reason why they'd dragged me down here in the middle of the night like some common criminal, and I came up empty.

Or at least empty of charges serious enough to warrant such treatment. Sure, I'd taken a piece of evidence from a crime scene without informing Stanton. And I'd broken the seal on the Marshall apartment so I could get that piece of evidence. So sue me, okay?

But none of that was worth arresting me over. And it certainly didn't deserve the hard-core treatment that I'd been subjected to since they'd showed up at my door.

Just what the hell was going on?

Eventually, I heard the door open and caught the scent of Stanton's usual brand of cheap cologne. The click of the lock as the door closed behind him was loud in the silence.

I heard the scrape of a chair against the floor tile and then the creak of the joints as Stanton settled into it. He fiddled with something on the tabletop for a moment and then began speaking.

"11:55 p.m., November 6. Interrogation of Jeremiah Hunt. Present with the suspect is Detective First Grade Miles Stanton, Homicide."

His fury was evident from his very first word and I knew I was in serious trouble. His formality also meant that he was taping the session; the sounds I'd heard must have been him turning on the tape recorder.

"The subject has received his Miranda warning and has waived his right to speak to an attorney."

That made me sit up a bit straighter. I'd been Mirandized back at my house during the initial arrest, that much was true, but I sure as hell hadn't waived my right to speak to anyone, least of all my attorney. Something wasn't right, wasn't right at all, and Stanton's next words really hit home.

"It's over, Hunt. We've got you cold."

I was honestly too surprised to answer him.

"Save yourself some trouble," he continued. "Spit it all out, every last detail, and maybe the judge will have some leniency. I'm certainly not going to recommend it, but hey, you might get lucky."

I shook my head. "I don't have any idea what you are talking about, Stanton."

"Right. And I'm the tooth fairy. Start writing, Hunt."

"I'm not kidding, Stanton. I don't know what you are talking about."

"Cut the bullshit, Hunt. I'm sick of listening to it."

I did what I could to hold my temper and tried to reason with him. "I'm not bullshitting you, Stanton. Why the hell am I in here?"

Stanton had less control of his temper than I did and he'd finally reached his limit. "Don't act stupid with me, asshole!" he shouted, his spittle peppering my face. "Did you think you could just keep stringing us along?"

There was a loud clatter as he kicked the chair out from behind him, and the next thing I knew he was right there on my side of the table, rage coming off him in waves. He leaned in close so that the recorder couldn't hear and whispered, "We've got you on video, asshole, and I'm going to do my best to see to it that you fry for what you've done."

Stanton's anger was so intense that I was suddenly

certain he wouldn't wait for the trial. He was going to take things into his own hands and become judge, jury, and executioner right then and there.

That's when the second voice spoke up.

"That's enough, Detective. Go get some coffee. Leave Mr. Hunt to me for a bit."

The other man had been so quiet, or I'd been so focused on Stanton, that I hadn't even known he was there.

I heard the door slam as Stanton left the interrogation room. I wondered how much of his anger had been an act. Was the newcomer supposed to play the good cop to Stanton's bad?

I didn't have long to wait to find out.

"My name is Robertson, Mr. Hunt. Special Agent Dale Robertson."

He paused, as if waiting for me to say something. What did he expect me to do? Break down and confess the minute I learned he was with the FBI? The guy had apparently been watching too much TV.

I had to restrain myself from laughing.

"You are under arrest for the murders of Brenda Connolly, James Marshall, and Hector Morales. I suggest you cooperate now. If you wait too long, I won't be able to help you."

It was standard cop talk, but I decided to play along and see what I could find out.

Acting indifferent to his proposal, I asked, "Since when is murder an FBI affair?"

"When it involves the deaths of more than one individual in more than one state, Mr. Hunt. But I'm sure you know that. What don't you just make everyone's lives easier and tell us why you did it. We have you on videotape, after all."

Videotape?

"I'm sorry," I said. "You have me on what?"

Robertson sighed. It was actually pretty good; he even sounded like someone who was tired of all the shenanigans.

"Didn't Detective Stanton tell you? At one thirty-five this afternoon we caught you on camera entering the building where Hector Morales lived. According to witnesses, you took the elevator to his tenth-floor apartment. A second camera just outside Mr. Morales's apartment picked you up again as you rang the bell. When he opened the door, you slit his throat. The camera caught every minute of it."

The FBI agent chuckled. "You might have gotten away with it at that point, given the wide-brimmed hat you were wearing, but like the stupid fuckup you are, you looked right up at the camera and gave us a perfect view of your face."

He tossed something across the table and when I picked it up I could feel the extra smoothness of the paper that told me it was a photograph.

I didn't have to ask who was in it.

"Stanton was right, Hunt. You're going to fry. So why not help us out and tell us what you did to the other forty-seven victims?"

42

now

It was obvious to me what had happened. The doppel-ganger, or fetch, had assumed my appearance to commit the next murder and made sure that the surveillance cameras had gotten a good look at him while doing so. I would have bet my left hand that the latest victim was unrelated to all the others, too, that he'd been chosen on the spur of the moment and wasn't part of the larger scheme the killer was following.

But how could I explain that to the police? There was no way they would believe me. They were already ignor-ing the fact that in the previous murders there were no obvious signs of a struggle nor an apparent cause of death, while this one had both. And it just happened to have been caught on camera, too? Did they think the killer suddenly had a lobotomy overnight? And if they couldn't see the obvious right before their eyes, how on earth did I expect them to manage the truth? Shape-changers and ghosts? Humans with magickal powers?

I could hear them laughing already.

The doppelganger had managed to take me out of the picture and throw the cops off the scent, all in one fell swoop. The creature was more intelligent than I had given it credit for.

It had brought me into the investigation, kept me running around in circles for days with false leads, and then, when the three of us—Dmitri, Denise, and I—had begun to close in on the reality behind the smoke screen, it had set me up as the fall guy with one carefully chosen crime scene.

I ground my teeth in frustration.

When I refused to say anything more, Agent Robertson informed me that I would be arraigned in the morning, an experience I wasn't looking forward to, and I was led off to a holding cell for the night. It seemed it was an open-and-shut case, at least where the latest killing was concerned. They'd have to jump through hoops to link me to the others, but I had no doubt that Robertson would find a way to do it, even if he had to bend the truth a little bit to make it work. He clearly thought I was responsible for all of them.

They gave me my phone call around seven that night. I called the only person I could think of. Denise. She wasn't in, so I left a message on her answering machine, letting her know what had happened. I didn't know what else to do. I couldn't imagine calling Anne after all these years and wouldn't want to drag her into this anyway. She'd gotten on with her life and didn't need me screwing it up again. I wasn't expecting the judge to grant me bail anyway, not with the evidence they had against me and the brutal nature of the crimes of which I was accused.

I was in very deep shit, and I knew it was going to be a long night.

That's why I was surprised when a guard appeared at the door to my cell just after nine. "Your attorney is here to see you," he said, as he took out a key, unlocked the door, and led me down the hall.

I didn't have an attorney, but I wasn't about to tell the guard that. I simply walked into the room, sat down at the table, and waited for the other man to be led into the room. When I heard him thank the guard, I knew who it was.

We both waited for the guard to leave. Attorney-client visits were supposed to be confidential, after all.

When he heard the clang of the cell door at the end of the block, Dmitri said, in a voice like breaking glass, "Denise is dead, Hunt."

"What?!"

He crossed the room and began pacing back and forth, his boots thumping against the concrete floor. He was clearly upset and getting more so by the minute. His words tumbled over each other. "We should have known better, Hunt. The damn thing is just too strong for us!"

"Slow down a minute, man. I can't understand you."

But the big Russian wasn't listening. "God's blood, Hunt! It's all my fault! If only I'd been a few seconds faster!"

I was getting scared now, and when I get scared, I get angry. I could see his vague outline going back and forth in front of me, and so I jumped up, grabbed him by the arms, and shook him until he stopped.

"Tell me what you're talking about! What happened to Denise?"

My anger startled him out of his panic. He stopped, took a deep breath and said, "The doppelganger killed her."

Four words.

Four little words.

That's all it took to turn my world upside down.

I released him and took a few shaky steps backward

until my knees hit the bench behind me and I dropped down onto it in stunned silence.

Denise? Dead?

"What happened?" I asked dully.

"When you didn't show up, we decided to give it a go on our own. We figured we'd just drop in, do a little scouting around, and then get the hell out of there."

Dmitri went on to describe how they'd arrived at the old hospital grounds, parked out of sight, and snuck into the main building through a broken window. They found tracks in the dust by the front doors and followed them into the depths of the building.

The fetch had surprised them in the darkness and overwhelmed Dmitri. "My head slammed into a support column and that was it. Lights out. The last thing I remember was the doppelganger carrying Denise off into the depths of the building. When I came to I was alone in the room with no idea which direction they had gone. Rather than wander around on my own, I found my way out and came looking for you. I heard the press conference on the radio and came right over." He even bent over, pulled his hair aside, and made me feel the lump on his head to prove he wasn't making it all up.

I barely acknowledged his injury; Denise was all that mattered right now. "So she was alive the last time you saw her."

"Yes, but . . ."

"No buts. We act on that assumption. It wouldn't have carried her off if it wanted her dead right away. It would have just killed her right then and there. Which means we have some time."

But how much time, I didn't know.

"Do you think you can find that spot again? Where the two of you were attacked?"

Dmitri thought about it for a moment. "Yeah, I can

find it," he said finally. I pretended to ignore the uncertainty I heard in his voice.

"Okay. We can't do anything while I'm locked up in here, so this is what we're going to do . . ."

When the guard came back, we were ready.

43

now

"Time's up, counselor," the guard said, opening the door of the cell and stepping to the side to let Dmitri squeeze past.

Because we had discussed it earlier, I knew what happened next. My partner in crime started to exit the cell, then spun to his left in midstride. The punch probably started somewhere down near his knees and by the time it connected with the guard's chin it had all the force of a freight train. I don't think the guy even knew what hit him. One minute he was probably smiling at Dmitri, enjoying his little display of power, and the next he was dropping to the floor like a sack of wet rice.

Lights out.

I can't even say I felt sorry for the guy. After all, he was barely paying attention. He deserved what he got.

There was some shuffling and then Dmitri was handing me a pair of handcuffs and a small snub-nosed revolver.

"I've got his badge and his service piece. The one I gave you is his backup gun," he said, as he dragged the guard's unconscious form farther into the cell. "It's loaded, so take care."

I'd never fired a gun in my life but figured the weapon wouldn't be all that hard to figure out. Just point and shoot, right? I slipped it into the rear waistline of my pants, hoping my long shirt would cover it sufficiently.

After that, we were ready to go.

The plan was for him to impersonate a plainclothes detective transporting a prisoner to the interview rooms on the second floor. What it lacked in complication it made up for in sheer audacity. After all, who expected a prisoner to simply stroll right out of One Schroeder Plaza under the cops' very noses?

I just hoped it would work, 'cause we were only going to get one chance. After that, they'd lock us up somewhere down in the basement and throw away the key.

I put the cuffs on loosely, without locking them, and held my hands behind my back, pretending to be a prisoner, while Dmitri guided me forward with his hand on one of my arms. I had my sunglasses with me, but due to the lighting I couldn't see much beyond the vague shapes of those around me. I was going to have to trust him to get us out of here.

We headed down the hall and turned the corner toward the guard station.

"Two of them," Dmitri said, meaning the number of police officers who were currently manning the desk, and I breathed a sigh of relief at the news. Two of them we could probably handle, given that we had the element of surprise, but any more than that would have been a problem.

As planned, Dmitri tried to get up close and personal, flashing his stolen badge to set them at ease while I stood docilely nearby. I heard him joke with the others in a low voice, there was the sound of a brief struggle, and then Dmitri was back at my side.

"All clear," he said.

We left one of them tied up with his belt and shoelaces behind the guard desk. We shanghaied the other into leading us down the back stairwell, bypassing the elevator, where we were sure to run into more people and thereby increase our chances of getting caught. Weaponless, and with his hands cuffed behind his back, Officer Dietrich was docile enough for even me to handle.

Dmitri was in the lead, with our hostage in the middle and me bringing up the rear. When we reached the first floor without incident, Dmitri turned to Dietrich and asked how to get out.

The officer indicated the door in front of us. "That leads to a small service hall off the central corridor. Turn left at the main corridor, cross the rotunda, and you'll be at the front doors."

Sounded easy enough.

That should have been our clue right there.

Dmitri cautiously opened the door and peered out. Finding the service corridor empty, he pulled us along behind him. We crept another ten feet forward and then waited while he checked out the next step.

"Pizdetz!"

From the tone of his voice I didn't need a translator to tell me that something wasn't right.

He reverted to English with his explanation. "Some idiot is holding a press conference in the middle of the rotunda. There is no way we are going to get past all that without being recognized."

I jerked on Dietrich's arm and jammed my revolver into his side so he got the message. "Is there another way out of here?"

His voice cracked as he said, "Across the hall. There is

another service corridor that leads to the morgue. You can get out that way."

I thought it over. We'd have perhaps ten seconds of exposure as we crossed the corridor and opened the service door. Fifteen seconds max. From a distance, Dmitri and I might pass for a couple of cops escorting a prisoner, but if Dietrich chose that moment to call attention to us, we'd be screwed.

You'll just have to see to it that he doesn't, I thought.

Turning to Dmitri, I said, "I don't see any other option, do you?"

"No," Dmitri answered, and followed it up with another long stream of Russian.

That was good enough for me.

I jammed the gun into Dietrich's side, told him I'd put a bullet in him if he opened his mouth to say anything, anything at all, and then followed Dmitri out into the hallway when he tugged on my arm.

The chatter from the press conference filtered down the hall to us, and I could tell just by the sound of it that it was going to be a big one. Apparently they hadn't started yet, but it couldn't be long now.

We were in the middle of the hallway when our luck ran out.

A voice rang out from inside the rotunda.

"Hey! Stop right there!"

Stanton!

"Let's go, people," Dmitri said nervously and pulled us after him.

"I said *stop*!" Stanton shouted. The sound of running feet quickly followed.

We crossed the last few steps and reached the door. Dmitri hauled it open, shoved our hostage inside, and then grabbed me by the arm as I followed.

"We're out of time, Hunt. If we don't stop them here they'll pin us down in the stairwell."

I couldn't believe what I was hearing. The big idiot wanted a confrontation when we were seconds away from escaping. We didn't have time for this!

"Don't be a fool, Dmitri. We can still do this."

But he didn't answer and it took me a heartbeat to realize that he had already headed off down the hall toward the oncoming group of cops.

So be it. One of us had to get out of here.

I kicked the door shut behind me and was about to get Dietrich to lead me down the stairs when an unbelievably loud roar sounded from the hallway we'd just left.

"What was *that*?" Dietrich asked, his voice shaking in fear.

I knew I should get going, knew I should be hightailing it down that hallway and out the morgue entrance before anyone could figure out what was happening, but I felt rooted to the floor with curiosity.

I wanted, no, needed, to know just what the hell had made that sound, too.

My hand was still holding on to the handcuffs Officer Dietrich was wearing so I pulled him back toward me and, with the gun in his side to keep him from trying anything stupid, made him open the door just a crack and look out.

"What's happening?" I asked.

He froze, tried to speak, and failed again.

I ground the muzzle of the revolver into his kidney.

"Talk to me, damn it! What do you see?"

His voice was small and tight when he said, "A polar bear."

What???

I'd had enough. My anger flared and before I could stop to think about what I was doing I gathered my will and "pushed" myself into my captive's head.

Unlike the smooth connection that had accompanied the link between Denise and me, this one hurt.

A lot.

Pain flared through my head, through the depths of my mind. It felt like someone was taking sandpaper to the back of my eyeballs, grinding it back and forth, over and over again. It went on for what seemed to be minutes, but in the end the pain stopped and once again I could see.

Next to me, I was dimly aware of Dietrich sinking to his knees and retching, but I didn't care. He wasn't a threat any longer; after all, not only was the man handcuffed, but he couldn't see me anyway.

Another roar split the air outside the service corridor and with it came several human shouts of fear.

Throwing caution to the wind, I pulled open the door and took a look for myself.

Looking through Whisper's eyes usually presented me with a riot of unearthly colors. Borrowing the sight of one of the Gifted was almost like seeing normally again. But doing so through the eyes of a Mundane was like looking at a scene left too long in the summer sun; the colors were faded, the edges fuzzy, as if the entire image was going to fade away to nothingness in the very near future.

But it was good enough for my purposes.

And, to my amazement, I saw that Dietrich was right!

A polar bear stood on its hind legs in the midst of the corridor, snarling and bellowing at the small, determined knot of policemen that hadn't fled when everyone else back near the press-conference stage had.

The creature was enormous, all yellow-white fur and primal muscle, and its very presence was confusing the hell out of the cops facing off against it. They didn't know whether to shoot it or simply try to subdue it; after all, polar bears were protected species, and where in God's name had this one come from anyway?

It took me another second or two to realize that I actually knew that particular polar bear.

"Well I'll be a son of a . . ."

Dmitri was a berserker.

First mentioned in the Norse saga, Vatnsdæla, the berserkers were described as elite warriors led by their king, Harald. They wore animal pelts on their heads and charged into battle in a ravaging frenzy, fighting so hard that they were nearly unstoppable. Of course, the bards hadn't quite gotten it right, never realizing that the berserkers were actually warriors who were so in touch with the totem spirits of the animals they respected that they could assume the physical properties of these beasts in battle, borrowing, if you will, their strength, cunning, and senses to accomplish things they never could have done as mere humans.

I knew the legends of course; any scholar of Old Norse worth their salt did, but I had never imagined I'd ever actually see one.

Even as I watched, three cops tried to rush Dmitri from the darkness of an unoccupied office to his left. I have no idea what they thought they were doing. He was a damned *polar bear*, for heaven's sake, but you had to give them credit for trying. Dmitri spun toward them with a quickness that belied his immense size, and with a blow from a paw bigger than my head he sent them scattering like tenpins.

I knew I couldn't linger any longer. Dmitri was buying me time to escape in order to save Denise, and I couldn't let either of them down.

I slipped back inside the service corridor, hauled Dietrich to his feet, and dragged him along behind me as I raced down the hall.

We burst through the basement doors, startling several people who were standing in the hallway, waiting for the elevator. I hollered something about a terrorist attack, which sent them all scattering in different directions, and then shot down the hallway to my left and through the big metal doors marked "Morgue."

No sooner had I done so than an alarm started blaring throughout the building and someone came on the intercom system to warn the employees that there were two dangerous fugitives loose in the building.

Thankfully the morgue was empty and no one stopped us on our way through the back door. We emerged onto the loading dock.

Through the eyes of my captive I saw a police car sitting ten feet to my right.

I froze, cursing my luck.

To have come so far . . .

After a moment, I dared to breathe again. No one got out of the cruiser. Apparently, all the cops were inside.

There were several other cars parked next to the cruiser. The fourth one in line, a dark green Chevy Tahoe, had unlocked doors and a spare set of keys in the glove box.

Some people just never learn.

I didn't think too much about it, just shoved my unwilling guest into the rear seat and hopped inside. Dietrich was whining piteously in the back, asking what I had done to his eyes, begging me to return his sight, but I didn't pay much attention; I only needed him for a few more minutes anyway.

I smoked rubber coming up the ramp, lost control, and bounced over the curb into the pedestrian square that spread out in front of the building.

People screamed and raced to get out of my way as I fought for control. As I spun the big vehicle around, I had an uninterrupted view of the front of the building just as Dmitri, back in human form, burst through the plate glass doors and rushed down the steps.

I gunned the engine and shot backward in reverse, skidding to a stop beside him.

"Come on!" I yelled, watching half a dozen more officers charge out of the front door behind him.

He stared at me dumbly, hesitating.

"Get the fuck in the car, Dmitri!" I screamed, as the officers went for their guns.

I think it was the screaming that did it. He grabbed the handle of the door behind me, wrenched it open, and fell into the backseat as I slammed my foot back down on the accelerator and set a new land speed record getting out of there.

44

now

Denise awoke to darkness.

She lay still, trying to unravel the fragmented cords of her memory. Her head was pounding and she was having trouble focusing. She was sure about one thing though—she wasn't getting up anytime soon. She was tied hand and foot, a situation she didn't like in the least. At least her hands were in front of her, rather than tied behind her back.

Thank Gaia for small favors.

She remembered making the drive to Danvers State with Dmitri, recalled how they had parked on one of the long unused driveways that led to the property. After hopping the fence, they'd found a broken window large enough to let them pass and had gone searching through the darkened interior, looking for the fetch.

As it turned out, the fetch had found them first.

Now she remembered the fight in the darkness, remembered the fetch tossing Dmitri aside and coming for her. She remembered fighting back, to no avail. At one point she'd stepped backward into nothingness, never seeing the rotted flooring until it was too late.

The fall had knocked her unconscious.

Why the fetch hadn't clambered down and finished her off was a mystery.

The reality of her situation hit home with a mental thud as she realized she was a captive somewhere in the darkness of the ruined old hospital, completely at the mercy of a creature as evil and deadly as any she'd ever encountered.

Easy there, girl, she thought. *Panicking won't help at this point.*

But her fear caused her heart to pound frantically, and it took her much longer than she thought it would to calm herself and consider the situation rationally.

She couldn't use her Art to call up some light or to free herself from her bonds, for any magickal working had somatic elements that required the use of her hands to be effective.

Which meant she was going to have to free herself the old-fashioned way, it seemed.

First, she had to be certain she was alone. For all she knew the fetch was sitting there in the darkness, watching her. The very thought brought goose bumps to her flesh, but she knew it was a possibility and so she sat still and listened carefully.

When no sound other than her own breathing reached her ears, she decided it was now or never.

Her eyes had adjusted well enough at this point to use the small bit of moonlight coming in through one of the broken windows near the ceiling of the room. By its light she discovered she was in a storeroom of some kind. Various pieces of discarded furniture, some intact, some barely holding together, were stacked along one wall, while the floor around her was covered with piles of moldy paper, the air filled with that peculiar smell of old paper and rat droppings.

Bracing her hands against the floor, she managed to get her knees underneath her. From there it was just a matter of taking it slowly and keeping her balance, until, several minutes and a handful of tries later, she stood on her own.

Now she had to get rid of her bonds.

By shuffling her feet forward a little bit at a time one after another, she was able to make her way over to the pile of furniture against the wall. In the dim light she picked out a metal desk that stood at the bottom of the pile and had seen better days. At some point in its long career the surface of the desk had buckled, causing one edge to split, and leaving a section of it jutting upward from the whole.

That was going to be her ticket to freedom.

She slowly clambered forward until she stood in front of the desk. She tested the tip of the edge with her finger, decided it was sharp enough for what she needed to do, and then got to work.

She put her hands over the edge, brought the rope in contact with the torn and twisted edge of the desk, and then began sawing her hands back and forth, back and forth.

It was slow going. The rope, while not exactly new, was still strong, and the fact that her feet were secured as tightly as her hands meant she slipped and fell more than once. Thankfully, none of her falls caused her serious injury.

By the time she was finished, her hands and wrists were bloody and raw, but she considered that a small price to pay for her freedom. She rubbed her arms, easing the muscles and getting her circulation back to normal.

When she could feel her hands well enough to make

use of them, she bent over and got right to work on the knots binding her legs.

At last she was free.

Satisfied with her efforts so far, Denise raised one hand, her palm cupped as if holding a ball. "Illuminante!" she said, in a voice sharp with command, and a split second later a ball of bright light filled her palm, shining upon the room around her and causing her to blink several times until her eyes could adjust to the sudden light.

She'd been right; she *was* in a storeroom. Besides the pile of furniture and several rows of metal filing cabinets, there were shelving units stocked full of boxes like those used to store medical records. Case numbers and what she took to be patient names were scrawled on the end of each one, a history of those who had visited the facility in the days before computerized record-keeping systems were invented. A row of windows close to the ceiling lined one wall and a single door with its own small window provided both entrance and egress from the room.

She was just about to head for the door when the sound of approaching footfalls reached her ears.

Denise had no idea of what had happened to Dmitri, and, who knew, maybe it was he who was approaching, come to rescue her, but she couldn't take that chance without knowing for sure. While she hoped it was Dmitri, it could just as easily be the fetch.

Afraid of being discovered before she was ready, Denise doused the light and then settled back into the position she'd been in when she had awakened, lying on the floor, her hands and feet clasped together as if still tightly bound.

Except this time, between her fingers, she also held the split end of a table leg. If she was discovered, she was determined not to go down without a fight.

Sibilant hissings and mutterings reached her ears.

She knew that nothing human made sounds like that.

Her heart grew cold as she realized that rescue was not at hand.

The footsteps drew closer and then stopped, right outside the door to her room.

A small click reached her ears, like that of a switch being thrown. Light blossomed on the other side of her closed eyelids, but Denise didn't have the courage to look just yet. Everything counted on the fetch, if that was indeed what it was, believing she was still incapacitated.

The light drew closer, and with it, her visitor.

She kept her eyes tightly shut, but she could feel it there, just on the other side of the window, watching. She felt goose bumps rising on her skin again and prayed the creature wouldn't notice, prayed they wouldn't give her away. If it entered the room, she would fight, that much was certain, but she didn't want to be forced to do so, not until she was ready. If she had to fight now, without a plan, she would most likely lose.

Denise could feel its eyes upon her and she willed herself to remain still, to keep her breathing easy and unhurried, as if she were still unconscious. *Don't move*, she told herself, over and over again. *Don't move.*

Just when she thought she couldn't hold her position another moment longer, the light outside the room dimmed as the fetch turned away.

Denise let out her breath in a long, slow stream and shifted her legs to relieve the cramp that had formed there.

As she did, her right foot jerked just a bit too far and smacked solidly into a stack of files piled up on the floor next to her.

They toppled over with a soft thump.

Instantly she froze, praying the sound had not been loud enough to attract the fetch's attention.

But it had.

The light outside the room suddenly flared and drew closer again.

Denise gripped the makeshift stake tighter and reviewed her options.

There was a rattling at the door, the click of a lock, and then a man dressed in coveralls like a maintenance worker was striding inside, headed right for her, an electric camping lantern held in one hand.

She didn't hesitate.

Surging to her feet, Denise threw up her arms, pointed at the oncoming stranger and shouted, "Ventus!" as loudly as she could.

A gale-force wind exploded into the room in response to her command. The boxes of files were swept off their shelves, flying like missiles directly at the newcomer, while the stacks of loose paper throughout the room spun up off the floor, surrounding him in a swirling vortex.

The man opened his mouth and screamed, a high-pitched shriek of rage and frustration that never could have been issued from a human throat. In its anger she could see its face begin to twitch and change, sliding from one set of features to another as it batted at the objects flying in its face.

Through the swirling chaos she could see that the path to the door was unguarded as the fetch stumbled to the side from the pressure of her attack.

Denise saw her chance.

Now! she thought.

She dashed for the door, her hands up to help keep the flying debris away from her face, hoping to get out into the hallway before the fetch could recover from the whirlwind surrounding it.

She'd gone only a few steps when something smashed into her shins and swept her feet out from under her. She struck the floor heavily, smacking her head against the concrete hard enough to disrupt her concentration and make her cry out in pain.

Fear kept her moving though, forced her to roll over as quickly as she could and to glance backward, knowing she needed to keep the fetch in sight. The light was no longer steady but was swinging back and forth across the room, and a moment later she saw why. The lantern was rolling on the floor by her feet, having apparently been hurled in her direction to stop her flight.

The fall hadn't done her much physical damage, but it had broken her concentration and that was enough to disrupt her focus. As a result, the whirlwind had slowed considerably. Even as she watched, the fetch forced its way through the swirling barrier and leapt at her.

It landed practically on top of her, and in the shifting light its face took on a particularly demonic hue. She could see that its flesh was covered with hundreds of tiny cuts thanks to all the flying paper, but that hadn't seemed to slow it down any. It bent over her and hissed its fury.

"Fuck you, asshole!" she snarled in return, and before it could do anything else, she kicked it square in the face with the heel of one foot.

The fetch went over backward.

Denise didn't wait around, twisting over and propelling herself up and forward with her hands and feet, headed for the door . . .

A hand seized her ankle in a vicelike grip. Almost immediately she began to slide backward as the fetch reeled her in like a fish on a hook.

"No!" she screamed. "No!"

With her free leg she kicked at the hand holding her, trying to break the fetch's hold, but it was no use. It pulled her closer and then rose to its feet, still holding her leg. It spun in place and flung her away toward the far side of the room with one mighty heave of its arms.

Denise flew through the air and slammed against the far wall, knocking the breath from her lungs. She fully expected it to leap after her and slaughter her where she lay, so it was with great surprise that she watched the fetch dash across the room in the other direction, disappearing out the door and slamming it closed once more behind it.

She was still a prisoner.

But, she thought, as dizziness and exhaustion claimed her, at least she was still alive. And that meant she wouldn't remain a prisoner for long.

45

now

Officer Dietrich was a gibbering wreck by the time we dumped him on a side street twenty minutes later. With the link between us dissipated, I was all but blind once more, so Dmitri took the wheel.

We dumped the stolen car shortly thereafter, knowing that soon there would be cops all over the streets looking for it. Dmitri left the engine running and the doors unlocked, trusting that some enterprising individual would 'jack it within minutes after we left the scene. If we were lucky, the cops would be too busy chasing the car to realize that we'd gotten away.

We took the subway back to where Dmitri had parked Denise's Charger, and then we drove calmly out of the city, leaving a hornet's nest of activity behind us.

"Where to?" Dmitri asked, as if he didn't already know.

I gave him the only possible answer.

"The Castle on the Hill."

Without a word, Dmitri turned north toward Danvers.

I could tell what he was thinking by the worried expression on his face. He thought we were too late.

To keep my mind off Denise's plight, I tried to sort out the events of the past few days, trying to put the various pieces together like some kind of enormous jigsaw puzzle. I knew I was missing something, something important, but I just couldn't put my finger on what it was.

When in doubt, start over from the beginning.

It was something my father used to say, back when I was a kid, and it had stuck with me all of these years. With nowhere else to start, it seemed as good an idea as any other.

Okay, I thought. *What exactly do I know?*

I had a series of killings going back at least fifteen years, all of which had been carried out by an as yet unidentified doppelganger that was targeting the Gifted. The killing spree had started slowly, with both time and distance between the individual attacks, but this had changed right about the time my daughter was taken. Somehow, her disappearance was connected to the most recent killings. That much was obvious. Even worse, the killer himself had arranged to bring me into the investigation, had used both ancient script and items stolen directly from my daughter to get my attention.

So what did the murders have to do with me?

That was a question I didn't know where to begin to answer. Prior to my meeting with the Preacher, I hadn't even known creatures like the doppelganger existed. I'd gone my merry way, unconcerned by and uninvolved with whatever mischief the supernatural denizens of the world chose to spread. I'd been the classic example of a mild-mannered college professor, for heaven's sake, without any enemies to speak of. And I'd have stayed that way too, if they hadn't taken Elizabeth.

Elizabeth.

That was it! It had to be.

I was asking myself the wrong question. It wasn't what I had to do with the murders, but rather what Elizabeth had to do with them that mattered.

Don't be an idiot, my conscience told me. *She was just a little girl when she was taken. What could she possibly have to do with it all?*

That was exactly what I had to find out. It couldn't be a coincidence that shortly after Elizabeth was taken the killings began to happen at a faster rate. Either her abduction had pushed the killer to a new timetable or she had provided him with something he had previously had to do without. My gut was telling me it was the latter, though I didn't have a clue what it might be.

Nor was I going to figure it out without more information. Hopefully, I was on my way to find it.

The State Lunatic Hospital at Danvers, also known as Danvers State Hospital, was built in 1878 at a cost of $1.5 million dollars. It was originally built to provide residential treatment and care to the mentally ill, though its charter was expanded once in 1889 to create a training program for nurses and again in 1895 to add a pathology research laboratory.

During the first few decades of its existence, Danvers was a model of humane treatment, including a site-wide policy on no restraints, but this gradually changed as the hospital soon was filled with far too many problem patients, from alcoholics and drug addicts to the criminally insane. By the 1950s the hospital was considered one of the worst in the region, using various types of shock therapy, lobotomies, and other such methods to make the patients manageable under conditions of extreme overcrowding.

The hospital itself was situated at the top of the Hathorne Hill, in a wooded area just north of the town of Danvers on Interstate 95. The centerpiece was the massive, fortress-like Kirkbride building, all Gothic spires and red brick, which earned the place its nickname of the Castle on the Hill. Eight wings jutted off to either side of the main building, four on each end, like the steps of some massive pyramid. The place had been closed since the early nineties and the state had done its best to discourage the usual trespassers with guard patrols and prosecution of those caught on the grounds.

It wasn't too long ago that I'd given some thought to making a trip out to the place. It had long been rumored to be haunted by the ghosts of those who had been held there over the years, and a certain morbid curiosity had made me want to see for myself if the rumors were true. I suspected that they were, as a place with that much emotional residue to it couldn't help but attract the dead like moths to a flame, but suspecting and knowing for certain were two different things. I'd even done a fair amount of research on the place, delving into its history and doing what I could to learn the general layout so I wouldn't be stumbling around blind in the dark when and if I decided to go.

I'd been surprised to learn that Danvers had once been called Salem Village, and that many of the events that led to the Salem Witch Trials, including the infamous trials themselves, had taken place in the vicinity of the hill on which the hospital now stood, and not in modern-day Salem. In fact, the spot on which the Kirkbride had been built had once contained the home of John Hathorne, one of the trial's judges and the only one never to recant his actions during the trials.

If that didn't make the place haunted, I didn't know what would.

Before I'd had the chance to act on my plans, however, the property had been sold to a consortium of new owners who intended to tear the whole place down and build luxury condominiums on the site. The occasional foot patrol was changed to twenty-four-hour coverage, and I decided the whole thing was too much of a bother.

It looked like I was finally going to get my chance to see it.

I was determined, however, not to make the same mistake that my partners had by walking in the front door. There were other ways into the complex, ways that the fetch and its master might not know about.

In fact, I was counting on it.

I was exhausted from all the time I'd spent linked to Dietrich but was too high on adrenaline and anxiety to rest. Even worse, I was jonesing for a cup of coffee something fierce. Going after the fetch without at least one cup of joe in my veins seemed almost, well, sacrilegious or something. At least lamenting my lack of coffee kept me occupied until we turned onto the property itself.

"Where, exactly, are we?" I asked, when Dmitri announced we had arrived.

"In the woods near the power plant at the bottom of the hill, like you asked."

An urban explorer I once spoke to had told me about the labyrinth of underground tunnels that connected much of the complex. The majority of them branched off from a central hub located behind the Kirkbride building, connecting that location to places like the male and female nurses' homes, the machine shops, and several of the other medical buildings, but the one I was interested in ran from the old steam-and-power-generating plant up the hill to the Kirkbride itself.

Of course, first we had to find the entrance.

"Guards?"

"Not for at least an hour or two. They don't patrol constantly," Dmitri said, and that solved the first of our problems.

We had no time to waste.

I got out of the car and stood there a moment, letting my senses adjust. It was dark enough under all the tree cover that I could see fairly well if I kept my sunglasses on. I could feel the place looming up the hill off to my left, like a dark stain against the late afternoon sky. The air had gotten cooler, and I knew with the prescience of the Oracle at Delphi that tonight would be the night I would have my answers.

Tonight I would know what had happened to Elizabeth.

Out here, away from the city, the darkness was nearly complete. The massive structure of the Kirkbride rose ahead of us in the distance, and from here it seemed to me as if it were covered with a dense web of pain and despair, the emotional and spiritual residue of all those who had lost so much of their lives inside its brick walls.

I didn't spend too much time looking at it; I'd see it soon enough, up close and personal, too. Instead, I turned to see if Dmitri was ready.

He was digging around in the trunk, muttering to himself in Russian, and when he straightened up I saw that he'd come armed for bear. A brace of pistols was strapped to his body in shoulder holsters, and he carried a sawed-off shotgun in one hand. He picked up a high-power flashlight for a moment, similar to the type that police officers carry, and then dropped it back into the trunk. Given that just a few hours before I'd seen him in the form of a massive polar bear, I wasn't worried too much about him being able to see in the dark.

I did have other concerns, though. Reaching into my pocket, I withdrew a silver necklace identical to the one I was currently wearing, complete with its own pendant of polished lodestone. I called Dmitri's name and when he glanced my way tossed it in his direction.

He caught it in one hand and gave it a quizzical look. "What's this?"

"A little extra insurance. Do me a favor and wear it, will ya?"

"Sure."

He slipped it over his head, and I felt a little better about bearding the dragon in its own den knowing he had it on him.

The generating plant was inside a square concrete blockhouse hidden among the trees. The wooden door was padlocked, but Dmitri, with one sharp swing with the butt of the shotgun, broke it open.

It was damp inside and smelled heavily of mildew. I could see the crumbled ruin of the boiler sitting off to the side of the diesel generator that had replaced it. The entrance to the maintenance tunnels turned out to be on the floor behind them both.

Dmitri hefted the iron manhole cover out of the way and we took a look at what we had. Steel brackets had been set into one side of the shaft to serve as a ladder; we quickly made use of them to reach the floor of the tunnel itself.

The passage was about eight feet in width and tall enough that we could both walk upright easily. The walls had been constructed of brick and then covered with a thin coat of mortar, much of which had crumbled away after so many years.

Without hesitation, we headed off into the darkness, Dmitri in the lead with me following close behind.

46

now

The tunnel ran for several hundred yards, turning a time or two before climbing steadily and depositing us into the generator room in the basement of the Kirkbride building.

So far, so good.

We'd managed to get inside the facility. Now all we had to do was find Denise. I'd also be looking for any evidence that might provide further information about the condition and whereabouts of my daughter, Elizabeth, but that went without saying. Once we had what we'd come for, the plan was to hotfoot it out of there and regroup to fight another day.

I should have known better.

The best laid plans never survive contact with the enemy and this one was far from that right from the get-go.

We hadn't been in the Kirkbride building for more than ten minutes before the psychic weight of it began to drag on me. The place was dripping with dark emotions: anger, hate, pain, envy, sorrow, despair; you name it, it was there. Madness ran beneath it all, corrupting the already corrupted in ways I never would have thought possible.

I wanted to close my eyes and run away, the desire pounding through my veins with all the force of some instinctive survival imperative, but a glimpse of Dmitri stoically pushing onward saved me from embarrassing myself. If he could deal with it, I told myself, then so could I.

That was before the ghosts started gathering, however.

At first there were just a few of them, watching us from the shadows. I would catch just a glimpse of a face or the faint sense of motion from out of the darkness where no motion should be.

While he couldn't see them the way I could, Dmitri must have felt them, for he grew tenser as our exploration continued and he began casting furtive glances over his shoulder with much greater frequency, searching for what his senses were telling him was there despite his inability to perceive it.

At that point, the ghosts hadn't done anything to prevent our forward motion, so we ignored them as best we could and continued on toward our goal. We passed a number of rooms set off to either side of the main corridor: a laundry, a kitchen, more than a handful of storage rooms filled with dusty piles of something or other.

When we reached the end of the hall, we found a staircase leading upward and continued that way.

They came for me in the stairwell, halfway between this floor and the next.

A group of ghosts had been waiting on the floor above and now began making their way down the stairs toward us, while at the same time the contingent that had been following us for the last fifteen minutes suddenly pushed up close behind, effectively trapping us between them.

Much to my shock, I recognized some of the faces,

having glimpsed them in the crowds that sometimes gathered outside my gate. An even bigger surprise was the sight of Scream standing among them as if he was their leader.

It was as if I had suddenly been betrayed by my best friend.

I was still standing there in shocked amazement when Whisper appeared beside me, reached up, and yanked my lodestone necklace off my neck, then tossed it into the darkness behind us.

As if that was some kind of a signal, the ghosts moved in.

Scream went straight for Dmitri, trying to use his ability to generate fear to incapacitate my partner, while the group that contained most of those I'd recognized rushed me in the wake of Whisper's betrayal.

I backpedaled as quickly as I could, still too stunned to do much else, trying to wrap my head around the idea that Whisper and Scream had quite effectively ambushed me. Had they been working for the fetch or its still-unseen master all along?

With my attention on the ghosts, I didn't see the bit of rubble in my path until it was too late to do anything about it. My legs got tangled and down I went.

I could hear Dmitri bellowing in anger and fighting back as hard as he could, but it's hard to defend yourself against a pack of marauding poltergeists, particularly without the right equipment. I couldn't see him, but I could imagine what was happening, how he would be swinging his massive fists only to have them pass right through his assailants.

I pushed myself into a sitting position just as the first of the ghosts surrounding me made its move. It rushed forward, passing physically through my body just as the ghost of Marshall had in his loft. And just as before, I saw snatches of the ghost's earthly memories, of the time before it had left its body on the other side of death. I was able to see the events that had led the ghost to this particular place and time, to experience them as if they were memories of my own, to feel all the pain and grief and despair that went along with them. I watched through the eyes of my mind as a stranger first approached and then killed him. I felt it in the depths of my being as a piece of the poor man's soul was torn from his dying corpse by the actions of the fetch. My body shook and shuddered, flailed against the cold cement on which it lay, while I could do nothing to stem the tide that engulfed me.

When it was over the next one stepped forward and repeated the process.

One after another, I watched them die. Their killers often wore a different face, but there was no question as to what I was seeing.

The ghosts had given me a front-row seat to their own murders at the hand of the fetch.

I lay there stunned, emotionally drained. To know that there had been multiple murders at the hands of the same individual was one thing; to watch them die, to feel their pain, that was something else entirely. I could feel tears running down my face, and I was unashamed. Suddenly I wanted to help them, not because it would help me discover what had happened to Elizabeth, but because it was the right thing to do. They hadn't deserved their fate and someone had to fight back on their behalf.

No sooner had I come to that conclusion than a final phantom entity approached from out of the darkness.

Whisper herself.

She stared at me without expression and then ran forward.

My mind recoiled from the onslaught of memories that weren't my own, but there was nothing I could do. In the midst of it, I learned why Abigail Matthews had been missing for so long.

In addition, I understood what connected these people together and what they had done to deserve such a fate.

Their selection as victims hadn't been random at all.

They'd been intentionally chosen by the fetch, chosen not for who they were but for who their ancestors had been.

And in the heart of that information was the answer to the puzzle we'd been trying to solve.

47

now

Denise regained consciousness for the second time in as many hours. She lay on the cold cement floor, still facing the wall she'd slammed into when the fetch had thrown her across the room after her escape attempt earlier.

For the life of her, she couldn't figure out how she could still be alive.

She rolled over and pushed herself into a seated position, her back against the wall. One quick look was all it took for her to recognize that, yes, she was still captive in the same room she'd been held in before. This time, however, the space around her was considerably messier, with discarded file boxes, folders, and mounds of paper scattered throughout the room.

There was also a light.

The electric lantern the fetch had been carrying earlier stood on the floor in the center of the room, pushing back the darkness with its soft glow.

A slender journal bound in what looked to her like genuine leather rested on the floor next to it.

She stared at it, dumbfounded.

The thing was bringing her reading material? What the hell?

Something was going on here, something she didn't completely understand. The fetch had had the opportunity to kill her not once, but twice now, and each time it had chosen not to do so. The bloodthirsty killer that had already slaughtered forty-seven other Gifted individuals had made a conscious decision to let her live.

Why? What does it want?

Obviously, it had something in mind for her. All she could think was that it needed to use her talents; otherwise, she figured, she'd already be as dead as the rest of them.

Maybe the book would hold some answers. The damned thing must have brought it for a reason.

Leery of hidden dangers, she used a minor cantrip to flip the book over a few times and then levitate it into the air. When that didn't trigger any defensive measures or cause it to vanish into thin air like the illusion she half expected it to be, she made a "come here" gesture with her right hand.

The journal shot through the air and came to rest in the palm of her outstretched hand.

It was old; that much was immediately obvious before she even opened it. It was hand-stitched, something they didn't do anymore, and the paper was of a quality and heft that would never be used in a commercial product in this day and age. Never mind the fact that it was yellowed with age.

The owner's name was written inside the front cover, along with the date.

JOHN HATHORNE
1696

Her interest went up considerably. She recognized the name; any practitioner of the Arts living in New England would, as Hathorne had been one of the judges presiding over the Salem Witch Trials in 1692. Never mind the first Magister named to that position in the New World.

If it was authentic, the journal in her hands was worth an incredible sum to the right parties.

Turning the pages, Denise discovered that Hathorne had written in a cramped spidery hand that time had made, for all practical purposes, illegible.

That wasn't going to stop a hedge witch of Denise's caliber, however.

She waved a hand over the open page, said a few words beneath her breath in a language that hadn't been spoken in over a thousand years, and channeled her will into the book before her.

The voice of the long dead Magister spoke from out of the darkness around her, reciting the words he had written on the page so long ago.

She hadn't even gotten through the first two pages before her heart began to beat faster and she realized that what she held in her hands might hold the answers to many of their questions.

From what she could gather, Hathorne and several other practitioners of the Art had faced off against a rogue mage in the fall of 1696. This was not in itself unusual in that day and age, she knew. The Americas had been considered a kind of Wild West for those early mages and more than a few had tangled with one another for various reasons, just as they did now in other parts of the world.

But what caught her attention was Hathorne's description of what happened when he and several of his cohorts cornered the rogue with the intention of permanently ending his rebellious activities.

But the sorcerer had made of himself a twin, a double of the most heinous kind, and set within its black heart a small portion of his own villainous soul in blasphemous parody of the Holy Creation. This twin, this terrible demon, was swift and fleet of foot and thereby escaped capture.

Because the doppelganger contained a portion of Eldredge's most unholy soul, we, the righteous judges appointed by God, could not carry out our intent to cleanse him of his darkness and set his soul free.

We therefore devised a new plan, this one being twofold. We would secure Eldredge's body inside a suitable container and then bury said container, hiding it away for generations to come and leaving the final resolution regarding the sorcerous witch to the hands of Almighty God and his most excellent Judgment Divine.

When the time came to carry out the deed, we surrounded Eldredge and his followers, and, after a fierce exchange of mystical energies, were able to subdue him appropriately. Winston secured an iron maiden and the sorcerer was bound and sealed inside the vessel. The lady was then wrapped tight with chains and the whole contraption buried deep beneath the surface of the earth where it could be guarded and watched as necessary.

Hathorne continued speaking but it soon became obvious that he'd said all he intended to say about the Eldredge incident. Eventually Denise waved her hands in a complicated pattern and released the spell's energy back into the air around her.

There was no need to hear the rest; she had what they were looking for.

Eldredge had created the fetch to carry out his evil plans.

And it was looking more and more likely that he was

still controlling it now, though how that was possible after all this time she didn't know.

One thing was certain: she intended to find out. Gaia willing, she'd put an end to it once and for all.

That line of thought brought her right back to the fetch and its reasons for giving her the information it had. She considered recent events for a few minutes and then drew some hasty conclusions, noting primarily that the fetch was up to something more than just what its master wanted.

It had to be; its behavior just couldn't be explained any other way. It had left the street artist's paintings to be discovered, the one clue that had led them directly to the Kirkbride. The fetch had passed up a chance to kill Hunt when the opportunity had presented itself and then had done the same with her on not one, but two separate occasions now. It had even locked her up in this room, which she had first taken as a sign that she was bait to draw in her friends, but which she now suspected might have simply been a means of keeping her out of harm's way.

Finally, the fetch had begun to feed them intelligence, revealing just who and what it was they were facing.

Which meant the fetch must want . . . Sweet Gaia!

She had to get out of here. She had to warn Hunt. She snatched up the journal and the light, then rushed over to the door of her makeshift cell.

As she expected, the door was unlocked.

That was all the invitation she needed. Moments later she was free of the storeroom and moving as quietly as she could through the deserted halls, searching for a way out.

48

now

Stanton brought his car slowly to a halt several yards behind the parked Charger. He had no idea if the vehicle was still occupied, and he wanted to give himself time to react if it was.

He knew he couldn't be more than ten, maybe fifteen, minutes behind the fugitives.

Spotting them climbing into that Charger in the aftermath of their escape had been pure luck. The decision to follow them on his own rather than haul them in then and there had been based on years of investigative experience. There was something strange going on, and Stanton was determined to understand just what it was before he collared Hunt and made him stand trial for as many of the Reaper cases as he could make stick.

Every passing second gave Hunt a bigger lead, but Stanton wasn't going to throw away his chance at redemption by being stupid now. He unsnapped his holster and drew his gun, his eyes never leaving the vehicle in front of him.

Still no movement.

Good.

Taking a deep breath to steady himself, he advanced swiftly on the other vehicle. He checked the backseat, then the front. His initial guess was correct; the car was empty.

Which meant they were on foot somewhere up ahead.

He'd already made the decision to follow them wherever they went, but there was a time for initiative and a time for decisions that would be remembered at a later date by those up the chain of command. Now that he knew where they were, going after the fugitive alone and without backup would come across as just showboating. He at least had to make the call.

He walked back to the cruiser he'd borrowed from the station lot and called it in. He identified himself to dispatch, let them know his location—his twenty—and then asked to be patched in to the Danvers police. Not five minutes after he hung up with Captain Stenck there were two squad cars pulling in behind his own. The officers got out and offered their assistance, just as they'd been ordered to do. Stanton wasn't surprised to discover he even knew one of them, Patrolman White, a solid officer who had recently been cited for bravery under fire on a cross-jurisdictional case Stanton had previously been involved with. The two men nodded at each other and introductions were made all around.

Stanton was pleased. Invoking the name of the task force had paid off. Now he had to get his man before the real task force got wind of what was going on and short-circuited his efforts.

The detective explained to the uniforms what they were up against and, satisfied that they understood the gravity of the situation, set out with them to find his two fugitives.

It didn't take long to discover their trail; the shattered

lock on the power station door was too recent to miss. So, too, was the open manhole cover that led into the tunnels below.

Never one to shy away from the difficult or the challenging, Stanton was the first man down the ladder. One by one, the others followed.

Flashlights came out, illuminating the tunnel ahead. Pistols came out as well; Stanton had told the uniforms working with him that both fugitives should be considered armed and dangerous. He'd purposely neglected to tell them that Hunt was blind because, at this point, he was no longer sure that was truly the case.

They had only traveled a couple hundred yards into the tunnel network when Stanton spotted a flash of movement up ahead. He signaled the others to stay quiet as they quickened their pace forward. A fork loomed ahead out of the darkness. When Stanton flashed his light down the left-hand passage, he was rewarded with a glimpse of Hunt's face as he was caught looking back down the tunnel at them.

"Freeze!" Stanton shouted, bringing his gun up but declining to fire because he knew he was too far away for the shot to be accurate.

Apparently Hunt had come to the same conclusion, for he didn't pay any attention to Stanton's command and quickly disappeared down the tunnel ahead of them.

"This way!" Stanton shouted, and took off in hot pursuit.

They chased Hunt through a series of quick turns and forked passages as he led them deeper into the tunnels. Hunt was unable to increase the distance between them, but at the same time, Stanton and his men were unable to close it. Several times the detective thought he had lost the trail, only to catch a glimpse of movement up ahead, movement that drew him forward once more.

In his eagerness, Stanton got out ahead of the others,

racing to close the gap between him and his quarry. Several minutes passed before he realized that he could no longer hear his colleagues' footfalls behind him nor could he see any sign of Hunt up ahead. Stanton slowed, and then came to a stop.

Silence filled the space around him.

He was alone.

He tried the radio, but all he got was static.

All this earth and concrete must be blocking the signal, he thought.

With his pulse quickening, he retraced his steps, concerned that Hunt had somehow doubled back on his people and ambushed them from the rear. He reached the first fork and turned right, confident in his direction. But by the time he reached the second, and then the third junction, he became less certain. Several minutes later he came to a halt once more.

There was no sign of the officers who had accompanied him into the tunnels.

Even worse, he realized he was now quite lost.

"Shit!"

With no other choice but to continue walking and hope that he either ran into his men or a section of the tunnel that looked familiar, Stanton took a few moments' rest and then headed off once more.

He had been on the go for ten, maybe fifteen minutes more when he heard sounds of struggle coming from up around a bend in the tunnel before him. Extinguishing his light, he crept forward in the darkness until he reached the turn. A faint light was coming from the other side.

Cautiously, he slowly eased his head out enough to see around the corner.

A lantern stood in the center of the tunnel ahead and by its light he could see Hunt kneeling in the semidarkness. He was rocking back and forth slightly, holding his stomach, as if in pain.

Stanton readied himself to charge around the corner and arrest the son of a bitch when something about Hunt's movements made him pause. A few seconds later he was glad he had.

As he watched, the skin at the top of Hunt's head slowly began to peel back away from his scalp. It rolled down the side of his face, exposing dark skin and eyes that gleamed silver. A weird keening noise was coming from Hunt's mouth; the sound sent shivers up Stanton's spine. It didn't seem even remotely human.

Hunt toppled over and began to twitch wildly, jerking back and forth in undulating rhythms. Stanton was reminded of the time he'd seen a giant boa shed its skin; Hunt's transformation was almost identical, his new flesh slowly emerging from the old.

By the time it was over several minutes later, something strange and altogether inhuman squatted on the ground in the length of tunnel ahead of Stanton. Even as he watched, the creature's apparently malleable skin shifted and reformed, until he was looking at the face of Patrolman White, one of the men he'd entered the tunnels with more than an hour before.

He froze.

When the fetch finished conforming its body so that it resembled the young police officer it had just gutted like a fish, it looked down the tunnel in Stanton's direction. Only the detective's inability to move saved him from being seen as he knelt there rigid in the darkness.

With a cry that never should have emerged from a human throat, the creature then moved off deeper into the tunnels.

After it was gone Stanton expelled the air in his lungs in a harsh rush, unaware until that moment that he'd been holding his breath.

What the hell was that thing?

How in God's name were they going to stop it?

He didn't know. Didn't have a clue. But he did know that stopping it was his responsibility.

And if he had any hope in hell of doing so, he couldn't let it get too far ahead.

He got up and carefully began to move down the tunnel in the direction the creature had taken, the darkness surrounding him like a huge stone just waiting to crush him beneath its weight.

The night I met Stanton was probably one of the worst nights of my life. I'd already lost my daughter, my wife, and my job. That night, I lost my self-esteem as well, and it would be a long climb back out of the pit before I found it again.

The idea to knock off the convenience store popped into my head as I walked past. It was late at night and the kid behind the counter didn't look like he knew his ass from his elbow. If I brought Scream in with me, the clerk would probably hightail it out of there, leaving me to rifle the cash register at my leisure. Besides, who would believe him when he said a blind guy had robbed the store?

Should work like a charm, *I thought.*

I tried not to be too obvious when I checked the aisles for other customers and then walked up to the clerk.

"Give me the cash," I said politely from behind my dark sunglasses, and then sotto voce called for Scream.

The kid outright laughed at me, until Scream showed up and sent him running off, shrieking, into the night.

I had my hand in the cash register when the off-duty cop who'd been in the beer cooler out back walked up.

"You sure you want to do that, dipshit?" he drawled.

Startled, I spun around, dropping my cane to the floor.

"Now I've seen it all," he said with a chuckle. "They teach you how to rob convenience stores at the Association for the Deaf and Blind?"

I tried to fake my way out of it. "The clerk took off. I was just trying to get my change."

"Yeah, right. Turn around and spread 'em."

He had me up against the counter and was frisking me when the three gang members came in the store behind us. I couldn't see them, but the aura of menace they exuded was hard to miss. Beside me, Whisper suddenly flickered into existence, an urgent expression on her face. She mimed the act of pulling a gun from beneath her shirt several times until I got it.

"Be careful, they're armed," I said softly to the cop beside me. That's when the shit hit the fan.

Turns out it was initiation night for the Wolverines and the price of membership was shooting a police officer. Bullets filled the air like angry wasps, but my warning had been enough to give Stanton the edge he needed. Rather than being caught unawares, he was ready to return fire the moment things spun out of control. When it was all over, the floor of the mini-market held not the body of a dead cop, but the corpses of three gangbangers instead. My warning had saved Detective Stanton's life. That and the fact that he couldn't prove I was robbing the store resulted in him letting me off with just a warning, but he apparently never forgot that the blind guy had somehow seen the hit coming long before he did.

And when he'd next come across a case that he couldn't

explain, he tracked me down and demanded my help. It was his interference, more than anything else, that stopped the long slide that I'd been on and put me back on the road to recovery, if not sanity.

Strange how everything comes around full circle, isn't it?

50

now

The ghosts dispersed shortly thereafter, leaving me lying at the bottom of the stairwell, dazed and bruised in their wake.

Seeing me there, Dmitri rushed back down the stairs to my side.

"Hunt! Are you all right?"

I nodded, then, "Yeah, I'm fine. Just banged up a bit."

He reached down and helped me back to my feet, a look of unease on his face.

"What the hell just happened?" he asked.

At first I was surprised by the question, but then I realized that, unlike me, he hadn't been able to see any of it. I did my best to explain, letting him know about the ghosts and what I had learned from them.

He seemed to accept the situation without much difficulty. I guess when you can turn into a polar bear at will, petty little things like ghosts don't bother you too much.

After giving me a few minutes to catch my breath, he

led us back up the stairs and into the east wing of the Kirkbride building, just as we'd intended.

We spent some time wandering through the halls until, a short time later, we found ourselves in an enormous room near the back of the building. The darkness of the place allowed me to see just fine. The floor stretched out before us, half the length of a football field if it was an inch. A glass ceiling soared high above and rows of windows lined the walls on three of the four sides. There were two doors on either side and one at the far end.

"What is this place?" Dmitri asked.

"Solarium, I think," I said, recognizing it from the plans I'd studied in the past.

The vegetation that had once grown here in neatly tended rows had run riot, filling the place with crawling vines and wide-leafed plants of various shapes and sizes. In the center of the room a dark and crippled old oak grew right up through the floor.

It was so strange to see a tree growing in the middle of the room that we had to wander over and take a look.

For the second time that night a feeling of unease settled over me, like a cold hand that danced down my spine and settled somewhere in my gut. It increased as I drew closer to the tree and then seemed to fade away again once I stood beneath its skeletal branches.

The tree wasn't just dying but diseased as well; a thick black tar-like substance spilled from cracks in its trunk. At some point in the past someone had tried digging into the earth in front of the tree, though they hadn't gotten too deep before the root system had stopped further efforts. A small plaque lay discarded in the loose earth nearby.

"On this spot once stood the home of Judge John Hathorne, Esquire," it read.

Seen through the gray filter that had become my sight,

the tree and its surroundings bore a sense of desolation and ruin that perfectly matched the uneasy feeling I had standing there.

It was time to move on.

Before I could make the suggestion to Dmitri, however, we heard someone approaching the nearest door; footfalls sounded loud in the stillness of the cavernous room.

Even as we turned to face the entrance, the door opened, revealing a figure standing there, a bright light in its hand.

The illumination blinded me and I instinctively turned away, shielding my eyes.

The light immediately dimmed and a voice said, "That's certainly not the reception a girl wants to get."

"Denise!" I shouted and rushed across the room toward her, snatching her up into my arms and swinging her about.

There was a long moment of surprised silence and then she said quite distinctly, "Put me down, Hunt."

I did as she asked and stepped back. She was giving me one of those looks that said I'd just embarrassed myself beyond belief, but I didn't care. Despite what I'd said to Dmitri earlier, until this moment I'd been half convinced that she was dead. Seeing her here, alive and well, had broken through my carefully controlled shell. Seems I was a bit more taken with her than I'd admitted even to myself.

Dmitri hurried over and the two of them spent a moment reassuring each other that they were all right.

"What happened?" Dmitri wanted to know, and I echoed his question.

Denise told us about her brief captivity at the hands of the fetch.

"This was there when I awoke the second time," she said, offering the journal to us. As we leafed through it she explained what she'd discovered; how Judge Hathorne's Circle had discovered the existence of the fetch and had ultimately faced off against its sorcerous creator, Nathan Eldredge, binding him into a mystical prison for what they'd hoped was all time.

In return, I told her of how we'd been cornered in the stairwell by the ghosts of the fetch's victims and what I had learned from them.

"The Magister told us that each of the victims was one of the Gifted, but the truth is even stranger than that. Each of the victims is in fact a direct descendant of one of the original members of Hathorne's Circle."

It sounded outrageous; I knew that, but as I watched Denise consider the implications I also knew that I was right.

Then Denise abruptly went still.

Seeing her reaction, both Dmitri and I spoke over each other, asking, "What?"

"Hathorne's Circle must have used some kind of ritual magick to bind Eldredge into the prison they fashioned for him. It was the only way to ensure that the spell would last for as long as they needed it to."

"So?"

"So a spell like that, one powerful enough to seal a fellow sorcerer outside of space and time, would have to be powered by human blood. An animal sacrifice just wouldn't do it."

I had this sudden image of Hathorne and his crew standing around an altar where a young woman waited for the knife. Shaking it off, I said, "I thought they were supposed to be the good guys?"

Denise gave me an irritated look. "They are. I wasn't implying they killed someone. They probably all gave up a little of their own blood to power the spell. It's how I would do it, if I was powerful enough to attempt something like that."

"And?"

"And if that's the case, then one way to reverse the spell would be to destroy the bloodlines whence it came. Blood symbolizes the power inherent in life; destroy the bloodline and you destroy the life, therefore you destroy the power of the spell. Killing the ancestors of the Twelve would release Eldredge from his cell."

"But why?" Dmitri asked. "What could he hope to gain?"

"Life," she replied, and suddenly I understood.

Eldredge had died because his physical body had been sealed away inside the mage's prison. But if he could reverse the magick that kept him there, offer a debt of blood larger than that given by those who had imprisoned him, he could return to the state he was in when he had first been sealed away. I explained as much to the others.

"Okay, say that's the case," Dmitri said, clearly trying to think it all through. "Then why would the fetch want to bring Hunt into the picture?"

Denise started to shake her head, indicating she didn't know, but I cut her off, a sudden suspicion forming in the back of my head.

"What would happen to the fetch if Eldredge was destroyed, Denise?"

She didn't hesitate. "Either the fetch would be destroyed or the bonds that tie the two together would be severed, releasing it to act on its own. Which is why we need to stop standing around, find the vile thing, and put an end to them both."

Dmitri agreed.

Tired of talking and filled with the need to take action, the two of them headed across the room toward the closed doors at the other end, intent on continuing their search.

My thoughts whirling, I barely noticed.

That was it, I thought. *That had to be it!*

Eldredge had been using the fetch to hunt down and slaughter its victims. Each death had brought Eldredge one step closer to his ultimate goal, that of bringing his physical form back to life. But each death had also strengthened the ties that bound Eldredge to his doppelganger creation as the sorcerer gained more and more of his old power back.

And the fetch didn't like it.

I imagined that it didn't want to spend the next four hundred plus years following Eldredge's orders. It wanted to strike out on its own, and it had dragged me into the picture to help it achieve that goal.

It was just conjecture at this point, but it was the only answer that made sense. Somehow, and I didn't know how, the fetch had learned about my affinity for ghosts and my ability to drive them off. It had then decided I was either capable enough or stupid enough to try to confront the real power behind the throne, so to speak. It then provided ample motive for me to get involved with the investigation, first with the strange writings on the walls of the crime scenes and then with charms from Elizabeth's bracelet.

It was also why the creature hadn't killed me when it had the chance back at my house or slain Denise when she'd been in its control. Doing either one would have spoiled its grand plan. It needed us to take out Eldredge.

I looked up, intending to tell the other two what I was thinking, when my heart froze in my chest.

Charging across the room toward me in its natural form was the fetch.

It must have come in through the entrance that Dmitri and I had used, and then snuck up as close as possible by hiding in the overgrown rows of vegetation between us.

Now, with the other two moving away and facing in the other direction, it was making its move.

It didn't matter that the fetch wanted me to destroy its master. Right now it was still under the sorcerer's control, and as a result it was going to try to slaughter me where I stood, for that was what its master wanted.

And my two best hopes for staying alive were halfway across the room.

I screamed.

5 1

now

I thought I was a goner.

I could see Dmitri going for the shotgun at his side; I knew it was no use. Even if he managed to get it up in time, at this distance I would be caught in the spreading path of the buckshot. He couldn't fire or he'd take me down at the same time.

I'm sorry, Elizabeth, I thought, as I braced myself for what was coming.

I had no illusions about getting out of there alive.

But as I was discovering every day, people can still surprise me.

The fetch closed the distance impossibly fast and launched itself in my direction, claws extended and mouth open wide.

As it did, a figure stepped out of one of the doors off to my right, firing as he came. The flashlight he held in his hands blinded me slightly, but I could still see enough to watch as the bullets struck the fetch in the face and neck, splashing blood all over me as it crashed to the floor less than a foot away.

In the sudden silence, I turned my head, amazed to be alive, and stared at Stanton as if he was a visitor from another planet.

"What in God's name is that thing?" he asked, fear and disgust evident in his tone as he shone his light on the bizarre creature at our feet.

I had to swallow hard to find my voice. It had been that close.

"It's a doppelganger."

"A doppa-what?" he asked.

"Doppelganger. German for double walker."

He brushed it off. The name didn't matter, not really. "I saw it, back there in the tunnels. It looked like you and then . . . then it didn't." He cocked his head at me in a questioning way, and I thought I saw his gun hand adjust slightly.

"Yeah." I looked him straight in the eyes as I said it, almost willing him to believe me. "It can do that. It can look like anyone it wants to, actually."

He stared at the fetch's corpse for a minute, then back at me. "You didn't kill that guy at the plaza, did you?"

"No."

He grunted. "I should've known better. You don't have it in ya. Couldn't even knock over a convenience store properly, never mind slash a guy's throat."

Stanton. Gotta love him.

Dmitri and Denise rushed up at that point and, seeing that they weren't a threat, Stanton ignored them, his interest on the body of the fetch in front of him instead.

"Are you all right?" they asked in unison, and I assured them that I was.

"Might be a good idea to stick together in the future, though," I said, all too uncomfortably aware that while they might be able to hold their own against a creature like the fetch, I was pretty far out of my element.

A gun went off, uncomfortably close, and we all turned to see Stanton turning away after putting another bullet into the fetch's skull from close range.

"What was that for?" I asked.

He shrugged. "Just playing it safe."

I have to say, I didn't blame him.

Something about the whole situation didn't feel right. The fetch had killed forty-seven other people without once being seriously injured, at least not enough to leave more than the slightest bit of trace evidence at the scenes. It was forged in magick, imbued with a portion of the soul of an undead sorcerer and sent out to claim its victims by impersonating those they knew. And yet here we were, a couple of misfits and a single police detective, and we were able to take it out with nothing more unusual than a pistol full of 9 mm bullets?

As if reading my mind, booming laughter rang out through the room unexpectedly.

It sounded as if it were coming from every direction at once and the four of us spun around, searching for where it originated but unable to get a lock on it as it echoed and crashed in the overlarge space.

Then, even as we watched, a whirlwind formed on the far side of the room, drawing dirt and dust and vegetation together in a churning mass that rose off the floor like a dust devil, writhing and turning about as within its depths something began to form.

A thunderclap sounded inside the confined space and the doors and windows along the walls suddenly flew open, the glass shattering and raining down in a deadly shower, the doors themselves flying off the hinges. Luckily all of us escaped unscathed.

As the dust settled and we dared to raise our heads again, we discovered that we were no longer alone.

At the other end of the room, where the whirlwind had been, the shade of Nathan Eldredge now stood before us.

I had been expecting some phantasmal form of one kind or another, a spectral presence like that of Whisper or Scream, but the success of his efforts to regain his physical form was very evident and, frankly, scared the hell out of me.

He was dressed in the clothing common to the time in which he'd been imprisoned: boots, breech pants, and a shirt that tied in front. A long, hooded cloak covered his frame and hid his face in shadow.

"Did you think my pet would be defeated so easily?" he asked, the words dripping with disdain.

The shade gestured with one hand, and behind us, the fetch came back to life, its arm lashing upward, claws extended, and disemboweled Stanton where he stood. The look of shocked surprise on the detective's face might have been comical if it hadn't been accompanied by the sight of his small intestines leaking out across his lap and falling onto his shoes. He stood there, staring back at us, and then the fetch swarmed up over his body and planted that circular mouth over Stanton's own. There was a strange sucking sound and right before our eyes Stanton's body seemed to collapse in on itself. I would have bet that his skin turned that peculiar shade of blue green that the fetch's other victims had as well. It was over in seconds; when the fetch was done it released Stanton's corpse and watched it topple over sideways. Then it fell upon us with a vengeance.

Dmitri's gun came up, faster than I thought him capable of, and he let loose with shot after shot, pummeling the fetch's form, blowing it from its feet and then driving it backward across the floor with the force of the gunfire.

When he ran out of shells he tossed the weapon away

and drew one of the two pistols he carried, continuing to fire until that, too, ran dry.

Meanwhile Denise threw her energies against the shade itself, conjuring up several blazing fireballs in each hand and hurling them in the shade's direction.

Unfortunately, neither tactic seemed to be doing much good. No sooner had Dmitri emptied an entire magazine of shells into the fetch than did it shift shape, expel the lead from its body, and reform again, good as new. Eldredge didn't even need that much effort; he simply waved his hands, summoning a shield of powerful energy to deflect Denise's attacks and send them bouncing harmlessly to either side.

The flashes of arcane brilliance had blinded me, so I didn't actually see Dmitri change, but one minute he was standing before the fetch in human form and the next he was towering over the other creature, his transformation to a polar bear complete.

I thought his sheer size and strength might be able to put an end to the fetch, but once again I was wrong. The creature's ability to shift in size and form, never mind its sheer speed, kept Dmitri from landing a solid blow, certainly not one strong enough to take the creature out of the fight. At the same time, the fetch was giving as good as it got, ducking beneath Dmitri's long arms or dodging his driving muzzle, and soon Dmitri's yellow-white fur was stained crimson in more than a handful of places.

There was no way that we could keep this up for long.

Even as I worked to figure a way out of this for all of us, Eldredge began to take the offensive, using his power to hurl chunks of masonry, tile, and shards of glass in our direction at impossible speeds. Denise did her best, conjuring an energy shield large enough to protect us both. Each time an object struck it, there was a blinding flash; in seconds I lost my ability to see all together.

Time was running out.

Eldredge's shade was incredibly powerful; that much was obvious. It would take the combined efforts of all three of us just to have an impact, it seemed. When you added in the strength, cunning, and physical agility of the fetch, we were clearly outclassed. I realized with sickening certainty that even Dmitri's prodigious strength would eventually wear out and we'd be left to face the two of them on our own.

Not a situation I wanted to be in.

All right, Hunt. Forget the fetch. Focus on the shade. Get rid of the shade first.

I thought furiously.

Technically speaking, the shade was just another form of ghost, albeit an enormously powerful one. And ghosts needed a fetter, a material object of some kind that was so important to them it formed a psychic bond powerful enough to keep them here.

Destroy the fetter and you destroy the shade!

But first we had to find the damn thing.

My first thought was that the fetch itself was the shade's fetter, but that didn't make sense. The fetch wanted to destroy its master and it wouldn't do anything to harm itself in the process, otherwise it would all have been for naught. The fetter had to be some other object.

But what?

Something Denise said earlier came back to me.

Hathorne and his precious Circle hadn't been able to destroy Eldredge, so they'd imprisoned his physical body in some kind of iron coffin and then buried him away somewhere for safekeeping.

Which meant that his earthly body was more than likely acting as his fetter!

Without anything else to go on, it was the best guess I had. And sometimes, guessers get lucky.

I had no idea where in heaven's name I was going to find the corpse of a sorcerer buried three hundred years ago, never mind do it in the next few minutes.

The situation seemed hopeless.

I glanced around frantically, my thoughts a scattered mess.

When the solution finally occurred to me, I wanted to kick myself for being so obtuse. As Denise worked to hold off the shade, I closed my eyes, cleared my thoughts, and called for Whisper.

Or, at least, that's what I tried to do.

Ever tried to clear your head in the midst of an argument? Being in the middle of a battle with arcane energies going off all around you, as two creatures out of myth and legend are facing off in a whirl of teeth and claws not ten feet away, might make it just a little bit tough to concentrate.

I cast a frantic glance at Denise, saw she was still holding her own, and I tried again, pushing my desire out into the world around me, struggling so hard to visualize the end result that my temples began to pulse in pain.

Still, my ghostly companion failed to appear.

Finally, out of options and knowing my time was fading fast, I did the only other thing I could think of to do.

I threw my head back and screamed for her at the top of my lungs.

"Whisper!"

When I looked down again, she was standing beside me, watching the fight between Denise and Eldredge with an unreadable expression on her face.

I knelt down beside her as fast as I could and pointed out our foe.

"I need to know where that man is buried, Whisper," I explained. "Can you do that for me? Can you show me where he is buried?"

I felt her squeeze my hand in reply. I wasn't ready for

the freight train of pain that poured through my head, however, and it nearly undid me. With my hands on the ground to hold me up, I fought back against it. When it passed a few seconds later, I opened my eyes.

A fine silvery cord stretched from the sorcerer's physical manifestation, across the room, and down into the roots of that old twisted oak.

I wanted to hit myself for being so stupid. Of course! Eldredge's coffin had been buried in the one place Hathorne could always watch over it—beneath the floor of his own house.

Now all I had to do was unearth it, open it up, and destroy the remains inside. Doing so should destroy the fetter. That would definitely disrupt whatever energy Eldredge was using to remain on this plane and send him back to hell where he belonged.

Trouble was, I didn't have several hours and a bunch of shovels at my disposal. I had to think of something else.

I hear a cry of pain from Denise; a frantic glance in her direction showed me that she was still fighting, but she couldn't keep it up at that pace for long. The shade's attacks were finally starting to breach the shield she'd conjured up to protect us; if I didn't do something soon we were toast.

Then it hit me. I might not be able to dig down to the coffin fast enough to do any good, but no one said I had to do things by the book anymore, either.

I shouted in Denise's direction, hoping to be heard above the din of the battle. "I need you to dig up that tree!"

She glanced at me, frowning. "You what?" she yelled, as she flung up another protective shield against the blasts of energy the enemy was still sending our way.

"The tree, Denise!" I shouted, pointing. "Rip up the tree!"

I could see she didn't understand why I was shouting about the tree, but that didn't stop her from doing what I'd asked. She faced the target, gathered her strength about her, and flung her hands out in front, shouting "Ventus!" as she did.

A hurricane-like wind tore through the solarium and burst against the trunk of the tree like a shot from a cannon. Branches cracked, leaves flew, and the old, diseased trunk tore itself free of the earth.

There, in the dark hollow beneath the roots, was an iron casket, bound in chains and sealed with large antique locks.

This time she didn't need to be told what to do. Anticipating my need, she raised her arms and sent another blast of power at the coffin, lifting it up and slamming it back down to earth hard enough to shatter the chains that bound it and spill the human remains it contained out on the ground.

In the midst of the pile, a human skull, yellow with age, stared out at me.

Now we were talking!

But by taking her attention off the shade and doing what I'd asked, Denise had let her guard down just enough, and the enemy wasted no time in taking advantage of it.

With a shout of anger the shade gestured in our direction again.

A furrow suddenly ripped down the floor at high speed, tearing the ceramic tiles free of their mooring and sending them flying every which way, their razor sharp edges seeking to tear the flesh from our bones. The explosion of force literally threw me to one side; I wasn't the shade's target.

Denise was.

The furrow roared across the space separating the two

of them as fast as a gunshot. I saw a blue shimmer rise up in front of her as she sought to impose some mystical barrier between her and the oncoming power blast, but she was a second too slow. I watched as she was picked up and tossed aside like a rag doll by the force of the strike, spinning away to slam into the nearest wall with a force that brought mortar, bricks, and ceiling down on her in a rumbling cascade.

At the same time the fetch finally wore Dmitri down to the point where it was able to slip through his defenses and land a stunning blow to the side of his head. Dmitri stumbled backward, slipping to one knee, and giving the fetch the chance to rush in close, inside the reach of those long arms. I could only watch in horror as the fetch lashed out, raking its claws across Dmitri's unprotected throat.

Blood splashed everywhere.

But Dmitri had no intention of going down alone. Even as the fetch slashed his throat, Dmitri's massive paw slammed into the fetch's chest. As Dmitri toppled over, he took the fetch down with him.

Then he collapsed, leaving them both unmoving and me on my own.

My conscience practically screamed at me to help him, but I knew there was nothing I could do. If I wanted to destroy the shade, I had to act now or I'd lose my chance.

I turned my back and raced for the coffin, avoiding several blasts of power the shade idly tossed in my direction along the way, and slid into the dirt beside it. Snatching the skull from out of the tangled pile of bones, I jumped to my feet, spun around, and held it up aloft so that Eldredge could see that I had it, shouting, "All right, you bastard, I've had enough. This is where this farce ends!"

As the shade stood watching, I raised the skull high

over my head and brought it crashing back down against the edge of the sarcophagus.

The iron rang with the impact and the aged relic shattered into dust with the force of the blow.

Expecting to see the shade vanish right before my eyes, I watched . . . only to have it break into another howling bout of laughter.

Not good.

Okay, I guess Eldredge's physical remains weren't the fetter after all.

Now I was really in trouble.

5 2

now

As I stood there, listening to that psycho laugh and waiting for the fetch to finish me off, the Magister's message of days before suddenly came back to me, like a voice speaking inside my head.

"When the living fail you, the dead shall do your bidding."

It had been such a strange statement that at the time I had brushed it aside, not even telling Denise what he had said.

Now I glanced toward my fallen companions and then back at the face of the shade, realizing as I did just what I had to do.

I snatched the harmonica from my pocket, brought it to my lips, and began to play, letting my passion and need dictate the tune.

Seeing what I was doing, Eldredge stopped toying with me and quickly readied another spell, no doubt intending to blast me into oblivion.

I didn't think about that, didn't think about my injured

friends, didn't think about my long-lost daughter, didn't think about all that had happened to bring us to this place and time. I squeezed my eyes shut to keep out the distractions and simply poured my heart into that song, letting my music do what all of our strength, intelligence, and planning had been unable to do.

One moment I was standing there alone, facing off against an enemy that had the power to wipe me from the face of existence, and the next I had the dead for company.

An army of ghosts stood at my back, called to me by the power of my song.

Scream stood prominently in the front ranks, his eyes ablaze, watching, waiting.

As I turned and met that unearthly gaze I understood at last, one father to another, the destiny that tied us together, and knew it was no accident that we both had been brought here to this place at this time. I had called him my devil incarnate, but in truth Scream was the instrument of my vengeance, the swift, sure hand of justice denied too long, and he waited now for me to command him, to unleash his judgment on the enemy that stood before us.

I was all too happy to oblige.

My song changed, increasing in volume and tempo, minor notes clashing with major ones in a strident wail that would have made me cringe in pain if I'd heard it in other circumstances, but now only made me smile, as the ghosts responded to the call buried deep in their hearts.

As one, they rushed forward toward the shade, screaming out their vengeance, like Valkyries come to claim one of their own.

The song that drove them forward had the opposite effect on the shade. It held him securely in its grip, preventing him from moving, from calling on his magick or finishing the spell that he had been readying to end the confrontation—and us. I watched his eyes widen in horror as he realized that the incorporeal form that had protected him from our prior efforts had now become his prison.

It took less than a handful of seconds for Scream and his allies to cross the length of the solarium and reach the shade. When they did they tore into him, all teeth and nails and claws, unleashing the fury they had been harboring ever since they had met their unjust ends at the hands of the sorcerer or the doppelganger he'd created. Eldredge began shrieking as, unable to move or defend himself, piece after piece of him was torn away and cast aside, his form gradually losing shape and coherence until, with a final, fading cry of rage and anguish, there was nothing left.

Silence fell.

As if on cue, the dead turned to face me.

I continued to play but let the tune morph into something smoother, gentler, a whispering brook rather than a raging whitewater torrent. As I did, one by one the ghosts began to fade, slowly at first and then with greater frequency, until only Scream remained.

Seeing that the music had no effect on him, I faltered to a stop and pulled the harmonica from my lips.

When he was sure I was watching, Scream turned to look at the closed door at the other end of the hall. Then he nodded once, and vanished of his own accord.

5 3

now

With Scream's departure I could turn my attention from the dead to the living. I could see Denise rising to her feet a short distance away; the shade's assault had sent her flying, but she'd apparently managed to cushion her fall and didn't seem too much the worse for it. Nothing time and a little rest wouldn't heal, at least.

Dmitri was another story. He was still conscious when I reached his side, though he was fading quickly. The fetch had cut a massive gash in the side of his neck, and his blood was pulsing out in rhythm with the beating of his heart. I clamped both hands over the wound, but I could still feel the hot leak of his blood against my skin. He wasn't going to last beyond a few more minutes.

"Don't you die on me, Dmitri!" I said through gritted teeth as he flailed vainly beneath my touch. "Don't you fucking die on me!"

And then Denise was there, her hands covering my own, a brilliant glow spilling from beneath her palms and down toward Dmitri's neck. I could feel the flesh beneath my hands literally knitting itself back together, the flow of blood slowing and then stopping completely. Dmitri struggled for a few seconds longer, until Denise waved a hand over his face and he fell into a deep sleep.

The glow from her hands died off. "You can let go now," she said. "He'll be all right. He's going to need more extensive work once we're out of here, but that should hold for the time being."

I slumped back on my heels, my heart and head pounding from all the adrenaline coursing through my system. I could feel Denise relaxing beside me as well.

We knelt beside him for several minutes, trying to catch our breath.

At last, I climbed to my feet and wearily turned my attention to the door that Scream had indicated. I needed to see what was in that room.

Crossing the solarium with heavy feet, I pushed gently against the door.

It swung open at my touch.

The room before me was almost an exact duplicate of the room in which Elizabeth had grown up. The walls had been painted the same luminescent pink that she had loved as a child. The bed was in the same place, against the left-hand wall. Opposite the door was her dresser. Someone had even painted a window on the right-hand side of the room in the exact position that the real one occupied.

I felt the hair on my body stand at attention.

My heart beat hollowly in my chest.

I forced my legs into motion and walked stiffly to the dresser. I opened the drawers and found clothes for a young girl there. Clothes I had no doubt that my daughter had worn, despite the thick layer of dust that now coated them.

Elizabeth had lived here. I knew it as surely as I knew my own name. I didn't know when or for how long, but the realization that she had been less than an hour's drive away at some point during the last several years was like a blow to the face.

If the ghost of my daughter hadn't stepped through the wall at precisely that moment, I would have collapsed to the floor.

As it was my heart went into overtime, hammering so hard that it was physically painful, and I fought to catch a breath.

She was a few years older than when I'd last seen her, which told me she'd survived for a long while after she'd been taken. Her hair hung down long and straight, partially obscuring her face, but I knew it was her.

How could I not?

I met her stare with my own and the words just bubbled up from inside me.

"I never stopped looking for you, Elizabeth," I said softly into the sudden silence that seemed to surround the two of us. "I never gave up, not even once."

Tears were dripping down my face, cutting tracks through the dirt and grime that had been left there by the battle.

"I tried, Beth. I tried so hard."

Elizabeth stepped closer, until she stood directly in front of me. She looked at me for a moment, studying the changes I'd been through, the scars and tattoos mute testimony to all I had done to find her, and then she did the totally unexpected.

She spoke.

"He made me find them, Daddy. I didn't want to, but he made me."

The anguish in her voice broke my heart.

I knew she was talking about the doppelganger's other victims, the Gifted descendants of Eldredge's original captors. Elizabeth must have been Gifted herself, and the shade and its fetch had made use of that gift against her will; it was the only answer that made sense for their taking her in the first place. It also made my daughter an unwilling participant in the murders of those victims, but I didn't care about that. All that mattered was taking away her pain.

"It's okay, sweetie. You did what you had to."

"But he hurt them, Daddy. He . . ."

I interrupted her. "Shsssh," I said gently. "That doesn't matter now, sweetie. He's not going to hurt anyone ever again."

She nodded, in that way kids do when they want to appear all grown up. Then she reached up and placed her hand against the side of my face, just as she'd done so many times in the early years, and while I could only barely feel her phantom touch, I felt a sudden surge of love and caring the likes of which I hadn't felt in ages.

"I love you," she said, and my heart broke for the second time in just as many minutes.

"I love you, too, sweetie," I choked out through my tears.

We stood there together again for the first time in years, and I felt like our positions had been reversed; I had become the child and she the parent. I was sobbing openly now, while she watched with patient eyes, eyes full of wisdom beyond her years, eyes that could truly see.

I wanted to crush her in my arms, to hold her forever, to take away all the fear and pain and despair that she must have felt in the past five years, but that was so far beyond my abilities that it almost didn't bear thinking about. She must have felt my emotions though, for she smiled a sad little smile and then touched her forehead to mine.

No sooner had she done so than a vision sprang forth deep within my mind, a montage of events that passed as swiftly as a summer breeze, but in that vision I found the answers to the questions I didn't have the heart to ask.

I saw how she'd been cared for, a prisoner, yes, but one with certain material comforts, like the room in which we now stood. I saw the way they'd forced her to use her gift, the physical strain that it had placed on her body, and how her heart had finally given out on her in the midst of one particularly grueling session. I even bore witness as the fetch had done all it could to bring her back, to no avail.

Then she pulled away again and the vision faded as swiftly as it had come.

At long last, I knew what had happened to my daughter.

She took her hand away from my cheek, stood on her tiptoes, and bent her face toward mine. I felt her lips against my cheek like the flutter of a butterfly's wings and her soft voice in my ear, "I have to go now, Daddy."

I stared at her, not understanding.

She gestured toward my pocket and mimed my playing my harmonica.

I shook my head.

No.

No way.

I couldn't do it.

She waited, then repeated her earlier statement, this time with a bit more emphasis.

"I *have* to go now, Daddy."

I had no idea what to do. The very thought of using my talent to send her away after searching for her for so long was heartbreaking, but the idea that I was holding her against her will was even worse. She deserved to rest, to move on to whatever came next.

I could not keep that from her.

I wiped at my face, trying to brush away the tears that seemed as if they never wanted to stop, and reluctantly nodded my head.

She needed my help. What kind of parent would I be if I denied her that?

I took the harmonica back out of my pocket, keeping my eyes fixed firmly on its worn and battered silver surface, afraid if I looked at Elizabeth again I would lose my nerve.

Slowly I brought that harmonica to my lips.

"Good-bye," I whispered and then began to play.

It was a sweet melody, a joyful happy tune, something I'd played for her as a child at bedtime when she had difficulty falling asleep.

I kept it up for several minutes, my eyes closed and tears streaming down my face, then wound slowly to a stop.

In the doorway, Denise said, "She's gone, Hunt."

I didn't need to open my eyes to know that.

In those last few moments I had felt her go.

And with her went the weight on my shoulders, the sense of failure and shame that I had carried with me every second of every minute of every day for the past five years.

For the first time in a long while, I could breathe easy.

"Are you okay?" Denise asked.

I nodded and then said it aloud, "Yeah. I'm okay."

I was, too.

With that out of the way, the first order of business was to get out of there. I knew Stanton wouldn't have come after me without some sort of backup; I just didn't know how long it would take for them to get here. Unless we intended to wait around and surrender to the police for crimes we didn't commit, it was time to get the hell out of there.

Denise agreed.

She knew that Dmitri kept a small safe house a half hour or so outside the city, a bolt-hole to run to if he needed to lie low for a while, for she'd made use of the place herself once when certain events had required it. She even thought she remembered how to get there.

That was good enough for me. It would give us a place to rest and nurse Dmitri back to health while we figured out our next move.

By sliding our shoulders under Dmitri's arms, we were able to get him up on his feet and support him between us. Then we slowly made our way across the room toward the now-shattered French doors.

As we shuffled along I thought I heard something rustle back in the direction of Stanton's corpse, but when I told Denise about it and she took a moment to look around, she didn't see anything. I wrote it off as my imagination and we kept going.

It was going to be a long haul back to the car.

54

now

It was only a few hours before Special Agent Dale Robertson arrived at the scene. By that time a cordon had been placed around the entire building and another around the solarium itself. Crime scene techs were swarming all over the place, putting up little flags to mark the evidence and making notations of this and that in their notebooks, recording it all so the entire scene could be reconstructed at a later date, should the need arise.

A lieutenant from the Danvers PD led him over to the body they'd discovered and subsequently identified as the missing Detective Stanton. There was a good deal of blood on the floor nearby, but Stanton's was the only body left behind.

Robertson stood over him, silently taking it all in.

Stanton's stomach had been torn open, and he'd died either from the wound or from blood loss shortly thereafter. Either way, it wasn't an easy way to go.

"You poor dumb bastard," Robertson said beneath

his breath. Rather than sharing what he knew with the other members of the task force, Stanton had tried to cowboy it on his own and had ended up paying the final price. When he'd found out about it, Robertson had been furious, but that didn't mean he couldn't feel some measure of sorrow at the death of one of his own. Even if the person in question had acted like an idiot in the process.

The special agent raised his head and looked around, watching his men swarm around the place like worker bees in the hive. By the time they were done, Robertson would know everything there was to know about what had happened here. All of that information would be tied into the rest of the data they'd collected and ultimately it would provide a better picture of the man they had been chasing for the last six months.

A man whose name they hadn't known until recently.

But those days were behind them.

Now they knew who they were chasing.

Now they knew the Reaper's identity.

"I'm coming for you, Jeremiah Hunt," the FBI special agent told the air around him, pronouncing Hunt's name slowly and distinctly, as if taking great pleasure in the fact of knowing it.

"I'm coming for you."

5 5

now

Dmitri's bolt-hole turned out to be a small, two-bedroom colonial in Norton, a little country town about forty-five minutes south of Boston. It had an attached garage without windows, so we were able to drive the Charger inside and close it up again behind us. Denise and I managed to manhandle him onto the couch in the living room, where she immediately went to work changing his bandages and checking on the state of his wounds.

Given the thick scent of blood that filled the air during the process, I was thankful I couldn't see anything.

I was sitting in the kitchen, nursing a cup of instant coffee I'd managed to put together from what I could find in the cabinets, when she joined me.

"How is he?" I asked, speaking softly so he couldn't overhear us from the other room.

Denise took the coffee cup out of my hand, took a long swig, and then sat down beside me. "He's going to have a nasty old scar, but he'll make it."

When I heard that, a massive weight that I hadn't even realized was there dropped off my shoulders.

Denise went on. "I had to reopen the temporary patch we'd put in place to clean the wound properly, so he lost a bit more blood, but he's a big guy and I think he can handle it just fine. I jump-started the healing process, and with a little of Gaia's grace and a few more healing treatments, I think he'll be back on his feet in no time."

She was tired. I could hear it in her voice; the working must have taken more out of her than she wanted to admit. I suggested she get some rest, and to my surprise she didn't argue at all, just wandered upstairs looking for a bedroom where she could crash.

Dmitri improved slowly but surely. While we waited, we had plenty of time to keep an eye on the news and get an understanding of just how much trouble we were actually in.

A lot, as it turned out.

I knew that I was already wanted for the murder of three people. Now they had added escaping from custody and suspicion of killing a cop to the list. My picture was all over the news, with warnings that I was likely armed and dangerous. They made no mention of my blindness, which I took to be odd until Denise suggested that warnings about a blind killer just wouldn't be taken seriously by the general public.

Denise was not mentioned in any of the broadcasts, nor was Dmitri. The former I expected, but not the latter. I thought they would have identified him from the surveillance cameras at One Schroeder Plaza as the accomplice who'd helped me break out of jail but maybe we got lucky. Then again, maybe they had identified him and they were just keeping that information to themselves for the time being.

Just thinking about it gave me a headache.

With Stanton dead, the chances of clearing my name looked pretty slim. He was the only one who knew that I'd been invited to the crime scenes at his request. He was the only one who had seen the fetch and knew what it was capable of. Just the videotape of me slashing that poor man's throat would be enough to convince a jury to send me to the chair, never mind my subsequent jail break and mad rush through the city.

I had to get away. Not just from the city, maybe even from the whole state. And with only a few lingering questions left to answer about Elizabeth's disappearance, I could finally do so without feeling as if I was abandoning her.

Denise and I were sitting in the kitchen, lingering over lunch, when I told her what I intended to do.

"Take me with you," she said, her gaze never leaving my own.

"What?"

"Take me with you. You're going to need someone to teach you, to help you channel your talent and learn to use it properly. Who better than me?"

She laughed, a sign of nervousness I'd never seen in her before, and then added, "Besides, it won't be long before the cops tie all of us together. I'd have to leave on my own at that point anyway."

Much to her surprise, I agreed. I wasn't sure what was going to happen between us, but I couldn't think of anyone else better suited to help me get back to normal, whatever that was these days. If I'd learned anything recently, it was that I no longer wanted to be alone. I needed someone like Denise to keep me grounded. The fact that I genuinely enjoyed her company made the decision an easy one to make.

"Looks like there will be three of us then," said a voice from the doorway, and we turned to find Dmitri standing there, listening in. He joined us at the table and we got down to some serious planning.

☩

With our decision to leave made, there was just one last thing I had to do.

I knew it was a risk, a huge risk in fact, but I had no choice. I couldn't leave without speaking to Anne one last time. I wouldn't have felt right otherwise. Regardless of what had happened between us since that terrible day, she had a right to know. Elizabeth was her daughter, too.

I chose my moment carefully, waiting until after the next session of healing magick, when both Dmitri and Denise were sleeping off the exhausting effects of their efforts, and then scribbled out a note to tell them where I'd gone. I also let them know that if I wasn't back in a few hours they should hit the road without me.

I slipped out the door and set off for the bus stop, a few blocks down the street. A stiff wind was blowing, making the already cold day seem that much colder, and I was thankful for the hooded sweatshirt I'd decided to wear under my leather coat. Besides protecting my ears from the biting wind, the hood also served to keep my features in shadow and cut down on the chance of someone recognizing me, a real concern. My face had been plastered all over the television since the discovery of Stanton's body and, unfortunately, there wasn't much I could do to change it. I'd dyed my hair surfer blond and grown a short goatee to break up the lines of my face, but that was the extent of the changes that I could manage. It would do for now, but I knew it wouldn't fool anyone who got a good long look.

I was lucky and caught a bus a few minutes after I arrived. Taking a seat to myself, I kept my head down and pretended to be asleep. Twenty minutes later, I exited the bus at the station in Braintree, made the quick walk to the commuter-rail station, and headed into the city proper.

Coming up on the lunch hour as we were, the commuter train wasn't very full and my anxiety about being seen dropped a few notches. Still, I kept my hood up and my face turned toward the window, but I didn't think any of the other passengers were paying too much attention to me, for which I was thankful. By the time I got off at Government Center, I was feeling pretty good about my mission.

While I hadn't kept in contact, I had continued to follow Anne's career and knew that she had risen to senior partner in the firm where she was employed. I also knew that she liked to grab a quick bite to eat alone at a nearby cafe. I shanghaied the sight of a local haunt and sat down on a bench nearby to wait for her.

Just as she was passing by me, I stood up and said quietly, "Hello, Anne."

She turned in my direction, probably expecting to see a colleague or a former client, and I watched her expression change from one of cheerful welcome to wariness as she sought to figure out who I was.

I reached up and pulled back my hood, forcing the smile to stay on my face. The next few seconds were critical.

"It's me, Anne. Jeremiah."

"Jeremiah?"

She took a step forward, and then went stiff when her brain caught up with her heart. From the fear in her eyes I knew that she had seen the news; hell, as my ex-wife she probably had already been questioned by the police, so I wasn't surprised by her reaction.

I kept my hands out in plain sight and tried to look as nonthreatening as possible. "I just need a second, that's all. Just long enough to say good-bye."

"Good-bye?"

For a woman who made her living arguing in court, she sure seemed at a loss for words. Not that I blamed her. I'm sure seeing me after all these years was a bit of a shock, especially knowing that I was wanted by the police on suspicion of multiple murders. I knew that I had to talk quickly before her good sense reasserted itself.

"I found her, Anne. After all these years I found her."

Whatever she had expected me to say, that apparently wasn't it. Her breath caught in her throat and she took another step forward, her hand unconsciously snatching at the sleeve of my coat.

"Elizabeth?" she whispered.

I nodded, the tears already forming in my eyes.

"Is she . . . ?" Even after all this time she couldn't bring herself to say it.

Shaking my head, I answered the question she had left unfinished. "No," I said gently. "She left us a few years ago. But at least now we know that she's no longer suffering."

She stumbled then and would have collapsed right there on the sidewalk if I hadn't caught her in my arms. I eased her over to the bench that I'd sat on while I had waited for her, and sat us down together. I guess hearing it said aloud by the one person you knew would never give up unless absolutely certain was more than she could handle. Like a dam that had burst wide open, she let it all out, all the years of wondering and waiting, all the pain and agony that such a thing can cause. Despite the fact that other people were looking at us closely as they walked past, increasing my chances of being seen and recognized, I just held her tight and let her cry until she was done.

That seemed to take forever, but was probably only a few minutes. The fact that my heart ached to hear her anguish told me that I wasn't as over us as I thought I was, but at this point that was just water under the bridge.

I waited until she had regained a bit of control and then said softly, "I've got to go, Anne. People are looking for me. I just didn't want to leave without you knowing that Beth was all right. No one can hurt her anymore, I promise you."

She nodded, wiping the tears from her eyes with the heels of her hands, a gesture I hadn't seen in years. I felt a sharp yank on the strings of my heart and knew I had to get out of there before I got her involved in this whole mess.

As I rose to leave, she grabbed my hand and looked up at me.

"Thank you," she said. "Thank you for never giving up. And thank you for telling me. Take care of yourself. If I can help with . . ."

She left the rest unfinished. What could she say really?

I nodded in reply, unable to speak. Then, without another word, I turned and made my way down the street.

I could feel her eyes upon me, but I didn't look back.

It was time to put the past behind me.

Time to start living again.

Jeremiah Hunt may have survived the terrifying, centuries-old creature that destroyed the lives of countless people and nearly got him killed, too. But his escape has made him a marked man, and his journey has just begun. Turn the page for a sneak peek at what happens next to Hunt, Dmitri, and Denise Clearwater in the next novel of the Jeremiah Hunt chronicle:

KING of the DEAD

JOSEPH NASSISE

Available in November 2012 from Tom Doherty Associates

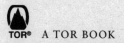

TOR® A TOR BOOK

I

Hunt

Life as an interstate fugitive isn't easy. It's not being on the run itself that's so difficult: mankind has been wandering from place to place since the dawn of human existence. No, it's the constant state of fear and anxiety that wears on you, little by little, bit by bit, until you're ready to turn yourself in to make it all stop.

Being on the run turns you into a virtual prisoner; all that's missing are the steel bars. You can't go out without worrying about being seen in public. If you do go out, you end up having a terrible time because you're constantly looking over your shoulder, wondering if you've been recognized. Then, when you've finally buckled under the strain of it all and retreated to whatever hole-in-the-wall place you're calling home that week, you spend the entire night waiting for that knock on the door, the one that heralds the arrival of the police who've come to drag your ass away to jail for the rest of your natural-born life. All that, and I didn't even mention the never-ending itch between your shoulder blades, that constant sense you're being hunted, tracked, like a fox fleeing before the hounds.

Fact is, life as a fugitive pretty much sucks.

You'll have to take my word for it when I tell you that it's even tougher when you're blind.

I know. Cry me a river, right?

We, meaning Dmitri Alexandrov, Denise Clearwater, and I, had been on the run for the last three months. We'd left Boston in early September, just a half step ahead of an FBI agent named Robertson. Mr. FBI was convinced I was the serial killer known as the Reaper, a particularly vicious monster he'd been hunting for more than a decade. He also thought I was responsible for the death of a homicide detective named Stanton. To be honest, I did have to take some responsibility for Miles's death; he wouldn't have been following me and ended up getting himself killed if I hadn't broken out of a holding cell at One Police Plaza.

Then again, if I hadn't been illegally imprisoned and accused of multiple homicides that I couldn't possibly have committed, I wouldn't have had to break out of jail in the first place.

Oh, what a tangled web we weave.

It all started with the kidnapping of my daughter, Elizabeth, five years before. I didn't know it then, but she'd been snatched by the supernatural equivalent of the man with a thousand faces: a doppelganger, or fetch as they were sometimes called, that could take the form of any creature it came into contact with. The fetch was the magically created twin of a sorcerer named Eldredge, who had been locked away in a mystical prison somewhere around the time the American colonies won independence. Eldredge eventually died, but not before he used the power that bound him to become a shade.

Shades are nasty business—incorporeal spirits imbued

with the intelligence and power that they had in life, with no expiration date for their hatred or their craving for vengeance. With the right ritual and no small measure of arcane energy, a shade can even regain its physical form, or, in the words of *Star Trek*'s Spock, create life from lifelessness. All Eldredge needed to do was track down and slaughter the last living relatives of those who had originally sealed him away in that mystical prison beneath the earth and he'd be home free.

It had taken him more than a decade, but he'd made good use of the time, sending his doppelganger crisscrossing the country, killing as it went. By the time I'd entered the picture, he was down to the final four or five.

If the doppelganger hadn't kidnapped my daughter, he probably would have succeeded.

Instead of completing the ritual and waltzing off into the sunset, he'd been forced to fight for his life, and, in the end, the three of us had cleaned his clock and put him down like the rabid dog he was.

Before we had, though, his pet fetch had disemboweled Stanton and nearly killed the three of us as well.

We'd survived and had taken out Eldredge, something a powerful group sorcerers two centuries before hadn't been able to do. The fairy tale ending I'd hoped for never materialized, though. I soon found out that while Elizabeth had been kidnapped by the fetch at Eldredge's command, she died in an accident almost a year before.

Sending her ghost on to the rest she deserved was one of the hardest things I'd ever done.

And what did we get for all our trouble?

Three months of living as fugitives, with no end in sight.

Which was why we were parked in an empty lot in the Warehouse District at midnight, trying to buy a set of fake IDs from a gangbanger named Carlos. He'd been recommended to us by the friend of a friend of someone Dmitri knew, which didn't put him too high on the trustworthy list, but at least it gave us a place to start. We needed those IDs. With them, and the security of being able to do simple daily tasks, we could start to build some semblance of a life. It wouldn't be what we'd had before; there was no way we could ever go back to that, but at least it would be better than what we had now.

Things had been going pretty well, too, until the punk in front of me stuck his gun in my face.

I was standing next to the door of my car when he arrived in his lowriding Impala, the booming beat of a bass drum pumping out of his open windows. I had to struggle to conceal my smirk as he got out of the car and sauntered over to me. He'd killed his headlights before doing so and that had allowed me to give him the once-over from behind my sunglasses without making it too obvious.

He was five seven, maybe five eight on a good day, which put him four inches shorter than me. He was dressed in a pair of baggy pants that were belted on halfway down his ass, revealing the top of his boxer shorts, and a dark formfitting long-sleeved shirt, the kind the bodybuilders wear. The whitest sneakers I'd ever seen and a red bandanna tied around his left arm completed his getup. He was trying too hard and it showed; he looked more like Hollywood's idea of a cholo than the real thing.

In the good ole days, before we had to run for the hills, Dmitri had owned and operated the best bar in all of Southie, which, when you think about it, was kind of unusual for a guy with the last name Alexandrov. But he'd successfully defended his territory against more than one attempt by the Irish mob to home in on it, and it wasn't until I'd known him for a few years that I'd discovered why. Besides being a mean son of a bitch, Dmitri had been one of the best fixers in the business. Information and equipment were his stock in trade; if you needed something, anything at all, you went to Dmitri.

It was his safe house that we'd been staying in for the last several weeks, and when it came time to establish a new set of identities for each of us, it was his expertise that allowed us to set up this meet.

Something went wrong, however. We were expecting a professional and ended up with the farm team instead.

This punk with the gun.

The acrid smell of gunpowder filled my nostrils, letting me know the weapon had been fired recently.

That wasn't a good sign, either. So far, our negotiations were off to a bad start.

I put my hands up without being asked and said in a soft, nonthreatening tone, "Easy, man. No need for that."

Carlos must have thought he was now the big man on campus for he turned his wrist so that the weapon was practically upside down and waggled it back and forth in front of my face. "Shut up and give me the money," he said with a sneer.

Nobody with an ounce of brains would fire a gun from that position and expect to hit anything with any degree of accuracy, so I could tell he was more bark than bite. If I could stall him for just a bit longer, I knew we could turn the tables on him, so I played the clueless white guy, full of indignation and completely out of his element.

"But we had a deal," I whined. "Two sets of IDs for ten grand."

Carlos grinned so wide that I could see the gold teeth in his mouth.

"I'm changing the deal, shithead. Give me the money before I put a cap in your ass!"

My whining tone did the trick. All he saw was some gringo in way over his head, which was exactly what I wanted him to see. It kept him focused on me and not on what was silently lumbering up behind him on all fours.

"Okay, okay. Take it easy," I said, looking down and to one side, signaling my submission in a way he'd instinctively understand. "I'm going to reach into my pocket and . . ."

"Stop talking and just do it, fool!"

I reached into the pocket of my coat and withdrew a thick envelope. I started to hand it over to him and then pulled back.

"The IDs . . ."

Carlos practically snarled as he snatched at the envelope in my hand. "Give me that!"

I pulled my hand back just enough to keep it out of his reach. The charade had gone on long enough. I glanced over his shoulder, saw what I was looking for, and dropped the scared-gringo act.

"You might want to look behind you first," I said, letting the boredom I was feeling with the whole situation color my voice.

Surprisingly, Carlos caught the change in tone. Maybe he was smarter than I was giving him credit for, or maybe he just had a finely tuned sense of survival, I don't know, but he seemed to recognize he was no longer in control of the situation. His eyes narrowed, and I could almost see the wheels turning in his head as he tried to figure out where the danger was coming from.

It didn't take long.

From directly behind him came a roar that suddenly split the night in two, shockingly close and loud enough to make my knees tremble involuntarily, despite the fact I'd known what was coming.

Poor Carlos didn't have any such warning and he nearly wet his pants as that cry sounded from directly behind him, so close that he could probably feel hot breath on the back of his neck. His eyes got as round as saucers and he frantically spun around and tried to bring his gun to bear at the same time.

Whatever it was that he expected to see there, I'm pretty sure that a ten-foot-tall polar bear wasn't it.

In the aftermath of my daughter Elizabeth's disappearance, I'd tried everything I could think of to discover what had happened to her. When, after a few years, I'd exhausted the usual methods, I'd delved into more esoteric ones. Things like divination, witchcraft, and black magick. It was in the course of those "investigations" that I'd encountered the Preacher.

To this day, I'm still not sure who or what he actually was or why he appeared to me, but it was through his help that I located a ritual that would let me see that which was unseen, and I'd used it in an effort to locate Elizabeth.

As is typical of dark magick, the ritual did exactly what it promised to do but not in the way I'd expected. Rather than helping me locate what was missing, it stole my natural sight and replaced it with something else, something I've come to call my ghostsight. Among other things, it lets me see the supernatural denizens of the world around me. It doesn't matter what they are, I can see them all: the good, the bad, and the scares-me-shitless.

I'm not completely blind. I can actually see better in complete darkness than most people can in broad daylight. I can no longer see colors—everything comes out in a thousand shades of gray—but at least I can see. The minute you put me in the light, however, everything goes dark. Direct sunlight is the equivalent of a complete whiteout for me; I can't even see the outline of my hand if I hold it directly in front of my face. All I see is white. Endless vistas of white. Electrical lights are almost as bad, though if I use a pair of strong UV sunglasses I can see the vague shapes and outlines of things around me.

Which was why I was standing in a dark alley at night wearing the darkest sunglasses I could find.

Thanks to my sight I'd known that Dmitri wasn't just a simple bartender, but I hadn't been able to pierce the glamour around him to know exactly *what* he was. It was when I was hunting for the fetch earlier that fall that I'd discovered he was a berserker.

First mentioned in the Norse saga *Vatnsdoela*, the berserkers were described as elite warriors that wore animal pelts on their heads and charged into battle in a ravaging frenzy, fighting so hard that they were nearly unstoppable. Of course, the bards hadn't quite gotten it right, never realizing that the berserkers were actually warriors that were so in touch with the totem spirits of certain animals that they could assume the physical properties of those beasts in battle, borrowing their strength, cunning, and senses to accomplish things they never could have done as mere humans.

Dmitri and I decided to play it safe for tonight's rendezvous, arriving early and having only one of us meet our intended contact. While I did that, Dmitri would remain out of sight, ready to come to my assistance if necessary.

Now we were glad that we'd taken the extra precaution.

Dmitri reared up on his hind legs, towering over Carlos. He opened his mouth and let loose another ground-shaking roar of challenge. That close, his teeth seemed bigger than my clenched fist.

To his credit, Carlos stood his ground and tried to bring his gun to bear, though what he thought a pistol was going to do against a brute like Dmitri was beyond me.

He needn't have bothered. Before he'd even managed

to move his arm a few inches it was intercepted by the swipe of a massive fur-covered paw. The impact sent Carlos spinning to the ground, and the gun went flying off into the darkness. Dmitri lumbered forward, straddled Carlos's body, and clamped his teeth firmly onto the back of the gangbanger's neck.

A few more ounces of pressure and bye-bye Carlos.

For the first time all night, our would-be thief did the smart thing.

He froze.

Smiling now, I put one hand on Dmitri's broad back and squatted down next to Carlos so that he could see me without having to move his head. This close, I could smell the stink of urine and feces that was coming off of him in waves. From the smell I knew he'd be a bit more receptive to our needs now that we'd gotten the preliminaries out of the way.

Good thing, too, since I was done dicking around.

"One word from me and my friend here will crush your head like an eggshell. *Comprende,* amigo?"

He opened his mouth, only to find that his fear had stolen his voice. He gaped like a fish a few times, vainly trying to get something out.

I took that as a yes.

"Where are the IDs?"

This time he managed to find his voice.

"Glove box," he gasped out.

I patted Dmitri on the back, rose to my feet, and walked over to the lowrider. I slid into the front seat, leaned over to the other side, and opened the glove box. Inside I found another pistol and a manila envelope containing the driver's licenses and passports that Carlos's organization had agreed to provide. I put the new IDs back in the envelope and then tucked it and the pistol into the pocket of my jacket.

Carlos had left the keys in the ignition, perhaps in

anticipation of a quick getaway after screwing us over. I took them with me as I got out of the car and threw them into the darkness as far as I could.

Once I had, I signaled for Dmitri to let Carlos up.

Dmitri growled low in his chest, expressing his annoyance at the idea and eliciting another whimper of fear from Carlos, but with a little encouragement Dmitri eventually backed off, moving to sit on his haunches at my side. Even seated, he towered over me.

"Not a particularly bright play, Carlos," I said, packing all the disdain for his intelligence that I could into the words. "But today must be your lucky day, for I've decided to let you go. Now get the hell out of here and don't even try to come back for your car."

Carlos didn't need to be told twice. He scrambled to his feet and ran off, never once looking back.

Dmitri turned his shovel-shaped head in my direction and grunted something.

Having no idea what he'd just said, one roar sounding pretty much like the next, I just stared at him blankly.

Another growl, a quick sensation of movement, and before I had time to look away, Dmitri was back in human form, standing in front of me completely naked and seemingly not bothered by it at all.

Catching a glimpse of what he was carrying around with him, I could understand why.

Some guys just get all the luck.

He walked over to Denise's car, a black Dodge Charger we'd borrowed for the evening's activities, and pulled on the extra set of clothes that he'd brought along for that purpose. I got in the passenger side, he slid in behind the wheel, and we took off in a spray of dirt and gravel.

Dmitri drove for a few blocks and then pulled into the parking lot of an all-night diner, finding a spot beneath one of the few streetlamps illuminating the lot.

"Give 'em here," he said.

I passed him the envelope containing the fake IDs.

Besides limiting my vision, the Preacher's ritual had also robbed me of my ability to see photographs or paintings of any kind. I could see the spot on the IDs where the images were supposed to be, but the images themselves were just flat black squares, making it impossible for me to judge how well the passports and driver's licenses had turned out.

Dmitri looked them over for a few minutes, even going so far as to hold them up to the light one at a time and turn them this way and that, before dropping them back into the envelope.

"Good enough, I think," he said, passing the envelope back to me, and I let out the breath I didn't know I'd been holding. If we'd gone through all this trouble only to end up with useless junk . . .

But we hadn't, and that was good. Really good. Having the IDs would at least provide us some small measure of protection, allow us to do simple things that other people took for granted, like cashing a paycheck or signing a long-term lease on a piece of property. Even opening up a bank account or getting a line of credit was now possible, though I didn't think I'd want to put our IDs up to that level of scrutiny unless it was absolutely necessary.

Dmitri started the car and pulled out into traffic, while I took out one of the prepaid cell phones we'd been using to communicate with one another and called to let Clearwater know we were on our way home.

If I'd known what she was going to drag us into less than seventy-two hours later, I might have tossed the phone out the window and told Dmitri to head south at the fastest possible speed, do not pass Go, do not collect two hundred dollars.

Unfortunately, I didn't.

2

Clearwater

Around her, the city burned.

She ran through the streets, the buildings on either side engulfed in writhing sheets of flame, tongues of green and blue mixed with those of red and yellow, evidence of the eldritch energies mixing with the natural ones. The heat pouring off the fire was intense; even from the middle of the street she could feel it beating against her flesh, sending rivulets of sweat running down her face. Smoke and soot and ash filled the air, limiting her ability to see as she ran, searching for something, though she couldn't remember who or what it was that she sought. Behind her, lost in the smoke and ash, something searched for her in turn.

She stumbled forward, looking for a street sign or some other landmark that would give her a better sense of her location, but all such markings seemed to have been removed, if they'd ever existed at all.

The thing behind her drew closer. She didn't know how she knew; she just did. The first twinges of panic rose to the surface of her mind, but she fought them back down.

Giving in was not an option; the thing behind her would catch her and that would be the end.

Of everything.

She couldn't let that happen!

The smoke grew thicker, darker, and she was forced to hold her arm over her mouth as she stumbled forward. Her breath was coming in short, sharp gasps as she struggled to draw enough oxygen from the polluted air, but she bravely fought forward.

Something moved in the ruins to her left and she turned in that direction, eyes straining to make out what it was in the glare of the flames, but it was gone as swiftly as it had come.

A wailing cry sounded from close behind, just beyond the nearest curtain of smoke, and her heart pounded to hear it.

Faster! You have to run faster! *a voice shouted at her from deep inside her mind.*

She pushed herself, drawing on the last of her reserves. Sweat poured down her face and plastered her hair against her scalp, while her clothing seemed weighted down with falling ash. She dodged wrecked cars and the shattered remains of crumbled homes, racing deeper into the darkness, searching for a way out.

She didn't see the jagged crack in the pavement until it was too late. Her foot caught on the edge and she fell, her hands coming up to protect her face as she slid across the harsh surface, leaving flesh and blood in her wake.

Already an inner voice was shouting at her, Get up! Get up! Get up!

She tried, really tried, but her right leg wouldn't support her and she fell back to the pavement, crying and screaming in pain and fear. She must have broken her ankle in the fall.

Unwilling to give in, she used her arms to pull herself forward, dragging her wounded leg behind her.

That wailing cry sounded again, this time from immediately behind her, and she knew she'd been found. She rolled over, bringing her hands up before her in defense, as she caught a glimpse of something monstrous looming against the darkness of the smoke surrounding them.

She screamed as the thing descended . . .

☩

The vision departed as swiftly and as unexpectedly as it had come. In its aftermath, Denise found herself standing before the big bay window in the living room. She was clad in the loose-fitting pajamas she'd pulled on when she went to bed earlier that evening and was shivering in the cold air. A portion of the window had been fogged over, as if someone had just breathed on it, and the outline of two words were clearly visible on its surface.

NEW ORLEANS.

Just seeing the words there made her nervous and so she reached up, intending to wipe them away. *Out of sight, out of mind*, she thought, rubbing her fingers across the glass, only to recoil in fear when the words did not disappear.

They couldn't.

They were written on the *outside* of the glass.

A shiver of arctic cold ran up her spine and she took a few steps back, unable to tear her gaze away from the letters as they slowly faded from view, seeming to mock her as they did so. Her thoughts raced through all the ways those words could have ended up on the window in front of her, each one more dangerous than the last . . .

"Are you okay, Denise?"

She screamed.

She couldn't help it. So great had been her concentration that she hadn't heard Hunt enter the room behind her. His sudden voice in the silence of the room shocked her almost as much as seeing the words on the window.

Almost.

She knew he'd react to her fear and so she quickly turned, waving her hand and intentionally laughing to keep him from learning how upset she actually was.

"Gaia, Hunt, you startled me!"

Moonlight spilled in through the windows, letting her see his face. His white eyes seemed to gleam of their own accord in the partial darkness and she wondered, not for the first time, exactly what the ritual he'd undergone had done to him.

"You looked like something scared you," he said. "Well, before I did, I mean."

She shook her head. "It was nothing—a bad dream, nothing more. I'll be fine. Your voice just surprised me, that's all. I didn't hear you come into the room."

He glanced past her to the window but apparently didn't find anything there to make him suspicious since he turned his attention back to her.

"You're sure?"

"Yes, of course. Go back to bed. I'm sorry I woke you."

Now it was his turn to brush it off. "You didn't. I was up anyway. Memories, ya know?"

She did know. She'd been there when the ghost of his daughter Elizabeth had asked him to use his power to release her into whatever it was that came next; it was the glimpse of the man she'd seen in that moment, the one who would have gladly given his life to save that of his little girl, that convinced her to join him when he was forced to flee the city.

"Really, I'm fine," she said, and smiled again to show that she meant it.

Whether he believed her or not, she couldn't tell, but he said good night, turned, and wandered off back in the direction of his bedroom at the rear of the house.

She stayed up after Hunt had gone to bed, settling onto the couch and staring out into the night's darkness, considering her next move. The visions had started two weeks before, and there was no denying the fact that they were coming more regularly now. Each time it was the same: she was trapped in the burning city while magick ran amok around her and something dark and twisted stalked her through the smoke and flames of the city streets.

She couldn't ignore the summons much longer. And there was no doubt about it, that's what it was—a summons. Gaia needed her assistance again, just as she'd been needed when the fetch and its master had begun slaughtering people in Boston, intent on disrupting the natural order of things. Then, like now, she'd begun having visions, images of her and Hunt and Dmitri wrapped up in their efforts to put a stop to what was to come. Most of those visions came true, as she knew they would. The longer she waited, the more fixed those events became in that future time line, as if her willingness to act sooner rather than later made a difference to the ultimate outcome. And maybe that was the point. You couldn't ignore a call from the Earth Mother any more than you could ignore gravity, not if you wanted to continue as a practitioner of the Art, and doing so could have dire consequences.

So why was she resisting?

The answer was right there, simply waiting for her to acknowledge it, and this time she did so.

She was afraid.

Facing off against the shade of Eldredge and his deadly fetch had nearly killed her and her friends. Going back into battle against the unknown a second time wasn't high on her list of favorite things right now.

What if this time they weren't strong enough?

No matter how long she sat there, she couldn't come up with an answer that satisfied her.